A MERRY HEART DOETH

GOOD LIKE A MEDICINE

All scripture references are taken from
the King James Version
Holy Bible

A MERRY HEART DOETH GOOD LIKE A MEDICINE

Carol Dold

AuthorHouse™
1663 Liberty Drive
Bloomington, IN 47403
www.authorhouse.com
Phone: 1-800-839-8640

© 2011 by Carol Dold. All rights reserved.

No part of this book may be reproduced, stored in a retrieval system, or transmitted by any means without the written permission of the author.

First published by AuthorHouse   10/14/2011

ISBN: 978-1-4670-6040-0 (sc)
ISBN: 978-1-4670-6039-4 (hc)
ISBN: 978-1-4670-6038-7 (ebk)

Library of Congress Control Number: 2011918363

Printed in the United States of America

Any people depicted in stock imagery provided by Thinkstock are models, and such images are being used for illustrative purposes only.
Certain stock imagery © Thinkstock.

This book is printed on acid-free paper.

Because of the dynamic nature of the Internet, any web addresses or links contained in this book may have changed since publication and may no longer be valid. The views expressed in this work are solely those of the author and do not necessarily reflect the views of the publisher, and the publisher hereby disclaims any responsibility for them.

CONTENTS

ACKNOWLEDGMENTS		vii
CHAPTER I	PASTOR'S POTSHOTS	1
CHAPTER II	ADMINISTRATIVE ANTICS	39
CHAPTER III	PINTSIZE PANDEMONIUM	57
CHAPTER IV	TEEN TIDAL WAVES	131
CHAPTER V	FAMILY FRENZY	179
CHAPTER VI	MATRIMONIAL MISFITS	199
CHAPTER VII	CARNAL COMMOTION	235
CHAPTER VIII	JAILBIRD JOLLIES	293
CHAPTER IX	SINKING SHIPS	311
CHAPTER X	HOLIDAY HILARITY	353
CHAPTER XI	SILLY SAINTS	361
CHAPTER XII	SATAN SHAKERS	455
CHAPTER XIII	ABOUT THE AUTHOR	481

ACKNOWLEDGMENTS

First, and foremost, I humbly thank our Lord Jesus Christ for His Word, His Blood, His Spirit. I am at a loss for words to adequately express how much His unfailing love, grace, and mercy have meant to me. But, perhaps, I can sum it up it these three scriptures:

Colossians 3:4: . . . Christ, who is our [my] life . . .

Galations 2:20: I am crucified with Christ: nevertheless I live; yet not I, but Christ liveth in me: and the life which I now live in the flesh I live by the faith of the Son of God, who loved me, and gave himself for me.

II Corinthians 9:15: Thanks be unto God for His unspeakable gift.

I also thank my beloved husband, Roger, whose gentleness and patience have melted glaciers of ice in my once cold heart. He has been a human refuge for my soul. Roger is full of enthusiasm for marriage, music, most sports, and, of course, above all, our Master, Lord, and Savior, Jesus Christ. He is a kind and wonderful man. I am proud to have him for my husband.

I thank my three beloved, amazing, awesome children, whose names I will list alphabetically because there is no competition where they are concerned. In a mother's heart, they each take first place. I could give you a list of their honorable accomplishments but that is not what I would want you to remember about them. What I would want imbedded in your mind is that they love God, love others, and love us. To me, love is the greatest thing that they can offer to society.

My beloved son, Clifford was born 7-7-81. He met and married Nicole from Wisconsin in 2005. They have three beautiful, irresistible children,

Wyatt (born 11-17-05); Liam (born 2-1-09), and Isabella (born 1-10-11) who have also stolen my heart.

My beloved son, Joey, born 10-26-83, met and married Kelly from Connecticut on October 11, 2008. They have two adorable bunnies, Callie and Bunny in their "hare salon."

My beloved daughter, Lisa, born 7-6-78, met and married Terence from Michigan on July 1, 2006. They have two energetic, salt and pepper Chihuahuas, Ginger (white) and Promise (black).

I would like to take a moment to mention that I also love Kelly, Nicole, and Terry (listed alphabetically because, again, there are no favorites where they are concerned.). I am privileged to have them in my life. My children picked very special mates to occupy their hearts and very special pets to warm their homes.

Roger and I, likewise, have three Chihuahuas living with us—two "chocolate pupcakes" named Moses and Joshua, and one "vanilla pupcake" named Buster.

I would also like to mention that it is my heart's desire that my husband, my children, their mates, and my grandchildren always have a heart totally devoted to our Lord Jesus Christ. Nothing could be a better, more lasting legacy than this.

And now, I invite you to come along with me onto the stage of laughter and drama, peril and pandemonium . . .

PASTOR'S POTSHOTS

Oh no! It's the Pastor!" shouted Mrs. Brown to her children. "Quick, put your toys away!"

"Tommy, turn that awful show off!" his mother shrieked.

Mrs. Brown was running around like a chicken with its head cut off!

"Mary!" her mother hollered, "Pick up all these clothes lying around and throw them in the bedroom. Oh," she added, "and find your Bible as fast as you can!"

Mary wasn't moving as quickly as her mother had expected. She glared at her with looks that could scare a cobra. "On the double and I mean it, Mary!" she demanded. "And put your Bible on the coffee table where Pastor Davison will see it!"

"And, Susie," her mother screeched, "for heaven sakes get those roller skates off the dining room table! And when you're finished doing that," she ordered, "put all the dishes out in the kitchen sink."

"But Mom," Susie objected, "the sink is already full."

"Then hide them in the oven!" she shot back. "I don't care what you do! Just get them out of sight!"

While the children were running around in a frenzy trying to do two weeks worth of housework in three minutes, their mother made a mad dash to the bedroom to comb her hair.

Meanwhile, the pastor had parked his car and was knocking at the door. "Why, what a pleasant surprise," said Mrs. Brown, catching her breath as she opened the door. "I've just been relaxing on the couch with a cup of coffee and my favorite book, the Gospel according to St. John," she told him.

"That's always been a favorite of mine as well," said the Pastor. As they exchanged greetings, he happened to notice her youngest child coloring and scribbling furiously all over the paneling. "I hate to be the one to tell you this, Mrs. Brown," he said, removing his coat, "But I'm afraid that the handwriting is on the wall.'"

HEBREWS 2:3: HOW SHALL WE ESCAPE, IF WE NEGLECT SO GREAT SALVATION . . .

"It seems we have a lot of perfect Christians around here, or so they think," said the pastor in a reprimand. "Therefore, I thought I'd have some folding chairs brought up here on the platform for those of you who have reached a plateau of sinless perfection and uncompromising holiness before the Lord. Then the rest of us will sit quietly and listen to your formula for attaining such a degree of unparalleled spirituality.

"How many chairs should I set up" asked one of the deacons trying to be helpful.

"On second thought don't bother, David," the pastor replied, motioning for him to sit back down. "I don't think we'll need more than *none*."

JOB 9:20: IF I JUSTIFY MYSELF, MINE OWN MOUTH SHALL CONDEMN ME: *IF I SAY* I *AM* PERFECT, IT SHALL ALSO PROVE ME PERVERSE.

II CORINTHIANS 10:18: FOR NOT HE THAT COMMENDETH HIMSELF IS APPROVED, BUT WHOM THE LORD COMMENDETH. [SEE PROVERBS 20:6 & 9; PSALM 14:2-3; ROMANS 3:19-20 & 23; ROMANS 7:24]

ECCLESIATES 7:20: FOR *THERE IS* NOT A JUST MAN UPON EARTH, THAT DOETH GOOD, AND SINNETH NOT.

JAMES 2:10: FOR WHOSOEVER SHALL KEEP THE WHOLE LAW, AND YET OFFEND IN ONE *POINT*, HE IS GUILTY OF ALL.

PSALM 130:3: IF THOU, LORD, SHOULDEST MARK INIQUITIES, O LORD, WHO SHALL STAND?

GALATIONS 4:16: AM I THEREFORE BECOME YOUR ENEMY, BECAUSE I TELL YOU THE TRUTH?

During a church service, one of the deacons handed the pastor a set of lost car keys.

Examining them closely, the pastor noticed the key chain bore a small emblem from a local casino. He dangled them in front of the congregation, snickering as he did so.

"If you're brave enough to come claim them," he said, pointing to the emblem, "they're yours!"

I CORINTHIANS 8:9: BUT TAKE HEED LEST BY ANY MEANS THIS LIBERTY OF YOURS BECOME A STUMBLINGBLOCK TO THEM THAT ARE WEAK.

ACTS 23:1: AND PAUL, EARNESTLY BEHOLDING THE COUNCIL, SAID, MEN *AND* BRETHREN, I HAVE LIVED IN ALL GOOD CONSCIENCE BEFORE GOD UNTIL THIS DAY.

II CORINTHIANS 6:3: GIVING NO OFFENCE IN ANY THING, THAT THE MINISTRY BE NOT BLAMED.

ACTS 24:16: AND HEREIN DO I EXERCISE MYSELF, TO HAVE ALWAYS A CONSCIENCE VOID OF OFFENCE TOWARD GOD, AND *TOWARD* MEN.

I JOHN 2:15-17: LOVE NOT THE WORLD, NEITHER THE THINGS *THAT ARE* IN THE WORLD. IF ANY MAN LOVE THE WORLD, THE LOVE OF THE FATHER IS NOT IN HIM. FOR ALL THAT *IS* IN THE WORLD, THE LUST OF THE FLESH, AND THE LUST OF THE EYES, AND THE PRIDE

OF LIFE, IS NOT OF THE FATHER, BUT IS OF THE WORLD. AND THE WORLD PASSETH AWAY, AND THE LUST THEREOF: BUT HE THAT DOETH THE WILL OF GOD ABIDETH FOR EVER.

EPHESIANS 5:11-12: AND HAVE NO FELLOWSHIP WITH THE UNFRUITFUL WORKS OF DARKNESS, BUT RATHER REPROVE *THEM*. FOR IT IS A SHAME EVEN TO SPEAK OF THOSE THINGS WHICH ARE DONE OF THEM IN SECRET.

As attendance increased steadily, the seating conditions in one church became unbearably crowded. Packed together like sardines, the pastor was eventually forced to break the large group into three separate services to accommodate all the people.

Making light of the situation, he joked one Sunday, "We have a service to fit your every mood. For example, the 8:00 a.m. individuals come stumbling in, drowsy-eyed, wearing pajamas and robes, with a Bible in one hand and a pillow in the other.

The 10:30 a.m. group comes trotting in with a Bible and toothbrush in one hand and a cup of coffee in the other.

And, last but not least," he chuckled, "the 11:30 a.m. crowd comes prancing in, alive and alert, with a Bible in one hand and a swimsuit and surf board in the other."

HEBREWS 10:25: NOT FORSAKING THE ASSEMBLING OF OURSELVES TOGETHER, AS THE MANNER OF SOME *IS;* BUT EXHORTING *ONE ANOTHER;* AND SO MUCH THE MORE, AS YE SEE THE DAY APPROACHING.

LUKE 4:16: AND HE [JESUS] CAME TO NAZARETH, WHERE HE HAD BEEN BROUGHT UP: AND, AS HIS CUSTOM WAS, HE WENT INTO THE SYNAGOGUE ON THE SABBATH DAY, AND STOOD UP FOR TO READ.

Noticing a few sleepers in the congregation each Sunday, Pastor Holden remarked, "It's a good thing that sleeping in church on Sunday isn't against

the law, because if it was," he laughed, "there is a few habitual offenders that I'd have to turn in for 'Indecent Composure.'"

ROMANS 13:11: AND THAT, KNOWING THE TIME, THAT NOW *IT IS* HIGH TIME TO AWAKE OUT OF SLEEP: FOR NOW *IS* OUR SALVATION NEARER THAN WHEN WE BELIEVED.

Reverend Thompson, shepherding a church of one thousand members, was addressing his congregation one Sunday on the topic of Bible prophecy and the soon coming of the Lord. "For those of you who miss the rapture, and get left behind," he said, reassuring them, "nine hundred seventy five helium-filled balloons will be stored in the church gymnasium. May the Lord be with you as you rise to meet him in the air."

I THESSALONIANS 4:16-17: FOR THE LORD HIMSELF SHALL DESCEND FROM HEAVEN WITH A SHOUT, WITH THE VOICE OF THE ARCHANGEL, AND WITH THE TRUMP OF GOD: AND THE DEAD IN CHRIST SHALL RISE FIRST: THEN WE WHICH ARE ALIVE AND REMAIN SHALL BE CAUGHT UP TOGETHER WITH THEM IN THE CLOUDS, TO MEET THE LORD IN THE AIR: AND SO SHALL WE EVER BE WITH THE LORD.

MATTHEW 25:6: AND AT MIDNIGHT THERE WAS A CRY MADE, BEHOLD, THE BRIDEGROOM COMETH; GO YE OUT TO MEET HIM.

MATTHEW 25:13: WATCH THEREFORE, FOR YE KNOW NEITHER THE DAY NOR THE HOUR WHEREIN THE SON OF MAN COMETH.

MARK 13:36: LEST COMING SUDDENLY HE FIND YOU SLEEPING. [SEE II THESSALONIANS 2:7-12]

Reverend Aubrey's weekly ordeal of watching children run down the aisles and swing from chandeliers was becoming highly irritating to himself and the other deacons. Short of using some "physical persuasion" they couldn't stop the rowdy, little rascals, who, on any day could outrun the pastor and his staff.

Fed up with their shenanigans, Reverend Aubrey appealed to their parents. "I think you should know," he said sternly to the mothers and fathers of

the children, "that, if you don't discipline your kids, we're going to have to hire a bouncer!"

PROVERBS 22:6: TRAIN UP A CHILD IN THE WAY HE SHOULD GO: AND WHEN HE IS OLD, HE WILL NOT DEPART FROM IT. [SEE DEUTERONOMY 6:5-9]

PROVERBS 23:13: WITHHOLD NOT CORRECTION FROM THE CHILD: FOR IF THOU BEATEST HIM WITH THE ROD, HE SHALL NOT DIE. [SEE PROVERBS 22:15]

PROVERBS 19:18: CHASTEN THY SON WHILE THERE IS HOPE, AND LET NOT THY SOUL SPARE FOR HIS CRYING.

(Author's note: Under no circumstances is this a license for child abuse! Loving correction is to be administered.)

In order to encourage good moral behavior and to unite the members in a common goal of striving for clean, upright living, several churches decided to have a contest to see whose congregation could last the longest without sinning. The members of each church were instructed to begin their quest for god1iness on the first day of the following month.

"Are there any other questions?" Pastor Coleman asked his church.

A gentleman in the front row raised his hand. "I have one," he replied "Go ahead," the Pastor remarked, motioning for the man to speak.

Well, I was just wondering, Reverend," he asked, "is there a prize or some reward that would give us incentive to make this all worthwhile?"

"There sure is!" shouted the Pastor. He picked up his Bible and waved it before the crowd. "How does eternal life sound?"

LUKE 6:23: REJOICE YE IN THAT DAY, AND LEAP FOR JOY: FOR, BEHOLD, YOUR REWARD IS GREAT IN HEAVEN. [SEE EPHESIANS 2:8-9 & GALATIONS 2:16]

(Author's note: Salvation is only provided through the shed blood of Jesus Christ and His grace. Our works do not save us but they do reveal us! If we truly have turned our lives over to Jesus Christ, works will follow our declaration of faith and repentance. In the same way that apple trees produce apples, pear trees produce pears, orange trees produce oranges, Christians produce Christ like actions.)

II CORINTHIANS 13:5: EXAMINE YOURSELVES, WHETHER YE BE IN THE FAITH; PROVE YOUR OWN SELVES. KNOW YE NOT YOUR OWN SELVES, HOW THAT JESUS CHIRST IS IN YOU, EXCEPT YE BE REPROBATES.

JEREMIAH 9:23-24: THUS SAITH THE LORD, LET NOT THE WISE *MAN* GLORY IN HIS WISDOM, NEITHER LET THE MIGHTY *MAN* GLORY IN HIS MIGHT, LET NOT THE RICH *MAN* GLORY IN HIS RICHES: BUT LET HIM THAT GLORIETH GLORY IN THIS, THAT HE UNDERSTANDETH AND KNOWETH ME . . .

"Broad is the road and narrow is the way that leads to destruction" bellowed an evangelist to the attentive city crowd who'd come to hear the fiery man of God preach. "For the penalty of sin is death and hell," he continued.

At that point, a giant, husky man—broad shouldered and muscular—with a very mean look on his face, rose to vehemently oppose the evangelist.

"I don't agree!" he shouted, as he slowly started walking toward the now mortified evangelist who was shaking from head to toe.

Trying to compose himself—despite knees knocking and a body that suddenly felt limp—he managed to sputter out a few feeble words. "I don't see why you don't believe the wages of sin are death," he said with a weak and squeaky voice, "when the Lord is about to make me an example of these very facts!"

MATTHEW 7:13-14: ENTER YE IN AT THE STRAIT GATE: FOR WIDE *IS* THE GATE, AND BROAD *IS* THE WAY, THAT LEADETH TO DESTRUCTION, AND MANY THERE BE WHICH GO IN THEREAT: BECAUSE STRAIT *IS* THE GATE, AND NARROW *IS* THE WAY, WHICH LEADETH UNTO LIFE, AND FEW THERE BE THAT FIND IT. [SEE ROMANS 6:23]

To generate a warm, friendly atmosphere among the brethren, Reverend Atkins generally started each service with a time of handshaking and hugging between those present at the Sunday worship services.

What began as an intended gesture of friendship, however, got carried away into what the Reverend sternly warned against: "harem hugging," as he called it.

"I challenge you to conduct yourselves in a dignified and respectable manner," he told his church. And to you young and old men alike," he said, "I want to say that I Thessalonians 5:26, 'Greet all brethren with an [a] holy kiss,' does not give you a license to charge toward every single woman like some romantic, love struck Romeo!"

TITUS 2:11-14: FOR THE GRACE OF GOD THAT BRINGETH SALVATION HATH APPEARED TO <u>ALL</u> MEN, TEACHING US THAT, DENYING UNGODLINESS AND WORLDLY LUSTS, WE SHOULD LIVE SOBERLY, RIGHTEOUSLY, AND GODLY, IN THIS PRESENT WORLD; LOOKING FOR THAT BLESSED HOPE, AND THE GLORIOUS APPEARING OF THE GREAT GOD AND OUR SAVIOUR JESUS CHRIST; WHO GAVE HIMSELF FOR US . . .

In Pastor Whitney's church, the nursery was always crowded and understaffed. "We desperately need help," he complained. "But where are the volunteers?"

He walked away from the pulpit toward the congregation to create a more informal, friendly approach. Then to put things on a lighter note he incorporated a little humor into his plea for assistance.

"The Bible says that when the heavenly trumpet sounds, we shall all be changed in the twinkling of an eye," he told them. "In the basement nursery, however, we have thirty little trumpets all sounding, and it takes a little longer than a twinkle to get them changed. In plain English," he said, "We could use a few diaper deacons down there!"

I CORINTHIANS 15:51-52: BEHOLD, I SHEW YOU A MYSTERY; WE SHALL NOT ALL SLEEP, BUT WE SHALL ALL BE CHANGED, IN A MOMENT, IN

THE TWINKLING OF AN EYE, AT THE LAST TRUMP: FOR THE TRUMPET SHALL SOUND, AND THE DEAD SHALL BE RAISED INCORRUPTIBLE, AND WE SHALL BE CHANGED.

Pastor Richardson, a new minister in the community, had a real burden for souls. Although church membership had grown, it seemed that the ratio of new believers hadn't increased.

He called in an evangelist friend of his asking him to do a week of revival meetings hoping to stir souls to repentance. Night after night, however, no one responded to the altar calls.

The pastor, himself, cried unto the Lord from the depths of his heart.

On the last night of the revival, the evangelist gave his usual altar call. Still no one went forward to receive Christ. After everyone left, the pastor confided in his friend. "As you know, Leonard, my father was a farmer who saw a few droughts in his time. And if he were here today," he said, "I think he'd definitely call this a crop failure!"

JEREMIAH 8:20: THE HARVEST IS PAST, THE SUMMER IS ENDED, AND WE ARE NOT SAVED.

JEREMIAH 29:13: AND YE SHALL SEEK ME, AND FIND *ME*, WHEN YE SHALL SEARCH FOR ME WITH ALL YOUR HEART.

PROVERBS 8:17: I LOVE THEM THAT LOVE ME; AND THOSE THAT SEEK ME EARLY SHALL FIND ME.

Deborah and Dan, a happy couple about to be wed, stood at the altar looking adoringly into each other's eyes.

After making the customary opening speech, the pastor asked the bride and groom to join hands and prepare to exchange their vows.

He turned to the groom and began, "Do you Dan, take Deborah to be your one and only wife for as long as she lives? And," he continued, "do you promise to be faithful to her through all the ups and downs of life,

in good times and in bad times, whether she is well or whether she is ill, whether she is prosperous or whether she is poor until death brings your union to a close?"

As Dan started to spout out an ecstatic 'I do,'" the pastor abruptly stopped him. "I must first inform you both," he said admonishing them, "this is not multiple choice."

I CORINTHIANS 13:4-7: CHARITY SUFFERETH LONG, AND IS KIND; CHARITY ENVIETH NOT; CHARITY VAUNTETH NOT ITSELF, IS NOT PUFFED UP, DOTH NOT BEHAVE ITSELF UNSEEMLY, SEEKETH NOT HER OWN, IS NOT EASILY PROVOKED, THINKETH NO EVIL; REJOICETH NOT IN INIQUITY, BUT REJOICETH IN THE TRUTH; BEARETH ALL THINGS, BELIEVETH ALL THINGS, HOPETH ALL THINGS, ENDURETH ALL THINGS.

Reverend Ingram was addressing his congregation on the subject of spiritual maturity. He began his presentation by holding up a diaper and bottle in one hand and a steak in the other. "Spiritually speaking," he asked his listeners, "Which group do you belong to?" He told them that just as a child grows to maturity so must a Christian learn to feed on the meat of the Word.

He went on to say that, although it is sweet to see a little baby holding its own bottle, it gets old fast. "When the baby turns sixteen years old and is still wearing diapers and sucking on a bottle, it just isn't cute anymore! It's even more disgusting," he remarked, "when he turns 21 and you have to part the whiskers to get the bottle in."

I CORINTHIANS 3:1-2: AND I, BRETHREN, COULD NOT SPEAK UNTO YOU AS UNTO SPIRITUAL, BUT AS UNTO CARNAL, EVEN AS UNTO BABES IN CHRIST. I HAVE FED YOU WITH MILK, AND NOT WITH MEAT: FOR HITHERTO YE WERE NOT ABLE TO BEAR IT, NEITHER YET NOW ARE YE ABLE.

Upon hearing some nasty gossip about one of the deacon's wives, Reverend Ingram stood at his pulpit and reprimanded the "tongue waggers." "There are some self-righteous saints among us," he stated angrily, "Who have a

lot of idle time on their hands. Because I don't know who they are," he said, "I'm having the deacons pass the offering plates to each one here today. They will be filled with peel and stick adhesive tape.

If you are one of the talebearers, then by all means, help yourself to a piece of tape. The best way to stamp out sin," he told them sharply, "Is to keep your mouth taped shut."

JAMES 3:7-10: FOR EVERY KIND OF BEASTS, AND OF BIRDS, AND OF SERPENTS, AND OF THINGS IN THE SEA, IS TAMED, AND HATH BEEN TAMED OF MANKIND: BUT THE TONGUE CAN NO MAN TAME; IT IS AN UNRULY EVIL, FULL OF DEADLY POISON. THEREWITH BLESS WE GOD, EVEN THE FATHER; AND THEREWITH CURSE WE MEN, WHICH ARE MADE AFTER THE SIMILITUDE OF GOD. OUT OF THE SAME MOUTH PROCEEDETH BLESSING AND CURSING. MY BRETHREN, THESE THINGS OUGHT NOT SO TO BE.

Reverend Brady was addressing a group of teens on the importance of total consecration to the Lord. "There is a fine group of young people represented here this evening," he told them. "As I look out over the crowd," he said, "I see clean cut, neatly dressed individuals sitting here.

"But," he continued, "our spiritual walk is something that requires so much more than just cleaning up the outside. Most of you here this evening have already given your hearts to Jesus," he said, "but it wouldn't hurt to give him that other one per cent above your neck!"

I TIMOTHY 4:12: LET NO MAN DESPISE THY YOUTH; BUT BE THOU AN EXAMPLE OF THE BELIEVERS, IN WORD, IN CONVERSATION, IN CHARITY, IN SPIRIT, IN FAITH, IN PURITY.

"If each of you here today were given an all-expenses-paid dream vacation of a lifetime, would you turn it down?" asked Pastor Jordan. "Of course you wouldn't if you had any sense," he said.

"If you were allowed to explore the vast empire of some celebrated person of nobility and stay as long as you desired," he went on, "would you turn down such an opportunity?

"Did you also know that Jesus Christ, the King of Kings and Lord of Lords has extended that very same invitation to each one of us?" he asked. "He wants us to join Him in a glorious paradise and live amidst the magnificent splendor of His love, His beauty, and the unparalleled adventure of His unending kingdom. He promises happiness, contentment, and joy throughout all eternity.

"If it was just a matter of 'cents,'" he told them, you'd probably all be tripping over one another to buy a ticket there, but access to God's kingdom," he said, "can't be bought with money.

Sadly, most of you won't have enough 'sense' to get there by the one and only way by which man can enter, namely, faith in Jesus Christ and his shed blood on the cross. But that, my friend," he told them, is the only payment He will accept for your ticket into heaven."

JOHN 14:2-3: IN MY FATHER'S HOUSE ARE MANY MANSIONS: IF *IT WERE* NOT *SO*, I WOULD HAVE TOLD YOU. I GO TO PREPARE A PLACE FOR YOU. AND IF I GO AND PREPARE A PLACE FOR YOU, I WILL COME AGAIN, AND RECEIVE YOU UNTO MYSELF; THAT WHERE I AM, *THERE* YE MAY BE ALSO.

PSALM 16:11: THOU WILT SHEW ME THE PATH OF LIFE: IN THY PRESENCE *IS* FULNESS OF JOY; AT THY RIGHT HAND *THERE ARE* PLEASURES FOR EVERMORE. [SEE REVELATION 21:7; MATTHEW 5:12; LUKE 6:23; I CORINTHIANS 2:9]

Elaine didn't know what to do with the big wad of bubblegum she'd been chewing. "Mom . . .," she said.

"Hush, her mother told her, not allowing her to finish speaking.

"You're in church," she whispered, "and you have to be quiet,"

"But Mom, I have to know what to do with . . ." Again, her mother cut her off, warning her not to say another word.

When her mother stood up to join the congregation in prayer, Elaine took the gum out of her mouth and, not knowing where to put it, stuck it on her mother's church bulletin. You guessed it! When her mother sat back down, the sticky mess was there to meet her.

Later that morning Elaine's mother went forward for prayer. Everyone noticed the church bulletin stuck on the back of her skirt.

When the pastor heard about it, he couldn't resist asking who had pinned the tail on the donkey.

Taking it all in stride, she chuckled and said, "Well, I guess it's my turn to be the 'butt' of the pastor's jokes."

NUMBERS 22:28-35: AND THE LORD OPENED THE MOUTH OF THE ASS, AND SHE SAID UNTO BALAAM, WHAT HAVE I DONE UNTO THEE, THAT THOU HAST SMITTEN ME THESE THREE TIMES? AND BALAAM SAID UNTO THE ASS, BECAUSE THOU HAST MOCKED ME: I WOULD THERE WERE A SWORD IN MINE HAND, FOR NOW WOULD I KILL THEE. AND THE ASS SAID UNTO BALAAM, *AM* NOT I THINE ASS, UPON WHICH THOU HAST RIDDEN EVER SINCE I *WAS* THINE UNTO THIS DAY? WAS I EVER WONT TO DO SO UNTO THEE? AND HE SAID, NAY. THEN THE LORD OPENED THE EYES OF BALAAM, AND HE SAW THE ANGEL OF THE LORD STANDING IN THE WAY, AND HIS SWORD DRAWN IN HIS HAND: AND HE BOWED DOWN HIS HEAD, AND FELL FLAT ON HIS FACE. AND THE ANGEL OF THE LORD SAID UNTO HIM, WHEREFORE HAS THOU SMITTEN THINE ASS THESE THREE TIMES? BEHOLD, I WENT OUT TO WITHSTAND THEE, BECAUSE *THY* WAY IS PERVERSE BEFORE ME. AND THE ASS SAW ME, AND TURNED FROM ME THESE THREE TIMES: UNLESS SHE HAD TURNED FROM ME, SURELY NOW ALSO I HAD SLAIN THEE, AND SAVED HER ALIVE. AND BALAAM SAID UNTO THE ANGEL OF THE LORD, I HAVE SINNED; FOR I KNEW NOT THAT THOU STOODEST IN THE WAY AGAINST ME: NOW THEREFORE, IF IT DISPLEASE THEE, I WILL GET ME BACK AGAIN. AND THE ANGEL OF THE LORD SAID UNTO BALAAM, GO WITH THE MEN: BUT ONLY THE WORD THAT I SHALL SPEAK UNTO THEE, THAT THOU SHALT SPEAK . . .

(Author's note: It is amazing to me that Balaam wasn't astounded by the talking donkey!)

While Pastor Burton was busy preaching a very thought—provoking message, he noticed an old gentleman "sawing logs" in the back corner. He kept an eye on the man, who, a half an hour later, still had not batted an eye nor raised an eyebrow. "I think we have a deep sleeper here among us," he said, approaching the back row.

Then, tapping the man's shoulder, he quoted Ephesians 5:14 to the snoozing saint: 'Awake thou that sleepest, and arise from the dead, and Christ shall give thee light.'"

I THESSALONIANS 5:5-6: YE ARE ALL THE CHILDREN OF LIGHT, AND THE CHILDREN OF THE DAY: WE ARE NOT OF THE NIGHT, NOR OF DARKNESS. THEREFORE LET US NOT SLEEP, AS *DO* OTHERS; BUT LET US WATCH AND BE SOBER.

"While television may have some merit," said Pastor Stan, "It certainly does everything it can to promote marital unrest."

Focusing on the group of ladies present, he began his message. Soap operas," he said cautioning them, "make extra marital affairs look normal and exciting.

"Commercials, likewise, are becoming more repugnant by the minute," he told them. "It's getting so that you can't even buy a soda without a half dressed woman standing behind it. They want you ladies to believe," he said, "that you'll look like her as soon as you've consumed one bottle." He glanced at his notes and continued talking.

"With all these housewives comparing themselves to soap opera queens and television goddesses," he told them, "is it any wonder that the average housewife ends up feeling like some worn out old tire with no tread?"

He looked across his audience. "Nevertheless ladies," he said sternly, "just because you watch soap operas is no reason to have one of your own. Whenever a strange man is in your house," he warned, "unless he has his

eyes on the meter, his hand on a plunger, or he's fixing some appliance, throw him out of there as fast as you can!"

PROVERBS 6:27: CAN A MAN TAKE FIRE IN HIS BOSOM, AND HIS CLOTHES NOT BE BURNED?

As Pastor Stewart was preaching one Sunday, a little girl wandered away from her mother and made her way up onto the pastor's platform. Her angelic little face was outlined with sandy brown curls. Pink satin ribbons adorned her hair. She immediately won the Pastor's heart. With her big brown eyes she looked innocently up at him as she tugged at his leg. He picked her up and smiled fondly at her. Then he walked over and sat down on his bench, holding her in his lap.

Everyone laughed and giggled. Her mother turned beet red. Then with one arm around the little girl and the other holding his microphone, he said, "I guess she's smart enough to know where to get the best seat in the house."

II TIMOTHY 3:5: AND THAT FROM A CHILD THOU HAST KNOWN THE HOLY SCRIPTURES, WHICH ARE ABLE TO MAKE THEE WISE UNTO SALVATION THROUGH FAITH WHICH IS IN CHRIST JESUS.

During the summer months, Reverend Jackson's congregation declined considerably. Although he took into account those away on vacation, the substantial reduction in attendance prompted him to bring it to the attention of his church.

"For those of you playing hooky during Sunday morning services to go fishing," he scolded, "all I can say is that I pray you catch a big fish." Pausing for a moment, he then added, "And I hope you catch that big fish the same way Jonah did!"

JONAH 1:17: NOW THE LORD PREPARED A GREAT FISH TO SWALLOW UP JONAH. AND JONAH WAS IN THE BELLY OF THE FISH THREE DAYS AND THREE NIGHTS.

JONAH 2:10: AND THE LORD SPAKE UNTO THE FISH, AND IT VOMITED OUT JONAH UPON THE DRY *LAND*.

"I think if most of us are honest," said Reverend Stevens from the pulpit, "We'll admit that most of the time we have a battle overcoming the flesh. If our nose isn't in somebody's business, our mouth is. And if our hands aren't into some kind of mischief our feet are heading toward it. But view your body as a vehicle," he said, "whose oil needs to be checked and spark plugs changed. If you maintain it, it should run fairly well in spite of the rust and corrosion.

"In other words," he told them, "keep putting the word of God into your mind and allow yourselves to be transformed by the renewing power of the Holy Spirit, and you should be able to give the Lord some pretty good mileage. But please," he warned them, "no reckless driving."

ROMANS 13:14: BUT PUT YE ON THE LORD JESUS CHRIST, AND MAKE NOT PROVISION FOR THE FLESH, TO FULFIL THE LUSTS THEREOF.

In God's army of believers," said Pastor Lyons, 'there are various levels of ministry. Some of you 'generals' have been serving the Lord for a long time and He as been able to trust you with greater responsibility. Others have just begun your training. All of you, though, have been commissioned by the Lord to go out into the world and preach the gospel to every living soul. The responsibility is awesome.

God has a job for each of us to do whether we are veterans or have just enlisted in his service. Be faithful in whatever assignment He gives you. And I pray," he told them earnestly, "that as each soldier leaves here today, the Lord will not find you 'missing in action.'"

JOHN 4:35: SAY NOT YE, THERE ARE YET FOUR MONTHS, AND THEN COMETH HARVEST? BEHOLD, I SAY UNTO YOU, LIFT UP YOUR EYES, AND LOOK ON THE FIELDS; FOR THEY ARE WHITE ALREADY TO HARVEST.

MATTHEW 9:37: THEN SAITH HE UNTO HIS DISCIPLES, THE HARVEST TRULY *IS* PLENTEOUS, BUT THE LABOURERS [LABORERS] *ARE* FEW;

[SEE ROMANS 1:16; ROMANS 10:14-15; MARK 16:15; PSALM 40:9-10; PSALM 66:16; PSALM 107:2; ACTS 1:8: ACTS 4:20: ACTS 5:42; ACTS 20:26-27]

ISAIAH 6:8: ALSO I HEARD THE VOICE OF THE LORD, SAYING, WHOM SHALL I SEND, AND WHO WILL GO FOR US? THEN SAID I, HERE *AM I*; SEND ME.

Upon hearing about a church that had turned a couple away because of their sloppy appearance and improper clothing, Reverend Fisher stood in the pulpit to explain his position on the matter.

"Do you see these bright red socks and this purple and orange striped tie," he said pointing to himself. "I have worn this ridiculous outfit to make it obvious that we have no dress code here. While we appreciate you wearing your best for the Lord, nevertheless," he said, "you are welcome to come as you are.

"Men, you may come with holes in your socks and five o'clock shadow.

"Ladies, you may come with runs in your nylons and curlers in your hair.

"Ladies and gentlemen," he continued, "whether it be suits or blue jeans, gowns or 'grubbies', everyone may wear what they wish. We will only refuse admission should you be daring enough to come strolling through the doors wearing something less than a fig leaf."

I SAMUEL 16:7: FOR THE LORD SEETH NOT AS MAN SEETH; FOR MAN LOOKETH ON THE OUTWARD APPEARANCE, BUT THE LORD LOOKETH ON THE HEART.

Nick was a church song leader, conservative in dress, and reserved in manner as well as appearance. One day he decided to take a daring plunge and change his hairstyle.

His thick, shiny, black hair would have been the envy of Samson, except that, following his visit to the hairdresser, it now looked like a frizzy mess sticking out in every direction.

The pastor, seizing every opportunity to add humor into his sermon, couldn't resist commenting on his new look. "The message I'm about to deliver," he said, "is guaranteed to curl your hair." Then looking over at Nick, he joked, "And I see he already heard it in our earlier service."

JOHN 12:3: THEN TOOK MARY A POUND OF OINTMENT OF SPIKENARD, VERY COSTLY, AND ANOINTED THE FEET OF JESUS, AND WIPED HIS FEET WITH HER HAIR.

"Mr. Morton, an undertaker from out of town, is here with us today," announced Reverend Bailey to his church. "He has been a close friend of mine for years. In fact, he told me just yesterday that, should the time come when I lay down on the job, he'll be happy to embalm me free of charge."

The congregation giggled as the minister continued. "And for those of you who will be checking out of the hotel of life within the next few days," he told them, "you are welcome to avail yourself of his services. But hurry;" he teased, "he'll only be here for the remainder of this week."

JOHN 11:25: JESUS SAID UNTO HER, I AM THE RESURRECTION, AND THE LIFE: HE THAT BELIEVETH IN ME, THOUGH HE WERE DEAD, YET SHALL HE LIVE.

"With the world series on tonight," said Pastor Jones, "I didn't expect to see so many faces here tonight. But," he continued, "I'll try to make this night worth your while."

After a heart stirring message, he had an altar call. Several people went forward to repent and give their lives to Jesus. Delighted with the results, the Pastor remarked, "I guess we're having our own world series here tonight.

There are some of you out there who are still at first base. Why don't you come forward," he urged them "while you still have time to make it.

"And there are some of you that were on second and third base that I see making your way down here."

Then he pointed to those already at the altar kneeling. "And these champions," he remarked joyously, "have already made a homerun!"

I JOHN 5:5: FOR WHATSOEVER IS BORN OF GOD OVERCOMETH THE WORLD: AND THIS IS THE VICTORY THAT OVERCOMETH THE WORLD, EVEN OUR FAITH.

At the conclusion of his message one evening, Pastor Parson opened a big box he had sitting next to his pulpit. "Could some able-bodied person assist me with this?" he asked, struggling to take out the first of a few heavy steel balls and chains he'd ordered.

"You're probably wondering just what this is all about," he told them, "so let me explain. We've got a few people among us," he said, "who are walking pretty close to the Lord. I don't know what I would do without these fine Christians, who, to the best of their ability are living for God in mind, body, and soul. Since I can't afford to lose these modern-day Enochs," he told them, smiling, "I'm hooking these balls 'n chains around their ankles so God doesn't try to pull a fast one!"

GENESIS 5:24: AND ENOCH WALKED WITH GOD: AND HE WAS NOT; FOR GOD TOOK HIM.

II KINGS 2:9-14: AND IT CAME TO PASS, WHEN THEY WERE GONE OVER, THAT ELIJAH SAID UNTO ELISHA, ASK WHAT I SHALL DO FOR THEE, BEFORE I BE TAKEN AWAY FROM THEE. AND ELISHA SAID, I PRAY THEE, LET A DOUBLE PORTION OF THY SPIRIT BE UPON ME. AND HE SAID, THOU HAST ASKED A HARD THING: *NEVERTHELESS, IF THOU SEE ME WHEN I AM* TAKEN FROM THEE, IT SHALL BE SO UNTO THEE; BUT IF NOT, IT SHALL NOT BE *SO*. AND IT CAME TO PASS, AS THEY STILL WENT ON, AND TALKED, THAT, BEHOLD, *THERE APPEARED* A CHARIOT OF FIRE, AND HORSES OF FIRE, AND PARTED THEM BOTH ASUNDER; AND ELIJAH WENT UP BY A WHIRLWIND INTO HEAVEN. AND ELISHA SAW *IT*, AND HE CRIED, MY FATHER, MY FATHER, THE CHARIOT OF ISRAEL, AND THE HORSEMEN THEREOF. AND HE SAW HIM NO MORE: AND HE TOOK HOLD OF HIS OWN CLOTHES, AND RENT THEM IN TWO PIECES. HE TOOK UP ALSO THE MANTLE OF ELIJAH THAT FELL FROM HIM, AND WENT BACK AND

STOOD BY THE BANK OF JORDAN; AND HE TOOK THE MANTLE OF ELIJAH THAT FELL FROM HIM, AND SMOTE THE WATERS, AND SAID, WHERE *IS* THE LORD GOD OF ELIJAH? AND WHEN HE ALSO HAD SMITTEN THE WATERS, THEY PARTED HITHER AND THITHER: AND ELISHA WENT OVER.

Reverend Andrews told his listeners one evening, "God sees all those ulterior motives that you think nobody knows about. When, for instance, you bragged to all your neighbors about buying the old widow Thompson a cherry pie," he said in a reprimanding tone, "why didn't you also tell them the only reason you gave it to her was because you forgot to add the sugar and remove the pits"

He looked out over the crowd and continued, "And when you took those boxes of Christmas candy up there to the nursing home to distribute, why didn't you tell them it was some you'd had laying around for the past four or five years?

And that potato salad you gave to your neighbor," he continued, "did you mention that it had been sitting out too long and you were afraid to eat it yourself?

"I certainly hope I didn't offend any innocent parties here tonight," he said, "But this sermon certainly gives you some 'food for thought.'"

GALATIONS 5:14: FOR ALL THE LAW IS FULFILLED IN ONE WORD, EVEN IN THIS; THOU SHALT LOVE THY NEIGHBOUR AS THYSELF. [SEE GALATIONS 6:2]

When the pastor arrived ten minutes late for a small church wedding, the family had become quite anxious, not quite so anxious as the flustered minister, however, who was about to make the unpardonable blunder of his ministerial experience. "I'm sorry for the delay," Reverend Smith apologized, "I got held over at a funeral, but now, without further ado, let us begin. Would everyone take their places, please."

Everyone scrambled to their seats as the radiant bride began to walk down the aisle escorted by her father. As she was joined by the happy groom, the pastor began the ceremony. "Dearly beloved," he said, "We are gathered here today on this solemn and mournful occasion . . .

PSALM 48:14: FOR THIS GOD *IS* OUR GOD FOR EVER AND EVER: HE WILL BE OUR GUIDE *EVEN* UNTO DEATH.

ADMINISTRATIVE ANTICS

Jim, a deacon of the church, was giving his testimony one evening. "My wife got born again several months before my own conversion," he said. "She asked me to leave the lukewarm church we were in to join one which was spirit-filled and full of life. I continued to stubbornly decline her offer, however.

"After months of nagging," he told them, "she decided to leave me on my own and, for the duration of each church service, sit across the street in the donut shop and wait for me. My slim, attractive wife was beginning to resemble a cream puff," he said, "and our marriage was 'literally coming apart at the seams.'

"For the sake of our marriage," he said, "I realized I had to do something fast. You guessed it, my friends," he told them, "I left the service one night to join my wife at the donut shop and I got saved in between a French pastry and a glazed donut!"

II CORINTHIANS 6:2: . . . BEHOLD, NOW IS THE ACCEPTED TIME: BEHOLD, NOW IS THE DAY OF SALVATION.

ROMANS 10:9-10: THAT IF THOU SHALT CONFESS WITH THY MOUTH THE LORD JESUS, AND SHALT BELIEVE IN THINE HEART THAT GOD HATH RAISED HIM FROM THE DEAD, THOU SHALT BE SAVED. FOR WITH THE HEART MAN BELIEVETH UNTO RIGHTEOUSNESS; AND WITH THE MOUTH CONFESSION IS MADE UNTO SALVATION. [SEE JOHN 14:6 & I JOHN 5:11-12]

As one of the church treasurers was addressing the congregation concerning finances, he concluded his message by saying, "Would you please spare our treasurers the irritation of sorting through the buttons, bobby pins, jewelry,

paperclips, croaking frogs, garden vegetables and other paraphernalia we find in the plates," he sighed.

"I think the Lord prefers direct deposit, cash, or checks that can be backed with something green," he continued, "and we don't mean lettuce."

As he glanced around at those in attendance, he could see that a number of members were now squirming in their seats. "We find that it makes it much easier to credit your account accurately," he told them, "when the tithe envelope includes currency rather than I.O.U. statements and last night's poker chips. Also, please," he urged, "no more blue ribbon squash in place of your ten percent."

PSALMS 116:12: WHAT SHALL I RENDER UNTO THE LORD FOR ALL HIS BENEFITS TOWARD ME? [SEE GENESIS 28:22 & MALACHI 3:8-11]

EXODUS 23:15: . . . NONE SHALL APPEAR BEFORE ME EMPTY . . . [SEE II CORINTHIANS 9:6]

GENESIS 28:22: . . . OF ALL THAT THOU SHALT GIVE ME I WILL SURELY GIVE THE TENTH UNTO THEE.

PROVERBS 3:9: HONOUR [HONOR] THE LORD WITH THY SUBSTANCE, AND WITH THE FIRSTFRUITS OF ALL THINE INCREASE . . .

"Where is Reverend Standish?" Deacon Jones asked Deacon Smith. "It's almost 11:00 a.m. and he's no where to be seen.

"Did you call his home?" Deacon Smith asked.

"Yes," replied Deacon Jones. "I checked with everyone except the morgue. I do hope," he remarked, "that we don't find him 'resting in the Lord' there."

"Well," replied Deacon Smith, "I suppose we can keep the people busy singing hymns and praying for another five or ten minutes."

At 11:15 a.m. Reverend Standish still had not arrived nor called.

"I guess one of us will have to preach this morning," said Deacon Jones. "Not me!" Deacon Smith quickly told him without apology. "I don't have any notes prepared."

"Then go ahead and take the offering," Deacon Jones told him. "I'm sure he'll be here within a matter of minutes."

By 11:30 a.m. the Reverend was still conspicuous by his absence. "We can't stall any longer," said Deacon Jones. We'll have to make an announcement. He walked up to the podium, took the microphone, and said, "Reverend Standish has apparently been detained for some reason. If he isn't here by 11:45 a.m." he teased, "we're going to send out a posse after him."

ROMANS 14:7: FOR NONE OF US LIVETH TO HIMSELF, AND NO MAN DIETH TO HIMSELF.

Arnold, the church treasurer, was counting the Sunday morning offering.

"It's a good thing I learned to count up to infinity," he kidded one of the other deacons. "If I was counting dollars, or even quarters, I'd feel it was worth the effort," he grumbled, "but each week we get the same infinite amount of pennies. Honestly," he sighed, "it's like counting the sands of the sea."

"You can say that again," replied Bernie, another deacon. "Sometimes I think they view us as nothing more than a glorified piggy bank!"

II CORINTHIANS 9:6-7: BUT THIS I SAY, HE WHICH SOWETH SPARINGLY SHALL REAP ALSO SPARINGLY: AND HE WHICH SOWETH BOUNTIFULLY SHALL REAP ALSO BOUNTIFULLY. EVERY MAN ACCORDINGAS HE PURPOSETH IN HIS HEART, *SO LET HIM GIVE;* NOT GRUDGINGLY, OR OF NECESSITY:FOR GOD LOVETH A CHEERFUL GIVER.

Although Reverend Donovan's church was steadily growing, he was always open to innovative ideas on how to recruit new members. During his board meeting, he would welcome any new suggestions to increase church attendance.

Hal, one of the deacons whose judgment the minister trusted implicitly, advised the Reverend to put a catchy phrase on their church billboard which faced a busy street.

"That's an excellent idea, Hal," Reverend Donovan told him. "And since it's your idea, I'll give you the liberty of taking on that responsibility yourself."

The following Sunday, as the minister drove into the church parking lot, he read the words to his reliable assistant: "COME 'N JOIN US ONE AND ALL FOR THE HAPPY HOUR FROM 9 : 00 A. M. TO 12:00 P.M. WHERE THE SERMONS ARE ON THE HOUSE!"

PSALMS 122:1: I WAS GLAD WHEN THEY SAID UNTO ME, LET US GO INTO THE HOUSE OF THE LORD.

Concerned about the nonchalant attitude in his church, Reverend Campbell stood in the pulpit criticizing his members because of their indifference to eternal matters. "How can you take this burden for souls so lightly?" he charged them. "Don't you care about the salvation of those that are dying everyday and going to a lake of fire without so much as even a prayer from any of you? He paced the floors and then continued.

"Week after week," he lamented, "souls drift in here from off the streets. Many of these poor sinners make their way up to altar, and yet," he said almost weeping, "not one of you will budge from your seats to come pray with them. I look out at scores of faces all glued to the clock," he said accusingly, "waiting for dismissal time. How can you be so numb to the needs of others and so lax in your own spiritual lives?" He went on. "And how long has it been," he asked, "since I've seen you, yourselves, at the altar? When, dear friends," he concluded, "was the last time I saw you stirred to tears?"

Later that afternoon, during a conversation with the minister, one of his deacons remarked, "I think what we have in this church, sir," he said regrettably, "is what you would call a 'severe draught.'"

REVELATION 3:15-16: I KNOW THY WORKS, THAT THOU ART NEITHER COLD NOR HOT: I WOULD THOU WERT COLD OR HOT. SO THEN BECAUSE THOU ART LUKEWARM, AND NEITHER COLD NOR HOT, I WILL SPUE THEE OUT OF MY MOUTH.

One evening one of the pastor's assistants was expounding on the various prayers one might offer unto the Lord. After discussing the "prayer of petition" and the "prayer of thanksgiving" in detail, he went on to illustrate the "prayer of adoration."

"Picture yourself," he told the congregation, "going down a steep, icy road during a blizzard. Your car has just gone out of control and you are now spinning and sliding off the road at an alarming ninety miles per hour. Your brakes have just gone out, your headlights have just shorted out, and your seatbelt is flexing like an elastic rubber band. The point I'm trying to make," he said, "is that, as your car flies into the tree just ahead of you, and your life flashes before your eyes, most of you will not be thinking about giving the Lord the "prayer of adoration."

ISAIAH 65:24: AND IT SHALL COME TO PASS, THAT BEFORE THEY CALL, I WILL ANSWER, AND WHILE THEY ARE YET SPEAKING I WILL HEAR.

After receiving a number of invalid and bounced checks, the church treasurers brought it to their minister's attention. The following Sunday, a message in the church bulletin read as follows: *It would be appreciated if, in the future, all checks made payable to "God" would be made out to our church instead. As you all know, the Lord has been on vacation for a couple thousand years and we're not sure just when he'll be back to endorse them.*

HEBREWS 10:37: FOR YET A LITTLE WHILE, AND HE THAT SHALL COME WILL COME, AND WILL NOT TARRY.

"Attention everyone," announced Deacon Bertram. "The pastor will be with us momentarily but before he comes to the podium, there are a few instructions I must give you. Clearing his throat, he began. "Please <u>do not enter</u> the church by using the back door," he told them. "Loitering in the parking lot is <u>prohibited</u> as a safety precaution. The gymnasium

is definitely <u>off limits</u> during the service, <u>trespassing</u> on the grass, or smoking on the premises. <u>Avoid</u> making unnecessary trips to and from the restroom while the pastor's message is being delivered. <u>No whispering or talking</u> during the service. Making change in the offering plate is <u>not allowed</u>. Cursing, swearing, and gossiping in the hallways is <u>forbidden</u>. <u>No</u> drinking of alcoholic beverages within or without the building will be tolerated. And above all, <u>no</u> throwing tomatoes or rotten eggs at the pastor during the parts of his sermon that you disagree with." Looking up from his notes, he concluded, "I hope that you will all make yourselves feel right at home."

ROMANS 6:12-13: LET NOT SIN THEREFORE REIGN IN YOUR MORTAL BODY, THAT YE SHOULD OBEY IT IN THE LUSTS THEREOF. NEITHER YIELD YE YOUR MEMBERS *AS* INSTRUMENTS OF UNRIGHTEOUSNESS UNTO SIN: BUT YIELD YOURSELVES UNTO GOD, AS THOSE THAT ARE ALIVE FROM THE DEAD, AND YOUR MEMBERS *AS* INSTRUMENTS OF RIGHTEOUSNESS UNTO GOD.

A visiting evangelist was invited to speak to a capacity crowd in a large church. After wetting their spiritual appetites with the story of Noah and the judgment flood, he began giving an altar call. "There are many here tonight, who, like Noah, are safe amidst the storm," he said, "but for those of you who aren't anchored in him, I suggest you put your life jackets on and start rowing toward this altar as fast as you can."

GENESIS 7:11-12 & 22-23: AND THE WINDOWS OF HEAVEN WERE OPENED. AND THE RAIN WAS UPON THE EARTH FORTY DAYS AND FORTY NIGHTS. ALL IN WHOSE NOSTRILS WAS THE BREATH OF LIFE, OF ALL THAT WAS IN THE DRY LAND, DIED. AND EVERY LIVING SUBSTANCE WAS DESTROYED WHICH WAS UPON THE FACE OF THE GROUND, BOTH MAN, AND CATTLE, AND THE CREEPING THINGS, AND THE FOWL OF THE HEAVEN; AND THEY WERE DESTROYED FROM THE EARTH: AND NOAH ONLY REMAINED ALIVE, AND THEY THAT WERE WITH HIM IN THE ARK.

Lynette, the church secretary was unable to locate the Pastor one afternoon so she called his wife at home. "Would you give this message to the Pastor as soon as possible?" she asked.

"Certainly," said his wife. "I'll stick a note inside the refrigerator as soon as we hang up."

"The refrigerator!" exclaimed Lynette.

"Sure," replied the Pastor's wife, "that's the first place he goes when he steps through these doors."

PSALMS 37:25: I HAVE BEEN YOUNG, AND NOW AM OLD; YET HAVE I NOT SEEN THE RIGHTEOUS FORSAKEN, NOR HIS SEED BEGGING BREAD.

I KINGS 17:16: *AND* THE BARREL OF MEAL WASTED NOT, NEITHER DID THE CRUSE OF OIL FAIL, ACCORDING TO THE WORD OF THE LORD, WHICH HE SPAKE BY ELIJAH.

GENESIS 21:19: AND GOD OPENED HER [HAGAR'S] EYES, AND SHE SAW A WELL OF WATER; AND SHE WENT, AND FILLED THE BOTTLE WITH WATER, AND GAVE THE LAD DRINK.

ISAIAH 41:17-18: *WHEN* THE POOR AND NEEDY SEEK WATER, AND *THERE IS* NONE, *AND* THEIR TONGUE FAILETH FOR THIRST, I THE LORD WILL HEAR THEM, *I* THE GOD OF ISRAEL WILL NOT FORSAKE THEM . . . I WILL MAKE THE WILDERNESS A POOL OF WATER.

PSALM 78:19: YEA, THEY SPAKE AGAINST GOD; THEY SAID, CAN GOD FURNISH A TABLE IN THE WILDERNESS?

Mr. Norton was anxiously hoping for a position on the church board. He prayed fervently over the matter as well as brushing up on his vocabulary, his manners, etc.

On the day of his interview, he went to special lengths to make sure that everything was in order, including a portfolio containing a list of his qualifications, record of faithful stewardship, and so forth. He shaved and showered, and put on his best suit.

"Mr. Norton is here," the secretary said, notifying the pastor and other board members.

"Please send him in," the Pastor instructed her.

As Mr. Norton seated himself and began shuffling through his papers, he was promptly informed that wouldn't be necessary.

"All we want to know," said one of the deacons is whether you own a set of matching cufflinks and a tie clip?"

"Yes," he replied, looking perplexed.

"Do you own at least two good suits?" the deacon asked him.

"Yes," he again nodded.

"That's good enough for us," the pastor said enthusiastically. "You're hired!"

ISAIAH 61:10: I WILL GREATLY REJOICE IN THE LORD, MY SOUL SHALL BE JOYFUL IN MY GOD; FOR HE HATH CLOTHED ME WITH THE GARMENTS OF SALVATION, HE HATH COVERED ME WITH THE ROBE OF RIGHTEOUSNESS.

GENESIS 3:21: UNTO ADAM ALSO AND TO HIS WIFE DID THE LORD GOD MAKE COATS OF SKINS, AND CLOTHED THEM. [SEE HEBREWS 9:22 & EPHESIANS 1:7; EPHESIANS 2:13-14; LEVITICUS 17:11; REVELATION 1:5; COLOSSIANS 1:14 & 20]

"And now here is Sally to make the weekly announcements," said the minister, calling his secretary to the platform.

Sally, who was always quite theatrical, glided up to the platform and began in her customary manner. First, she blew her nose and arranged her papers. Then she walked over to the minister, adjusted his tie and refolded his handkerchief. "Now that we've got things up here straightened out," she said, looking over the top of her glasses and adding a firmness to her voice, "We can get down to the business of getting some things out there straightened out."

LAMENTATIONS 3:40: LET US SEARCH AND TRY OUR WAYS AND TURN AGAIN TO THE LORD.

When the Pastor introduced Mr. Joles, the Principal of their Christian affiliated school, the gentleman stumbled up to the platform blurry-eyed and momentarily disoriented. With a face flushed from embarrassment, he quickly collected himself and then commenced with his speech. "I want you all to know," he said, pointing to himself, "this principal does not indulge in alcoholic beverages. What you see here are the lingering effects of some strong cough syrup which I have been using to nurse this bad cold."

The pastor, also seated on the platform, got up, chuckled, and said, "Mr. Joles, would you please tell me where I can get some of that same medicine?"

"Why certainly, pastor," Mr. Joles jokingly replied, "But first tell me how to find that yard sale where you purchased that outstanding bow tie!"

A MERRY HEART DOETH GOOD LIKE A MEDICINE . . . PROVERBS 17:22

"Marlene, I'd like to see you after church." Deacon Conally told her. "It's very important so please meet the pastor and myself in his office immediately following the service."

"Is anything wrong?" Marlene asked the deacon and her pastor when they were behind closed doors.

"Deacon Conally has had a vision concerning you," her pastor said. "He would like to share it with you."

Marlene, who had just seated herself, looked at him with surprise. "Me?" she exclaimed. "Please tell me about it."

"I had this dream in which I saw you sharing the gospel with thousands." he said quietly. "I wouldn't have thought much of it except that my wife had the same identical dream a few days later."

"His wife, not knowing he'd had the same dream, told him about it," Marlene's pastor told her.

At that instant, Marlene slumped over in her chair.

"Hmmm," Deacon Conally said to the minister. "Either she was slain in the spirit or she's just fainted from shock!"

As soon as Marlene revived, she asked the deacon, "Did you by any chance see my two little adorable poodles at my side?"

GENESIS 41:32: AND FOR THAT THE DREAM WAS DOUBLED UNTO PHARAOH TWICE; *IT IS* BECAUSE THE THING *IS* ESTABLISHED BY GOD, AND GOD WILL SHORTLY BRING IT TO PASS.

II CORINTHIANS 13:1: . . . IN THE MOUTH OF TWO OR THREE WITNESSES SHALL EVERY WORD BE ESTABLISHED.

JOB 33:14-17: FOR GOD SPEAKETH ONCE, YEA TWICE, *YET MAN* PERCEIVETH IT NOT. IN A DREAM, IN A VISION OF THE NIGHT, WHEN DEEP SLEEP FALLETH UPON MEN, IN SLUMBERINGS UPON THE BED; THEN HE OPENETH THE EARS OF MEN, AND SEALETH THEIR INSTRUCTION, THAT HE MAY WITHDRAW MAN *FROM HIS* PURPOSE, AND HIDE PRIDE FROM MAN.

HABAKKUK 2:3: FOR THE VISION *IS* YET FOR AN APPOINTED TIME, BUT AT THE END IT SHALL SPEAK, AND NOT LIE: THOUGH IT TARRY, WAIT FOR IT; BECAUSE IT WILL SURE COME, IT WILL NOT TARRY.

JEREMIAH 1:12: . . . FOR I WILL HASTEN MY WORD TO PERFORM IT.

NUMBERS 23:19: GOD *IS* NOT A MAN THAT HE SHOULD LIE; NEITHER THE SON OF MAN, THAT HE SHOULD REPENT: HATH HE SAID, AND

SHALL HE NOT DO *IT?* OR HATH HE SPOKEN, AND SHALL HE NOT MAKE IT GOOD? [SEE DEUTERONOMY 18:22]

PSALM 89:34: MY COVENANT WILL I NOT BREAK, NOR ALTER THE THING THAT IS GONE OUT OF MY LIPS.

JOSHUA 23:14: . . . NOT ONE THING HATH FAILED OF ALL THE GOOD THINGS WHICH THE LORD YOUR GOD SPAKE CONCERNING YOU; ALL ARE COME TO PASS UNTO YOU, *AND* NOT ONE THING HATH FAILED THEREOF.

II CORINTHIANS 1:20: FOR ALL THE PROMISES OF GOD IN HIM *ARE* YEA, AND IN HIM AMEN, UNTO THE GLORY OF GOD BY US.

ECCLESIASTES 3:11: HE HATH MADE EVERY THING BEAUTIFUL IN HIS TIME . . .

ROMANS 4:20-21: HE (ABRAHAM) STAGGERED NOT AT THE PROMISE OF GOD THROUGH UNBELIEF; BUT WAS STRONG IN FAITH, GIVING GLORY TO GOD; AND BEING FULLY PERSUADED THAT, WHAT HE HAD PROMISED, HE WAS ABLE ALSO TO PERFORM. [SEE JOB 33:14-17]

PINTSIZE PANDEMONIUM

"In the beginning God created the heavens and the earth," said Miss Woods, the primary Sunday school teacher.

Little Jimmy raised his hand, wiggling it back and forth until the teacher called on him.

"Yes, Johnny," said the teacher. "I just want to know," he said in earnest, "What mistakes he made after that."

DEUTERONOMY 32:4: *HE IS* THE ROCK, HIS WORK IS PERFECT . . .

PSALM 18:30: *AS FOR* GOD, HIS WAY *IS* PERFECT . . .

While doing her housework one day, Diane discovered her little boy hiding under her bed. "Johnny, for heaven's sake," his mother beckoned, "get out from underneath my bed. What are you doing under there anyway?"

"I'm hiding from God," came the timid, squeaky reply.

"Well, hide somewhere else," she told him. "All that dust will rub off on your clean clothes."

"But Mom," Johnny replied, "God will find me if I hide someplace else. It's dark under here and He won't be able to see me."

"What kind of mischief have you been into, Johnny?" his mother asked, suspiciously.

"Enough to get God pretty upset," he answered. First He saw me let the air out of your tires. Then He saw me pull your towels off the clothesline,

- 57 -

but what really got him mad," he told his mother, "was when He saw me turn on the garden hose and spray our next door neighbor, Mrs. Adams, and her dog."

PSALMS 116:15: PRECIOUS IN THE SIGHT OF THE LORD *IS* THE DEATH OF HIS SAINTS.

ST. MATTHEW 10:19-20: BUT WHEN THEY DELIVER YOU UP, TAKE NO THOUGHT HOW OR WHAT YE SHALL SPEAK: FOR IT SHALL BE GIVEN YOU IN THAT SAME HOUR WHAT YE SHALL SPEAK. FOR IT IS NOT YE THAT SPEAK, BUT THE SPIRIT OF YOUR FATHER WHICH SPEAKETH IN YOU.

It was a hot, humid, summer day and little Laura's father was out mowing their huge backyard. "Please go in the house and get me a glass of pop," he told his daughter, as he stopped to rest for a minute.

A few minutes later, Laura returned with a cola for her father. "Is pop good for you, daddy?" she asked.

"I should say not!" he quickly answered. "God wants us to put things that are good for us in our bodies. In fact," he said, "I shouldn't even be drinking this. It's like putting poison in my body."

"Probably 'cause it's got all that kitty litter in it," his daughter agreed.

"Kitty litter?" he asked, laughing. "Where did you come up with that notion, sweetheart?"

"Well, daddy, it says so right on the bottle," she stated in a matter-of fact manner. She hurried into the house, grabbed the bottle of pop, and ran over to her father with it. "See!" she said pointing at the words 'half *liter*'!

I CORINTHIANS 6:20: FOR YE ARE BOUGHT WITH A PRICE: THEREFORE GLORIFY GOD IN YOUR BODY, AND IN YOUR SPIRIT, WHICH ARE GOD'S.

Sweetie, give your allowance to me. That way it wont get lost.
Yah, it'll just get spent!

Paula and her six-year old son were shopping at a mall. As they stepped into an elevator and pushed the button to the third floor, it suddenly occurred to Bobby that there must be an elevator somewhere that would lead to heaven.

"Mom," her son asked, "Does it say in the Bible where the elevator is that reaches to heaven, or is God just going to drop a big rope down for us when it's time to go?"

ROMANS 8:11: BUT IF THE SPIRIT OF HIM THAT RAISED UP JESUS FROM THE DEAD DWELL IN YOU, HE THAT RAISED UP CHRIST FROM THE DEAD SHALL ALSO QUICKEN YOUR MORTAL BODIES BY HIS SPIRIT THAT DWELLETH IN YOU.

II CORINTHIANS 4:14: KNOWING THAT HE WHICH RAISED UP THE LORD JESUS SHALL RAISE UP US ALSO BY JESUS, AND SHALL PRESENT *US* WITH YOU.

JOHN 11:25: JESUS SAID UNTO HER, I AM THE RESURRECTION, AND THE LIFE: HE THAT BELIEVETH IN ME, THOUGH HE WERE DEAD, YET SHALL HE LIVE.

JOHN 14:19: . . . BECAUSE I LIVE, YE SHALL LIVE ALSO.

ACTS 26:8: WHY SHOULD IT BE THOUGHT A THING INCREDIBLE WITH YOU, THAT GOD SHOULD RAISE THE DEAD?

REVELATION 1:18: *I AM* HE THAT LIVETH, AND WAS DEAD; AND, BEHOLD, I AM ALIVE FOR EVERMORE, AMEN; AND HAVE THE KEYS OF HELL AND OF DEATH.

As Bonnie and her daughter arrived at the church parking lot to drop off a couple of boxes of used clothing, they noticed a wedding in progress.

"Can we stay here until the bride and groom come out, mom?" Misty pleaded.

"I suppose it would be alright," her mother replied. "Besides, it will take a few minutes to set these things inside the back door." While removing some of the boxes from the back seat, she asked, "Do you want to wait in the car?"

"Yes, Mom," exclaimed Misty. "I don't want to miss seeing the bride when she comes out of the church. I bet her dress will be beautiful!"

When Bonnie returned to the car, her daughter told her that the bride and groom still had not come out of the church. "It's taking them forever to get out here," her daughter complained.

Then she happened to notice the "Just married" sign on the back of the parked limousine. "Look at that, mom," she said disapprovingly. "They've just got married and already they're telling everybody all their business!"

REVELATION 22:17: AND THE SPIRIT AND THE BRIDE SAY, COME, AND LET HIM THAT HEAREH SAY, COME. AND LET HIM THAT IS ATHIRST COME. AND WHOSOEVER WILL, LET HIM TAKE THE WATER OF LIFE FREELY.

A couple that generally attended church regularly had been missing for several weeks. They were unable to be reached by phone.

The pastor and his wife decided to call upon the family to see why they'd been absent for so long. "Perhaps there's been a serious illness in the family," Pastor Ellington told his wife. "Either that, or maybe they're having some serious spiritual problems.

When they arrived at the couple's home, Jimmy, their small nephew, answered the door.

"Are your mother and father home?" Pastor Ellington asked him, mistakenly thinking he was one of their children.

Not recognizing the minister and his wife and having watched a few too many spy movies, Jimmy gave them a scrutinizing look. Then, with an outstretched hand, he demanded to see some identification.

The pastor and his wife continued to be gracious as they stood there with their Bibles in hand. They were, however reaching the end of their patience with Jimmy when he gradually closed them out leaving only an open crack in the door. Adding further insult to the occasion, he asked them, "Do you have a search warrant?"

REVELATION 3:20: BEHOLD, I STAND AT THE DOOR, AND KNOCK: IF ANY MAN HEAR MY VOICE, AND OPEN THE DOOR, I WILL COME IN TO HIM, AND WILL SUP WITH HIM, AND HE WITH ME.

A teenage girl was babysitting for her neighbor one evening. One of the children she was watching was sitting on the floor using a lot of slang words as he played imaginary games with his toys.

"Honey," the babysitter said gently, "You really shouldn't use slang. God really doesn't like to hear it and He watches and listens to everything we do. I hope that you start choosing your words more carefully," she encouraged him.

"But there's slang in the Bible," Johnny insisted innocently.

"Who told you that?" the babysitter asked in disbelief.

Johnny looked at her as if she had been living on some other planet. I thought everybody had heard the story," he said, "about David and his 'slang' shot"

I SAMUEL 17:37: DAVID SAID MOREOVER, THE LORD THAT DELIVERED ME OUT OF THE PAW OF THE LION, AND OUT OF THE PAW OF THE BEAR, HE WILL DELIVER ME OUT OF THE HAND OF THIS PHILISTINE. AND SAUL SAID UNTO DAVID, GO, AND THE LORD BE WITH THEE. [SEE JOHN 15:5; ZECHARIAH 4:6; PSALM 44:6]

I SAMUEL 17:49: AND DAVID PUT HIS HAND IN HIS BAG, AND TOOK THENCE A STONE, AND SLANG IT, AND SMOTE THE PHILISTINE IN HIS FOREHEAD, THAT THE STONE SUNK INTO HIS FOREHEAD; AND HE FELL UPON HIS FACE TO THE EARTH.

One afternoon Olivia was rearranging the pictures in her daughter, Brenda's bedroom. As she began pounding the nails in the wall to hang the pictures, her small daughter watched fearfully. As she glanced down at her little girl, she noticed the fretful look on her face.

"What's the matter, honey?" she asked, concerned. "Don't you like these pictures mommy bought for your room?"

"It's not that, mommy," Brenda replied anxiously. "Just be careful when you're pounding those nails in. Remember," she warned, "that's how Jesus got hurt."

GALATIONS 2:20: I AM CRUCIFIED WITH CHRIST: NEVERTHELESS I LIVE; YET NOT I, BUT CHRIST LIVETH IN ME: AND THE LIFE WHICH I NOW LIVE IN THE FLESH, I LIVE BY FAITH OF THE SON OF GOD, WHO LOVED ME AND GAVE HIMSELF FOR ME. [SEE PHILIPPIANS 3:7-10; JOHN 13:37; ACTS 20:24; ACTS 21:13]

ROMANS 12:1-2: I BESEECH YOU THEREFORE, BRETHREN, BY THE MERCIES OF GOD, THAT YE PRESENT YOUR BODIES A LIVING SACRIFICE, HOLY, ACCEPTABLE UNTO GOD, *WHICH IS* YOUR REASONABLE SERVICE. AND BE NOT CONFRMED TO THIS WORLD: BUT BE YE TRANSFORMED BY THE RENEWING OF YOUR MIND, THAT YE MAY PROVE WHAT IS THAT GOOD, AND ACCEPTABLE, AND PERFECT, WILL OF GOD.

MATTHEW 22:37-39: JESUS SAID UNTO HIM, THOU SHALT LOVE THE LORD THY GOD WITH ALL THY HEART, AND WITH ALL THY SOUL, AND WITH ALL THY MIND. THIS IS THE FIRST AND GREAT COMMANDMENT. AND THE SECOND IS LIKE UNTO IT, THOU SHALT LOVE THY NEIGHBOUR [NEIGHBOR] AS THYSELF.

"Mom," said Gary, "Mrs. Williams, our Sunday school teacher, told the story about Samson and Delilah this morning, but I missed part of it because I had to go to the restroom."

"It's certainly a sad story, honey," his mother said. "Poor Samson had no idea what kind of woman he got tangled up with. Delilah was one

scheming lady. I just hope that when you grow up, son," she continued, "you don't lose your *principles* to a pretty face."

"Mom," Gary said, "Mrs. Williams didn't mention anything about Samson losing any of his *pencils*. She just told us he lost his hair. But that's when I left to go to the restroom. Do you know how he got scalped?" her son asked. "I just love those old cowboy and Indian stories."

JUDGES 16:19 & 21-22 & 30: AND SHE MADE HIM SLEEP UPON HER KNEES; AND SHE CALLED FOR A MAN, AND SHE CAUSED HIM TO SHAVE OFF THE SEVEN LOCKS OP HIS HEAD; AND SHE BEGAN TO AFFLICT HIM, AND HIS STRENGTH WENT FROM HIM . . . BUT THE PHILISTINES TOOK HIM, AND PUT OUT HIS EYES, AND BROUGHT HIM DOWN TO GAZA, AND BOUND HIM WITH FETTERS OF BRASS; AND HE DID GRIND IN THE PRISON HOUSE. HOWBEIT THE HAIR OF HIS HEAD BEGAN TO GROW AGAIN AFTER HE WAS SHAVEN . . . SO THE DEAD WHICH HE SLEW AT HIS DEATH WERE MORE THAN *THEY* WHICH HE SLEW IN HIS LIFE.

"Mom," said six-year-old Marvin, "Can Jesus go faster than a loaded gun?"

"He sure can," his mother replied, smiling at his foolish question.

"Is he more powerful than a train?" he asked.

"Why, yes," she answered, "as a matter of fact, He is."

"Mom, do you think he can jump over great big buildings?"

"Without a doubt," she replied, shaking her head at his silliness.

"What a relief!" exclaimed Marvin. "I sure was worried that superman might have one up on Him."

ISAIAH 46:5: TO WHOM WILL YE LIKEN ME, AND MAKE *ME* EQUAL, AND COMPARE ME, THAT WE MAY BE LIKE?

ISAIAH 45:5-6: I *AM* THE LORD AND *THERE IS* NONE ELSE, *THERE IS* NO GOD BESIDE ME . . . I *AM* THE LORD, AND *THERE IS* NONE ELSE.

REVELATION 22:13: I AM ALPHA AND OMEGA, THE BEGINNING AND THE END, THE FIRST AND THE LAST.

ISAIAH 44:6: I *AM* THE FIRST, AND I *AM* THE LAST; AND BESIDE ME *THERE IS* NO GOD.

EPHESIANS 1:19-21: AND WHAT *IS* THE EXCEEDING GREATNESS OF HIS POWER TO US-WARD WHO BELIEVE, ACCORDING TO THE WORKING OF HIS MIGHTY POWER, WHICH HE WROUGHT IN CHRIST, WHEN HE RAISED HIM FROM THE DEAD, AND SET *HIM* AT HIS OWN RIGHT HAND IN THE HEAVENLY *PLACES*, FAR ABOVE ALL PRINCIPALITY, AND POWER, AND MIGHT, AND DOMINION, AND EVERY NAME THAT IS NAMED, NOT ONLY IN THIS WORLD, BUT ALSO IN THAT WHICH IS TO COME:

PHILIPPIANS 2:9-11: WHEREFORE GOD ALSO HATH HIGHLY EXALTED HIM, AND GIVEN HIM A NAME WHICH IS ABOVE EVERY NAME: THAT AT THE NAME OF JESUS EVERY KNEE SHOULD BOW, OF *THINGS* IN HEAVEN, AND *THINGS* IN EARTH, AND *THINGS* UNDER THE EARTH; AND *THAT* EVERY TONGUE SHOULD CONFESS THAT JESUS CHRIST *IS* LORD, TO THE GLORY OF GOD THE FATHER.

I TIMOTHY 1:17: NOW UNTO THE KING ETERNAL, IMMORTAL, INVISIBLE, THE ONLY WISE GOD, *BE* HONOUR [HONOR] AND GLORY FOR EVER AND EVER. AMEN.

"Can I make my own breakfast this morning?" Lisa asked her mother.

"As long as you don't use the stove," her mother replied. "And please, honey, clean up after yourself," she instructed her eight year old.

Her mother went upstairs to make the beds. When she came down, she smelled something burning.

"I thought I told you not to use the stove," she gently scolded.

"I didn't mom," her daughter said. "I made myself some toast.

"It looks like charred remains," she teased. "And if I don't see Blackie pretty soon and hear the sound of her contented purring I'm going to assume she wound up on your plate instead of that toast!

"But mom," Lisa answered innocently, "I like to fix my food the same way you do."

I TIMOTHY 4:4-5: FOR EVERY CREATURE OF GOD *IS* GOOD, AND NOTHING TO BE REFUSED, IF IT BE RECEIVED WITH THANKSGIVING: FOR IT IS SANCTIFIED BY THE WORD OF GOD AND PRAYER.

(Author's funny note: Please folks, don't fry the family pets!)

Returning home from shopping one afternoon, a detour in the road caused Bobbie Jo to be momentarily confused. She backed her car up and circled through a huge senior citizen structure. In awe of the tall building, her four-year-old daughter squealed with glee, "Is this where God lives, momma?"

"No, honey," her mother laughed, being amused by the remark. "He lives in heaven.

Silently pondering the information for a moment, she then asked her mother, "Oh, did He give you His address?"

ISAIAH 66:1: THUS SAITH THE LORD, THE HEAVEN IS MY THRONE, AND THE EARTH IS MY FOOTSTOOL . . .

"Mommy," asked Andrea, "Why is it raining so hard outside. Is there going to be a flood?"

"No honey, don't worry," her mother said, comforting her. "It's been said that when it rains very hard it means that God is crying because of all the sin in the world."

"Mommy," her daughter asked, "The next time you talk to God, would you please tell him to stop crying on the day that we go to the zoo?"

GENESIS 9:15-16: AND I WILL REMEMBER MY COVENANT, WHICH *IS* BETWEEN ME AND YOU AND EVERY LIVING CREATURE OF ALL FLESH; AND THE WATERS SHALL NO MORE BECOME A FLOOD TO DESTROY ALL FLESH. AND THE BOW SHALL BE IN THE CLOUD; AND I WILL LOOK UPON IT, THAT I MAY REMEMBER THE EVERLASTING COVENANT BETWEEN GOD AND EVERY LIVING CREATURE OF ALL FLESH THAT *IS* UPON THE EARTH.

Upon retiring one evening, Harold, the proud father of a five year old child, tiptoed in his son's bedroom to take a peek at the "sleeping beauty." He leaned over and kissed little Tommy and then began to straighten his son's covers. To his surprise, he found Tommy fully dressed from head to toe, complete with suit, tie, and even dress shoes!

Gently awakening his sleepy-eyed son, he asked why he was wearing his best clothes instead of pajamas.

"Because daddy," replied the boy, "My Sunday school teacher said Jesus is coming soon and I want to be ready when He comes."

LUKE 12:40: BE YE THEREFORE READY ALSO: FOR THE SON OF MAN COMETH AT AN HOUR WHEN YE THINK NOT.

HEBREWS 9:28: SO CHRIST WAS ONCE OFFERED TO BEAR THE SINS OF MANY; AND UNTO THEM THAT LOOK FOR HIM SHALL HE APPEAR THE SECOND TIME WITHOUT SIN UNTO SALVATION. [SEE II CORINTHIANS 5:21]

Eddie lived in a small town right next door to the police station. One day he went inside and marched up to the counter. "I want to file a missing person's report, sir" said eleven-year-old Eddie as he stood there.

"Son, how long has the party been missing?" the policeman asked him compassionately.

"It's not a party, sir," he answered politely. "He's a person; and He's been missing for 2,000 years." The serious look on Eddie's face convinced the police officer that the boy actually believed his own story.

"Son, I'm very sorry," replied the policeman, "but if he's been missing 2,000 years it's because he's already died."

"No! No! You're wrong," insisted Eddie. "He's alive! I know he is!" he exclaimed. "My Sunday school teacher said so and she never lies."

"I think I'm beginning to get the picture," said the policeman. "By any chance would this missing person happen to be named Jesus Christ?"

"Yes, sir!" He answered excitedly. "It's Jesus Christ, my Lord and Savior," replied the boy.

"I'm not sure I'll be able to find Him for you, son," the police officer told him, "but I think the best place for us to start looking is up!"

ACTS 1:11: . . . YE MEN OF GALILEE, WHY STAND YE GAZING UP INHEAVEN? THIS SAME JESUS, WHICH IS TAKEN UP FROM YOU INTO HEAVEN, SHALL SO COME IN LIKE MANNER AS YE HAVE SEEN HIM GO INTO HEAVEN.

ACTS 1:3: TO WHOM ALSO HE SHEWED [SHOWED] HIMSELF ALIVE AFTER HIS PASSION BY MANY INFALLIBLE PROOFS, BEING SEEN OF THEM FORTY DAYS, AND SPEAKING OF THE THINGS PERTAINING TO THE KINGDOM OF GOD: [I CORINTHIANS 15:3-8; ROMANS 8:11; II CORINTHIANS 4:14;]

REVELATION 1:18: I AM HE THAT LIVETH, AND WAS DEAD; AND, BEHOLD, I AM ALIVE FOR EVERMORE . . .

"Mom," Sarah asked excitedly, "could we have Reverend Applebee over for supper tonight?

"Not tonight, Sarah," her mother answered. "We wouldn't have enough time to get things ready."

"Then how about this Saturday?" she pleaded.

"I suppose Saturday would be fine," her mother agreed. "but why are you so anxious to have him dine with us?" "Because," Sarah replied, "I want to help you fix all of 'his' favorite things to eat."

"I guess I could unthaw that roast I have in the freezer," her mother said.

"No, Mom, he wouldn't like that," Sarah told her.

"Then what did you have in mind, honey?" her mother asked.

"I thought we could make popcorn balls and hotdogs said Sarah," licking her lips. "And then for dessert we could have chocolate cupcakes and popsicles. But, mom, if you'd rather have cotton candy instead of popcorn balls," she said, "it's okay with me."

PSALMS 128:2: FOR THOU SHALT EAT THE LABOUR [LABOR] OF THINE HANDS: HAPPY SHALT THOU BE, AND IT SHALL BE WELL WITH TREE.

Two children sat on the curb discussing the mysteries of God. "Where do you think God came from?" Bobby asked Matthew.

"Well," he said, scratching his forehead, "I'm not sure if he was hatched from an egg or if he came from another planet."

"Probably from another planet," said Matthew, "Because my mom told me about the trinity."

"What's the trinity?" Bobby wondered.

"Oh, that's where you have three people all getting along with each other all the time," he replied, "and that could only happen on another planet."

I JOHN 5:7: FOR THERE ARE THREE THAT BEAR RECORD IN HEAVEN, THE FATHER, THE WORD, AND THE HOLY GHOST: AND THESE THREE

ARE ONE. [SEE JOHN 17:5, 21-22 & 24, REVELATION 3:21; ACTS 7:56; HEBREWS 12:2]

EPHESIANS 4:6: ONE GOD AND FATHER OF ALL, WHO IS ABOVE ALL, AND THROUGH ALL, AND IN YOU ALL.

COLOSSIANS 2:6, & 9-10: AS YE HAVE THEREFORE RECEIVED CHRIST JESUS THE LORD, SO WALK YE IN HIM: . . . FOR IN HIM DWELLETH ALL THE FULNESS OF THE GODHEAD BODILY. AND YE ARE COMPLETE IN HIM, WHICH IS THE HEAD OF ALL PRINCIPALITY AND POWER: [SEE JOHN 1:18; JOHN 5:37; JOHN 14:6]

Several children were asked to participate in their church program, with each given a special memory verse to say before the seated guests.

When it was little Herb's turn, he was a bit flustered and couldn't recall the exact wording of the verse he was to quote.

A laughing audience clapped to his version of Matthew 19:24: "And again I say unto you, it is easier for a *cannibal* to go through the eye of a *beetle*, than for a rich man to enter into the kingdom of God."

MATTHEW 19:24: AND AGAIN I [JESUS] SAY UNTO YOU, IT IS EASIER FOR A CAMEL TO GO THROUGH THE EYE OF A NEEDLE, THAN FOR A RICH MAN TO ENTER INTO THE KINGDOM OF GOD.

LUKE 18:18-24: AND A CERTAIN RULER ASKED (JESUS), SAYING, GOOD MASTER, WHAT SHALL I DO TO INHERIT ETERNAL LIFE? AND JESUS SAID UNTO HIM, WHY CALLEST THOU ME GOOD? NONE IS GOOD, SAVE ONE, THAT IS, GOD. THOU KNOWEST THE COMMANDMENTS, DO NOT COMMIT ADULTERY, DO NOT KILL, DO NOT STEAL, DO NOT BEAR FALSE WITNESS, HONOUR THY FATHER AND MOTHER. AND HE SAID, ALL THESE HAVE I KEPT FROM MY YOUTH UP. NOW WHEN JESUS HEARD THESE THINGS, HE SAID UNTO HIM, YET LACKEST THOU ONE THING: SELL ALL THAT THOU HAST, AND DISTRIBUTE UNTO THE POOR, AND THOU SHALT HAVE TREASURE IN HEAVEN: AND COME, FOLLOW ME. AND WHEN HE HEARD THIS, HE WAS VERY SORROWFUL: FOR HE WAS VERY RICH. AND WHEN JESUS SAW THAT

HE WAS VERY SORROWFUL, HE SAID, HOW HARDLY SHALL THEY THAT HAVE RICHES ENTER INTO THE KINGDOM OF GOD!

"Mom, how come I can't go outside after dark?" whined seven-year-old Leslie.

"It's not safe," answered her mother, "and besides that," she said, "when it gets dark it means that it's time to come in, take a bath, and get things ready for school tomorrow."

"But why isn't it safe when it's dark outside?" Leslie persisted "Are there spooks and ghosts that will get me?"

"No honey, there's no such thing as ghosts," she replied, "but just as there are good people in the world, there are also bad people. Do you understand now," she asked her, taking her pajamas out of the dresser drawer, "why I can't allow you out after dark?"

"Yes, Mom," answered Leslie, "But I was just wondering . . . if a bad person was to get me, would I go to heaven?

"Why, of course you would," replied her mother, "But I'm sure nothing like that will ever happen."

"Well, if something happens to me, mom," she asked, "do you want me to pray that something really bad happens to you so you can come to heaven with me?"

LUKE 19:13: . . . OCCUPY TILL I COME.

"It's time to say prayers," Brad told his son, Bobby, as he tucked him into bed.

"No, I don't want to say prayers," Bobby protested.

"Do you want God to feel sad?" his dad asked, trying to be persuasive."

"Okay, dad, but let's wait 'til tomorrow night," his son said, "because He told me He's already gone to bed."

PROVERBS 17:6: CHILDREN'S CHILDREN *ARE* THE CROWN OF OLD MEN; AND THE GLORY OF CHILDREN *ARE* THEIR FATHERS.

"Mom," Andrew asked, "If I die before you do, would you and dad put me in a jet?"

"Now why would you want to be put in an airplane?" his mother laughed.

"It's not funny," he cried.

"Okay, honey," she said, "if that's what you want."

"Make sure it's a jet, mom," he told her.

"Why a jet? She asked.

"So I can get a head start to heaven," he replied.

REVELATION 21:3-4: AND I HEARD A GREAT VOICE OUT OF HEAVEN SAYING, BEHOLD, THE TABERNACLE OF GOD *IS* WITH MEN, AND HE WILL DWELL WITH THEM, AND THEY SHALL BE HIS PEOPLE, AND GOD HIMSELF SHALL BE WITH THEM, *AND BE* THEIR GOD. AND GOD SHALL WIPE AWAY ALL TEARS FROM THEIR EYES; AND THERE SHALL BE NO MORE DEATH, NEITHER SORROW, NOR CRYING, NEITHER SHALL THERE BE ANY MORE PAIN: FOR THE FORMER THINGS ARE PASSED AWAY.

Seeing pyramids for the first time on television, little Charlotte was curious to learn about the huge, triangular structures. "Are those big tents for people to stay in when their family goes camping?" she asked her grandmother.

"No, honey," her grandmother replied, smiling at her.

"Those are pyramids," she explained, "and they were used a very, very long time ago to bury important people who died such as kings and people of nobility.'

"Oh," Charlotte replied. "Is that where our other pastor is buried?"

"No dear," her grandmother grinned imagining how her deceased pastor would have laughed at hearing such a thing.

"Then if he's not in there, grandma," asked Charlotte, trying to figure it all out, "did somebody roll his body out and take him to heaven?"

JOHN 5:24-25: VERILY, VERILY, I SAY UNTO YOU, HE THAT HEARETH MY WORD, AND BELIEVETH ON HIM THAT SENT ME, HATH EVERLASTING LIFE, AND SHALL NOT COME INTO CONDEMNATION; BUT IS PASSED FROM DEATH UNTO LIFE. VERILY, VERILY, I SAY UNTO YOU, THE HOUR IS COMING, AND NOW IS, WHEN THE DEAD SHALL HEAR THE VOICE OF THE SON OF GOD: AND THEY THAT HEAR SHALL LIVE. [SEE ROMANS 8:1-2; I JOHN 8-9]

JOHN 5:28-29: MARVEL NOT AT THIS: FOR THE HOUR IS COMING, IN THE WHICH ALL THAT ARE IN THE GRAVES SHALL HEAR HIS VOICE, AND SHALL COME FORTH; THEY THAT HAVE DONE GOOD, UNTO THE RESURRECTION OF LIFE; AND THY THAT HAVE DONE EVIL, UNTO THE RESURRECTION OF DAMNATION. [SEE DANIEL 12:2; I JOHN 2:3-4; EZEKIEL 18:24 & 26-27; II THESSALONIANS 1:8-9]

(Author's note: After reading the following scriptures, you will know that only the blood of Jesus Christ is sufficient to make atonement for the soul: Leviticus 17:11; Exodus 12:13; Ephesians 1:7; Ephesians 2:13-14; Colossians 1:14 & 20 Hebrews 9:22; & John 14:6. However, although works do not save us, they do prove us!]

HEBREWS 9:27: AND AS IT IS APPOINTED UNTO MEN ONCE TO DIE, BUT AFTER THIS THE JUDGEMENT. [SEE LUKE 16:19-31 & LUKE 12:20]

REVELATION 20:11-15: AND I SAW A GREAT WHITE THRONE, AND HIM THAT SAT ON IT, FROM WHOSE FACE THE EARTH AND THE HEAVEN

Mom when I go to heaven can I do some of the stuff you never let me do down here on earth? I want to watch scarey classics like shark horror stories.
Don't worry, son you'll be experiencing your own close encounters of another kind!

FLED AWAY; AND THERE WAS FOUND NO PLACE FOR THEM. AND I SAW THE DEAD, SMALL AND GREAT, STAND BEFORE GOD; AND THE BOOKS WERE OPENED: AND ANOTHER BOOK WAS OPENED, WHICH IS *THE BOOK* OF LIFE: AND THE DEAD WERE JUDGED OUT OF THOSE THINGS WHICH WERE WRITTEN IN THE BOOKS, ACORDING TO THEIR WORKS. AND THE SEA GAVE UP THE DEAD WHICH WERE IN IT; AND DEATH AND HELL DELIVERED UP THE DEAD WHICH WERE IN THEM: AND THEY WERE JUDGED EVERY MAN ACCORDING TO THEIR WORKS. AND DEATH AND HELL WERE CAST INTO THE LAKE OF FIRE. THIS IS THE SECOND DEATH. AND WHOSOEVER WAS NOT FOUND WRITTEN IN THE BOOK OF LIFE WAS CAST INTO THE LAKE OF FIRE.

Every six weeks, a certain church offered classes for a low fee on Friday evenings to enrich the spiritual growth of its members. To meet the various age levels of its members, classes were provided from young children to adults.

One mother and her fourth-grade daughter, Linda, were enrolled in their respective classes.

Linda always looked forward to joining her other classmates for Bible stories and craft projects. When the six weeks were completed, sometimes her mother would take a six week break before enrolling again.

When the mail arrived one afternoon, Linda brought the letters into the house and laid them on the table. "Hey, Mom," she said motioning for her attention, "Are we taking another class at church?"

"No, dear," her mother replied.

Linda looked puzzled. "Then why," she asked, "does this letter say 'First Class Mail'?"

COLOSSIANS 1:10: . . . WALK WORTHY OF THE LORD UNTO ALL PLEASING, BEING FRUITFUL IN EVERY GOOD WORK, AND INCREASING IN THE KNOWLEDGE OF GOD."

Katie came skipping into the house looking for her grandmother. "Granny!" she shouted, "Where are you?"

"Out in the kitchen," her grandmother replied.

Katie hurried to the kitchen. "Granny," she said, "I've got a riddle for you." She smiled from ear to ear as if she had the world's best kept secret.

"What's your riddle?" her grandmother asked, putting some cookies in the oven.

"What special thing did God make for Adam and Eve when they were in the garden of Eden?" she asked. "It was big enough to reach all the way to heaven," Katie told her, "but small enough to hide under a leaf."

"I can't possibly imagine," said her grandmother, "but I can see that you're going to burst if you don't tell me. So go ahead," she teased, "and impart your infinite wisdom to your grandmother."

Katie giggled. "It's easy, granny," she told her. "He made Adam and Eve a cell phone so that they could call Him whenever they needed to borrow his riding lawn mower or some garden tools from His garage."

PSALM 32:7: THOU *ART* MY HIDING PLACE; THOU SHALT PRESERVE ME FROM TROUBLE; THOU SHALT COMPASS ME ABOUT WITH SONGS OF DELIVERANCE. SELAH.

JEREMIAH 36:26: . . . THE KING COMMANDED JERAHMEEL THE SON OF HAMMELECH, AND SERAIAH THE SON OF AZRIEL, AND SHELEMIAH THE SON OF ABDEEL, TO TAKE BARUCH THE SCRIBE AND JEREMIAH THE PROPHET: BUT THE LORD HID THEM.

"Mom," said eight-year-old Lisa, "I wish I could look up past the clouds and take a peek at heaven. I would love to see all the animals, and the games and toys that are up there. Do you think," she asked eagerly, "that we will get to have everything we want?"

"I don't know what God has in store for us, sweetie,' replied her mother, "but I'm sure it will be wonderful just because Jesus our Lord is there."

"I know, mom," her daughter said, "but what I'm wondering is whether I'll be able to eat pickles and ride my bike," she said.

Her mother hugged her. "I'm certain, Lisa," she said, "that when you get to heaven you'll be able to eat all the pickles you want and ride your bike to your heart's content. After all," she said, "why would God take away the two things people love to do most in life."

REVELATION 21:7: HE THAT OVERCOMETH SHALL INHERIT ALL THINGS; AND I WILL BE HIS GOD, AND HE SHALL BE MY SON.

I CORINTHIANS 2:9: . . . EYE HATH NOT SEEN, NOR EAR HEARD, NEITHER HAVE ENTERED INTO THE HEART OF MAN, THE THINGS WHICH GOD HATH PREPARED FOR THEM THAT LOVE HIM.

"What are you doing, Mama," asked Buffy?

"I'm getting things ready for a barbecue," she replied. "It's such a nice day outside, I thought perhaps we'd eat dinner out on the patio. Does that sound like fun to you?"

"It sure does!" exclaimed Buffy. "What are we having for dinner?"

"Barbecued spare ribs," her mother answered.

"Oh," said Buffy, wanting to show her mother how smart she was, "that's the same thing God used to make Eve."

GENESIS 2:21-23: AND THE LORD GOD CAUSED A DEEP SLEEP TO FALL UPON ADAM, AND HE SLEPT: AND HE TOOK ONE OF HIS RIBS, AND CLOSED UP THE FLESH INSTEAD THEREOF; AND THE RIB, WHICH THE LORD GOD HAD TAKEN FROM MAN, MADE HE A WOMAN, AND BROUGHT HER UNTO THE MAN. AND ADAM SAID, THIS *IS* NOW BONE OF MY BONES, AND FLESH OF MY FLESH: SHE SHALL BE CALLED WOMAN, BECAUSE SHE WAS TAKEN OUT OF MAN.

After scraping his knees all up in a bad fall, little Matthew limped into the house to be consoled by his mother.

She hugged him and then carefully washed the injured area, putting some salve on his knees. As she was patching up his wounds, she began praying over him.

"Mom," he interrupted her teary-eyed. "If God heals, how come my knees are still bleeding?"

She kissed her son on the cheek and said, "Because, honey, sometimes God likes to use up the bandages in His medicine cabinet."

PSALMS 103:2-4: BLESS THE LORD, O MY SOUL, AND FORGET NOT HIS BENEFITS: WHO FORGIVETH ALL THINE INIQUITIES: WHO HEALETH ALL THY DISEASES; WHO REDEEMETH THY LIFE FROM DESTRUCTION; WHO CROWNETH THEE WITH LOVINGKINDNESS AND TENDER MERCIES;

PSALM 68:19: BLESSED *BE* THE LORD, *WHO* DAILY LOADETH US *WITH BENEFITS, EVEN* THE GOD OF OUR SALVATION . . .

"Look what Tammy and I made!" said Gerald to his mother, proudly holding up the pictures they had drawn.

"My, you certainly are playing nice together this afternoon," their mother replied, smiling pleasantly at their pictures.

"That's because I'm glad I have an *older* sister," said Gerald. "I can remember how lonesome I used to get before she was born."

JOSHUA 1:9: . . . THE LORD THY GOD *IS* WITH THEE WHITHERSOEVER THOU GOEST. [SEE PSALM 34:19]

ISAIAH 43:2: WHEN THOU PASSEST THROUGH THE WATERS, I *WILL BE* WITH THEE; AND THROUGH THE RIVERS, THEY SHALL NOT OVERFLOW THEE: WHEN THOU WALKEST THROUGH THE FIRE, THOU

SHALT NOT BE BURNED; NEITHER SHALL THE FLAME KINDLE UPON THEE.

DANIEL 3:23-25 & 27: AND THESE THREE MEN, SHADRACH, MESHACH, AND ABEDNEGO, FELL DOWN BOUND INTO THE MIDST OF THE BURNING FIERY FURNACE. THEN NEBUCHADNEZZAR THE KING WAS ASTONIED, AND ROSE UP IN HASTE, *AND* SPAKE, AND SAID UNTO HIS COUNSELLORS, DID NOT WE CAST THREE MEN BOUND INTO THE MIDST OF THE FIRE? THEY ANSWERED AND SAID UNTO THE KING, TRUE, O KING. HE ANSWERED AND SAID, LO, I SEE FOUR MEN LOOSE, WALKING IN THE MIDST OF THE FIRE, AND THEY HAVE NO HURT; AND THE FORM OF THE FOURTH IS LIKE THE SON OF GOD . . . AND THE PRINCES, GOVERNORS, AND CAPTAINS, AND THE KING'S COUNSELLORS, BEING GATHERED TOGETHER SAW THESE MEN, UPON WHOSE BODIES THE FIRE HAD NO POWER, NOR WAS AN HAIR OF THEIR HEAD SINGED, NEITHER WERE THEIR COATS CHANGED, NOR THE SMELL OF FIRE HAD PASSED ON THEM.

PSALM 46:1: GOD IS OUR REFUGE AND STRENGTH, A VERY PRESENT HELP IN TROUBLE.

HEBREWS 13:5: . . . I WILL NEVER LEAVE THEE, NOR FORSAKE THEE.

MATTHEW 28:20: . . . LO, I AM WITH YOU ALWAYS, EVEN UNTO THE END OF THE WORLD. [SEE ISAIAH 43:2]

JOHN 14:23: JESUS ANSWERED AND SAID UNTO HIM, IF A MAN LOVE ME, HE WILL KEEP MY WORDS: AND MY FATHER WILL LOVE HIM, AND WE WILL COME UNTO HIM, AND MAKE OUR ABODE WITH HIM.

PSALM 23:4: . . . THOU *ART* WITH ME . . .

PSALM 34:18: THE LORD *IS* NIGH UNTO THEM THAT ARE OF A BROKEN HEART . . .

JAMES 4:8: DRAW NIGH TO GOD, AND HE WILL DRAW NIGH TO YOU . . .

"Momma," asked Randy, her inquisitive ten-year-old, "Why did God make computers so hard to understand?"

"They are quite complicated to figure out, aren't they?" she agreed.

"They sure are, mom," he sighed. "That must be why God's lost track of all of us down here."

HEBREWS 4:13: NEITHER IS THERE ANY CREATURE THAT IS NOT MANIFEST IN HIS SIGHT: BUT ALL THINGS *ARE* NAKED AND OPENED UNTO THE EYS OF HIM WITH WHOM WE HAVE TO DO.

PSALM 139:1-4 & 7-10: O LORD, THOU HAST SEARCHED ME, AND KNOWN *ME*. THOU KNOWEST MY DOWNSITTING AND MINE UPRISING, THOU UNDERSTANDEST MY THOUGHT AFAR OFF. THOU COMPASSEST MY PATH AND MY LYING DOWN, AND ART ACQUAINTED *WITH* ALL MY WAYS. FOR *THERE IS* NOT A WORD IN MY TONGUE, *BUT*, LO, O LORD, THOU KNOWEST IT ALTOGETHER . . . WHITHER SHALL I GO FROM THY SPIRIT? OR WHITHER SHALL I FLEE FROM THY PRESENCE? IF I ASCEND UP INTO HEAVEN, THOU *ART* THERE: IF I MAKE MY BED IN HELL, BEHOLD, THOU *ART THERE*. *IF* I TAKE THE WINGS OF THE MORNING, *AND* DWELL IN THE UTTERMOST PARTS OF THE SEA; EVEN THERE SHALL THY HAND LEAD ME, AND THY RIGHT HAND SHALL HOLD ME. [SEE JOB 42:2; ACTS 1:24; ACTS 15:8; PROVERBS 15:3; PSALM 94: 7 & 9; JEREMIAH 1:5; EZEKIEL 11:5; I CHRONICLES 28:9; II CHRONICLES 16:9]

EZEKIEL 49:16: BEHOLD, I HAVE GRAVEN THEE UPON THE PALMS OF *MY* HANDS . . .

LUKE 12:5-7: ARE NOT FIVE SPARROWS SOLD FOR TWO FARTHINGS, AND NOT ONE OF THEM IS FORGOTTEN BEFORE GOD? BUT EVEN THE VERY HAIRS OF YOUR HEAD ARE ALL NUMBERED. FEAR NOT THEREFORE: YE ARE OF MORE VALUE THAN MANY SPARROWS.

JEREMIAH 31:3: THE LORD HATH APPEARED OF OLD UNTO ME, *SAYING*, YEA, I HAVE LOVED THEE WITH AN EVERLASTING LOVE: THEREFORE WITH LOVINGKINDNESS HAVE I DRAWN THEE.

Rodney, a curious eight-year-old owner of one hamster, three goldfish, and a jar full of night crawlers, had now found a large turtle wandering along the river bank behind his family's home.

His mother, however, did not share his delight and was not enthused at the prospect of having another creature roaming about the house. "Please keep Herman (as they fondly called him) outside," she told him.

"But he'll run away, Mom," her son argued. "Then put him on a leash,' she joked.

A few minutes later, Rodney returned with his turtle. "Mom," he cried, "It's impossible to put a collar around Herman's neck. He keeps sticking his head back in his shell.

"Oh, alright then," said his soft-hearted mother, giving in to her son. "Bring him back in the house."

Then, referring to Herman, she muttered, "I suppose it's like the Good Book says . . . "a man's woes shall be they of his own household."

MATTHEW 10:36: AND A MAN'S FOES *SHALL BE* THEY OF HIS OWN HOUSEHOLD.

"God sure has blessed us, hasn't he, Mom?" said little Lori to her mother.

"Indeed he has, honey," her mother replied. "We have a lot to be thankful for. In fact, the "lot" our farm is sitting on! Yes," she agreed, "He's given us abundant blessings."

"He sure has, Mom," exclaimed Lori with glee. Referring to her brother, she remarked, "He gave Tommy a lizard, a toad, three guppies, and a snail."

"Yes," said her mother cringing and looking a bit squeamish.

"And he gave me a cat, two little kittens, and an aquarium. And," she added, "He gave you and dad chickens, cows, and pigs."

"Do you think God will give us a new horse this year, mom?" Lori asked. "I've missed Brownie ever since we had to put her down."

"I don't know, Lori," her mother answered. "But if God blesses us with more animals, we can build our own ark!"

"Yes," Lori replied, "And we can hire Noah to be our manure manager."

GENESIS 7:9: THERE WENT IN TWO AND TWO UNTO NOAH INTO THE ARK, THE MALE AND THE FEMALE, AS GOD HAD COMMMANDED NOAH.

Rachel came running into the house screaming as though she'd just been chased by a swarm of angry bees.

"It's only a little mosquito bite," her mother reassured her.

"Mommy," the four year old asked, "When we get to heaven will there be bugs up there?"

"I don't know, dear," her mother answered, wiping away the tears. "But if there are, I'm sure they'll be good bugs."

"Well, if I see any bugs," her daughter asked, "is it alright if we move?"

ISAIAH 11:6-9: THE WOLF ALSO SHALL DWELL WITH THE LAMB, AND THE LEOPARD SHALL LIE DOWN WITH THE KID; AND THE CALF AND THE YOUNG LION AND THE FATLING TOGETHER; AND A LITTLE CHILD SHALL LEAD THEM. AND THE COW AND THE BEAR SHALL FEED; THEIR YOUNG ONES SHALL LIE DOWN TOGETHER: AND THE LION SHALL EAT STRAW LIKE THE OX. AND THE SUCKING CHILD SHALL PLAY ON THE HOLE OF THE ASP, AND THE WEANED CHILD SHALL PUT HIS HAND ON THE COCKATRICE DEN. THEY SHALL NOT HURT NOR DESTROY IN ALL MY HOLY MOUNTAIN: FOR THE EARTH SHALL BE FULL OF THE KNOWLEDGE OF THE LORD, AS THE WATERS COVER THE SEA.

"Tommy, this is the best work you've ever done!" his teacher said praising him.

"Thank you, Miss Marvin," he beamed.

"Honestly, I can't get over this essay," she said. "It's truly remarkable. If I didn't know better, I'd almost think you copied it. Knowing what an honest boy you are, however," she said, "I'm certain you must have written it yourself."

"I did have a little help," Tommy admitted.

"Your parents?" she asked.

"No, it was a Ghost writer," Tommy replied.

"Now Tommy, I know better than that," Miss Marvin remarked

"I'm telling the truth," he insisted. "I prayed and asked the Lord for help."

"Oh, I see," said his Christian teacher smiling. "When you said you had a Ghost writer you meant the Holy Ghost!"

JOHN 16:13-14: HOWBEIT WHEN HE, THE SPIRIT OF TRUTH, IS COME, HE WILL GUIDE YOU INTO ALL TRUTH: FOR HE SHALL NOT SPEAK OF HIMSELF; BUT WHATSOEVER HE SHALL HEAR, *THAT* SHALL HE SPEAK: AND HE WILL SHEW [SHOW] YOU THINGS TO COME. HE SHALL GLORIFY ME [JESUS] . . .

HEBREWS 12:2; LOOKING UNTO JESUS THE AUTHOR AND FINISHER OF OUR FAITH; WHO FOR THE JOY THAT WAS SET BEFORE HIM ENDURED THE CROSS, DESPISING THE SHAME, AND IS SET DOWN AT THE RIGHT HAND OF THE THRONE OF GOD.

Leaving church one night, Louise was pulled over by the police about two miles down the road.

"Do you know why I stopped you?" asked the officer?"

"No," replied Louise, looking discouraged. "But I have a feeling this ticket is going to cost me a small fortune." She thought about her missing headlight, broken windshield, and other defective items on her car that he must have already noticed.

Just as the officer started to explain why he'd pulled her over, her son, Alfred, interrupted the officer excitedly. "I know why, sir! I know why!" he exclaimed, his arms flailing. "You pulled my mom over," he said, "to give her some tickets to the circus."

LUKE 6:38: GIVE, AND IT SHALL BE GIVEN UNTO YOU; GOOD MEASURE, PRESSED DOWN, AND SHAKEN TOGETHER, AND RUNNING OVER, SHALL MEN GIVE INTO YOUR BOSOM. FOR WITH THE SAME MEASURE THAT YE METE WITHAL IT SHALL BE MEASURED TO YOU AGAIN.

TEEN TIDAL WAVES

A group of Christian teens stood outside a triple x-rated movie theatre passing out gospel tracts and other Christian literature as the crowd came out.

The jeering looks they received were followed by verbal ridicule and scorn. Not swayed by the mocking remarks, laughter, or pointing fingers poking fun, they continued to suffer humiliation for the furtherance of the gospel.

Addressing one of the scoffers, Alex, one of the teens commented, "You really should treat us with a little more consideration and respect. After all," he told them, "we are an endangered species."

I JOHN 3:13: MARVEL NOT, MY BRETHREN, IF THE WORLD HATE YOU.

I PETER 2:9: BUT YE *ARE* A CHOSEN GENERATION, A ROYAL PRIESTHOOD, AN HOLY NATION, A PECULIAR PEOPLE; THAT YE SHOULD SHEW FORTH THE PRAISES OF HIM WHO HATH CALLED YOU OUT OF DARKNESS INTO HIS MARVELLOUS LIGHT.

II TIMOTHY 2:3: THOU THEREFORE ENDURE HARDNESS AS A GOOD SOLDIER OF JESUS CHRIST.

ROMANS 8:16: FOR I RECKON THAT THE SUFFERINGS OF THIS PRESENT TIME ARE NOT WORTHY TO BE COMPARED WITH THE GLORY WHICH SHALL BE REVEALED IN US.

II CORINTHIANS 4:17: FOR OUR LIGHT AFFLICTION, WHICH IS BUT FOR A MOMENT WORKETH FOR US A FAR MORE EXCEEDING *AND* ETERNAL WEIGHT OF GLORY;

A teenage youth group was having a car wash in their church parking lot to earn money for an outing they had planned. "Get your car washed here!" they hollered at passersby. "Get your car washed dirt cheap," they yelled, trying to flag down customers. As the cars began to pull in, one teenager was overheard saying to the driver, "Oh, by the way, sir, when I finish with your car, if you want your mind washed, too, just step inside the church and you can have that done for free."

PSALM 51:7: . . . WASH ME, AND I SHALL BE WHITER THAN SNOW. [SEE ISAIAH 1:18]

ROMANS 12:2: . . . BE YE TRANSFORMED BY THE RENEWING OF YOUR MIND . . .

I THESSALONIANS 4:7: FOR GOD HATH NOT CALLED US UNTO UNCLEANESS, BUT UNTO HOLINESS.

Two teenagers who were reading the scripture, "Flee fornication . . ." joked with each other. "Does this mean the bugs have to stop their immoral fooling around.?" one of them asked the other.

"If they do," said the other, "somebody should let them know that at the rate they're multiplying, God is sure to notice before long!"

I CORINTHIANS 6:13 & 18-20: . . . NOW THE BODY *IS* NOT FOR FORNICATION, BUT FOR THE LORD; AND THE LORD FOR THE BODY . . . FLEE FORNICATION. EVERY SIN THAT A MAN DOETH IS WITHOUT THE BODY; BUT HE THAT COMMITTETH FORNICATION SINNETH AGAINST HIS OWN BODY. WHAT? KNOW YE NOT THAT YOUR BODY IS THE TEMPLE OF THE HOLY GHOST *WHICH IS* IN YOU, WHICH YE HAVE OF GOD, AND YE ARE NOT YOUR OWN? FOR YE ARE BOUGHT WITH A PRICE: THEREFORE GLORIFY GOD IN YOUR BODY, AND IN YOUR SPIRIT, WHICH ARE GOD'S.

I PETER 1:18-19: FORASMUCH AS YE KNOW THAT YE WERE NOT REDEEMED WITH CORRUPTIBLE THINGS, *AS* SILVER AND GOLD, FROM YOUR VAIN CONVERSATION *RECEIVED* BY TRADITION FROM YOUR FATHERS; BUT WITH THE PRECIOUS BLOOD OF CHRIST, AS OF A LAMB WITHOUT BLEMISH AND WITHOUT SPOT:

I CORINTHIANS 10:8: NEITHER LET US COMMIT FORNICATION, AS SOME OF THEM COMMITTED, AND FELL IN ONE DAY THREE AND TWENTY THOUSAND.

PROVERBS 6:24-28: . . . KEEP THEE FROM THE EVIL WOMAN, FROM THE FLATTERY OF THE TONGUE OF A STRANGE WOMAN. LUST NOT AFTER HER BEAUTY IN THINE HEART; NEITHER LET HER TAKE THEE WITH HER EYELIDS. FOR BY MEANS OF A WHORISH WOMAN *A MAN IS BROUGHT* TO A PIECE OF BREAD: AND THE ADULTERESS WILL HUNT FOR THE PRECIOUS LIFE. CAN A MAN TAKE FIRE IN HIS BOSOM, AND HIS CLOTHES NOT BE BURNED? CAN ONE GO UPON HOT COALS, AND HIS FEET NOT BE BURNED? [SEE GENESIS 39:7-12]

PROVERBS 2:18: FOR HER HOUSE INCLINETH UNTO DEATH, AND HER PATHS UNTO THE DEAD.

I PETER 2:11: DEAR BELOVED, I BESEECH *YOU* AS STRANGERS AND PILGRIMS, ABSTAIN FROM FLESHLY LUSTS, WHICH WAR AGAINST THE SOUL; [SEE GENESIS 34:2; PROVERBS 7:1-27; II SAMUEL 12:1-14; II SAMUEL 13:1-32]

Two teens, Andrew and Richard, were arguing over who had the most problems. "I've got a father who thinks he's Lucifer's right arm. He's a self appointed judge, jury, and hangman. And my mother," he said, "is a ticking time bomb."

"You think you got it bad," muttered Richard. I've got homework that's stacked a mile high and I can't even remember which grade it's from! I've got an ex girlfriend that left me for the football captain, half of his teammates, the student council president, and most of the school body.

"And if all that isn't bad enough, I've got a mother who says, 'In everything give thanks!'"

PHILIPPIANS 4:4: REJOICE IN THE LORD ALWAY: AND AGAIN I SAY, REJOICE.

I THESSALONIANS 5:18: IN EVERY THING GIVE THANKS: FOR THIS IS THE WILL OF GOD IN CHRIST JESUS CONCERNING YOU.

EXODUS 16:8: . . . YOUR MURMURINGS *ARE* NOT AGAINST US, BUT AGAINST THE LORD.

I CORINTHIANS 10:10-11: NEITHER MURMUR YE, AS SOME OF THEM ALSO MURMURED, AND WERE DESTROYED OF THE DESTROYER. NOW ALL THESE THINGS HAPPENED UNTO THEM FOR ENSAMPLES [EXAMPLES]: AND THEY ARE WRITTEN FOR OUR ADMONITION . . .

Clyde was a teenager who had a big problem with compulsive lying. His stories were so far-fetched that one would have to search for any kind of credibility. If he accidentally nicked his finger on a tin can while making soup, he'd swear he was attacked in a dark alley by a blood thirsty street gang all carrying machetes.

Arriving at church one Sunday morning with a slight sunburn, he began telling everyone, including the pastor, that he'd done a back float clear across the Pacific in the hot, blistering sun. "Dad let me use his boat," he told everyone, "and it capsized. With only rainwater to hydrate me and the cold, Pacific waves to carry me," he dramatized, "I drifted across the deep, shark-infested waters of the ocean, dodging razor-sharp teeth."

"Clyde" the pastor told him, "exaggerating is just another form of lying."

"Don't worry, Pastor," remarked Clyde, putting his arm around him, "I'll be praying for you to get victory over it."

PROVERBS 12:22: LYING LIPS ARE ABOMINATION TO THE LORD: BUT THEY THAT DEAL TRULY ARE HIS DELIGHT.

III JOHN 4: I HAVE NO GREATER JOY THAN TO HEAR THAT MY CHILDREN WALK IN TRUTH.

"Are you still on that religious kick? Janice asked Tina, her freshman roommate. "I'm warning you," she said firmly, "if you don't watch out, you're going to be labeled a 'fanatic.'

"Some of the other girls on our floor have caught you reading that silly Bible of yours and" she continued, "there's a lot of snickering and whispering going on behind your back. I just thought you'd want to know."

Tina went right on reading, totally absorbed in her Bible as if she hadn't heard a word her roommate had said.

Trying to distract her, Janice asked her to help with her false eyelashes. "I can't seem to get these on," she said. "and I have a date this evening. Would you help me?"

While Tina was helping Janice, she began sharing about the Apostle Paul's letters to the Corinthians. "They're very thought provoking," she remarked.

"What are you reading all that nonsense for?" Janice snapped.

"I can't help it" said Tina. "I've always loved reading other people's mail and especially God's!"

JOHN 5:39: SEARCH THE SCRIPTURES; FOR IN THEM YE THINK YE HAVE ETERNAL LIFE: AND THEY ARE THEY WHICH TESTIFY OF ME.

JOHN 5:46: FOR HAD YE BELIEVED MOSES, YE WOULD HAVE BELIEVED ME: FOR HE WROTE OF ME.

I CORINTHIANS 2:2: FOR I DETERMINED NOT TO KNOW ANY THING AMONG YOU, SAVE JESUS CHRIST, AND HIM CRUCIFIED.

Ever since learning about the end time apocalyptic scenario foretold in the books of Revelation, Daniel, Matthew, Luke, II Thessalonians, Joel, etc., 17-year-old Donald had become obsessed with the whole matter.

He would shudder at the very sight of a "six" because of the three-digit code 666, identifying a Satanic beast called the "antichrist" whose worldwide dominion will cause catastrophic consequences for all living under his tyrannical control.

Donald's mother and father had read about this terrifying event in the Bible. They had shared these scriptures with their children wanting to make sure that their hearts were right before the Lord in order to escape this future holocaust.

It is referred to as the "great tribulation" or "the time of Jacob's trouble" (Jeremiah 30:7) in which a diabolical global leader comes to power half way through the seven year tribulation period and demands to be worshipped as God.

One afternoon, however, Donald got a little carried away with his vivid imagination. He was down the block getting acquainted with some new neighbors. He remembered his mother's instructions to call home by 2:00 p.m. because of an appointment he had. "May I use your telephone to call my mother?" he asked them.

"Sure," his new friend told him, "just go on in the house and my parents will show you where the phone is at."

As Donald was dialing his mother's number, he noticed that the new neighbors' phone number began with a 666. He dropped the receiver, left, and ran home as fast as he could. "Mom! Call the police right away," he exclaimed, gasping. "I've found the man whose the antichrist beast and he's living right here on our block!"

LUKE 21:36: WATCH YE THEREFORE, AND PRAY ALWAYS, THAT YE MAY BE ACCOUNTED WORTHY TO ESCAPE ALL THESE THINGS THAT SHALL COME TO PASS . . . [SEE I THESSALONIANS 5:4; REVELATION 3:10]

MATTHEW 24:21-22: FOR THEN SHALL BE GREAT TRIBULATION, SUCH AS WAS NOT SINCE THE BEGINNING OF THE WORLD TO THIS TIME, NO, NOR EVER SHALL BE. AND EXCEPT THOSE DAYS SHOULD BE SHORTENED, THERE SHOULD NO FLESH BE SAVED: BUT FOR THE ELECT'S SAKE THOSE DAYS SHALL BE SHORTENED.

DANIEL 12:1: . . . AND THERE SHALL BE A TIME OF TROUBLE, SUCH AS NEVER WAS . . .

REVELATION 13:8: AND ALL THAT DWELL UPON THE EARTH SHALL WORSHIP HIM, WHOSE NAMES ARE NOT WRITTEN IN THE BOOK OF LIFE OF THE LAMB SLAIN FROM THE FOUNDATION OF THE WORLD.

REVELATION 13:16-18: AND HE CAUSETH ALL, BOTH SMALL AND GREAT, RICH AND POOR, FREE AND BOND, TO RECEIVE A MARK IN THEIR RIGHT HAND, OR IN THEIR FOREHEADS: AND THAT NO MAN MIGHT BUY OR SELL, SAVE HE THAT HAD THE MARK, OR THE NAME OF THE BEAST, OR THE NUMBER OF HIS NAME. HERE IS WISDOM. LET HIM THAT HATH UNDERSTANDING COUNT THE NUMBER OF THE BEAST: FOR IT IS THE NUMBER OF A MAN; AND HIS NUMBER IS SIX HUNDRED THREESCORE AND SIX. [SEE MATTHEW 24:21-22; I THESSALONIANS 2:1-12; DANIEL 9:27; REVELATION 13:12-18]

REVELATION 14:11: AND THE SMOKE OF THEIR TORMENT ASCENDETH UP FOR EVER AND EVER: AND THEY HAVE NO REST DAY NOR NIGHT, WHO WORSHIP THE BEAST AND HIS IMAGE, AND WHOSOEVER RECEIVETH THE MARK OF HIS NAME.

A group of teens were putting on a series of short skits for the parents of vacation Bible school students. Hoping to stimulate interest in eternal matters among some of the unsaved parents who were present, they rehearsed their presentation on hell fire.

The first skit included two boys, each in a bear costume and another posing as a conservation officer. "And now a word from someone 'beary' concerned," said the teen in the bear costume. "I just finished taking a tour of hell," he said. "and forget about the forest fires up here," he told them, "we've got something a lot bigger going on down there."

ISAIAH 5:14: THEREFORE HELL HATH ENLARGED HERSELF, AND OPENED HER MOUTH WITHOUT MEASURE.

Following their Bible study and devotions one evening, Linda, a teenager related to her mother her ambivalent feelings toward God. "How could a good God allow the children of Israel to go through all that suffering and hardship?" she asked. "Pharaoh was so cruel and wicked using them as slaves. And then God made things worse by getting them in more trouble with Pharaoh."

"Honey, don't question God's strategy," her mother said. "That story had a happy ending because God delivered the people of Israel from Pharaoh and that awful time of bondage in Egypt. He sent terrible plagues to persuade Pharaoh to let the people go. He even turned their rivers to blood.

"Mom," her daughter said, "I guess you could say that God was out painting the town red!"

EXODUS 7:17: THUS SAITH THE LORD, IN THIS THOU SHALT KNOW THAT I AM THE LORD: BEHOLD, I WILL SMITE WITH THE ROD THAT IS IN MINE HAND UPON THE WATERS WHICH ARE IN THE RIVER, AND THEY SHALL BE TURNED TO BLOOD.

"May I speak to you a minute, Jeff," Pastor Frazier asked the teen, pulling him aside.

"Sure, what is it?" replied Jeff, thinking that the Pastor was about to pat him on the back for all the money they had collected during their recent car wash.

"It's because I'm concerned about your spiritual welfare that I must bring this to your attention," said Pastor Frazier solemnly. "I've heard a rumor that you've been involved in some despicable debauchery, cunning concupiscence, and deviate degradation." Looking Jeff straight in the eye, he continued. "and it's only because I'm worried about you committing further acts of lewd lasciviousness that I have felt compelled to discuss this with you.

"Wow, Pastor Frazier," replied Jeff scratching his head. "Are you sure I'm guilty of all that stuff? I'm not even sure I can spell any of it."

GALATIONS 5:19-21: NOW THE WORKS OF THE FLESH ARE MANIFEST, WHICH ARE THESE; ADULTERY, FORNICATION, UNCLEANESS, LASCIVIOUSNESS, IDOLATRY, WITCHCRAFT, HATRED, VARIANCE, EMULATIONS, WRATH, STRIFE, SEDITIONS, HERESIES, ENVYINGS, MURDERS, DRUNKENNESS, REVELLINGS, AND SUCH LIKE: OF THE WHICH I TELL YOU BEFORE, AS I HAVE ALSO TOLD YOU IN TIME PAST, THAT THEY WHICH DO SUCH THINGS SHALL NOT INHERIT THE KINGDOM OF GOD.

COLOSSIANS 3:5-6: MORTIFY THEREFORE YOUR MEMBERS WHICH ARE UPON THE EARTH; FORNICATION, UNCLEANNESS, INORDINATE AFFECTION, EVIL CONCUPISCENCE, AND COVETOUSNESS, WHICH IS IDOLATRY: FOR WHICH THINGS' SAKE THE WRATH OF GOD COMETH ON THE CHILDREN OF DISOBEDIENCE:

II TIMOTHY 2:19: NEVERTHELESS THE FOUNDATION OF GOD STANDETH SURE, HAVING THIS SEAL, THE LORD KNOWETH THEM THAT ARE HIS. AND, LET EVERY ONE THAT NAMETH THE NAME OF CHRIST DEPART FROM INIQUITY.

It had been several weeks since Kathy had been present in her Sunday school class. She had always been faithful in church attendance. Recently, however, she had gotten involved with the wrong crowd and strayed away from the Lord.

When she received a loving letter from her Sunday school teacher telling her how much she'd been missed, it prompted her to return to church.

As she entered her classroom that Sunday for the first time in weeks, everyone hugged her and told her how much she'd been missed.

"Kathy," asked her teacher, "Where have you been these past few weeks?"

Not wanting to elaborate on her backslidden condition, she joked, "I just didn't want to wear out my welcome."

I JOHN 3:1-3: BEHOLD, WHAT MANNER OF LOVE THE FATHER HATH BESTOWED UPON US, THAT WE SHOULD BE CALLED THE SONS OF GOD: THEREFORE THE WORLD KNOWETH US NOT, BECAUSE IT KNEW HIM NOT. BELOVED, NOW ARE WE THE SONS OF GOD, AND IT DOTH NOT YET APPEAR WHAT WE SHALL BE: BUT WE KNOW THAT, WHEN HE SHALL APPEAR, WE SHALL BE LIKE HIM; FOR WE SHALL SEE HIM AS HE IS. AND EVERY MAN THAT HATH THIS HOPE IN HIM PURIFIETH HIMSELF, EVEN AS HE IS PURE.

While driving home after church one evening, Alice detected an unusually moody, quietness about her daughter. For several months, she had been praying that her daughter would make a deeper commitment to the Lord. "Are you feeling alright," she asked Melissa tenderly.

Melissa, who had been feeling convicted about not going to the altar and dedicating her life to Christ, replied. "Oh, it's nothing more than a mild case of being torn asunder!"

HEBREWS 4:12: FOR THE WORD OF GOD IS QUICK, AND POWERFUL, AND SHARPER THAN ANY TWOSIDED SWORD, PIERCING EVEN TO THE DIVIDING ASUNDER OF SOUL AND SPIRIT, AND OF THE JOINTS AND MARROW. AND IS A DISCERNER OF THE THOUGHTS AND INTENTS OF THE HEART.

Doug, a theatrical teenager, came into his Sunday school class wearing a life jacket and carrying an oar. "What are you doing with that stuff?" asked one of the other classmates.

"It should be obvious," said Doug. "I want to be prepared just like Noah was. And," he added, "'when the enemy comes in like a flood,' I just hope I can find a life boat lying around somewhere."

LUKE 21:25-27: AND THERE SHALL BE SIGNS IN THE SUN, AND IN THE MOON, AND IN THE STARS; AND UPON THE EARTH DISTRESS OF NATIONS, WITH PERPLEXITY; THE SEA AND THE WAVES ROARING; MEN'S HEARTS FAILING THEM FOR FEAR, AND FOR LOOKING AFTER THOSE THINGS WHICH ARE COMING ON THE EARTH: FOR THE POWERS OF HEAVEN SHALL BE SHAKEN. AND THEN SHALL THEY SEE

THE SON OF MAN COMING IN A CLOUD WITH POWER AND GREAT GLORY. AND WHEN THESE THINGS BEGIN TO COME TO PASS, THEN LOOK UP, AND LIFT UP YOUR HEADS; FOR YOUR REDEMPTION DRAWETH NIGH.

A teenager was overheard praying one evening, *Lord I know I should intercede for my enemies, so I ask you to bless that low down, despicable creep who stole my new bike. Bless that rotten scoundrel, Lord, and give him Your mercy. Meet his every need. Amen and amen. Oh, and P.S., Lord, I know I'm always asking things of You, so if You don't want to answer this one particular prayer, it'll be just fine and dandy with me.*

MATTHEW 6:15: BUT IF YE FORGIVE NOT MEN THEIR TRESPASSES, NEITHER WILL YOUR FATHER FORGIVE YOUR TRESPASSES. [SEE MATTHEW 18:21-35; COLOSSIANS 3:13; EPHESIANS 4:32; PSALM 119:165]

HEBREWS 12:14-15: FOLLOW PEACE WITH ALL *MEN*, AND HOLINESS, WITHOUT WHICH NO MAN SHALL SEE THE LORD: LOOKING DILIGENTLY LEST ANY MAN FAIL OF THE GRACE OF GOD; LEST ANY ROOT OF BITTERNESS SPRINGING UP TROUBLE *YOU*, AND THEREBY MANY BE DEFILED.

"Bradley," his mother said angrily, "why is it that you always act like an angel in church but then the rest of the week you behave like the devil, himself? I can't get you to mind your father or me," she scolded.

"In fact, Bradley," she went on, "you haven't done a single thing your father asked you to do this week. The lawn hasn't been mowed. The grass is so high," she told him, "that your father has to chop and hack his way out to the car everyday.

Your room is still a mess, too" she hollered. "It looks like it was hit by 200 mile per hour gale force winds! And all you want to do, Bradley," she hollered, "is run with your derelict friends. I thought when you invited Christ into your life," she continued, "that things would be different, but so far the only time you act like a saint is in front of the pastor and the youth group leader."

"Whoa Mom!" said Bradley, "Don't be so hard on me. After all," he told her, "I do have some redeeming qualities. I picked some pretty good parents to raise me."

GALATIONS 5:25: IF WE LIVE IN THE SPIRIT, LET US ALSO WALK IN THE SPIRIT.

While Reverend James was addressing his congregation on the subject of fear, he felt compelled to ask each person to come forward and kneel at the altar who was battling this problem.

"Why didn't you go up for deliverance," one teenage girl asked her twin sister. You know how frightened you are of everything, including your own shadow."

"I would have gone up front," whispered her sister timidly, "But I was too afraid."

PSALM 56:3: WHAT TIME I AM AFRAID, I WILL TRUST IN THEE.

ISAIAH 26:3: THOU WILT KEEP *HIM* IN PERFECT PEACE, WHOSE MIND IS STAYED ON THEE.

"In this week's Sunday school lesson we will study the life of Moses and the ten commandments," said Mrs. Adams to her teenage group. "I was just wondering," she asked, "how many of you know the entire ten commandments by heart?"

As she called upon those who had raised their hands, she noticed one young man sitting in the back row who hadn't responded. "Harold," she asked, "You didn't raise your hand. Do you know the ten commandments?"

"Do I know them? Yes, Mrs. Adams," he told her. "I know everyone of them. And," he added, "if you check with the police department, they will verify that very fact."

EZEKIEL 18:23 & 30: HAVE I ANY PLEASURE AT ALL THAT THE WICKED SHOULD DIE? SAITH THE LORD GOD: AND NOT THAT HE SHOULD

RETURN FROM HIS WAYS AND LIVE? . . . REPENT, AND TURN *YOURSELVES* FROM ALL YOUR TRANSGRESSIONS; SO INIQUITY SHALL NOT BE YOUR RUIN.

"Whew!" said Darrin to his father. 'I never thought I'd be able to say it," he told him, "but I've finally reached the book of Revelation. I plowed through the Old Testament book by book and the New Testament book by book. Some of those chapters in the Old Testament seemed so long," he said. "For a while there, I felt like I was wandering around for forty years going in circles with the children of Israel."

"I'm very proud of you Darrin," said his father, beaming with delight. "I knew you could do it if you stuck with it. You just wait and see," he said, "the Lord will bring many of those scriptures to mind when you need them."

"I hope there was some purpose in it all," said Darrin, putting his Bible away. "Because right now all I can say is that, when the Lord wrote the Bible, he certainly was long-winded!"

About that time, Darrin's little brother walked in, overhearing the conversation. "Dad," he asked, "I know God wrote the Bible but who was the clown that wrote all those 'begets?'"

II TIMOTHY 3:16-17: ALL SCRIPTURE IS GIVEN BY INSPIRATION OF GOD, AND IS PROFITABLE FOR DOCTRINE, FOR REPROOF, FOR CORRECTION FOR INSTRUCTION IN RIGHTEOUSNESS: THAT THE MAN OF GOD MAY BE PERFECT, THROUGHLY FURNISHED UNTO ALL GOOD WORKS.

II PETER 1:20-21: KNOWING THIS FIRST, THAT NO PROPHECY OF THE SCRIPTURE IS OF ANY PRIVATE INTERPRETATION. FOR THE PROPHECY CAME NOT IN OLD TIME BYTHE WILL OF MAN: BUT HOLY MEN OF GOD SPAKE *AS THEY WERE* MOVED BYTHE HOLY GHOST. [SEE ACTS 1:16]

HEBREWS 4:12: FOR THE WORD OF GOD *IS* QUICK, AND POWERFUL, AND SHARPER THAN ANY TWOEDGED SWORD, PIERCING EVEN TO THEDIVIDING ASUNDER OF SOUL AND SPIRIT, AND OF THE JOINTS

AND MARROW, AND *IS* A DISCERNER OF THE THOUGHTS AND INTENTS OF THE HEART.

No sooner than thirteen-year-old Richard phoned his school classmate, he realized he'd dialed the wrong party.

"I'm sorry," he said, not recognizing the voice at the other end. "I must have dialed the wrong number."

"On the contrary, young man," responded the woman who had answered his call. "This may be the first time you ever dialed the right number!" With that she began expounding on the gospel telling him all about Jesus Christ and His saving grace.

When she finished, he said, "Thanks, miss, I got saved when I was five, but it never hurts to take a refresher course."

JAMES 5:20: LET HIM KNOW, THAT HE WHICH CONVERTETH THE SINNER FROM THE ERROR OF HIS WAY SHALL SAVE A SOUL FROM DEATH, AND SHALL HIDE A MULTITUDE OF SINS.

Two teenagers were discussing the difficulties they were having in trying to walk in the Spirit and live a life that would be pleasing unto the Lord. When it comes to my walk with God, said Todd, "It seems like I'm either crawling, falling, or stalling."

"You're not alone," his friend said sympathetically. "Because whenever the Lord looks my way, I'm usually doing one of three things: committing, omitting, or considering!"

ROMANS 6:14: FOR SIN SHALL NOT HAVE DOMINION OVER YOU . . .

JOHN 15:4-5: ABIDE IN ME . . . FOR WITHOUT ME YE CAN DO NOTHING.

PHILIPPIANS 1:6: BEING CONFIDENT OF THIS VERY THING, THAT HE WHICH HATH BEGUN A GOOD WORK IN YOU WILL PERFORM *IT* UNTIL THE DAY OF JESUS CHRIST.

PHILIPPIANS 2:13: FOR IT IS GOD WHICH WORKETH IN YOU BOTH TO WILL AND TO DO OF *HIS* GOOD PLEASURE.

II TIMOTHY 1:12: . . . FOR I KNOW WHOM I HAVE BELIEVED, AND AM PERSUADED THAT HE IS ABLE TO KEEP THAT WHICH I HAVE COMMITTED UNTO HIM AGAINST THAT DAY.

I THESSALONIANS 5:24: FAITHFUL *IS* HE THAT CALLETH YOU, WHO ALSO WILL DO *IT*.

JUDE 24: NOW UNTO HIM THAT IS ABLE TO KEEP YOU FROM FALLING, AND TO PRESENT *YOU* FAULTLESS BEFORE THE PRESENCE OF HIS GLORY WITH EXCEEDING JOY.

I THESSALONIANS 3:13: TO THE END HE MAY STABLISH YOUR HEARTS UNBLAMEABLE . . .

PROVERBS 24:16: FOR A JUST *MAN* FALLETH SEVEN TIMES, AND RISETH UP AGAIN . . .

Frank, a teenager, was going through some times of testing. He was at a point in his life where he had to make some crucial decisions about his future plans. He asked his closest friend, Devon, to pray over his situation.

"I'd be glad to earnestly intercede for you," said Devon. "Let's take it to the Lord right now. "Lord," he cried, in his most pleading voice, "bless Frank and meet all his needs. Amen."

Though he tried not to show it, Paul was a bit peeved with his friend. The prayer had taken all of about ten seconds.

"Well," said Devon, "That takes care of that. You ought to get some serious results now because the Bible says in James 5:16 that 'the effectual, fervent prayer of a righteous man availeth much.'"

"I'm not sure God heard your prayer, Devon," Frank told him. "You said it so fast that it flew past Him like a supersonic missile!"

I SAMUEL 12:23: MOREOVER AS FOR ME, GOD FORBID THAT I SHOULD SIN AGAINST THE LORD IN CEASING TO PRAY FOR YOU . . .

EPHESIANS 6:18: PRAYING ALWAYS WITH ALL PRAYER AND SUPPLICATION IN THE SPIRIT, AND WATCHING THEREUNTO WITH ALL PERSEVERANCE AND SUPPLICATION FOR ALL SAINTS . . .

ROMANS 1:9: FOR GOD IS MY WITNESS, WHOM I SERVE WITH MY SPIRIT IN THE GOSPEL OF HIS SON, THAT WITHOUT CEASING I MAKE MENTION OF YOU ALWAYS IN MY PRAYERS;

FAMILY FRENZY

Mary, a struggling divorcee, was doing her best to live on a limited budget. Since the breakup of her marriage, she no longer had a husband to provide for her needs. It seemed as though one thing after another kept falling apart, particularly her car.

After a number of huge auto repair bills, her son-in-law suggested she purchase a new car and recommended the place he thought she would get the best deal.

"I'll have to pray about it first," Mary told him, "And wait for the leading of the Lord."

Her son-in-law, not quite the spiritual veteran his mother-in-law was, sarcastically replied. "I thought Jesus was a carpenter," he said. "Nobody told me he was also a mechanic."

PROVERBS 3:5-6: TRUST IN THE LORD WITH ALL THINE HEART; AND LEAN NOT UNTO THINE OWN UNDERSTANDING. IN ALL THY WAYS ACKNOWLEDGE HIM, AND HE SHALL DIRECT THY PATHS.

While the Peterson family was having their evening devotions, their son, Arnold, interrupted the discussion to ask a question he'd been wondering about for some time.

"Why does God have so many different names?" he asked. "He has more aliases than a check forger."

"Shame on you, Arnold," scolded his father. "You're being irreverent. He has a lot of names because there are many facets of his mighty power. As

As for me and my house, we will 'unnerve' the Lord.

an omnipotent being, he is a healer, a savior, a father, a king, a comforter, and so on."

"But,' asked Arnold, "Wearing that many hats isn't he going to have an identity crisis?"

ISAIAH 9:6: FOR UNTO US A CHILD IS BORN, UNTO US A SON IS GIVEN: AND THE GOVERNMENT SHALL BE UPON HIS SHOULDER: AND HIS NAME SHALL BE CALLED WONDERFUL, COUNSELLOR, THE MIGHTY GOD, THE EVERLASTING FATHER, THE PRINCE OF PEACE.

"Let's pray over our family, children," Reba said as she was driving to the grocery store. "I've been so busy running errands today that I nearly forgot to ask for God's protection and blessing over each one of you.

Then glancing up at her rearview mirror, she quickly eyed each one. "Settle down back there," she instructed them. When they stopped fidgeting and became quiet, she told them to bow their heads and close their eyes.

Ricky, her youngest son, who was peeking out out of one eye at his mother as she began to pray, interrupted. "Mom," he said. "Aren't you going to close your eyes too?"

"I would be glad to close my eyes, Ricky," replied his mother, "but the other drivers wouldn't appreciate it."

MATTHEW 6:9-13: AFTER THIS MANNER THEREFORE PRAY YE: OUR FATHER WHICH ART IN HEAVEN, HALLOWED BE THY NAME. THY KINGDOM COME. THY WILL BE DONE IN EARTH, AS *IT IS* IN HEAVEN. GIVE US THIS DAY OUR DAILY BREAD. AND FORGIVE US OUR DEBTS, AS WE FORGIVE OUR DEBTORS. AND LEAD US NOT INTO TEMPTATION, BUT DELIVER US FROM EVIL: FOR THINE IS THE KINGDOM, AND THE POWER, AND THE GLORY, FOR EVER. AMEN.

"When are you going to start increasing my allowance, dad?" Jane asked her father with a hopeful look on her face.

"Jane, you're not getting extra for doing things you're already paid to do," he told her. "No one gives me a bonus for taking out the garbage, mowing the lawn, and fixing things around here. I do it because it's my responsibility, and," he said, "I expect you to do the same!"

"But dad," she pleaded, "Can't you put something green in my hand so I can go shopping with my friends today?"

"If you want something green, here it is," her father retorted. He generously sprinkled some green powder cleanser on a scrub brush and handed it to her. "Now please go clean the bathroom, young lady, and then you can go shopping with your friends."

Jane walked away disappointed and pouting but her father noticed that she did clean the bathroom until it was spotless. In fact, it was glistening!

"Jane," he mentioned, complimenting her, "You did a fine job on the bathroom." He reached in his pocket and handed her $40. "Here's something green," he said, smiling with a change of heart.

"Thanks, dad," Jane said, hugging him, "and remember, next time you need the bathroom cleaned, you've got a ready and willing scum scooper living right here in your house.!"

COLOSSIANS 3:20: CHILDREN, OBEY YOUR PARENTS IN ALL THINGS: FOR THIS IS WELL PLEASING UNTO THE LORD.

With scarcely enough time to fix breakfast before Sunday morning church services, Judy, a busy housewife and mother scurried about to prepare a delicious breakfast for her family. The table, laid out with bacon 'n eggs, biscuits, cereal, toast, and juice was left untouched except for a couple of small glasses of orange juice that were gulped down by the children within a matter of seconds.

Running a little late, Judy urged her husband to take a shortcut to church. The children, confused by a different route, began asking questions.

"Mom, are we going out to breakfast first?" asked Cindy, their youngest daughter.

"Yah, Mom," said Wendy, the oldest girl, "Where are we going to eat breakfast at?"

Remembering her unappreciated efforts in the kitchen, their mother replied, "Where are we going to eat breakfast at? At lunch, that's where!"

MATTHEW 7:7-11: ASK, AND IT SHALL BE GIVEN YOU; SEEK, AND YE SHALL FIND; KNOCK, AND IT SHALL BE OPENED UNTO YOU: FOR EVERY ONE THAT ASKETH RECEIVETH; AND HE THAT SEEKETH FINDETH; AND TO HIM THAT KNOCKETH IT SHALL BE OPENED. OR WHAT MAN IS THERE OF YOU, WHOM IF HIS SON ASK BREAD, WILL HE GIVE HIM A STONE? OR IF HE ASK A FISH, WILL HE GIVE HIM A SERPENT? IF YE THEN, BEING EVIL, KNOW HOW TO GIVE GOOD GIFTS UNTO YOUR CHILDREN, HOW MUCH MORE THALL YOUR FATHER WHICH IS IN HEAVEN GIVE GOOD THINGS TO THEM THAT ASK HIM. [SEE PHILIPPIANS 4:19]

Mrs. Anderson and her children were on their way home from Sunday night services when their car stalled at an intersection. The children pointed out the window at the changing traffic lights, paying no attention to their mother's predicament.

"It's green!" shouted Susie.

"Now it's yellow!" squealed Sally.

'Look, it's red again," said Sammy.

"Now it's blue!" exclaimed Susie.

"Traffic lights aren't blue," said Sammy.

"This one is," said Susie, looking out the back window. "And it's sitting right on top of that police car that's behind us."

"As if things aren't already bad enough!" complained their mother. "He'll probably give me a ticket."

"Don't worry, Mom," said Sammy, reassuring her. "He looks like a nice man."

"Yes, he looks like Uncle Henry, Mom," Susie told her. "Maybe he'll give us a sucker just like Uncle Henry does when he comes over."

"I'm sure he will have something for us," their mother said sighing, "but I don't think it will be suckers."

ROMANS 8:28: AND WE KNOW THAT ALL THINGS WORK TOGETHER FOR GOOD TO THEM THAT LOVE GOD, TO THEM WHO ARE THE CALLED ACCORDING TO HIS PURPOSE.

"Don't you think it's about time you children gave your lives to Jesus?" Marie asked her five youngsters. "There is nothing more important than making a decision to live for God," she added.

"But Mom," said Eddie, the mathematical genius of the family. "Between the five of us kids, we've already been baptized 14,235 times."

"How do you figure?" his mother asked.

"Because," said Eddie, giggling, "that's how many baths we've taken altogether.

His mother shook her head at his silliness and replied, "You need to invite Jesus in your heart before you get baptized," she said. "Don't you think you're getting the 'cart before the horse?'"

"No, mom," Eddie laughed, "but we might be getting the cart before the hose!"

JOHN 3:5-7: JESUS ANSWERED, VERILY, VERILY, I SAY UNTO THEE, EXCEPT A MAN BE BORN OF WATER [A PHYSICAL BIRTH] AND *OF* THE SPIRIT [A SPIRITUAL BIRTH], HE CANNOT ENTER INTO THE

KINGDOM OF GOD. THAT WHICH IS BORN OF THE FLESH IS FLESH; AND THAT WHICH IS BORN OF THE SPIRIT IS SPIRIT. MARVEL NOT THAT I SAID UNTO THEE, YE MUST BE BORN AGAIN.

Donna and Dale, a couple with four children were looking for a house close to the school and church they attended.

Their pastor recommended a nice home he'd seen that was for sale only a few blocks away. He pointed out all of the fine features of the area and indicated that it was a neighborhood with kind, considerate homeowners, such as himself.

A month after the couple had moved into their new home, Dale began grumbling. "I have here in my hand a gas bill, an electric bill, a phone bill, a car insurance payment, and a house payment," he told Donna murmuring. "And the worst part of it is, they belong to my neighbor! The mailman is not only giving me my bills," he complained, "but everyone else's. And I thought this was a friendly neighborhood!"

I PETER 2:13: SUBMIT YOURSELVES TO EVERY ORDINANCE OF MAN FOR THE LORD'S SAKE . . .

Helen, a housewife, had been wanting some new furniture to replace her badly worn couch, loveseat, and recliner.

On her birthday her husband decided to surprise her with the new furniture she'd been eyeing.

While she was busy arranging the new pieces and admiring its flawless beauty, she hadn't noticed one of her children come wandering into the room with a small plastic cup of grape juice in his hand. Like an accident looking for a place to happen, before she could speak, he had already spilled and splattered it all over the new tan couch.

Absolutely horrified by the sight, she cried out, "God, you changed the water into wine. Now, please, I beg you to change the wine into water. Because, if you don't Lord," she said, fearfully, you'll be seeing me face to face.

You know when my husband sees this catastrophe, he's going to send me into orbit!"

PSALM 118:17-18: I SHALL NOT DIE, BUT LIVE, AND DECLARE THE WORKS OF THE LORD. THE LORD HATH CHASTENED ME SORE: BUT HE HATH NOT GIVEN ME OVER UNTO DEATH.

DEUTERONOMY 4:4: BUT YE THAT DID CLEAVE UNTO THE LORD YOUR GOD *ARE* ALIVE EVERY ONE OF YOU THIS DAY.

PROVERBS 3:25-26: BE NOT AFRAID OF SUDDEN FEAR, NEITHER OF THE DESOLATION OF THE WICKED, WHEN IT COMETH. FOR THE LORD SHALL BE THY CONFIDENCE, AND SHALL KEEP THY FOOT FROM BEING TAKEN.

PROVERBS 14:26: IN THE FEAR OF THE LORD *IS* STRONG CONFIDENCE: AND HIS CHILDREN SHALL HAVE A PLACE OF REFUGE.

PSALMS 118:6: THE LORD IS ON MY SIDE; I WILL NOT FEAR: WHAT CAN MAN DO UNTO ME?

PSALM 121:8: THE LORD SHALL PRESERVE THY GOING OUT AND THY COMING IN FROM THIS TIME FORTH, AND EVEN FOR EVERMORE.

Every week Mrs. Wilson and her husband drove to church separately. She would take their three children and leave twenty minutes early so that she could take care of preparations for her Sunday school class. Her husband would join her later for church.

One morning, however, because her husband's car needed repairs, they had agreed to ride together in her car. Preoccupied with the morning's activities, she forgot about the arrangements they had made and she left early without him. When she arrived at the sanctuary, she gasped. "Oh no!" she cried, "I forgot and left my husband behind!"

"I've heard of women forgetting their purse, or even their Bible," quipped one of the church members, "but this is the first time I've heard of someone leaving their husband behind!"

"Well," remarked another church member, "that's one way to drop 200 lbs. quickly!"

PHILIPPIANS 3:13-14: FORGETTING THOSE THINGS WHICH ARE BEHIND, AND REACHING FORTH UNTO THOSE THINGS WHICH ARE BEFORE, I PRESS TOWARD THE MARK FOR THE PRIZE OF THE HIGH CALLING OF GOD IN CHRIST JESUS.

A a young boy watched his mother and father each place a handful of coins and bills into the offering plate as it was passed to them. He couldn't forget about all the money he saw them put into the plate that morning.

On the way home, he asked his father, "Daddy, how much does it cost to go to church on Sunday"

His dad glanced back at the boy and said, "Oh, it costs the same as it always has, son—your life!"

MATTHEW 10:38-39: AND HE THAT TAKETH NOT HIS CROSS, AND FOLLOWETH AFTER ME, IS NOT WORTHY OF ME. HE THAT FINDETH HIS LIFE SHALL LOSE IT: AND HE THAT LOSETH HIS LIFE FOR MY SAKE SHALL FIND IT.

LUKE 9:23: AND HE SAID TO *THEM* ALL, IF ANY *MAN* WILL COME AFTER ME, LET HIM DENY HIMSELF, AND TAKE UP HIS CROSS DAILY, AND FOLLOW ME.

LUKE 14:27: AND WHOSOEVER DOTH NOT BEAR HIS CROSS, AND COME AFTER ME, CANNOT BE MY DISCIPLE. [SEE LUKE 17:33; GALATIONS 2:20; ROMANS 12:1-2]

One morning the Smith family overslept and were rushing around to get ready for church. The children's father, trying to expedite things by assigning each a task, became very annoyed with his daughter because she wasn't following instructions. Exasperated, he grumbled to his wife, "You know, Marie, if I told Lucy to go out the front door, she'd go out the back. And if I told her to go out the back, she'd go out the front. And if I told her to go out the side door, she'd go out the window!"

PROVERBS 20:24: MAN'S GOINGS *ARE* OF THE LORD; HOW CAN A MAN THEN UNDERSTAND HIS OWN WAY?

PSALMS 37:23: THE STEPS OF A GOOD MAN ARE ORDERED BY THE LORD: AND HE DELIGHTETH IN HIS WAY.

PROVERBS 16:9: A MAN'S HEART DEVISETH HIS WAY: BUT THE LORD DIRECTETH HIS STEPS.

PSALM 31:15: MY TIMES *ARE* IN THY HAND.

A mother and her three children stopped at a fast food restaurant for lunch. As the children reached for their hamburgers, she gently scolded them saying, "First we are going to bow our heads and give thanks for this food."

Her son, was looking out the window through the corner of his eye while she said the grace. "May I add a quick note?" he interrupted his mother.

"Uh . . . sure, Tommy," she said, rather surprised at his willingness to pray in public.

"Lord, besides our food, we want to also thank You for the new car that we are about to receive since someone just sped off with our old one."

LUKE 6: 29: AND UNTO HIM THAT SMITETH THEE ON THE *ONE* CHEEK OFFER ALSO THE OTHER; AND HIM THAT TAKETH AWAY THY CLOAK FORBID NOT TO *TAKE THY* COAT ALSO. GIVE TO EVERY MAN THAT ASKETH OF THEE; AND OF HIM THAT TAKETH AWAY THY GOODS ASK THEM NOT AGAIN.

"Shannon, I want you to do the dishes," her mother told her, "When you're finished you can go over to your girlfriend's house.

About ten minutes later Shannon skipped out the door. When her mother went into the kitchen to inspect her work, however, she was irritated to discover that only half of the dishes had been done. "Shannon" she yelled out the back door, get in this house this instant!"

"What's the matter, Mom?" asked Shannon, acting as if she didn't have the vaguest idea of what she'd done wrong.

"Shannon," her mother hollered, "just look at this mess."

"But, Mom," whined Shannon. "I did half the dishes. If I have to do the rest, I won't have time for anything else.

Angered by her daughter's irresponsible attitude, she asked, "Do I only drive you half way to school each day? Or do I only help you with half of your homework? Or when I go to the shoe store," she went on, "do I buy you only one tennis shoe? Or when I do the wash, do I only do half of your clothes? Or when I iron your blouses," she continued, "do I only press one side? And when you and your twin sister were born," she underscored looking directly into her eyes, "did I only bring one of you home?"

"I'm sorry, mom," said Shannon. "You made your point. I guess I have some 'half baked' ideas when it comes to doing chores.'

COLOSSIANS 3:17: AND WHATSOEVER YE DO IN WORD OR DEED, *DO* ALL IN THE NAME OF THE LORD JESUS, GIVING THANKS TO GOD AND THE FATHER BY HIM.

MATRIMONIAL MISFITS

A firm believer in commitment to one's marriage, Pastor Lane thought it would be lovely gesture to have every married couple in his congregation stand up and repeat their wedding vows.

"Whether you are newly married or have been 'enduring' for years," he joked, "I would like you to come up to the altar, take the arm of your spouse, and prepare to exchange vows." He told them that when everyone was present he would begin the ceremony.

As he was waiting for the marriage partners to make their way up front, he noticed one woman, teary-eyed, stomping furiously down the aisle in the opposite direction.

Signaling one of the deacons, he whispered, "Please go and find out what's the matter with that lady."

Later, after the service had concluded, the deacon related the problem to the pastor. "It was just a slight marital misunderstanding," the deacon said. "Her husband told her that the only way he'd take her arm again in matrimony was if he could re-attach it to some other woman's body!"

EPHESIANS 5:28-29: SO OUGHT MEN TO LOVE THEIR WIVES AS THEIR OWN BODIES. HE THAT LOVETH HIS WIFE LOVETH HIMSELF. FOR NO MAN EVER YET HATED HIS OWN FLESH; BUT NOURISHETH AND CHERISHETH IT, EVEN AS THE LORD THE CHURCH . . .

"Are you having another affair with the pastor, Loretta?" her jealous husband asked accusingly.

"Whatever would make you think such a ridiculous thing?" his wife replied angrily.

Because you seem to be spending all your time up there at the church," he snarled. "And all you ever say is 'the pastor this and the pastor that.'"

"Nonsense!" shouted Loretta. "I go there to draw closer to the Lord."
"If that doesn't beat all!" he yelled. "Now you're after the both of them!"

LUKE 2:49: . . . I MUST BE ABOUT MY FATHER'S BUSINESS.

"Harriet, where's my white shirt?" her husband, Rex, asked.

"It's in the basement, dear, with the rest of the dirty clothes," she replied nonchalantly.

"Harriet, darling, there are no black socks in my drawer."

"They're all in the hamper, honey," she answered, polishing her fingernails.

"Harriet, dearest, where are my black pants?" he asked, searching through the clutter and piles of clothes in the closet.

"They're at the cleaners, sweetie," she responded.

"Harriet," growled her husband as he watched her polish her nails and apply her makeup, "What do you do all day besides restore antiques?"

JOB 29:14: I PUT ON RIGHTEOUSNESS, AND IT CLOTHED ME . . .

A couple in love decided to set the date for their wedding. Unfortunately, the prospective groom was an avid sportsman who wanted everything to revolve around his fishing, hunting, and ballgame schedule.

The minister's secretary tried to be as flexible as possible but it seemed that every date she had available for the pastor to perform the ceremony only conflicted with the groom's hunting and fishing plans.

Meg, his fiancé, tried to be understanding. "That's okay, honey," she said, "go ahead and enjoy yourself. I know how important hunting season is to you. We can get married at a later date. And besides," she told him, "I'll have you all to myself on our honeymoon."

Looking at her blankly, he replied, "Oh, did you want to come along on that too?"

JAMES 1:5: IF ANY OF YOU LACK WISDOM, LET HIM ASK OF GOD, THAT GIVETH TO ALL *MEN* LIBERALLY, AND UPBRAIDETH NOT; AND IT SHALL BE GIVEN HIM.

Popping in from work one afternoon, Michael overheard his wife discussing the pros and cons of their up and down marriage. "There are days," said Connie to her friend, grumbling, "when 'til death do us part,' certainly tempts me."

At that point, her husband made his presence known. As he entered their family room, he threw in his two cents on the matter. Pointing to the regrettable skull and crossbones imbedded with indelible ink on his arm, he commented, "Marriage is like a tattoo, Connie," he told her, "Good or bad, you're stuck with it for life!"

"Yah," his wife retorted, "but a tattoo doesn't try to get the last word in!"

EPHESIANS 5:33: NEVERTHELESS, LET EVERY ONE OF YOU IN PARTICULAR SO LOVE HIS WIFE EVEN AS HIMSELF; AND THE WIFE *SEE* THAT SHE REVERENCE *HER* HUSBAND.

A henpecked husband was complaining about his marriage to his co-worker, "My wife never knows when to quit spouting off," he said. "The brakes that would stop most women are missing in her! From the time she slithers out of bed in the morning until she falls asleep at night," he went on, "she gripes incessantly. Her mouth is like a cesspool of constant criticism, all targeted at me of course! Each word is like an accurately aimed missile, intended to sabotage our marriage. I'm at the point," he said, "where I need to enlist some outside help.

"Well," replied his co-worker supportively, "If a nagging woman is like a dripping pipe, I think what you need is a plumber—and right away. Tell him," he joked, "to shut that faucet off right away!"

PROVERBS 19:13: THE CONTENTIONS OF A WIFE *ARE* A CONTINUAL DROPPING.

PROVERBS 11:22: *AS* A JEWEL OF GOLD IN A SWINE'S SNOUT, *SO IS* A FAIR WOMAN WHICH IS WITHOUT DISCRETION.

After a nasty argument with her husband, Carla remembered the words of Jesus about loving those that wrong you. So, although she was till seething inside, she managed to spout out a feeble but somewhat sincere "I love you" to her husband. *There! I did it! I fulfilled my Christian duty*, she told herself.

No sooner than those words were out of her mouth, however, a damn of hatred broke loose within. She put her hands on her hips, raised her eyebrows and remarked, "Like I said, I love you, darling. I love you. I love you. I love you . . . less and less every day!"

MARK 3:24: AND IF A KINGDOM BE DIVIDED AGAINST ITSELF, THAT KINGDOM CANNOT STAND.

"This marriage is like Mt. Saint Helen's and it's about to blast wide open!" Marvin told his friend.

"How can it be that bad, buddy?" his friend asked him. "You just got married a couple days ago. You have a beautiful wife, a great house, two well behaved dogs, and you both have six digit salaries."

"Yes, you're right," he admitted.

"Then what's wrong, pal?" he asked.

"Well," Marvin replied, "I just discovered that my wife was . . . um . . . er . . .

"Come on, spit it out, buddy," his friend coaxed, looking bewildered.

Marvin took a deep breath and then blurted out what he was having difficulty trying to divulge. "I just discovered," he said reluctantly, that my wife was my . . . um . . . er . . . my former neighbor's "former" brother!"

GENESIS 6:5: AND GOD SAW THAT THE WICKEDNESS OF MAN *WAS* GREAT IN THE EARTH, AND *THAT* EVERY IMAGINATION OF THE THOUGHTS OF HIS HEART *WAS* ONLY EVIL CONTINUALLY.

II CORINTHIANS 11:14: AND NO MARVEL; FOR SATAN HIMSELF IS TRANSFORMED INTO AN ANGEL OF LIGHT.

"Honey," Sandra said gently to her husband, "It wouldn't hurt you to get a haircut. I noticed a sign in the barber shop we just passed and the price on the window looked very reasonable."

Not wanting to part with his curly locks, he objected. "Have you forgotten, Sandra," he replied sarcastically, "that it took several years to grow this head of hair? And besides," he told her, "this is Sunday and they wouldn't be open."

"Yes, honey, they are," she told him, ignoring the meanness and sarcasm in his voice. "The sign in the window says 'Open,' she said. "I saw several people in there."

"If they're open on Sunday," he snapped, "Then they're a bunch of heathens; and I won't let some atheist stand within ten feet of me with a blade in his hand."

"Honey, you're being ridiculous," she told him. "Lot's of people work on Sunday—doctors, caregivers, desk clerks at hotels, waiters and waitresses at restaurants, gas station attendants, and the list goes on. Even the Pastor works on Sunday," she said, trying to persuade him. "There are lots of people who want to be in church on Sunday but they can't" she continued, "because they're scheduled to work.

"Well," he relented, "I guess you've got a point, but so far as my hair is concerned, the only way it's coming off is old age balding or a head on collision with a lawnmower!"

ROMANS 14:5-6: ONE MAN ESTEEMETH ONE DAY ABOVE ANOTHER: ANOTHER ESTEEMETH EVERY DAY *ALIKE*. LET EVERY MAN BE FULLY PERSUADED IN HIS OWN MIND. HE THAT REGARDETH THE DAY, REGARDETH *IT* UNTO THE LORD; AND HE THAT REGARDETH NOT THE DAY, TO THE LORD HE DOTH NOT REGARD *IT* . . .

"Marilyn," cried Kathy, "My husband has gotten so out of control. He smashes up our place whenever he feels like it, shouts and swears at the kids continually, finds fault with everything they do, and threatens to beat us up whenever things don't go his way. What should I do?" she cried in desperation.

"Don't take the law into your own hands," her friend advised. 'Do what the Bible says to do."

"And what's that?" Kathy asked.

"Well," said Betty, "Have the pastor baptize him."

"But, Betty," Kathy replied, "Baptism comes after a person is saved," she said, "and my husband obviously has not repented and accepted Christ as his savior."

"He will when the pastor holds him down long enough," her friend snickered.

MARK 1:4-5: 7-8: JOHN DID BAPTIZE IN THE WILDERNESS, AND PREACH THE BAPTISM OF REPENTANCE FOR THE REMISSION OF SINS. AND THERE WENT OUT UNTO HIM ALL THE LAND OF JUDAEA, AND THEY OF JERUSALEM, AND WERE ALL BAPTIZED OF HIM IN THE RIVER OF JORDAN, CONFESSING THEIR SINS . . . AND [JOHN] PREACHED, SAYING, THERE COMETH ONE MIGHTIER THAN I AFTER ME, THE LATCHET OF WHOSE SHOES I AM NOT WORTHY TO STOOP DOWN

AND UNLOOSE. I INDEED HAVE BAPTIZED YOU WITH WATER: BUT HE SHALL BAPTIZE YOU WITH THE HOLY GHOST.

ACTS 11:16: . . . JOHN INDEED BAPTIZED WITH WATER; BUT YE SHALL BE BAPTIZED WITH THE HOLY GHOST.

Each week Barbara would come strolling into church with her husband, Luke, lagging twenty or more feet behind her. Although he was vehemently opposed to coming, he would do so for the sake of keeping peace with his wife. He let it be known, however, that he resented every minute that he had to spend within the confines of the sanctuary. He would twitch and turn and growl at regular intervals to show his glaring disapproval of the Sunday gathering.

One particular Sunday, when the service concluded and Barbara and Luke were leaving, he felt a tap on his shoulder as they were pushing through the crowd. Luke turned around to see who it was.

"Nice to see you again, Luke," said the Pastor kindly. 'And, Lord willing, we'll see you again next Sunday."

Luke looked at the Pastor with piercing, cold eyes and spouted, "Is that a threat?"

JEREMIAH 17:9: THE HEART IS DECEITFUL ABOVE ALL THINGS, AND DESPERATELY WICKED. WHO CAN KNOW IT?

"Meg," said Pastor Parks, "Would you go into my office and try consoling Mrs. Benson. She's in there sobbing uncontrollably," he said compassionately. "I can't get a word out of her as to what's wrong. Maybe she needs to confide in another woman."

"Sure, I'll he happy to help, Pastor," said his secretary.

About a half an hour later, after Mrs. Benson had cried buckets of tears, she came out of the office with Mrs. Benson.

As soon as the woman had left, Meg relayed their conversation to the pastor.

"We talked about rice," she told him.

"Rice?" asked the pastor, looking bewildered.

"Yes," replied Meg. "Mrs. Benson, who, as you know, is a newlywed, said that it hadn't even been swept away before her husband started having an affair."

PROVERBS 7:22 & 27: HE GOETH AFTER HER STRAIGHTWAY, AS AN OX GOETH TO THE SLAUGHTER . . . HER HOUSE *IS* THE WAY TO HELL, GOING DOWN TO THE CHAMBERS OF DEATH.

JOB 31:1 & 11: I MADE A COVENANT WITH MINE EYES; WHY THEN SHOULD I THINK UPON A MAID? . . . FOR THIS *IS* AN [A] HEINOUS CRIME . . .

GENESIS 39:7-10: AND IT CAME TO PASS AFTER THESE THINGS, THAT HIS MASTER'S WIFE CAST HER EYES UPON JOSEPH; AND SHE SAID, LIE WITH ME. BUT HE REFUSED, AND SAID UNTO HIS MASTER'S WIFE, BEHOLD, MY MASTER WOTTETH NOT WHAT *IS* WITH ME IN THE HOUSE, AND HE HATH COMMITTED ALL THAT HE HATH TO MY HAND; *THERE IS* NONE GREATER IN THIS HOUSE THAN I; NEITHER HATH HE KEPT BACK ANY THING FROM ME BUT THEE, BECAUSE THOU *ART* HIS WIFE: HOW THEN CAN I DO THIS GREAT WICKEDNESS, AND SIN AGAINST GOD? AND IT CAME TO PASS, AS SHE SPAKE TO JOSEPH DAY BY DAY, THAT HE HEARKENED NOT UNTO HER, TO LIE BY HER, *OR* TO BE WITH HER.

Angela was a single, Christian lady, not getting any younger, whose steady boyfriend, Eddie, had a habit of giving her everything but proposals. In this particular case "steady" meant nothing more than one, continuous flow of dirty clothes which he expected Angela to launder, press, and alter as well.

After many long, tedious months of washing, sewing, mending, and pressing his clothes, the only addition to Angela's hope chest was a few more grey hairs, a pair of rough, red scaly hands, and a lot of bottles of fabric softener but still no proposal.

Her not-so-subtle hints and suggestions of taking him on a scenic tour of all the local Laundromats only reached very deaf ears.

One night, as she reached the end of her spin cycle, she realized she had also reached the end of her rope. When Eddie, her boyfriend, dropped by to pick up his clothes, she spouted out more steam than her iron could ever possibly match. After giving him quite a tongue lashing for his thoughtlessness, she informed him that her dryer was the only thing in the house that was still "cool," calm and collected, but only because it was no longer working.

"Furthermore," she declared, "the next time I carry an eight pound load into the house, it better be wrapped in a pink or blue blanket and followed by a proud husband and father!

And in case I haven't made myself perfectly clear, Eddie," she stated emphatically, "I've just pressed your last shirt. The way I see it ironing is like sex," she told him. "It only comes after marriage.

I TIMOTHY 5:18: FOR THE SCRIPTURE SAITH, THOU SHALT NOT MUZZLE THE OX THAT TREADETH OUT THE CORN. AND, THE LABOURER [LABORER] *IS* WORTHY OF HIS REWARD.

During an explosive argument, Marilyn unleashed her anger on her husband. "You're nothing but a contemptible, ill-mannered, uncivilized, foul-mouthed, stubborn old mule" she shouted, "and I must've been plum loco to have married you. Further more," she ranted, "You're not fooling anybody with that phony, hypocritical act of yours."

Keeping his calm, her husband coolly replied, "If I'm all of those things, then it certainly doesn't say much for the kind of company you keep."

I PETER 3:1-2,& 4: LIKEWISE, YE WIVES, *BE* IN SUBJECTION TO YOUR OWN HUSBANDS; THAT, IF ANY OBEY NOT THE WORD, THEY ALSO MAY WITHOUT THE WORD BE WON BY THE CONVERSATION OP THE WIVES; WHILE THEY BEHOLD YOUR CHASTE CONVERSATION *COUPLED* WITH FEAR . . . BUT *LET IT BE* THE HIDDEN MAN OF THE HEART, IN THAT WHICH IS NOT CORRUPTIBLE, *EVEN THE ORNAMENT* OF A MEEK AND QUIET SPIRIT, WHICH IS IN THE SIGHT OF GOD OF GREAT PRICE.

"Pastor," complained Larry, the situation at home has gotten progressively worse since the last time I spoke with you. My wife, Edie, just walks away whenever I mention the Lord. I've tried to ignite some interest in the Bible, but she's like a dead battery in an old car. There isn't even a spark of enthusiasm."

"Hmmm, said the Pastor, tapping his pencil on his desk. "Lifeless, hey?"

"That's right, Pastor," said Larry regrettably.

"Then I don't see any other way around this," the Pastor told him. "It sounds to me like you have no other alternative," he said, "but to call a wrecker and have her towed away."

PROVERBS 16:20: HE THAT HANDLETH A MATTER WISELY SHALL FIND GOOD . . .

"Did you hear about the Millers?" one church member, Anita, asked another.

"Yes, I heard about them," the other one admitted.

"Everyone thought they had the perfect marriage," said Anita. "They were always doing things together and helping each other."

"Yes," said the other member, "And in church he always had his arm around her. They seemed so happy together."

"It's certainly a shame," remarked Anita. "And now, after fifteen years of marriage, they've parted and are on very bad terms. And" she said, "from what I've heard, they said the last place they'd ever be was in the same room together."

'Hmmm," said the other member, pondering the situation, "that certainly poses an interesting problem."

"What?" asked Anita curiously.

"Well," said the other member, "Since they both dearly love the pastor, I just hope that when everything gets split in half, he doesn't get dissected in the process!"

I KINGS 3:16-27: THEN CAME THERE TWO WOMEN, *THAT WERE* HARLOTS, UNTO THE KING, AND STOOD BEFORE HIM. AND THE ONE WOMAN SAID, O MY LORD, I AND THIS WOMAN DWELL IN ONE HOUSE; AND I WAS DELIVERED OF A CHILD WITH HER IN THE HOUSE. AND IT CAME TO PASS THE THIRD DAY AFTER THAT I WAS DELIVERED, THAT THIS WOMAN WAS DELIVERED ALSO: AND WE *WERE* TOGETHER; *THERE WAS* NO STRANGER WITH US IN THE HOUSE, SAVE WE TWO IN THE HOUSE. AND THIS WOMAN'S CHILD DIED IN THE NIGHT; BECAUSE SHE OVERLAID IT. AND SHE AROSE AT MIDNIGHT, AND TOOK MY SON FROM BESIDE ME, WHILE THINE HANDMAID SLEPT, AND LAID IT IN HER BOSOM, AND LAID HER DEAD CHILD IN MY BOSOM. AND WHEN I ROSE IN THE MORNING TO GIVE MY CHILD SUCK, BEHOLD, IT WAS DEAD: BUT WHEN I HAD CONSIDERED IT IN THE MORNING, BEHOLD, IT WAS NOT MY SON, WHICH I DID BEAR. AND THE OTHER WOMAN SAID, NAY; BUT THE LIVING *IS* MY SON, AND THE DEAD *IS* THY SON. AND THIS SAID NO; BUT THE DEAD *IS* THY SON, AND THE LIVING *IS* MY SON. THUS THEY SPEAK BEFORE THE KING. THEN SAID THE KING, THE ONE SAITH, THIS *IS* MY SON THAT LIVETH, AND THY SON *IS* THE DEAD: AND THE OTHER SAITH, NAY; BUT THY SON *IS* THE DEAD, AND MY SON *IS* THE LIVING. AND THE KING SAID, BRING ME A SWORD. AND THEY BROUGHT A SWORD BEFORE THE KING. AND THE KING SAID, DIVIDE THE LIVING CHILD IN TWO, AND GIVE HALF TO THE ONE, AND HALF TO THE OTHER. THEN SPAKE THE WOMAN WHOSE THE LIVING CHILD

WAS UNTO THE KING, FOR HER BOWELS YEARNED UPON HER SON, AND SHE SAID, O MY LORD, GIVE HER THE LIVING CHILD, AND IN NO WISE SLAY IT. BUT THE OTHER SAID, LET IT BE NEITHER MINE NOR THINE, *BUT* DIVIDE *IT*. THEN THE KING ANSWERED AND SAID, GIVE HER THE LIVING CHILD, AND IN NO WISE SLAY IT: SHE *IS* THE MOTHER THEREOF.

MATTHEW 7:12: THEREFORE ALL THINGS WHATSOEVER YE WOULD THAT MEN SHOULD DO TO YOU, DO YE EVEN SO TO THEM . . .

Every Sunday Leonard, an elderly gentleman, would stroll into church with a large, brown suitcase in hand.

After several Sundays of seeing this, Pastor Jefferson's curiosity got the best of him. "Perhaps I'm being forward," he remarked to the man, "but why do you bring your suitcase to the service each week?"

"To be perfectly honest," replied Leonard, "I come every Sunday planning to leave my wife after church lets out. But then, Pastor, you preach on mercy, compassion, and forgiveness, and I end up going back home to give her another chance."

Then, looking down at his suitcase with a gleam in his eye," he continued, "But I'm earnestly waiting for the Sunday to come when you preach 'Go ye into all the world' and when that happens, I'm making a mad dash toward the farthest place away from home I can find!"

MARK 16:15: . . . GO YE INTO ALL THE WORLD, AND PREACH THE GOSPEL TO EVERY CREATURE.

Giving a blow-by-blow detailed account of her shattered marriage, Jill sobbed before her pastor. "Half the time I'm running around like a scared rabbit," she cried. "I've tried everything under the sun but he continues to be spiteful, malicious and often acts like a mad dog. In fact, Pastor, she continued, if he had two more legs and a tail I could write it off as distemper and have him put to sleep.

"Hmm . . ." said the pastor, "it could be that all he needs is a rabies shot. But if that doesn't change his disposition," he said, "maybe you should consider doing the Christian thing and having him put out of his misery."

PROVERBS 8:33: HEAR INSTRUCTION, AND BE WISE, AND REFUSE IT NOT.

Two women, Brenda and Dee, were having lunch together. Both were bemoaning the fact that their husbands were unfaithful. Brenda had started the conversation by giving Dee a tearful account of what had happened. She also gave a graphic description of her husband's mistress. Brenda made it sound as if her husband had just fallen in love with the world's first platinum blond gorilla.

"She must look absolutely grotesque," said Dee wondering how her attractive friend could have ever lost to such a frightful looking monster as that "other woman." "And what's more," said Brenda, "She's nothing but a Jezebel!"

"It does sound like her soul is a few shades darker than her hair," replied Dee.

HEBREWS 13:4: MARRIAGE IS HONORABLE [HONORABLE] IN ALL, AND THE MARRIAGE BED UNDEFILED BUT WHOREMONGERS AND ADULTERERS GOD WILL JUDGE.

Troubled by a shaky marriage, Martha decided to seek counseling. "I don't know why he's talking about leaving," she told her friend sadly. "He knew before we were married that I hate to cook and do housework. And just because I've gained a little weight," she said, "is no reason to hold it against me. Lord knows, I've tried to make this marriage work, ordering his favorite meals from every drive through restaurant I can find. But," she continued, "nothing pleases him. Just three or four months ago I dusted the whole house, but do you think he noticed? No, he was too busy complaining about our unmade bed and the stacks of dirty dishes. What does he think I am?," she grumbled, "an on call maid service?"

"What are you planning to tell the pastor in your counseling session?" Tonya, her friend asked? "Are you going to admit that you're not the best housekeeper and that you don't feed your husband good home cooked meals And," she added, "are you going to tell him that you were a size six when you got married and that now you're a size sixty?"

"Oh, I'll just state the facts, Tonya" she replied. Then thinking over what her friend had said and coming to terms with her fault in the marriage, she said, "But pray that I have strep throat and a severe case of laryngitis when I'm in his office."

JAMES 5:16: CONFESS *YOUR* FAULTS ONE TO ANOTHER, AND PRAY ONE FOR ANOTHER . . .

"Pastor Cardwell," cried Debbie, "I thought marriage was going to be different. I've always dreamed of what it would be like to walk down the aisle in a beautiful gown and look up into the eyes of some prince."

"You just got married last month," interrupted the pastor. "Surely the honeymoon isn't over yet."

"Yes, it is," she said, wiping the tears from her eyes. "I thought I was getting love and romance, but all I've seen so far is dirty socks and sweaty t-shirts."

"But Debbie," the pastor told her, "dirty clothes come with marriage."

"I know, pastor," she cried, "but the dirty clothes belong to my brother."

"Debbie," the pastor asked her, "you just got married. Why is your brother there?"

"He's been staying here waiting until my husband gets back from a camping trip he went on with his friend. He wants to give him a friendly pat on the back with a two by four."

"Debbie," the pastor cautioned her, "while I agree that your husband should be home with his new bride, I don't think your brother should be beating him up over a camping trip with his buddy.

"I agree, pastor," Debbie said, "but the thing he doesn't appreciate is that my husband's friend was about to become my brother's future wife!"

PROVERBS 14:12: THERE IS A WAY WHICH SEEMETH RIGHT UNTO A MAN, BUT THE END THEREOF *ARE* THE WAYS OF DEATH.

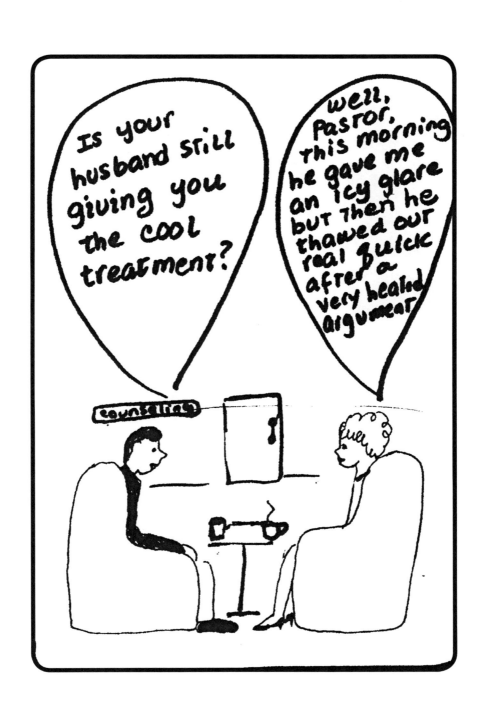

CARNAL COMMOTION

"Dad," Ron said excitedly, bursting into his father's den, "I'm in love! I met the most gorgeous girl tonight. What a knock out! She's got a face and figure that's just outa' sight. Wait 'til you meet her, dad!" he exclaimed, "you'll agree that she's just the neatest thing that could happen to a guy."

"Did you meet her in your youth group at church, Ron?" his father asked.

"No . . . uh . . . not exactly, dad," Ron answered.

"Is she a born-again Christian who loves Jesus and is living for him?" Ron's father asked.

"No . . . uh . . . not exactly, dad," Ron said, reluctantly, "but I can tell you one thing," he told him, "she's really nice. I told her I was rich and had a lot of nice clothes, and she even offered to take me to the cleaners some day."

I PETER 5:8: BE SOBER, BE VIGILANT; BECAUSE YOUR ADVERSARY THE DEVIL, AS A ROARING LION, WALKETH ABOUT, SEEKING WHOM HE MAY DEVOUR:

"Excuse me, sir," whispered a woman who had come into church late, "Would you mind moving down a few seats to make room for my daughter and myself?"

As she stood there waiting, the man in the back row didn't budge. She quietly repeated herself, thinking that possibly he hadn't heard. Still he ignored her and didn't move. Feeling awkward, she looked around for other seats but couldn't locate any, so she tapped him on the shoulder

and again asked if he might move down a couple of spaces. "Listen, lady," came the nasty reply, "I've got squatters rights!"

PHILIPPIANS 2:3: *LET* NOTHING *BE DONE* THROUGH STRIFE OR VAINGLORY; BUT IN LOWLINESS OF MIND LET EACH ESTEEM OTHER BETTER THAN THEMSELVES.

Oscar was a middle-aged man not yet established in the Lord. As he staggered toward the church from the parking lot, he felt someone gently take his arm, guiding him toward the door.

His eyes, blurry and bloodshot, made it difficult for him to make out the face of his pastor. Nevertheless, with slurred speech, stammering and wheezing, he managed to blurt out an enthusiastic "Ga . . . ga . . . good morning, your re . . . reverence!"

"Good morning, Oscar," replied the Pastor kindly while eyeing the leftovers of his night's activity. He noticed a bottle of whiskey protruding from the side pocket of his suit jacket. Hanging out of his back pocket was a white trail of toilet paper as long as a bridal train.

If that wasn't bad enough, to the pastor's further astonishment, he noticed he was using a pool stick in place of a cane. And last but not least, a couple packages of cigars slipped down through his pant leg laying on the floor before the pastor.

"Uh . . . er . . . Pa . . . Pa . . . Pastor," stuttered Oscar, squinting his eyes, his body swaying back and forth trying to maintain his balance, "I'm not too steady today or sh . . . sh . . . sure of anything. Whatever I did last na . . . na . . . night, the ca . . .ca . . . consequences seem to be fa . . . fa . . . following me around this ma . . . ma . . . morning!"

NUMBERS 32:23: . . . BE SURE YOUR SIN WILL FIND YOU OUT . . .

As the offering plate was passed from person to person, the church usher would wait for it to reach the end of the row. About three quarters of the way down, however, he noticed a man handling the bills and coins that had already been tossed in the plate.

I can't help but notice That Bible I gave you last week is tossed out with The garbage
Oh...a...er... I was just trying to witness to The garbage man.
HOLY Bible

Questioning his motives, the usher leaned over a couple of people and gave the gentleman a look of disapproval as he reached for the plate.

"Don't worry," whispered the man, surrendering it. "I was just fighting the urge to yield to temptation."

PSALM 7:8: THE LORD SHALL JUDGE THE PEOPLE: JUDGE ME, O LORD, ACCORDING TO MY RIGHTEOUSNESS, AND ACCORDING TO MINE INTEGRITY *THAT IS* IN ME.

(Author's note: Any righteousness that we have is not because of ourselves but because we have allowed God to take the reins of our life and produce His righteousness in us.)

II CORINTHIANS 8:21: PROVIDING FOR HONEST THINGS, NOT ONLY IN THE SIGHT OF THE LORD, BUT ALSO IN THE SIGHT OF MEN. [SEE ACTS 24:16]

II CORINTHIANS 6:2: RECEIVE US; WE HAVE WRONGED NO MAN, WE HAVE CORRUPTED NO MAN, WE HAVE DEFRAUDED NO MAN. [SEE ACTS 5:1-10]

THE LORD KNOWETH HOW TO DELIVER THE GODLY OUT OF TEMPTATIONS II PETER 2:9

PHILIPPIANS 2:13: FOR IT IS GOD WHICH WORKETH IN YOU BOTH TO WILL AND TO DO OF *HIS* GOOD PLEASURE.

PSALM 7:9: O LET THE WICKEDNESS OF THE WICKED COME TO AN END; BUT ESTABLISH THE JUST; FOR THE RIGHTEOUS GOD TRIETH THE HEARTS AND REINS.

Anne, A Christian divorcee, had just been through a very frightening experience and was relating it to Jim, a close friend. Apparently, someone had broken into her home and threatened to do her great bodily harm.

Jim, whose friendship with her was developing into a romantic interest, was mentioning the awful experience to one of the church deacons. As he

began telling the story, however, he suffered an embarrassing slip of the tongue. "It was just terrible, Deacon Dan," he exclaimed, "They tried to do her 'great body' harm."

II CORINTHIANS 10:5: CASTING DOWN IMAGINATIONS, AND EVERY HIGH THING THAT EXALTETH ITSELF AGAINST THE KNOWLEDGE OF GOD, AND BRINGING INTO CAPTIVITY EVERY THOUGHT TO THE OBEDIENCE OF CHRIST.

Debbie and Denise were sunbathing in Debbie's backyard when they spotted two men approaching them. "Oh no," muttered Debbie, nudging her friend, "Look whose coming!" Denise looked up and saw two well-dressed men, wearing suits and ties, carrying Bibles under their arms.

"It's too late to make a mad dash for the house," Denise said, trying to reach her towel so that she could cover her scantily clad body. Wouldn't you know," she grumbled, "just when we're wearing hardly more than a fig leaf, some preachers would have to show up."

Only seconds later, the gentlemen were standing in front of them with the two girls blushing from embarrassment.

"I'm Mr. Woods," said one of the men, introducing himself, "And this is Mr. Snyder to my left."

"Could you come back later?," asked Debbie, "We really aren't decent as you can see."

"Don't worry about that," said Mr. Woods, pretending not to notice. "This will only take a minute.

"Yes," said Mr. Snyder, clearing his throat, "We just want to read the New Testament." Then eyeing the pretty girls, he added, "In its entirety."

PROVERBS 21:2: EVERY WAY OF A MAN *IS* RIGHT IN HIS OWN EYES: BUT THE LORD PONDERETH THE HEARTS.

MATTHEW 5:28-29: BUT I SAY UNTO YOU, THAT WHOSOEVER LOOKETH ON A WOMAN TO LUST AFTER HER HATH COMMITTED ADULTERY WITH HER ALREADY IN HIS HEART. AND IF THY RIGHT EYE OFFEND THEE, PLUCK IT OUT, AND CAST *IT* FROM THEE: FOR IT IS PROFITABLE FOR THEE THAT ONE OF THY MEMBERS SHOULD PERISH, AND NOT *THAT* THY WHOLE BODY SHOULD BE CAST INTO HELL.

II SAMUEL 11:2-4: AND IT CAME TO PASS IN AN EVENINGTIDE, THAT DAVID AROSE FROM OFF HIS BED, AND WALKED UPON THE ROOF OF THE KING'S HOUSE: AND FROM THE ROOF HE SAW A WOMAN WASHING HERSELF; AND THE WOMAN *WAS* VERY BEAUTIFUL TO LOOK UPON. AND DAVID SENT AND ENQUIRED AFTER THE WOMAN. AND *ONE* SAID, IS NOT THIS BATHSHEBA, THE DAUGHTER OF ELIAM, THE WIFE OF URIAH THE HITTITE? AND DAVID SENT MESSENGERS, AND TOOK HER; AND SHE CAME IN UNTO HIM, AND HE LAY WITH HER . . .

II SAMUEL 12:9-13: [AND THE LORD SENT A MESSAGE TO DAVID BY WAY OF NATHAN THE PROPHET] WHEREFORE HAST THOU DESPISED THE COMMANDMENT OF THE LORD, TO DO EVIL IN HIS SIGHT? THOU HAST KILLED URIAH THE HITTITE WITH THE SWORD, AND HAST TAKEN HIS WIFE *TO BE* THY WIFE, AND HAST SLAIN HIM WITH THE WORD OF THE CHILDREN OF AMMON. NOW THEREFORE THE SWORD SHALL NEVER DEPART FROM THINE HOUSE; BECAUSE THOU HAST DESPISED ME, AND HAST TAKEN THE WIFE OF URIAH THE HITTITE TO BE THY WIFE. THUS SAITH THE LORD, BEHOLD, I WILL RAISE UP EVIL AGAINST THEE OUT OF THINE OWN HOUSE, AND I WILL TAKE THY WIVES BEFORE THINE EYES, AND GIVE *THEM* UNTO THY NEIGHBOUR [NEIGHBOR], AND HE SHALL LIE WITH THY WIVES IN THE SIGHT OF THIS SUN. FOR THOU DIDST *IT* SECRETLY: BUT I WILL DO THIS THING BEFORE ALL ISRAEL, AND BEFORE THE SUN. AND DAVID SAID UNTO NATHAN, I HAVE SINNED AGAINST THE LORD . . .

"Pastor," said Wilbur, "I want you to know that nothing would stop me from coming here each week. If my car broke down, I'd take a taxi. And if the taxi didn't show up, I'd take a bus. And if the busses quit running, I'd

hitchhike. And if no one picked me up, I'd walk. And if I couldn't walk, I'd crawl. Nothing would keep me out of this church!"

The following week, however, the pastor noticed that Wilbur was not there. The pastor called him thinking something serious must have happened to prevent him from being there.

"Well, pastor," he said answering the phone, "the reason I didn't come is quite simple. Just as I was about to pull into my favorite parking spot at the church," he said, "someone else took it. And by the time I ran up to the store to buy some eggs and finished sabotaging his car," he told him, "the service was already almost over with."

EPHESIANS 4:26: BE YE ANGRY, AND SIN NOT: LET NOT THE SUN GO DOWN UPON YOUR WRATH:

PROVERBS 6:16-19: THESE SIX THINGS DOTH THE LORD HATE: YEA, SEVEN ARE AN ABOMINATION UNTO HIM: A PROUD LOOK, A LYING TONGUE, AND HANDS THAT SHED INNOCENT BLOOD, AN HEART THAT DEVISETH WICKED IMAGINATIONS, FEET THAT BE SWIFT IN RUNNING TO MISCHIEF, A FALSE WITNESS THAT SPEAKETH LIES, AND HE THAT SOWETH DISCORD AMONG BRETHREN.

During the church service, a young man left to use the men's room. When he returned to the sanctuary, he couldn't recall in which row he'd been sitting. Looking in the general area where he'd been, he noticed the short, curly brown hair of his wife and hastened to his seat.

As soon as he was seated, however, he realized that the lady next to him was not his wife after all. "Oops, wrong wife and wrong row," he whispered to her as he got back up. Then glancing down at her, he whispered, "But it was nice while it lasted."

PROVERBS 31:10: WHO CAN FIND A VIRTUOUS WOMAN? FOR HER PRICE *IS* FAR ABOVE RUBIES . . .

While backsliding, Jenny let a lot of things slide besides her spiritual life.

After disregarding several bills, collection agencies began sending threatening notes. Not easily intimidated, she would often respond to these statements by sending a sympathy card in place of money.

The phone company, however, was not impressed by her warped sense of humor. "You aren't fooling us," they told her. "We've got your number."

PROVERBS 13:18: POVERTY AND SHAME SHALL BE TO HIM THAT REFUSETH INSTRUCTION: BUT HE THAT REGARDETH REPROOF SHALL BE HONOURED.

Describing her former husband, Phyllis commented to her friend, "He was the kind of notorious fellow that would make God turn gray overnight. He didn't consider a day complete until he'd broken all ten commandments—at least twice over.

But now, thank God, from what I've heard," she said, "he committed himself-to God!

The deacons no longer have to pry his hands from the offering plate or the waists of women during handshake time. And it's been a big relief to the pastor since he got saved. Now he no longer has to dodge flying objects fired from my ex-husband's peashooter during the sermons that he's taken issue with, which, judging from the bullet-ridden body of the pastor, have been many.

ROMANS 5:18-19: THEREFORE AS BY THE OFFENCE OF ONE [ADAM] *JUDGMENT CAME* UPON ALL MEN TO CONDEMNATION; EVEN SO BY THE RIGHTEOUSNESS OF ONE [CHRIST] *THE FREE GIFT CAME* UPON ALL MEN UNTO JUSTIFICATION OF LIFE. FOR AS BY ONE MAN'S [ADAM] DISOBEDIENCE MANY WERE MADE SINNERS, SO BY THE OBEDIENCE OF ONE [CHRIST] SHALL MANY BE MADE RIGHTEOUS.

After receiving a number of delinquent notices in the mail regarding their unpaid gas bill, Gail asked her husband, "Honey, should we leave the gas company in jeopardy or send them the twenty bucks we owe them?"

"Are you kidding?" answered her husband. "They wouldn't even know what to do with all that money!"

"But honey," she said trying to persuade him to assume responsibility for their debts, "Since it's now within our means, don't you think we should pay our bill and keep them from plummeting to near bankruptcy?"

ROMANS 13:7: RENDER THEREFORE TO ALL THEIR DUES: TRIBUTE TO WHOM TRIBUTE IS DUE; CUSTOM TO WHOM CUSTOM; FEAR TO WHOM FEAR; HONOUR [HONOR] TO WHOM HONOUR [HONOR].

"Candice, would you watch your sister today while I take care of some errands?" her mother asked.

"Sure, Mom," replied Candice, sounding almost too willing.

"Now you girls be good," their mother told them; "and remember, Candice, you're responsible for your sister, so keep an eye on her."

"I will, Mom, don't worry," she said, promising to watch her sister and stay out of trouble.

When Candice's mother returned three hours later, she heard a buzzing sound coming from the kitchen. She nearly fainted when she saw what was happening. Candice had the mixer on full speed and the blenders were splattering gooey chocolate in every direction. "Oh no!" her mother shouted. "I'm sorry, mom," she apologized. "All I wanted to do was make you a cake but the blender got loose. Mom," she exclaimed, "It's like it had a mind of its own!"

"Asking you to help me out, Candice," her mother hollered while cleaning up the mess "is like leaving a bull to stand guard in a china shop!"

Suddenly, Candice started to cry. Her mother realized that perhaps she had wounded her spirit. "I apologize, Candice. Would you forgive me?" she said softly, putting her arm around her. "You were just trying to make a cake. And don't worry," she teased, wiping the tears from her daughter's

eyes, "if your cake doesn't turn out and it's durable enough," she said, "we can always use it for a door stopper."

DEUTERONOMY 6:5-9: AND THOU SHALT LOVE THE LORD THY GOD WITH ALL THINE HEART, AND WITH ALL THY SOUL, AND WITH ALL THY MIGHT. AND THESE WORDS, WHICH I COMMAND THEE THIS DAY, SHALL BE IN THINE HEART: AND THOU SHALT TEACH THEM DILIGENTLY UNTO THY CHILDREN, AND SHALT TALK OF THEM WHEN THOU SITTEST IN THINE HOUSE, AND WHEN THOU WALKEST BY THE WAY, AND WHEN THOU LIEST DOWN, AND WHEN THOU RISEST UP. AND THOU SHALT BIND THEM FOR A SIGN UPON THINE HAND, AND THEY SHALL BE AS FRONTLETS BETWEEN THINE EYES. AND THOU SHALT WRITE THEM UPON THE POSTS OF THY HOUSE, AND ON THY GATES. [SEE DEUTERONOMY 30:6 & EZEKIEL 36:26-27]

ISAIAH 54:13: AND ALL THY CHILDREN *SHALL* BE TAUGHT OF THE LORD; AND GREAT *SHALL BE* THE PEACE OF THY CHILDREN.

PSALM 112:2: [THE RIGHTEOUS BELIEVER] HIS SEED SHALL BE MIGHTY UPON EARTH: THE GENERATION OF THE UPRIGHT SHALL BE BLESSED.

PSALM 115:14: THE LORD SHALL INCREASE YOU MORE AND MORE, YOU AND YOUR CHILDREN.

"Who is that at the door?" Marie asked her husband, Calvin, hearing the door bell ring.

"It's Mrs. Sanford again," Marie's husband answered, exasperated as he looked out the window. "I'll get the door."

"Hello, Calvin," Mrs. Sanford said. "I was just wondering if you could spare twenty dollars until next Friday. I'm a little short this week," she told him.

"No, Mrs. Sanford," Calvin replied gruffly, "I don't have a spare dollar to lend you." He abruptly ended their conversation and closed the door.

Lord, I vow never to sin again. If I do you may cause my car to lose control and hit a brick building, but, Lord please make sure I'm not in my vehicle when that happens! If I'm still alive after that you can cause an earthquake to swallow me up. S.O.S. S.O.S. But please make sure I'm off the ground when that happens! And if I'm still in one piece after that you can cause tons of poisonous snakes to bite me but please make sure that I'm not around when that happens! And if I'm still alive after all these calamities, please remind me never even to make foolish vows again!

Then turning to his wife, he complained, "First she started with a cup of sugar. Then it was a carton of milk, then a carton of eggs. Last week she needed a ride to the store and asked for ten dollars to cover the shortage on her groceries. This week she borrowed the garden hose and our can opener. What does she think we're running here—a free shopping center?"

His wife sat silently listening.

"And why am I feeling like such a heel?" he added. "Probably because a guilty conscience cometh with an empty hand," she replied, grinning. "I call it Proverbs 32:1"

PROVERBS 28:27: HE THAT GIVETH UNTO THE POOR SHALL NOT LACK: BUT HE THAT HIDETH HIS EYES SHALL HAVE MANY A CURSE.

Two well-known evangelists were arguing over some doctrinal differences of which they were diametrically opposed.

"There is no doubt in my mind," said Fred dogmatically, "that the Lord intended baptism to be done by total immersion after we've repented and acknowledged Christ as Lord and Savior through His shed blood on the cross."

Jack replied, "It's not whether we sprinkle or immerse that matters," he said. He went on to explain his position on the matter.

"I'm sorry," Fred told him, "but I cannot align myself with your view point on the matter." He continued to give his own perspective on why total immersion was necessary.

With neither party able to reach an agreement on the issue, Jack finally remarked, "I don't see it that way, Fred, but if immersion is what you want, immersion is what you'll get. Meet me at Niagara Falls around noon."

(Author's note: Like Fred, I personally believe in total immersion. In Matthew 4:6 & 16 we read about total immersion. Jesus left us an example. We are always to follow the example He sets.

However, any debates regarding contrary points of view should always be addressed with a spirit of humility and love and never with arrogance.

This does not mean, however, that we can ever compromise our beliefs. It simply means that whenever and wherever possible we exercise caution in the way that we present our case or approach our differences.)

EPHESIANS 4:15: BUT SPEAKING THE TRUTH IN LOVE . . .

ACTS 15:36-41: AND SOME DAYS AFTER PAUL SAID UNTO BARNABAS, LET US GO AGAIN AND VISIT OUR BRETHREN IN EVERY CITY WHERE WE HAVE PREACHED THE WORD OF THE LORD, *AND SEE* HOW THEY DO. AND BARNABAS DETERMINED TO TAKE WITH THEM JOHN, WHOSE SURNAME WAS MARK. BUT PAUL THOUGHT [IT] NOT GOOD TO TAKE HIM WITH THEM, WHO DEPARTED FROM THEM FROM PAMPHYLIA, AND WENT NOT WITH THEM TO THE WORK. AND THE CONTENTION WAS SO SHARP BETWEEN THEM, THAT THEY DEPARTED ASUNDER ONE FROM THE OTHER: AND SO BARNABAS TOOK MARK, AND SAILED UNTO CYPRUS; AND PAUL CHOSE SILAS, AND DEPARTED, BEING RECOMMENDED BY THE BRETHREN UNTO THE GRACE OF GOD. AND HE WENT THROUGH SYRIA AND CILICIA, CONFIRMING THE CHURCHES.

PROVERBS 18:19: A BROTHER OFFENDED *IS HARDER TO BE WON* THAN A STRONG CITY: AND *THEIR* CONTENTIONS *ARE* LIKE THE BARS OF A CASTLE.

PSALMS 133:1: BEHOLD, HOW GOOD AND HOW PLEASANT IT IS FOR BRETHREN TO DWELL TOGETHER IN UNITY. [SEE HEBREWS 12:14; JOHN 13:35 & ROMANS 14:19; & I CORINTHIANS 1:11-13]

I CORINTHIANS 3:3-4: FOR YE ARE YET CARNAL: FOR WHEREAS *THERE IS* AMONG YOU ENVYING, AND STRIFE, AND DIVISIONS, ARE YE NOT CARNAL, AND WALK AS MEN? FOR WHILE ONE SAITH, I AM OF PAUL; AND ANOTHER, I AM OF APOLLOS; ARE YE NOT CARNAL?

Ted, a Christian landlord, was trying to project a kind and godly image to his boarders. He often bent the rules to be accommodating to his renters

and, whenever possible, granted additional privileges. He even allowed them to keep pets.

One of his tenants, however, owned a mean and noisy cat. The animal was always snarling and scratching at his screen door drooling as he gazed hungrily at the landlord's beloved parakeet. The poor bird was usually shaking on its perch whenever the cat was in sight.

The landlord tolerated the situation as long as he could, but one day when he noticed Whiskers, the cat, tearing at his screen door and threatening the very survival of his parakeet, he became more than just annoyed by the situation.

"Whiskers is ruining my screen," he told his tenant and wearing out his welcome. And," he added, "when it comes to pets, my bird has seniority rights here."

LUKE 12:6: ARE NOT FIVE SPARROWS SOLD FOR TWO FARTHINGS, AND NOT ONE OF THEM IS FORGOTTEN BEFORE GOD?

MATTHEW 10:29: ARE NOT TWO SPARROWS SOLD FOR A FARTHING? AND ONE OF THEM SHALL NOT FALL ON THE GROUND WITHOUT YOUR FATHER. [SEE ECCLESIASTES 3:20-21]

Arriving early for Sunday night services, Eric, a new Christian, watched with reverent admiration as one of the veteran members of the church was kneeling in prayer at the altar, pouring out his soul unto God. *That man must truly love the Lord,* he thought to himself. *There he is, before church has even begun—up at the altar interceding for the lost souls of friends and relatives.*

Because the loud whisperings of the prayer warrior were not decipherable from a distance, Eric decided to quietly eavesdrop by tiptoeing past the man. *It will give me a better idea of how to pray for my own family's needs,* he thought.

As he slipped past the man unnoticed, just as he expected, he found him praying fervently for those who were dear to his heart.

"And Father God," he heard the man pray, "Watch over all my loved ones, including my daily compounded interest, hallelujah, my local checking accounts, my multiple statewide savings accounts, amen and amen, my stocks 'n bonds, praise His holy name, yes, and even my petty cash fund; but most of all, precious Lord, my hidden safe deposit box and my bursting Swiss bank account. Amen and amen."

PHILIPPIANS 3:18-19: (FOR MANY WALK, OF WHOM I HAVE TOLD YOU OFTEN, AND NOW TELL YOU EVEN WEEPING, *THAT THEY ARE* THE ENEMIES OF THE CROSS OF CHRIST: WHOSE END IS DESTRUCTION, WHOSE GOD IS THEIR BELLY, AND WHOSE GLORY IS IN THEIR SHAME, WHO MIND EARTHLY THINGS. [SEE COLOSSIANS 3:2]

LUKE 12:15-20: AND HE [JESUS] SAID UNTO THEM, TAKE HEED, AND BEWARE OF COVETOUSNESS: FOR A MAN'S LIFE CONSISTETH NOT IN THE ABUNDANCE OF THE THINGS WHICH HE POSSESSETH. AND HE SPAKE A PARABLE UNTO THEM, SAYING, THE GROUND OF A CERTAIN RICH MAN BROUGHT FORTH PLENTIFULLY: AND HE THOUGHT WITHIN HIMSELF, SAYING, WHAT SHALL I DO BECAUSE I HAVE NO ROOM WHERE TO BESTOW MY FRUITS? AND HE SAID, THIS WILL I DO: I WILL PULL DOWN MY BARNS, AND BUILD GREATER; AND THERE WILL I BESTOW ALL MY FRUITS AND MY GOODS. AND I WILL SAY TO MY SOUL, SOUL, THOU HAST MUCH GOOD LAID UP FOR MANY YEARS; TAKE THINE EASE, EAT, DRINK, *AND* BE MERRY. BUT GOD SAID UNTO HIM, *THOU* FOOL, THIS NIGHT THY SOUL SHALL BE REQUIRED OF THEE: THEN WHOSE SHALL THOSE THINGS BE, WHICH THOU HAST PROVIDED? [SEE ECCLESIASTES 2:26 & JOB 27:16-17]

MARK 8:36: FOR WHAT SHALL IT PROFIT A MAN, IF HE SHALL GAIN THE WHOLE WORLD, AND LOSE HIS OWN SOUL?

PROVERBS 11:4: RICHES PROFIT NOT IN THE DAY OF WRATH . . .

PSALM 37:35-36: I HAVE SEEN THE WICKED IN GREAT POWER, AND SPREADING HIMSELF LIKE A GREEN BAY TREE. YET HE PASSED AWAY, AND, LO, HE *WAS* NOT: : YEA, I SOUGHT HIM, BUT HE COULD NOT BE FOUND.

JOB 20:27-29: THE HEAVEN SHALL REVEAL HIS INIQUITY; AND THE EARTH SHALL RISE UP AGAINST HIM. THE INCREASE OF HIS HOUSE SHALL DEPART, *AND HIS GOODS* SHALL FLOW AWAY IN THE DAY OF HIS WRATH. THIS *IS* THE PORTION OF A WICKED MAN FROM GOD, AND THE HERITAGE APPOINTED UNTO HIM BY GOD.

JOB 27:8-9: FOR WHAT *IS* THE HOPE OF THE HYPOCRITE, THOUGH HE HATH GAINED, WHEN GOD TAKETH AWAY HIS SOUL?

I TIMOTHY 6:5 . . . MEN OF CORRUPT MINDS, AND DESTITUTE OF THE TRUTH, SUPPOSING THAT GAIN IS GODLINESS: FROM SUCH WITHDRAW THYSELF.

Diane and Phil, two Christian newlyweds, were undecided about where they wanted to worship. Diane suggested they attend several churches until they were able to find one that suited both of them.

After trying out all the churches within their area, they still had not found a church that satisfied them.

Phil, becoming frustrated with their search for the right place to worship, remarked to his new bride, "In every church we attend, I hear the minister say, 'This is the house of the Lord.' We've been in dozens of sanctuaries," he said, "and they all say, 'This is the house of the Lord.' I've come to the conclusion," he told his wife, Diane, "that either God owns a whole lot of real estate or some of these places are just using His name in vain."

PSALM 127:1: EXCEPT THE LORD BUILD THE HOUSE, THEY LABOUR [LABOR] IN VAIN THAT BUILD IT: EXCEPT THE LORD KEEP THE CITY, THE WATCHMAN WALKETH *BUT* IN VAIN.

MATTHEW 7:24-27: THEREFORE WHOSOEVER HEARETH THESE SAYINGS OF MINE, AND DOETH THEM, I WILL LIKEN HIM UNTO A WISE MAN, WHICH BUILT HIS HOUSE UPON A ROCK: AND THE RAIN DESCENDED, AND THE FLOODS CAME, AND THE WINDS BLEW, AND BEAT UPON THAT HOUSE; AND IT FELL NOT: FOR IT WAS FOUNDED UPON A ROCK. AND EVERY ONE THAT HEARETH THESE SAYINGS OF MINE, AND DOETH THEM NOT, SHALL BE LIKENED UNTO A FOOLISH MAN, WHICH

BUILT HIS HOUSE UPON THE SAND: AND THE RAIN DESCENDED, AND THE FLOODS CAME, AND THE WINDS BLEW, AND BEAT UPON THAT HOUSE; AND IT FELL: AND GREAT WAS THE FALL OF IT.

Bertha, one of the church spinsters, noticed a new woman coming to church each week with a different man at her side. "Have you seen that Jezebel who comes here?" she asked this one and that one, spreading as much malicious gossip as possible. "Every week she's courting someone different. She obviously has more boyfriends than an alley has cats. If you ask me," she fumed, "I think she certainly has her nerve coming here and making a mockery out of the house of the Lord.

One Sunday, when her anger had reached its pinnacle, she approached the woman. "Are you a missionary or a hooker?" she asked her sarcastically.

"Oh," replied the woman indignantly, "1 didn't know my brothers and I had to join a club to attend here.

MATTHEW 7:1: JUDGE NOT, THAT YE BE NOT JUDGED. [SEE ROMANS 2:1-3]

ROMANS 2:21: THOU THEREFORE WHICH TEACHEST ANOTHER, TEACHEST THOU NOT THYSELF?

LUKE 6:31: AND AS YE WOULD THAT MEN SHOULD DO TO YOU, DO YE ALSO TO THEM LIKEWISE.

LUKE 6:36-37: BE YE THEREFORE MERCIFUL, AS YOUR FATHER ALSO IS MERCIFUL. JUDGE NOT, AND YE SHALL NOT BE JUDGED: CONDEMN NOT, AND YE SHALL NOT BE CONDEMNED: FORGIVE, AND YE SHALL BE FORGIVEN.

JAMES 2:13: FOR HE SHALL HAVE JUDGMENT WITHOUT MERCY, THAT HATH SHEWED NO MERCY . . .

PSALM 18:25: WITH THE MERCIFUL THOU WILT SHEW THYSELF MERCIFUL . . . [SEE JOHN 13:35 & I JOHN 4:11

As the unfortunate owner of a complete line of dilapidated junk vehicles, each valued at less than $150, Alvin was rather touchy whenever the subject of cars was brought up.

With one or the other of these automobiles continually breaking down and leaving him with no means of transportation, he was always having to shell out money for taxies or tow trucks, not to mention tickets he received for defective vehicle equipment.

"I turn green with envy every time someone I know gets a new car," he said, feeling guilty. "There they are driving a Cadillac, a Jaguar, or a Rolls Royce while I stall out in some junker that looks as if it came out last place in a demolition derby" he told his friend.

"When I get to heaven," he added with disgruntlement, "If the Lord hands me the keys to anything over ten years old, I'm going to run out of the pearly gates and marry the first woman I see sitting behind the steering wheel of a brand new car."

PSALM 20:7: SOME *TRUST* IN CHARIOTS, AND SOME IN HORSES: BUT WE WILL REMEMBER THE NAME OF THE LORD OUR GOD.

LUKE 12:32: FEAR NOT, LITTLE FLOCK; FOR IT IS YOUR FATHERS GOOD PLEASURE TO GIVE YOU THE KINGDOM.

Katie had been praying for more courage in her life. Ever since she had viewed a television movie about a hero who, though he was completely surrounded and outnumbered by the enemy, wouldn't back down on his convictions, she, too wanted to have that kind of courage,

She had always admired people who, in the face of danger, stuck to their values and beliefs no matter what the cost. She thought about Daniel in the Lions den, Shadrach, Meshech, and Abednego in the fiery furnace, the Apostle Paul, and so many others named in Hebrews chapter 11 who displayed such heroic behavior even in the most fearful circumstances.

"Give me the strength to be true to you, Lord," she cried unto the Lord.

Now is the time, the Lord impressed in her mind. *You must learn to be brave in the small things first.*

Oh no! Katie thought, remembering a lie she had told her husband. *Surely, you don't mean now, Lord.*

Yes, now, the words echoed in her mind. *Now.*

Why is it, Father, she prayed, *that you always answer these kind of prayers right away?*

LUKE 16:10: HE THAT IS FAITHFUL IN THAT WHICH IS LEAST IS FAITHFUL ALSO IN MUCH; AND HE THAT IS UNJUST IN THE LEAST IS UNJUST ALSO IN MUCH.

I CORINTHIANS 4:2: MOREOVER IT IS REQUIRED IN STEWARDS, THAT A MAN BE FOUND FAITHFUL.

I JOHN 2:28: AND NOW, LITTLE CHILDREN, ABIDE IN HIM; THAT, WHEN HE SHALL APPEAR, WE MAY HAVE CONFIDENCE, AND NOT BE ASHAMED BEFORE HIM AT HIS COMING. [SEE EPHESIANS 5:27 & II CORINTHIANS 5:15]

Lord, prayed Jim, *You know I would have read my Bible today, but I was busy doing Your will helping Widow Johnson. And,* he prayed, *I would have gone to prayer meeting tonight, but again, I was doing Your will assisting her with her errands.*

I understand that you were detained, said a convicting inner voice. *It must have been time-consuming as well as exhausting to unscrew those two burned out, one-hundred watt light bulbs from the ceiling of the widow Johnson, who, as we both know, has the beauty of Bathsheba, the craftiness of Delilah and the scruples of Jezebel.*

PSALMS 44:21: SHALL NOT GOD SEARCH THIS OUT? FOR HE KNOWETH THE SECRETS OF THE HEART.

When Natalie returned home one evening after dining out with her husband, she realized that she'd left her rings in the ladies' room at the restaurant where they'd been. Her husband was angry with her since they were quite valuable. "How could you have done such a thing?" he asked her.

"I removed them to wash my hands," she told him with regret. "I feel just sick about losing them."

She quickly phoned the restaurant and asked them to check the ladies' room for her, but they returned momentarily to give her the bad news that they had neither been turned in nor found in the ladies' room.

"Well," she said, trying to be strong, "I've given everything I own to God. And whoever took them is going to have a hard time hiding them in a spot where He wouldn't think to look."

LUKE 15:4-10: WHAT MAN OF YOU, HAVING AN HUNDRED SHEEP, IF HE LOSE ONE OF THEM, DOTH NOT LEAVE THE NINETY AND NINE IN THE WILDERNESS, AND GO AFTER THAT WHICH IS LOST, UNTIL HE FIND IT? AND WHEN HE HATH FOUND *IT*, HE LAYETH *IT* ON HIS SHOULDERS, REJOICING.

. . . WHAT WOMAN HAVING TEN PIECES OF SILVER, IF SHE LOSE ONE PIECE, DOTH NOT LIGHT A CANDLE, AND SWEEP THE HOUSE, AND SEEK DILIGENTLY TILL SHE FIND *IT?* AND WHEN SHE HATH FOUND *IT*, SHE CALLETH *HER* FRIENDS AND *HER* NEIGHBOURS [NEIGHBORS] TOGETHER, SAYING, REJOICE WITH ME; FOR I HAVE FOUND THE PIECE WHICH I HAD LOST. LIKEWISE, I SAY UNTO YOU, THERE IS JOY IN THE PRESENCE OF THE ANGELS OF GOD OVER ONE SINNER THAT REPENTETH.

PSALM 38:18: FOR I WILL DECLARE MINE INIQUITY; I WILL BE SORRY FOR MY SIN. [SEE PSALM 51:1-17 & LAST PART OF ISAIAH 66:2; I JOHN 1:7-9; ISAIAH 55:7]

"I am so devastated over having my home ransacked by that burglar," Jan told her sister. "I feel so violated by that intruder!"

"Well, you have every right to feel that way," her sister said, trying to console her. "What a low down creep!"

A few days later the perpetrator was arrested. Eventually, he was convicted of the crime.

As Jan and her sister were leaving the courtroom, they overheard someone remark that the criminal was a pretty nice looking guy.

Jan quickly turned around to throw in her two cents. "He may be nice looking but my stolen jewelry definitely won't match his orange jumpsuit!"

MATTHEW 6:19-21: LAY NOT UP FOR YOURSELVES TREASURES UPON EARTH, WHERE MOTH AND RUST DOTH CORRUPT, AND WHERE THIEVES BREAK THROUGH AND STEAL: BUT LAY UP FOR YOURSELVES TREASURES IN HEAVEN, WHERE NEITHER MOTH NOR RUST DOTH CORRUPT, AND WHERE THIEVES DO NOT BREAK THROUGH NOR STEAL: FOR WHERE YOUR TREASURE IS, THERE WILL YOUR HEART BE ALSO.

COLOSSIANS 3:2: SET YOUR AFFECTION ON THINGS ABOVE, NOT ON THINGS ON THE EARTH.

(Author's note: It's not wrong to have nice things as long as you aren't controlled by them or turned to bitterness because of them.

There are many in the Bible who possessed great wealth, but they used their blessings to be a blessing.

As long as we are helping more than we are hoarding then we have peace with God. At any time, however, that our possessions are taken, we must always maintain an attitude of forgiveness.)

A Christian businessman was having lunch with a colleague. "It seems like I'm always tied up in a business meeting," he told his associate. "Last week I missed my daughter's birthday party.

This week I couldn't get free to take my wife out for our anniversary.

Yesterday, my son broke his arm and my schedule was so heavy that I never even got home to autograph his cast.

And with the way things are going, when the rapture occurs," he sighed, "I'll probably be held over in an all day staff meeting."

PSALM 127:1: EXCEPT THE LORD BUILD THE HOUSE, THEY LABOUR [LABOR] IN VAIN THAT BUILD IT: EXCEPT THE LORD KEEP THE CITY, THE WATCHMAN WAKETH *BUT* IN VAIN.

A couple of girls were soaking up the sun and enjoying an afternoon at the beach when a man passed by that caught their eye. He was covered from head to toe with the most offensive skin disorder that anyone could possibly imagine.

"Isn't he grotesque!" one of the girls commented with a look of disgust.

"Yes," she said, covering a giggle, "just gross!"

Overhearing their remarks, he stopped to talk to them.

"Excuse me, girls." he said, "but I couldn't help but overhearing your 'flattering' comments." Then pointing to himself, he added, "But if you're making fun of this body, it's only borrowed."

"Borrowed?" they said, laughing.

"That's right," he replied, confidently, "And I'll be getting my new one very soon if the Lord doesn't tarry."

I CORINTHIANS 6:19-20: WHAT? KNOW YE NOT THAT YOUR BODY IS THE TEMPLE OF THE HOLY GHOST *WHICH IS* IN YOU, WHICH YE HAVE OF GOD, AND YE ARE NOT YOUR OWN? FOR YE ARE BOUGHT WITH A PRICE: THEREFORE GLORIFY GOD IN YOUR BODY, AND IN YOUR SPIRIT, WHICH ARE GOD'S.

I PETER 1:18-19: FORASMUCH AS YE KNOW THAT YE WERE NOT REDEEMED WITH CORRUPTIBLE THINGS, AS SILVER AND GOLD, FROM YOUR VAIN CONVERSATION *RECEIVED* BY TRADITION FROM YOUR FATHERS; BUT WITH THE PRECIOUS BLOOD OF CHRIST, AS OF A LAMB WITHOUT BLEMISH AND WITHOUT SPOT.

PHILIPPIANS 3:20-21: FOR OUR CONVERSATION IS IN HEAVEN; FROM WHENCE ALSO WE LOOK FOR THE SAVIOUR [SAVIOR], THE LORD JESUS CHRIST: WHO SHALL CHANGE OUR VILE BODY, THAT IT MAY BE FASHIONED LIKE UNTO HIS GLORIOUS BODY, ACCORDING TO THE WORKING WHEREBY HE IS ABLE EVEN TO SUBDUE ALL THINGS UNTO HIMSELF.

II CORINTHIANS 5:1-2: FOR WE KNOW THAT IF OUR EARTHLY HOUSE OF *THIS* TABERNACLE WERE DISSOLVED, WE HAVE A BUILDING OF GOD, AND HOUSE NOT MADE WITH HANDS, ETERNAL IN THE HEAVENS. FOR IN THIS WE GROAN, EARNESTLY DESIRING TO BE CLOTHED UPON WITH OUR HOUSE WHICH IS FROM HEAVEN.

I CORINTHIANS 15:42-44, 49, & 53: SO ALSO *IS* THE RESURRECTION OF THE DEAD. IT IS SOWN IN CORRUPTION; IT IS RAISED IN INCORRUPTION: IT IS SOWN IN DISHONOUR [DISHONOR]; IT IS RAISED IN GLORY: IT IS SOWN IN WEAKNESS; IT IS RAISED IN POWER: IT IS SOWN A NATURAL BODY; IT IS RAISED A SPIRITUAL BODY. THERE IS A NATURAL BODY, AND THERE IS A SPIRITUAL BODY . . . . . AND AS WE HAVE BORNE THE IMAGE OF THE EARTHY [EARTHLY], WE SHALL ALSO BEAR THE IMAGE OF THE HEAVENLY . . . . . FOR THIS CORRUPTIBLE MUST PUT ON INCORRUPTION, AND THIS MORTAL *MUST* PUT ON IMMORTALITY.

You're hot stuff! Demetrius said to himself as he stood in front of his mirror admiring himself. *On a scale of one to ten, you're a twenty.* In fact, he told himself, *you're off the charts!*

And my teacher said I was no mathematician, he muttered. egotistically. *Boy, was she wrong. Just this week alone, I've counted up to at least ten girls I could've had.*

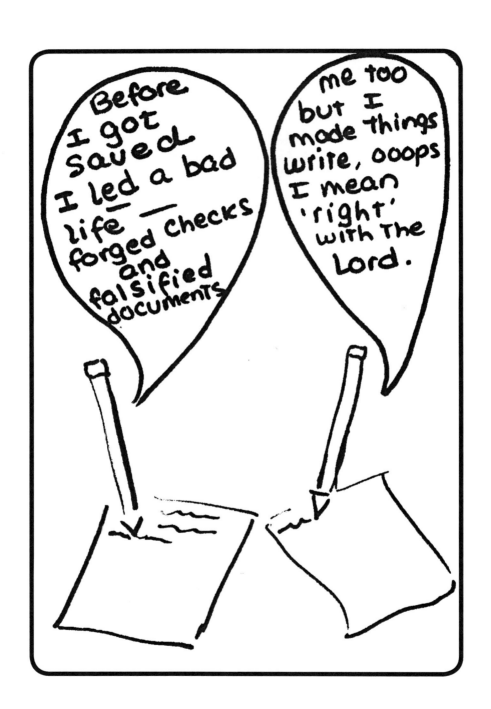

So who needs teachers and books? With this build, some nice threads, and a couple of parents that are loaded, I can have the world by the tail. Yah, you handsome devil! Your looks are going to pay off, he smiled. *I guess I add new meaning to the words "face value."*

PROVERBS 26:12: SEEST THOU A MAN WISE IN HIS OWN CONCEIT? *THERE IS* MORE HOPE OF A FOOL THAN OF HIM.

PROVERBS 27:2: LET ANOTHER MAN PRAISE THEE, AND NOT THINE OWN MOUTH; A STRANGER, AND NOT THINE OWN LIPS.

PSALM 131:1: LORD, MY HEART IS NOT HAUGHTY, NOR MINE EYES LOFTY . . .

ISAIAH 2:11-12: THE LOFTY LOOKS OF MAN SHALL BE HUMBLED, AND THE HAUGHTINESS OF MEN SHALL BE BOWED DOWN, AND THE LORD ALONE SHALL BE EXALTED IN THAT DAY. FOR THE DAY OF THE LORD OF HOSTS *SHALL BE* UPON EVERY *ONE THAT IS* PROUD AND LOFTY, AND UPON EVERY *ONE THAT IS* LIFTED UP; AND HE SHALL BE BROUGHT LOW.

PROVERBS 8:13: THE FEAR OF THE LORD IS TO HATE EVIL: PRIDE, AND ARROGANCY, AND THE EVIL WAY, AND THE FROWARD MOUTH, DO I HATE.

PROVERBS 16:18: PRIDE *GOETH* BEFORE DESTRUCTION, AND AN [A] HAUGHTY SPIRIT BEFORE A FALL.

PROVERBS 18:7: A FOOL'S MOUTH *IS* HIS DESTRUCTION, AND HIS LIPS ARE THE SNARE OF HIS SOUL. [SEE PROVERBS 6:2 & PROVERBS 27:19]

Frank had a knack for playing poker. His card-playing buddies began to marvel at what they thought was an incredible streak of luck.

"How do you do it?" they asked with astonishment. "We know the cards aren't marked. You're wearing a sleeveless shirt so we know you haven't got any aces up your sleeve and yet," they said, bewildered, "every week you clean us out."

Frank's uncanny ability to win had each one of them completely baffled.

"It's easy to explain," he said nonchalantly. "I used to live completely for God. The devil is just making sure I don't go back!"

II PETER 3:17: YE THEREFORE, BELOVED, SEEING YE KNOW *THESE THINGS* BEFORE, BEWARE LEST YE ALSO, BEING LED AWAY WITH THE ERROR OF THE WICKED, FALL FROM YOUR OWN STEDFASTNESS.

PSALM 111:10: THE FEAR OF THE LORD *IS* THE BEGINNING OF WISDOM: A GOOD UNDERSTANDING HAVE ALL THEY THAT DO *HIS* COMMANDMENTS . . . [SEE I JOHN 2:3-4]

A Sunday school teacher asked her teenage class if they knew who would be among the blessed group to enter the New Jerusalem. "Who will be present at the Marriage Supper of the Lamb?" she challenged them.

A freckle-faced boy in the front row was waving his hand excitedly. "Yes, Darryl," the teacher said, calling on him. "Well," replied Darryl, "There will be all different kinds of people in heaven—tall, born-again people, short, born-again people, thin born-again people, fat born-again people, smart born-again people, dumb born-again people, young born-again people, old born-again people, black, white, yellow, and red born-again people, and then there'll be all those born-again oddballs like the ones in this class who get in by the skin of their teeth."

I CORINTHIANS 3:15: IF ANY MAN'S WORK SHALL BE BURNED, HE SHALL SUFFER LOSS: BUT HE HIMSELF SHALL BE SAVED; YET SO AS BY FIRE.

"I know you've been going through some very difficult times, Mildred," Fran, a church member, told her. "If there is ever a time I can be of help, just let me know. If you need someone to talk to or someone to pray with you, don't hesitate to give me a call day or night," she said.

Taking Fran at her word, Mildred started calling—morning, noon, and night, and in between. After about a week of exhausting non-stop calls that would begin as early as 4:30 a.m. and not end 'til after midnight Fran

was going out of her mind. "When does that woman sleep?" she aked a friend with amazement.

During her next conversation with Mildred, Fran told her that it would be necessary to make a few changes in the offer she'd extended. "You are still welcome to call me day or night," she said, but only from 11:00 a.m. to 11:01 a.m. and from 7:00 p.m. to 7:01 p.m.

I PETER 4:8: AND ABOVE ALL THINGS HAVE FERVENT CHARITY AMONG YOURSELVES: FOP CHARITY SHALL COVER THE MULTITUDE OF SINS.

"My, how quiet it is in here," said Mrs. Howell, the nursery supervisor to the workers. "I can't remember when it's ever been so tranquil in this room before. I don't know what method you've employed," she said, smiling, "but the children in the nursery are behaving like little angels this morning.

"Whew! That was certainly a close call," Denise whispered to one of the other workers as soon as Mrs. Howell left. "If she had come in here ten minutes ago, my husband would probably have made her stand to attention," she said nervously. "He's been coming on like some kind of army drill sergeant with these two-year-olds," she remarked.

"Five minutes after he started watching these kids, he'd already court-martialed three of them, sending them to the corner. And the rest he kept marching single file around the room until they were ready to drop from sheer exhaustion. And if that wasn't enough," she continued, "after they marched, he made them stand saluting during one of his longwinded prayers.

"The reason Mrs. Howell found them being so tranquil and well behaved," she laughed, "is because they're too tired to do anything else! But I think," she added, "unless the service is over soon and their parents arrive promptly, there may be a huge conspiracy to go A.W.O.L."

PHILIPPIANS 4:21: SALUTE EVERY SAINT IN CHRIST JESUS.

Chuck was telling his friend, Neil, about how to look spiritual when you're not. "It's easy," he said. "I do it all the time."

"What do you mean?" asked Neil, eager to learn the 'tricks of the trade.'

"Just follow these five simple steps," replied Chuck, naming them: "First, you say 'Praise God' whenever you answer the phone. After all, it might be the pastor on the other end of the line—or one of his deacons checking up on you. You never know what spies he has on your tail," he told him.

Second," he said, "wear a cross around your neck and hang your head a lot, especially in church. Someone might be looking at you out of the corner of your eye so it's always good to be on the safe side.

"Third," he continued, "keep your Bible dusted at all times. The pastor likes to make unannounced visits. You have to be wise to his ways.

"Fourth," he said, "always throw something in the offering plate, even if it's only a nickel. No one will notice the difference anyway.

"And last, but above all," Chuck instructed him, "always answer the door on your knees. It makes people think you've just been praying."

EPHESIANS 6:6-7: NOT WITH EYESERVICE, AS MENPLEASERS; BUT AS THE SERVANTS OF CHRIST, DOING THE WILL OF GOD FROM THE HEART; WITH GOOD WILL DOING SERVICE, AS TO THE LORD, AND NOT TO MEN:

JOHN 12:43: FOR THEY LOVED THE PRAISE OF MEN MORE THAN THE PRAISE OF GOD.

GALATIONS 1:10: . . . DO I SEEK TO PLEASE MEN? FOR IF I YET PLEASED MEN, I SHOULD NOT BE THE SERVANT OF CHRIST.

MATTHEW 15:8-9: THIS PEOPLE DRAWETH NIGH UNTO ME WITH THEIR MOUTH, AND HONOURETH [HONORETH] ME WITH *THEIR* LIPS; BUT THEIR HEART IS FAR FROM ME. BUT IN VAIN DO THEY WORSHIP ME . . . [SEE LUKE 18:10-14 & II CORINTHIANS 10:18]

MATTHEW 23:28: . . . EVEN SO YE ALSO OUTWARDLY APPEAR RIGHTEOUS UNTO MEN, BUT WITHIN YE ARE FULL OF HYPOCRISY AND INIQUITY.

II TIMOTHY 3:5: HAVING A FORM OF GODLINESS, BUT DENYING THE POWER THEREOF . . .

LUKE 16:15: AND HE [JESUS] SAID UNTO THEM, YE ARE THEY WHICH JUSTIFY YOURSELVES BEFORE MEN; BUT GOD KNOWETH YOUR HEARTS:FOR THAT WHICH IS HIGHLY ESTEEMED AMONG MEN IS ABOMINATION IN THE SIGHT OF GOD.

MATTHEW 7:21-23: NOT EVERY ONE THAT SAITH UNTO ME, LORD, LORD, SHALL ENTER INTO THE KINGDOM OF HEAVEN; BUT HE THAT DOETH THE WILL OF MY FATHER WHICH IS IN HEAVEN. MANY WILL SAY TO ME IN THAT DAY, LORD, LORD, HAVE WE NOT PROPHESIED IN THY NAME? AND IN THY NAME HAVE CAST OUT DEVILS? AND IN THY NAME DONE MANY WONDERFUL WORKS? AND THEN WILL I PROFESS UNTO THEM, I NEVER KNEW YOU: DEPART FROM ME, YE THAT WORK INIQUITY.

"It's been weeks and weeks since Ward has been in church," Pastor Carlson said to his deacon. "I think I'll drop by his house this week and find out what's wrong.

"That's a good idea," his deacon replied. "Maybe he needs to know he's been missed."

That week, Pastor Carlson stopped over to see Ward. "Make yourself comfortable," Ward told the Pastor, pouring him a glass of ice tea. "I hope it tastes okay," he said, "I don't have a wife, so I have to do these things myself.

"It's fine," replied the Pastor, trying to keep the first swallow down. "A bit tart, but fine."

"Are you sure it's not too bitter?" asked Ward. "I like a touch a lemon."

"While we're on the subject of bitter," said Pastor Carlson, trying to work the conversation into a spiritual one, "I was just wondering why we haven't seen you in church for such a long time."

"To be honest," said Ward, "I'm on strike right now, but" he said, "the Lord and I are negotiating and we should be able to reach a settlement before long."

I KINGS 18:21: . . . HOW LONG HALT YE BETWEEN TWO OPINIONS? IF THE LORD BE GOD, FOLLOW HIM: BUT IF BAAL, THEN FOLLOW HIM . . .

JOSHUA 5:13: . . . *ART* THOU FOR US, OR FOR OUR ADVERSARIES?

LUKE 16:13: NO SERVANT CAN SERVE TWO MASTERS: FOR EITHER HE WILL HATE THE ONE, AND LOVE THE OTHER; OR ELSE HE WILL HOLD TO THE ONE, AND DESPISE THE OTHER. YE CANNOT SERVE GOD AND MAMMON.

JOSHUA 24:15: AND IF IT SEEM EVIL UNTO YOU TO SERVE THE LORD, CHOOSE YOU THIS DAY WHOM YE WILL SERVE . . . BUT AS FOR ME AND MY HOUSE, WE WILL SERVE THE LORD.

EXODUS 32:26: THEN MOSES STOOD IN THE GATE OF THE CAMP, AND SAID, WHO *IS* ON THE LORD'S SIDE? *LET HIM COME* UNTO ME . . .

JAMES 4:4: . . . KNOW YE NOT THAT THE FRIENDSHIP OF THE WORLD IS ENMITY WITH GOD? WHOSOEVER THEREFORE WILL BE A FRIEND OF THE WORLD IS THE ENEMY OF GOD. [SEE I JOHN 2:15-17]

Pastor Kelly reprimanded his church one morning about the sin of self righteousness. "Jesus had a lot to say about the Pharisees and Sadducees and their pious act before men. Their long prayers of vain repetition were strictly for man's benefit and not the Lord's. We are admonished by the Lord," he instructed them, "to worship Him not just from the lips but from the heart. There is also that other group of people," he said, "who are too heavenly minded to be any earthly good."

"Not me!" shouted one lady, drawing attention to herself and disrupting the service. "I'm so down to earth, Pastor, that I can give you all the dirt you want!"

PROVERBS 17:28: EVEN A FOOL, WHEN HE HOLDETH HIS PEACE, IS COUNTED WISE.

Two young women, Sylvia and Alice, both deep in their faith, were sharing things with each other that the Lord had been dealing with them about. "Recently," said Alice, "the Lord has been impressing on my mind to make a list of people whom I offended in the past." She added, "I want to write and ask forgiveness of each one whom I hurt by my actions."

The other girl, Sylvia, whose beauty had been the downfall of scores of broken-hearted men during her scarlet years, sighed, and said, "It's a nice gesture, Alice, but I'm afraid I couldn't afford all that postage!"

MATTHEW 6:14-15: FOR IF YE FORGIVE MEN THEIR TRESPASSES, YOUR HEAVENLY FATHER WILL ALSO FORGIVE YOU: BUT IF YE FORGIVE NOT MEN THEIR TRESPASSES, NEITHER WILL YOUR FATHER FORGIVE YOUR TRESPASSES. [SEE ACTS 24:16; MATTHEW 18:21-22 & 33; PROVERBS 18:19; HEBREWS 12:14-15; ROMANS 12:17-21; I CORINTHIANS 13:4-7; PSALM 133:1]

EPHESIANS 4:32: AND BE YE KIND ONE TO ANOTHER, TENDERHEARTED, FORGIVING ONE ANOTHER, EVEN AS GOD FOR CHRIST'S SAKE HATH FORGIVEN YOU.

COLOSSIANS 3:13: FORBEARING ONE ANOTHER, AND FORGIVING ONE ANOTHER, IF ANY MAN HAVE A QUARREL AGAINST ANY: EVEN AS CHRIST FORGAVE YOU, SO ALSO *DO* YE.

ROMANS 14:19: LET US THEREFORE FOLLOW AFTER THE THINGS WHICH MAKE FOR PEACE . . .

A couple had lied on their income tax form and were being invested by the I.R.S. They were feeling very apprehensive about the situation.

A friend tried to console them. "Don't be upset by all this," she told them. 'God forgives and forgets."

"We know God forgives and forgets," the woman answered. "But how do we get the Internal Revenue Service to do the same?"

(Author's note: God forgives but He expects us to make restitution!)

ACTS 17:30: AND THE TIMES OF THIS IGNORANCE GOD WINKED AT; BUT NOW COMMANDETH ALL MEN EVERY WHERE TO REPENT.

PROVERBS 6:30-31: *MEN* DO NOT DESPISE A THIEF, IF HE STEAL TO SATISFY HIS SOUL WHEN HE IS HUNGRY; BUT *IF* HE BE FOUND, HE SHALL RESTORE SEVENFOLD . . .

PROVERBS 28:13: HE THAT COVERETH HIS SINS SHALL NOT PROSPER: BUT WHOSO CONFESSETH AND FORSAKETH *THEM* SHALL HAVE MERCY.

Every few years a certain church updated its directory, making corrections and adding the names, addresses, and phone numbers of its new members. It also included a family photograph.

When Mrs. Gates received her directory, she quickly turned to the page containing her family's portrait. She held up the page for her family and her daughter's friend, Barbara, to see, proudly displaying the picture of the happy foursome.

Barbara couldn't resist poking fun at the photo. She put one hand over her mouth and gasped. Then, with her other hand, she pointed at the picture. "I've seen those people on a wanted poster!" she joked, "and they're armed and dangerous!"

ACTS 17:6: . . . THESE THAT HAVE TURNED THE WORLD UPSIDE DOWN [FOR CHRIST] . . .

In church one Sunday Pastor Elton was delivering a hair raising account of the things forecast in Revelation. When he got to chapter 16, a lady in the congregation yelled and screamed to the top of her voice. "Madam, please,' said the Pastor, "There is no need for such a demonstration. A simple 'Amen' will be sufficient."

Calming herself down, she apologized, "I'm sorry for that loud outburst, Pastor," she said, "but I wasn't reacting to the coming tribulation. I was addressing the present one!"

She glared at her twelve year old. "My son took a caterpillar out of his pocket," she said, "and put it on my arm."

Then she leaned over to her son and whispered in his ear, "If you think the tribulation sounds bad," she told him, "you just wait to see what's coming when we get home!"

AMOS 5:18-20: WOE UNTO YOU THAT DESIRE THE DAY OF THE LORD! TO WHAT END *IS* IT FOR YOU? THE DAY OF THE LORD *IS* DARKNESS, AND NOT LIGHT. AS IF A MAN DID FLEE FROM A LION, AND A BEAR MET HIM; OR WENT INTO THE HOUSE, AND LEANED HIS HAND ON THE WALL, AND A SERPENT BIT HIM. *SHALL* NOT THE DAY OF THE LORD *BE* DARKNESS, AND NOT LIGHT? EVEN VERY DARK, AND NO BRIGHTENESS IN IT?

DANIEL 5:27: . . . THOU ART WEIGHED IN THE BALANCES, AND ART FOUND WANTING.

REVELATION 6:15-17: AND THE KINGS OF THE EARTH, AND THE GREAT MEN, AND THE RICH MEN, AND THE CHIEF CAPTAINS, AND THE MIGHTY MEN, AND EVERY BONDMAN, AND EVERY FREE MAN, HID THEMSELVES IN THE DENS AND IN THE ROCKS OF THE MOUNTAINS; AND SAID TO THE MOUNTAINS AND ROCKS, FALL ON US, AND HIDE US FROM THE FACE OF HIM THAT SITTETH ON THE THRONE, AND FROM THE WRATH OF THE LAMB: FOR THE GREAT DAY OF HIS WRATH IS COME; AND WHO SHALL BE ABLE TO STAND? [SEE II PETER 3:10-11; MATTHEW 24:21; DANIEL 12:1]

"I've prayed, I've fasted, and I've sought the Lord," cried Marie, feeling defeated because of her queen size figure. "Everything I wear is so tight and uncomfortable and I don't have a bit of energy.

"Last night, when I had to go upstairs to shut the bedroom window, I felt like I was climbing Mount Everest. By the time I got to the top," she said, "I was thoroughly exhausted carrying all this weight. I don't know what to do," she continued. "All I do is look at food and I gain weight."

"Honey," said her friend, sympathetically. "Just give it to the Lord."

"I tried to," she said, "but I don't think He wants it either.

HEBREWS 12:1-2: WHEREFORE SEEING WE ALSO ARE COMPASSED ABOUT WITH SO GREAT A CLOUD OF WITNESSES, LET US LAY ASIDE EVERY WEIGHT, AND THE SIN WHICH DOTH SO EASILY BESET US, AND LET US RUN WITH PATIENCE THE RACE THAT IS SET BEFORE US. LOOKING UNTO JESUS THE AUTHOR AND FINISHER OF OUR FAITH; WHO FOR THE JOY THAT WAS SET BEFORE HIM ENDURED THE CROSS, DESPISING THE SHAME, AND IS SET DOWN AT THE RIGHT HAND OF THE THRONE OF GOD.

As Jan was witnessing to a co-worker in her office, her boss, Mrs. Davis, an unbeliever, overheard her sharing Christ.

"There'll be no preaching one's religion in this office" she scolded her angrily. "If we want a sermon we can get one at church."

Later that same day, while Jan, her boss, and some of the other employees were in the elevator leaving for lunch, Jan was subjected to hearing a steady flow of cuss words uttered by her boss, most of which included the Lord's name being taken in vain.

"I thought you told us there was no preaching allowed in this place," Jan remarked to her boss coolly at the risk of being fired.

"What are you talking about?" her boss retorted.

"You were just using the Lord's name and you told me we weren't allowed to do so," Jan answered.

"That's different," snapped Mrs. Davis. "I was only using it in vain."

EXODUS 20:7: THOU SHALT NOT TAKE THE NAME OF THE LORD THY GOD IN VAIN; FOR THE LORD WILL NOT HOLD HIM GUILTLESS THAT TAKETH HIS NAME IN VAIN.

MATTHEW 12:36: BUT I SAY UNTO YOU, THAT EVERY IDLE WORD THAT MEN SHALL SPEAK, THEY SHALL GIVE ACCOUNT THEREOF IN THE DAY OF JUDGMENT. FOR BY THY WORDS THOU SHALT BE JUSTIFIED, AND BY THY WORDS THOU SHALT BE CONDEMNED.

"Brace yourself," Pastor Tyson told his audience, if you're not already a Christian, you're about to receive the most important news of your life."

With excitement in his voice, he told them how Jesus Christ could give them a new lease on life. "He wants to change your life in a miraculous, powerful way. He wants to make you an over comer by the 'word of your testimony' and the 'blood of the Lamb.' He wants to comfort you, guide you, and lift you up through the presence of His Holy Spirit. He wants to make all things new and give you a fresh start and a clean slate. And He wants to make you a joint—heir and a partaker of his divine nature, and," he added, "He wants to reassure you of an eternal home in heaven with Him where the Bible says there will be pleasures for ever more!"

As he continued with his message one lady leaned over and whispered to her friend, "Cynthia, we've been sitting here on these hard pews while he drags on and on about who knows what. When is he going to give us the important news he promised us?"

I JOHN 2:25: AND THIS IS THE PROMISE THAT HE HATH PROMISED US, *EVEN* ETERNAL LIFE.

I PETER 1:4: . . . AN INHERITANCE INCORRUPTIBLE, AND UNDEFILED, AND THAT FADETH NOT AWAY, RESERVED IN HEAVEN FOR YOU . . .

I CORINTHIANS 1:18: FOR THE PREACHING OF THE CROSS IS TO THEM THAT PERISH FOOLISHNESS; BUT UNTO US WHICH ARE SAVED IT IS THE POWER OF GOD.

I CORINTHIANS 2:14: BUT THE NATURAL MAN RECEIVETH NOT THE THINGS OF THE SPIRIT OF GOD: FOR THEY ARE FOOLISHNESS UNTO HIM: NEITHER CAN HE KNOW *THEM*, BECAUSE THEY ARE SPIRITUALLY DISCERNED.

While working in the church nursery, one of the workers commented unkindly about several of the children. "See that little monster over there in the pink dress?" asked the helper. "She looks like an angel but," she criticized, "if her mother doesn't do something with her," she whispered, "she will be a runaway teenager by the time she's twelve. And that other child is just as bad," she said pointing at a little boy. "He's a little brat so keep your eye on him, too."

After listening to the helper go on for about ten minutes non stop about this one and that one, the other woman beckoned lovingly to the little girl in the pink dress and then to another energetic youngster, "Come to Mommy, Melissa and Mark," she said, waiting to see the expression on the lady's face.

PROVERBS 26:22: THE WORDS OF A TALEBEARER ARE AS WOUNDS, AND THEY GO DOWN INTO THE INNERMOST PARTS OF THE BELLY.

JAILBIRD JOLLIES

"Chaplain Olson," said Tom, during their visit, "I sure am glad I gave my life to Jesus. He's given me a purpose and a reason for living that I never knew existed. In spite of these bars," he said, smiling, "I have found a meaning to my life that gives me unspeakable joy. Needless to say," he went on, "without God's comforting presence, this would be a dismal place to wake up to each day.

"I must confess, though," he continued, "that I do find myself reminiscing about the past from time to time. I used to call it 'the good ole days.'"

"Yes," the chaplain remarked, "I understand."

"As you know, chaplain," Tom confessed, "my favorite pass time before coming to the Lord was . . . um . . . er . . . robbing banks. And occasionally," he said, "I still dream of taking a quiet stroll through the vaults of the United States treasury."

JOB 23:10: BUT HE KNOWETH THE WAY THAT I TAKE: *WHEN* HE HATH TRIED ME, I SHALL COME FORTH AS GOLD.

"Chaplain," said Barney, a convicted criminal, "You've heard that expression 'God helps them who help themselves.' Well, don't believe it," he said. "I tried helping myself to some cold cash and it got me a lot of years in this slammer!

EXODUS 20:15: THOU SHALT NOT STEAL.

A prison chaplain was doing follow ups on his new converts. He wrote one inmate, Bill, who was serving a life sentence in a state correctional facility. In his letter he inquired about his spiritual growth. *"Has God*

spoken to your heart, Bill, about any particular aspect of ministry during your incarceration?"

"Not exactly," was the reply that came back shortly, "But," Bill wrote, *"I've volunteered for the vengeance department if he needs any help in that area!"*

ROMANS 12:19-21: DEARLY BELOVED, AVENGE NOT YOURSELVES. BUT *RATHER* GIVE PLACE UNTO WRATH: FOR IT IS WRITTEN, VENGEANCE IS MINE: I WILL REPAY, SAITH THE LORD. THEREFORE IF THINE ENEMY HUNGER, FEED HIM; IF HE THIRST, GIVE HIM DRINK: FOR IN SO DOING THOU SHALT HEAP COALS OF FIRE ON HIS HEAD. BE NOT OVERCOME OF EVIL, BUT OVERCOME EVIL WITH GOOD.

I THESSALONIANS 5:15: SEE THAT NONE RENDER EVIL FOR EVIL UNTO ANY *MAN;* BUT EVER FOLLOW THAT WHICH IS GOOD, BOTH AMONG YOURSELVES, AND TO ALL *MEN.*

Sitting behind bars feeling discouraged about his lot in life, one convict wrote to his chaplain: *Dear Chaplain Freedman, Did you ever feel like everybody had their hooks in you? Every which way I turn, somebody's after a piece of my hide. This facility and the warden want my time; the girls want my body, the wife wants my throat, the devil wants my soul, the I.R.S wants my money, and if that's not asking enough,* he wrote, *God wants my heart. Isn't there anything left over for me to keep?"*

About a week later came the brief reply: *"Yes, beloved brother in Christ, you get to keep your sanity!"*

ISAIAH 26:3: THOU WILT KEEP *HIM* IN PERFECT PEACE, *WHOSE* MIND *IS* STAYED *ON THEE:* BECAUSE HE TRUSTETH IN THEE.

PHILIPPIANS 4:7: AND THE PEACE OF GOD, WHICH PASSETH ALL UNDERSTANDING, SHALL KEEP YOUR HEARTS AND MINDS THROUGH CHRIST JESUS.

ISAIAH 9:6: . . . THE PRINCE OF PEACE . . .

"Chaplain, I've only been doing time for six months," cried Dan, "And already I'm going berserk. I feel like a caged animal just screaming to get out," he agonized. "I've prayed to God, but my prayers just seem to bounce off the ceiling."

"Well, there's a good explanation for that," said the chaplain. "If you're prayers aren't getting past the ceiling, it's probably because there's two more floors on top of yours."

ACTS 16:25: AND AT MIDNIGHT PAUL AND SILAS PRAYED, AND SANG PRAISES UNTO GOD: AND THE PRISONERS HEARD THEM.

II CORINTHIANS 3:17 . . . WHERE THE SPIRIT OF THE LORD IS, THERE IS LIBERTY.

ISAIAH 61:1-3: THE SPIRIT OF THE LORD GOD *IS* UPON ME; BECAUSE THE LORD HATH ANOINTED ME TO PREACH GOOD TIDINGS UNTO THE MEEK; HE HATH SENT ME TO BIND UP THE BROKENHEARTED, TO PROCLAIM LIBERTY TO THECAPTIVES, AND THE OPENING OF THE PRISON TO *THEM THAT ARE* BOUND; TO PROCLAIM THE ACCEPTABLE YEAR OF THELORD, AND THE DAY OF VENGEANCE OF OURGOD; TO COMFORT ALL THAT MOURN; TO APPOINT UNTO THEM THAT MOURN IN ZION, TO GIVE UNTO THEM BEAUTY FOR ASHES, THE OIL OF JOY FOR MOURNING, THE GARMENT OF PRAISE FOR THE SPIRIT OF HEAVINESS; THAT THEY MIGHT BE CALLED TREES OF RIGHTEOUSNESS, THELPLANTING OF THE LORD, THAT HE MIGHT BE GLORIFIED.

PSALM 102:17 & 19-20: HE WILL REGARD THE PRAYER OF THE DESTITUTE, AND NOT DESPISE THEIR PRAYER . . . FOR HE HATH LOOKED DOWN FROM THE HEIGHT OF HIS SANCTUARY; FROM HEAVEN DID THE LORD BEHOLD THE EARTH; TO HEAR THE GROANING OF THE PRISONER . . .

"I wouldn't be here if you hadn't named me as an accomplice," complained Andy to his cohort in crime. "It's because of you that we're both going to spend the next twenty years behind bars. I knew I couldn't trust you," he said accusingly, glaring at the man. "And after all I did for you, teaching

you the ropes and cutting you in," he said, vengefully. "And this is the way you repay me for all my generosity toward you."

Andy paced back and forth in his cell furious over his incarceration. "All I've got to say, pal," he said sarcastically, "is the next time you decide to unburden your soul, please let me put you in a permanent coma before you start talking!"

LUKE 12:2-3: FOR THERE IS NOTHING COVERED, THAT SHALL NOT BE REVEALED; NEITHER HID, THAT SHALL NOT BE KNOWN. THEREFORE WHATSOEVER YE HAVE SPOKEN IN DARKNESS SHALL BE HEARD IN THE LIGHT; AND THAT WHICH YE HAVE SPOKEN IN THE EAR IN CLOSETS SHALL BE PROCLAIMED UPON THE HOUSETOPS.

"Here's your mail," said Chaplain Irwin's secretary handing him his letters. As he opened the first letter, he read, *Greetings in the name of the Lord. My name is Sherman. I'm an inmate here at the State Correctional facility doing a 20 year stretch. Things are going as well as can be expected, but there are a few things I have need of since becoming a Christian. To further enhance my spiritual growth, could you possibly send me the following list of things, Chaplain: ONE KING JAMES VERSION BIBLE, two hacksaws, ONE PICTURE OF JESUS, one box of dynamite, ONE EVANGELISTIC MAGAZINE, two packs of matches, ONE SOUL WINNER'S KIT INCLUDING TRACTS, one change of clothes, one ticket to any foreign country, and ONE DEVOTIONAL BOOKLET.*

Sherman concluded his letter to Chaplain Irwin by asking for prayer and assuring him *that any implements of the Lord that were sent would be greatly appreciated.*

PROVERBS 3:27: WITHHOLD NOT GOOD FROM THEM TO WHOM IT IS DUE, WHEN IT IS IN THE POWER OF THINE HAND TO DO IT.

Although Jason was a convict with a lot of time ahead, his confinement didn't stop him from dreaming of matrimonial bliss.

Searching for the comfort that belonging to someone brings, he wrote his chaplain: *Dear Sir, I'll get right to the point. I'm looking for a wife. Do*

you know of any young woman in her twenties who would be interested in becoming a lawfully wedded pen pal for the next 80 to 200 years til the soaring price of stamps us do part.

Jason's letter continued, *I would be willing to devote all my time (and believe me, Chaplain, I've got a lot to spare) unselfishly. As a new Christian, you could tell her that I no longer indulge in sex, drinking, gambling, cold blooded murder, or smoking. What's more, Chaplain, I'm the domesticated, stay-at-home type since maximum security makes it rather difficult to do otherwise.*

His letter ended, *I'll be anxiously awaiting your reply. Just try not to keep me waiting too long or I may resort to something desperate—like natural death.*

PHILIPPIANS 4:6: BE CAREFUL FOR NOTHING; BUT IN EVERY THING BY PRAYER AND SUPPLICATION WITH THANKSGIVING LET YOUR REQUESTS BE MADE KNOWN UNTO GOD.

I JOHN 3:21-22: BELOVED, IF OUR HEART CONDEMN US NOT, *THEN* HAVE WE CONFIDENCE TOWARD GOD. AND WHATSOEVER WE ASK, WE RECEIVE OF HIM, BECAUSE WE KEEP HIS COMMANDMENTS, AND DO THOSE THINGS THAT ARE PLEASING IN HIS SIGHT.

HEBREWS 4:15: LET US THEREFORE COME BOLDLY UNTO THE THRONE OF GRACE, THAT WE MAY OBTAIN MERCY, AND FIND GRACE TO HELP IN TIME OF NEED.

In a small, suburban town an enormous house fire was raging out of control on one of its busy streets. Throngs of curious spectators from blocks around came to view the blazing inferno.

Jill, a local church member, decided to turn what seemed to be a flaming disaster into an opportunity for God. Accompanied by Ted, a new convert who was also an ex convict, they began passing out Christian literature to the gathered crowd.

Unfortunately, some of the pamphlets were not well received and quickly tossed to the ground.

Ted, who was still a diamond in the rough, so to speak, had quite an over zealous attitude to win souls. He became increasingly agitated and most impatient with those who would not receive the good news of salvation. "Drop that tract and you'll be hitting the pavement right along with it," he snarled as he passed out each little booklet.

Needless to say, there were 100% conversions that evening!

PROVERBS 11:30: THE FRUIT OF THE RIGHTEOUS IS A TREE OF LIFE: AND HE THAT WINNETH SOULS IS WISE.

PROVERBS 14:25: A TRUE WITNESS DELIVERETH SOULS . . .

JAMES 5:20: LET HIM KNOW, THAT HE WHICH CONVERTETH THE SINNER FROM THE ERROR OF HIS WAY SHALL SAVE A SOUL FROM DEATH, AND SHALL HIDE A MULTIDUDE OF SINS.

I PETER 4:8: AND ABOVE ALL THINGS HAVE FERVENT CHARITY AMONG YOURSELVES: FOR CHARITY SHALL COVER THE MULTITUDE OF SINS.

John, a Christian inmate at a correctional facility, was having a real problem overcoming his cynical attitude toward one of his superiors. He was a big burly guard who seemed to delight in provoking the inmate's wrath. He would make unnecessary demands and take away privileges that would reduce one's existence to nothingness.

Passing by John's cell one day, the guard rattled his bars and made his usual sarcastic remarks. John, who was reading his Bible at the time, looked up at the guard and said, "I've just been reading about the golden rule. Why don't you step behind these bars and I'll show you how it works when I'm not obeying it."

I PETER 2:20: FOR WHAT GLORY IS IS, IF WHEN YE BE BUFFETED FOR YOUR FAULTS, YE SHALL TAKE IT PATIENTLY? BUT IF WHEN YE DO WELL, AND SUFFER FOR IT, YE TAKE IT PATIENTLY, THIS IS ACCEPTABLE WITH GOD.

After spending most of his life serving the devil, Felix, a converted convict, wrote and asked his chaplain to send him as many tracts as he could spare.

I feel I could be very useful to the Lord if I just had the necessary tools to do so, he wrote his chaplain.

Just as he had requested, scores of tracts arrived shortly after he had written. He rejoiced over the package including a variety of different tracts, including some that resembled a twenty dollar bill.

This particular tract was to be folded in half, thus giving the appearance of lost currency. When the "twenty-dollar bill" was picked up and unfolded, however, the other half contained the message of salvation.

In a letter of appreciation to the chaplain, Felix wrote: *When some of these tough guys find out they've been conned by a phony twenty dollar bill, they're bound to␣co something drastic. Because I have not yet felt the call to martyrdom* he continued, *I wrote your name legibly on each one!*

II TIMOTHY 3:12: YEA, AND ALL THAT LIVE GODLY IN CHRIST JESUS SHALL SUFFER PERSECUTION. [SEE II CORINTHIANS 11:23-28; I JOHN 3:13; II TIMOTHY 2:3]

ACTS 7:54-55 & 59: WHEN THEY [THE UNBELIEVERS] HEARD THESE THINGS, THEY WERE CUT TO THE HEART, AND THEY GNASHED ON HIM WITH *THEIR* TEETH. BUT HE [STEPHEN, BEING FULL OF THE HOLY GHOST, LOOKED UP STEDFASTLY INTO HEAVEN, AND SAW THE GLORY OF GOD, AND JESUS STANDING ON THE RIGHT HAND OF GOD . . . AND THEY STONED STEPHEN, CALLING UPON *GOD*, AND SAYING, LORD JESUS, RECEIVE MY SPIRIT.

ACTS 21:13: THEN PAUL ANSWERED, WHAT MEAN YE TO WEEP AND TO BREAK MINE HEART? FOR I AM READY NOT TO BE BOUND ONLY, BUT ALSO TO DIE AT JERUSALEM FOR THE NAME OF THE LORD JESUS.

Sarah, a feisty young woman with 20/20 vision, was looking out her window one night when she spotted a teenage boy in the process of swiping two tires she had laying out back of her house.

A fast thinker, she called the police and then ran out the back door with her son's toy pistol, pointing it at the teen. "Put those back!" she demanded. He scrambled to put the tires back fearing she might be trigger happy and unaware that it was only a toy.

"Now listen," she said, "Is that your ten-speed over there?" "Yes, miss," he said, his voice quivering. "Would you like to ride that bike without pedals?" she asked him.

"No, miss," he said, shaking his head. "Well, I think you can understand then, why I also would not like to drive my car around without tires."

She then admonished him to give the Lord a try. "You'll find," she said, "That time spent in church goes by much more quickly than it does in the county jail."

(Author's note: Generally speaking, it is best to leave these matters totally in the hands of the police. Things could have backfired and Sarah could have gotten hurt!)

I PETER 4:1: FORASMUCH THEN AS CHRIST HATH SUFFERED FOR US IN THE FLESH, ARM YOURSELVES LIKEWISE WITH THE SAME MIND: FOR HE THAT HATH SUFFERED IN THE FLESH HATH CEASED FROM SIN;

PROVERBS 16:6: BY MERCY AND TRUTH INIQUITY IS PURGED: AND BY THE FEAR OF THE LORD *MEN* DEPART FROM EVIL.

PSALM 119:67, 71, & 75: BEFORE I WAS AFFLICTED I WENT ASTRAY: BUT NOW HAVE I KEPT THY WORD . . . *IT IS* GOOD FOR ME THAT I HAVE BEEN AFFLICTED; THAT I MIGHT LEARN THY STATUTES . . . I KNOW, O LORD, THAT THY JUDGMENTS *ARE* RIGHT, AND *THAT* THOU IN FAITHFULNESS HAST AFFLLICTED ME.

HOSEA 5:15: . . . IN THEIR AFFLICTION THEY WILL SEEK ME EARLY.

PSALM 78:34: WHEN HE SLEW THEM, THEN THEY SOUGHT HIM: ANDTHEY RETURNED AND ENQUIRED EARLY AFTER GOD. [SEE PSALM 78:62]

JOB 5:17-18: BEHOLD, HAPPY IS THE MAN WHOM GOD CORRECTETH: THEREFORE DESPISE NOT THOU THE CHASTENING OF THE ALMIGHTY: FOR HE MAKETH SORE, AND BINDETH UP: HE WOUNDETH, AND HIS HANDS MAKE WHOLE.

HEBREWS 12:11: NOW NO CHASTENING FOR THE PRESENT SEEMETH TO BE JOYOUS, BUT GRIEVOUS: NEVERTHELESS AFTERWARD IT YIELDETH THE PEACEABLE FRUIT OF RIGHTEOUSNESS UNTO THEM WHICH ARE EXERCISED THEREBY.

A prisoner had been feeling convicted about not witnessing to the other inmates on his block. Day after day, he would try to ignore the guilt he felt about being a "silent Christian."

One night, before the lights were shut off, he was reading page 1668 of his Bible. Every passage he read only seemed to remind him of his obligation to share Christ with his fellow man. He tossed and turned in his bed trying to think of a way to share Christ, but all the speeches he rehearsed in his mind only left him feeling all the more inadequate. Then suddenly, as he was lying there, an idea came into his mind.

The next day he made a sign and wore it around his neck. Before the guards ordered him to remove it, he had already attracted plenty of interest from several of the inmates who'd seen the sign. It enabled him to share Christ spontaneously and to find the verses in the Bible he was looking for without hesitation. All the sign said was simply: READ PAGE 1668.

ROMANS 10:14: HOW THEN SHALL THEY CALL ON HIM IN WHOM THEY HAVE NOT BELIEVED? AND HOW SHALL THEY BELIEVE IN HIM OF WHOM THEY HAVE NOT HEARD? AND HOW SHALL THEY HEAR WITHOUT A PREACHER?

Ned and Sidney, two convicts, both Christians, got into a violent argument that led to a vicious fight in the prison cafeteria.

Ned had started the fight over some remarks that Sidney had made about him. Even though the Lord was dealing with Ned's heart about making amends, he continued to spew forth venomous and hard hitting remarks.

One night, however, as he lay thinking about the whole incident, he realized that his own behavior had brought reproach on the Name of Christ and had also ruined his own testimony.

"I'm sorry," he told Sidney the next time he saw him. "I ask you to forgive me."

"I accept your apology, Ned," he replied. "Actually," he said, "Ever since you knocked my tooth out, I haven't had any pain from that cavity that was bothering me. And," he continued, "as far as my broken nose is concerned, I guess it will teach me to keep it out of everyone else's business."

ROMANS 14:13: LET US NOT THEREFORE JUDGE ONE ANOTHER ANY MORE: BUT JUDGE THIS RATHER, THAT NO MAN PUT A STUMBLINGBLOCK OR AN OCCASION TO FALL IN *HIS* BROTHER'S WAY.

PROVERBS 26:20: WHERE NO WOOD IS, *THERE* THE FIRE GOETH OUT: SO WHERE *THERE IS* NO TALEBEARER, THE STRIFE CEASETH.

I JOHN 4:11: BELOVED, IF GOD SO LOVED US, WE OUGHT ALSO TO LOVE ONE ANOTHER.

I JOHN 4:20: IF A MAN SAY, I LOVE GOD, AND HATETH HIS BROTHER, HE IS A LIAR: FOR HE THAT LOVETH NOT HIS BROTHER WHOM HE HATH SEEN, HOW CAN HE LOVE GOD WHOM HE HATH NOT SEEN.

I JOHN 3:15: WHOSOEVER HATETH HIS BROTHER IS A MURDERER: AND YE KNOW THAT NO MURDERER HATH ETERNAL LIFE ABIDING IN HIM.

JOHN 13:35: BY THIS SHALL ALL *MEN* KNOW THAT YE ARE MY DISCIPLES, IF YE HAVE LOVE ONE TO ANOTHER.

I PETER 4:15: BUT LET NONE OF YOU SUFFER AS A MURDERER, OR *AS* A THIEF, OR *AS* AN EVILDOER, OR AS A BUSYBODY IN OTHER MEN'S MATTERS.

"I was just wondering," said an inmate to his chaplain,

"Is heaven as great as people make it out to be?"

"Oh, it's far beyond your fondest imaginations," his chaplain told him.

"Now that I'm a Christian," the inmate asked, "does that mean that I'm definitely going to heaven?"

Why, of course it does," said Chaplain Williams reassuring him. "Son, your past is forgiven, forgotten and under the blood of Christ."

"In that case," said the prisoner, "If heaven has that much to offer, I'd like to send the warden there as soon as possible."

II CORINTHIANS 12:1-4: IT IS NOT EXPEDIENT FOR ME DOUBTLESS TO GLORY. I WILL COME TO VISIONS AND REVELATIONS OF THE LORD. I KNEW A MAN IN CHRIST ABOVE FOURTEEN YEARS AGO, (WHETHER IN THE BODY, I CANNOT TELL; OR WHETHER OUT OF THE BODY, I CANNOT TELL: GOD KNOWETH;) SUCH AN ONE CAUGHT UP TO THE THIRD HEAVEN. AND I KNEW SUCH A MAN, (WHETHER IN THE BODY, OR OUT OF THE BODY, I CANNOT TELL: GOD KNOWETH;) HOW THAT HE WAS CAUGHT UP INTO PARADISE, AND HEARD UNSPEAKABLE WORDS, WHICH IT IS NOT LAWFUL FOR A MAN TO UTTER. [SEE I CORINTHIANS 2:9; REVELATION 21:1-27; REVELATION 22:1-5; MATTHEW 5:12; LUKE 6:23; JOHN 14:1-3; & ISAIAH 51:11]

Two men got into a fight in the prison yard. It turned out to be a knock-down, drag out affair with the one fellow turning the other into near mincemeat. He lay on the ground, surrounded by the other inmates, bruised and bleeding, with his ego more injured than his body.

A few weeks later, the cuts and bruises had healed but the anger was still festering inside. "I owe that dirty buzzard one," he told another inmate.

"But," he said, "being the kind and considerate man that I am, I won't lay another hand on him."

"Yah," another inmate piped in, "You'll let someday else do it for you!"

ROMANS 13:8: OWE NO MAN ANY THING, BUT TO LOVE ONE ANOTHER: FOR HE THAT LOVETH ANOTHER HATH FULFILLED THE LAW.

SINKING SHIPS

"I won't stand for this!" shouted Gordon angrily. "I want to see my attorney!"

The Lord looked at Gordon as he screamed, ranted, and raved, not feeling the least bit intimidated.

"I'm not about to spend the next trillion years in hell over a few petty charges of sin and lasciviousness. You're trying to make me look like a common criminal," he charged the Lord. "And I won't tolerate this kind of treatment!" Then pointing his finger at the Lord he yelled, "I not only want to see my attorney, I demand to see him!"

"He's over there, Gordon," replied the Lord, pointing to a dejected looking soul. I just finished with him. He didn't have much of a defense either."

ISAIAH 2:22: CEASE YE FROM MAN, WHOSE BREATH IS IN HIS NOSTRILS: FOR WHEREIN IS HE TO BE ACCOUNTED OF?

An elderly man, standing in line for the judgment bragged to the fellow behind him. "This should only take a matter of minutes," he said smugly. "I've never killed anybody. I wouldn't hurt a fly. I've never smoked, drank, cussed, or gambled. I guess in my case it's all pretty cut 'n dried as far as the Lord is concerned.

When his turn came, however, he turned white as a ghost, suddenly became faint and began gasping with astonishment at the mass of black marks against him.

"And that's just the first page," said the Lord. "Shall we continue with the other list of indictments against you?" "No thanks, Your Honor," said

the man despondently. But then perking up a bit, he asked, "I was just wondering, Lord, would you consider a plea of temporary insanity?"

LUKE 18:14: FOR EVERYONE THAT EXALTETH HIMSELF SHALL BE ABASED . . .

I CORINTHIANS 11:31: FOR IF WE WOULD JUDGE OURSELVES, WE SHOULD NOT BE JUDGED. [SEE II CORINTHIANS 10:18 & JAMES 2:10]

PSALM 130:3: IF THOU, LORD, SHOULDEST MARK INIQUITIES, O LORD, WHO SHALL STAND?

"But Lord," argued Agnes, "I did a lot of things for you during my life. When did you ever see me miss a Sunday? You know yourself I was the best dressed woman in church. I spent a lot of money on clothes to look nice for you.

"Was it really for me, Agnes?" the Lord asked her. "Never mind that," she remarked, "how about all those pies and cakes I donated to the church bake sale?"

"And you let everybody know that it was you who donated them, didn't you?" the Lord reminded her.

"Never mind that. Lord," Agnes went on. "How about all that money I gave you one year for charity? There was at least a thousand dollars in that envelope, in case you didn't notice." "But Agnes," the Lord told her, "you robbed from your tithe money to give to charity.

"Never mind that, Lord," she said, "look at all the time I spent serving you."

"Serving me, Agnes?" The Lord shook his head. "How many precious souls have you to lay at my feet?"

"Never mind that Lord," Agnes continued, I was busy taking care of church business."

"And while you were doing that, Agnes, did you take time to get born-again?" the Lord asked.

"Never mind that," she answered, "there's more important things to do for you that performing silly rituals."

"Agnes," the Lord said, indicting her, "You're under arrest for impersonating a believer."

MATTHEW 7:21-23: NOT EVERY ONE THAT SAITH UNTO ME, LORD, LORD, SHALL ENTER INTO THE KINGDOM OF HEAVEN; BUT HE THAT DOETH THE WILL OF MY FATHER WHICH IS IN HEAVEN. MANY WILL SAY TO ME IN THAT DAY, LORD, LORD, HAVE WE NOT PROPHESIED IN THY NAME? AND IN THY NAME CAST OUT DEVILS? AND IN THY NAME DONE MANY WONDERFUL WORKS? AND THEN WILL I PROFESS UNTO THEM, I NEVER KNEW YOU: DEPART FROM ME, YE THAT WORK INIQUITY.

On judgment day, Lois hung her head shamefully as the Lord read off an unending list of dastardly sins that, until now, had never caught up with her.

When the Lord finally reached the conclusion of her blunders he said, "I'm sorry, Lois, but I'm going to have to throw the book at you."

"I know," said the unfortunate woman, "But I just hope it isn't the thick, enlarged print, hardback red-letter edition. Those kind hurt!"

I CORINTHIANS 3:13: EVERY MAN'S WORK SHALL BE MADE MANIFEST: FOR THE DAY SHALL DECLARE IT, BECAUSE IT SHALL BE REVEALED BY FIRE; AND THE FIRE SHALL TRY EVERY MAN'S WORK OF WHAT SORT IT IS.

II CORINTHIANS 5:10: FOR WE MUST ALL APPEAR BEFORE THE JUDGMENT SEAT OF CHRIST; THAT EVERY ONE MAY RECEIVE THE THINGS *DONE* IN *HIS* BODY, ACCORDING TO THAT HE HATH DONE, WHETHER *IT BE* GOOD OR BAD. [SEE REVELATION 20:11-15]

Thought 4 the day

Heaven is lavish...

But hell is "lava"-ish

HEBREWS 9:27: AND AS IT IS APPOINTED UNTO MEN ONCE TO DIE, BUT AFTER THIS THE JUDGMENT.

ROMANS 14:12: SO THEN EVERY ONE OF US SHALL GIVE ACCOUNT OF HIMSELF TO GOD.

"Goodbye Garcia," said the Lord in parting. "By the life that you led, you have chosen your own eternal destiny."

"I thought I could get some justice up here," Garcia ranted. "But I can see that you're no different than anyone else. You discriminate against minorities!"

"Not so," replied the Lord. "And in hell you'll find that you're among the vast majority of others, like yourself, who followed the path of destruction rather than the path of the Savior.

"If that isn't a double injustice," objected Garcia. "Now you're discriminating against majorities!" Giving the Lord an evil look, he hollered "I demand a trial by an impartial jury!"

JOHN 3:16: FOR GOD SO LOVED THE WORLD, THAT HE GAVE HIS ONLY BEGOTTEN SON, THAT WHOSOEVER BELIEVETH IN HIM SHOULD NOT PERISH, BUT HAVE EVERLASTING LIFE.

ACTS 10:34-35: THEN PETER OPENED *HIS* MOUTH, AND SAID, OF A TRUTH I PERCEIVE THAT GOD IS NO RESPECTER OF PERSONS: BUT IN EVERY NATION HE THAT FEARETH HIM, AND WORKETH RIGHTEOUSNESS, IS ACCEPTED WITH HIM.

Your portion, Edith, along with so many others here today, is hell," the Lord told a woman at the judgment.

Upon hearing the solemn news, she said sarcastically, "Surely a gracious and merciful God like You will reconsider my fate."

"I'm sorry, Edith," He replied, "but your fate is permanently sealed.

"Where is the nearest pay phone?" she asked, trying to conceal her impatience and disgust.

"We don't use phones up here," the Lord told her.

"But Lord," she responded with an angry urgency in her voice, "there must be one around here somewhere!"

"What do you need one for?" the Lord asked her.

"I want to call someone for some quick cash," she replied indignantly, "in hopes that a decent and fair judge such as Yourself will allow me to post bond."

PSALM 12:3-4: THE LORD SHALL CUT OFF ALL FLATTERING LIPS, *AND* THE TONGUE THAT SPEAKETH PROUD THINGS: WHO HAVE SAID, WITH OUR TONGUE WILL WE PREVAIL; OUR LIPS *ARE* OUR OWN: WHO *IS* LORD OVER US?

EXODUS 5:2: AND PHARAOH SAID, WHO IS THE LORD, THAT I SHOULD OBEY HIS VOICE TO LET ISRAEL GO? I KNOW NOT THE LORD, NEITHER WILL I LET ISRAEL GO.

"The good news, Percival," the Lord told the young man on judgment day, "is that you're not going to hell today but . . ."

Before the Lord could finish, Percival began bouncing up and down like a beach ball. Ecstatic with joy at the prospect of spending eternity in paradise, he could barely contain himself. After a number of somersaults and back flips, the Lord finally managed to get him settled down.

"Percival," said the Lord with regret in His voice, "You didn't let me finish. True, the good news is that you're not going to hell today," he told him, "but, unfortunately, my foolish friend, the bad news is that you're going tomorrow—just as soon as the devil can find a place to put you. He says that right now there's standing room only."

ISAIAH 5:14: THEREFORE HELL HATH ENLARGED HERSELF, AND OPENED HER MOUTH WITHOUT MEASURE: AND THEIR GLORY, AND THEIR MULTITUDE, AND THEIR POMP, AND HE THAT REJOICETH, SHALL DESCEND INTO IT.

ISAIAH 14:9: HELL FROM BENEATH IS MOVED FOR THEE TO MEET *THEE* AT THY COMING.

As Kirk looked over his new surroundings in hell, his heart sank. "This isn't at all like I pictured the place," he told the devil. "I thought it would look light a wild nightclub. I figured there would be partying, dancing, wine, women, and song. Instead," he moaned, "there's nothing here but darkness, desolation, suffering, and loneliness!"

"The last laugh is on you, hey?" the devil chuckled, tormenting him.

'How long do you expect to keep me here?" Kirk cried in despair.

The devil laughed loudly and then replied, "Oh, about a half past forever!"

PROVERBS 15:24: THE WAY OF LIFE *IS ABOVE* TO THE WISE, THAT HE MAY DEPART FROM HELL BENEATH.

JOB 20:29: THIS IS THE PORTION OF A WICKED MAN FROM GOD, AND THE HERITAGE APPOINTED UNTO HIM BY GOD.

"Depart from Me" the Lord told Connie. "You have danced your way into hell."

"Will I still be able to party and get high down there?" the teen asked.

"No one makes merry down there," the Lord told her.

"Well, whatever it's like," she said, "it has to be better than home. Mom and dad were such party poopers—always making me go to church Sunday morning, Sunday night, and Wednesday, too. Sometimes they even made me go Friday night to some boring revival meeting. It was such a drag

spending all that time in church. They stole three months of my life before they quit living for You.

"You won't have to worry about being dragged to church where you're going," interrupted the Lord. "In fact, where you're headed," he told her, "there's no fellowship at all. You'll never see another human being again."

II THESSALONIANS 2:12: THAT THEY ALL MIGHT BE DAMNED WHO BELIEVED NOT THE TRUTH, BUT HAD PLEASURE IN UNRIGHTEOUSNESS.

I TIMOTHY 5:6: BUT SHE THAT LIVETH IN PLEASURE IS DEAD WHILE SHE LIVETH.

How do you want to execute judgment?" said Gabriel as he presented the Lord with the Book of Life. "There's so many people standing in line over there," he said. "Take a look for yourself." As God looked out upon the endless mass of faces, he was shocked. "Heavenly days," he exclaimed, "Did I really make that many people?"

"Have you got any suggestions where we should start, Gabriel?" he asked the angel.

"They probably should be judged in alphabetical order," replied Gabriel.

"That's as good an idea as any," agreed the Lord.

After sentencing a countless number of pathetic individuals, including the self righteous, the indifferent, and the lovers of darkness and evil, God said, "You know, Gabriel, I think we need a new cookie cutter. These batches didn't turn out like I hoped they would."

MATTHEW 23:33: YE SERPENTS, YE GENERATION OF VIPERS, HOW CAN YE ESCAPE THE DAMNATION OF HELL?

EZEKIEL 18:30 & 32: . . . REPENT, AND TURN *YOURSELVES* FROM ALL YOUR TRANSGRESSIONS; SO INIQUITY SHALL NOT BE YOUR RUIN . . .

FOR I HAVE NO PLEASURE IN THE DEATH OF HIM THAT DIETH, SAITH THE LORD GOD: WHEREFORE TURN *YOURSELVES*, AND LIVE YE.

HEBREWS 12:25: . . . FOR IF THEY ESCAPED NOT WHO REFUSED HIM THAT SPAKE ON EARTH, MUCH MORE SHALL NOT WE ESCAPE, IF WE TURN AWAY FROM HIM THAT SPEAKETH FROM HEAVEN. [SEE PROVERBS 1:24-30]

"Heaven help me!" exclaimed Mildred to her friend Ethel at the judgment. "Did you see who just got his walking papers?"

"No," replied Ethel. "It was our very own Pastor Simpson," Mildred said, stammering with amazement. "He was such a man of God," she added.

"You're right," said Ethel. "He was always preaching on the goodness of God and the brotherhood of man. And he packed so much into those fifteen minute sermons."

"And what about his tremendous burden for the souls on the French Riviera?" added Mildred in agreement. "Did you ever see such devotion to missions? Bless his heart," she added, "he was always willing to sacrifice his own family time with his wife and kids to go and minister to those dear people on the beach front."

"I suddenly have a sick feeling in the pit of my stomach," moaned Ethel. "If someone as saintly as him didn't make it," she said fearfully, "do you know who else is about to get the ax?"

MATTHEW 23:27: WOE UNTO YOU, SCRIBES AND PHARISEES HYPOCRITES! FOR YE ARE LIKE UNTO WHITED SEPULCHRES, WHICH INDEED APPEAR BEAUTIFUL OUTWARD, BUT ARE WITHIN FULL OF DEAD MEN'S BONES, AND OF ALL UNCLEANESS. EVEN SO YE ALSO OUTWARDLY APPEAR RIGHTEOUS UNTO MEN, BUT WITHIN YE ARE FULL OF HYPOCRISY AND INIQUITY.

"This certainly isn't Alaska!" exclaimed John to his wife, Lena.

"I think we're dressed rather warmly for the occasion," she responded. "All of these fur wraps are causing me to perspire."

"I agree," replied her husband removing his heavy sheepskin coat.

Later, as they were standing before the Lord in judgment, John asked, "Lord, can we expect the weather to be warm like this year 'round?"

"Well," replied the Lord, "where you're going the climate is even much warmer than this!"

REVELATION 9:2: AND HE OPENED THE BOTTOMLESS PIT; AND THERE AROSE A SMOKE OUT OF THE PIT, AS THE SMOKE OF A GREAT FURNACE.

PSALM 11:6: UPON THE WICKED HE SHALL RAIN SNARES, FIRE, AND BRIMSTONE, AND AN HORRIBLE TEMPEST: THIS SHALL BE THE PORTION OF THEIR CUP.

MARK 9:44: WHERE THEIR WORM DIETH NOT, AND THE FIRE IS NOT QUENCHED.

"Here's a basket of fruit, Lord," Sheila told the Lord at the judgment, hoping to find favor with Him.

"I'm sorry, Sheila," replied the Lord, "but I don't accept bribes, and besides there's a few ingredients missing."

Sheila looked perplexed. "But Lord, I put every kind of fruit imaginable in this basket—apples, oranges, bananas, pineapples, grapes, and so on."

"I appreciate that," said the Lord, "but I still must refuse your gift, because the fruits that are missing are the only ones for which I have an appetite."

"But what could possibly be missing?" she asked.

"To be specific," replied the Lord, "the fruits of repentance!"

MATTHEW 7:20: WHEREFORE BY THEIR FRUITS YE SHALL KNOW THEM, [SEE MATTHEW 3:10]

LUKE 3:8-9: BRING FORTH THEREFORE FRUITS WORTHY OF REPENTANCE . . . EVERY TREE THEREFORE WHICH BRINGETH NOT FORTH GOOD FRUIT IS HEWN DOWN, AND CAST INTO THE FIRE. [SEE MATTHEW 13:18-23]

HEBREWS 6:8-9: BUT THAT WHICH BEARETH THORNS AND BRIERS *IS* REJECTED, AND *IS* NIGH UNTO CURSING; WHOSE END *IS* TO BE BURNED. BUT, BELOVED, WE ARE PERSUADED BETTER THINGS OF YOU, AND THINGS THAT ACCOMPANY SALVATION . . .

LUKE 13:1-5: THERE WERE PRESENT AT THAT SEASON SOME THAT TOLD HIM OF THE GALILAEANS, WHOSE BLOOD PILATE HAD MINGLED WITH THEIR SACRIFICES. AND JESUS ANSWERING SAID UNTO THEM, SUPPOSE YE THAT THESE GALILAEANS WERE SINNERS ABOVE ALL THE GALILAEANS, BECAUSE THEY SUFFERED SUCH THINGS? I TELL YOU, NAY: BUT, EXCEPT YE RELPENT, YE SHALL ALL LIKEWISE PERISH. OR THOSE EIGHTEEN, UPON WHOM THE TOWER IN SILOAM FELL, AND SLEW THEM, THINK YE THAT THEY WERE SINNERS ABOVE ALL MEN THAT DWELT IN JERUSALEM? I TELL YOU, NAY: BUT, EXCEPT YE REPENT, YE SHALL ALL LIKEWISE PERISH.

PROVERBS 29:1: HE, THAT BEING OFTEN REPROVED HARDENETH *HIS* NECK, SHALL SUDDENLY BE DESTROYED, AND THAT WITHOUT REMEDY.

"Just give me one good reason why I should be banished to hell," Elaine protested at the judgment. "I've been an upstanding citizen all my life. You ought to see my fireplace mantle, Lord," she said. "It's loaded with all kinds of meritorious awards. I would've brought them along with me today," she added, haughtily, "if I had known you were going to be holding court here today. I was even recognized by the mayor once in honorable mention."

"I saw all your awards. Elaine," the Lord replied. "I was there when you received every one of them."

"Thank heavens," exclaimed Elaine. "Then what's all this talk about hell?"

There's one other award you received," the Lord told her. "It's the one that will keep you out of heaven."

"Which one is that?" asked Elaine, looking baffled.

"The one you were given each time you rejected Me—too afraid of what your friends might think."

"What award are you talking about?" she asked.

The Lord looked sadly at her and answered, "A coward."

REVELATION 21:8: BUT THE FEARFUL, AND UNBELIEVING, AND THE ABOMINABLE, AND MURDERERS, AND WHOREMONGERS, AND SORCERERS, AND IDOLATERS, AND ALL LIARS, ALL HAVE THEIR PART IN THE LAKE WHICH BURNETH WITH FIRE AND BRIMSTONE: WHICH IS THE SECOND DEATH. [SEE GALATIONS 2:16 & EPHESIANS 2:8-9]

HEBREWS 11:24-26: BY FAITH MOSES, WHEN HE WAS COME TO YEARS, REFUSED TO BE CALLED THE SON OF PHARAOH'S DAUGHTER; CHOOSING RATHER TO SUFFER AFFLICTION WITH THE PEOPLE OF GOD, THAN TO ENJOY THE PLEASURES OF SIN FOR A SEASON; ESTEEMING THE REPROACH OF CHRIST GREATER RICHES THAN THE TREASURES IN EGYPT: FOR HE HAD RESPECT UNTO THE RECOMPENCE OF THE REWARD.

"Am I getting a blue ribbon for good behavior?" Robert asked the Lord on judgment day.

"No," answered the Lord, shaking his head.

"Am I getting the red carpet treatment for keeping the ten commandments?" Robert continued.

"No," replied the Lord, again shaking his head.

"Am I getting a fresh coat of yellow paint for my halo?" he persisted.

"I'm afraid not," answered the Lord.

"Then what am I getting?" Robert joked. "A white wash for my crimson sins?"

"What you're getting," answered the Lord, "is a black mark throughout all eternity."

AMOS 5:18: WOE UNTO YOU THAT DESIRE THE DAY OF THE LORD! TO WHAT END IS IT FOR YOU? THE DAY OF THE LORD IS DARKNESS, AND NOT LIGHT.

MATTHEW 13:49-50: SO SHALL IT BE AT THE END OF THE WORLD: THE ANGELS SHALL COME FORTH, AND SEVER THE WICKED FROM AMONG THE JUST, AND SHALL CAST THEM INTO THE FURNANCE OF FIRE: THERE SHALL BE WAILING AND GNASHING OF TEETH. [SEE MATTHEW 13:41-42 & MARK 9:44]

"I've been in the garbage business all my life," Nick told the Lord on judgment day. "I thought things would change when I got up here, and now here you are, Lord, giving me more of the same."

"You spent your days picking up other people's garbage, Nick," the Lord told him, "but you failed to get rid of your own."

"Does this mean I'll be picking up trash cans in hell?" Nick asked the Lord.

"Not unless you can work in the dark," replied the Lord.

MATTHEW 8:12: BUT THE CHILDREN OF THE KINGDOM SHALL BE CAST OUT INTO OUTER DARKNESS: THERE SHALL BE WEEPING AND GNASHING OF TEETH.

"So long, Theodore," the Lord said at the judgment "I'm sorry it had to turn out this way."

"Then there's nothing I can do to change your mind, Lord?" Theodore asked wistfully.

"Nothing," replied the Lord. "It's too late for that."

"I never had time to read the Bible, Lord," Theodore said. "Is there anything in there about hell?"

"More than you can imagine," answered the Lord.

"Putting it in the simplest terms," Theodore asked, "how would you describe it?"

"Like a major heat wave," the Lord told him."

LUKE 16:19-30: THERE WAS A CERTAIN RICH MAN, WHICH WAS CLOTHED IN PURPLE AND FINE LINEN, AND FARED SUMPTUOUSLY EVERY DAY: AND THERE WAS A CERTAIN BEGGAR NAMED LAZARUS, WHICH WAS LAID AT HIS GATE, FULL OF SORES, AND DESIRING TO BE FED WITH THE CRUMBS WHICH FELL FROM THE RICH MAN'S TABLE: MOREOVER THE DOGS CAME AND LICKED HIS SORES. AND IT CAME TO PASS, THAT THE BEGGAR DIED, AND WAS CARRIED BY THE ANGELS INTO ABRAHAM'S BOSOM: THE RICH MAN ALSO DIED, AND WAS BURIED; AND IN HELL HE LIFT UP HIS EYES, BEING IN TORMENTS, AND SEETH ABRAHAM AFAR OFF, AND LAZARUS IN HIS BOSOM. AND HE CRIED AND SAID, FATHER ABRAHAM, HAVE MERCY ON ME, AND SEND LAZARUS, THAT HE MAY DIP THE TIP OF HIS FINGER IN WATER, AND COOL MY TONGUE; FOR I AM TORMENTED IN THIS FLAME. BUT ABRAHAM SAID, SON, REMEMBER THAT HOU IN THY LIFETIME RECEIVEDST THY GOOD THINGS, AND LIKEWISE LAZARUS EVIL THINGS: BUT NOW HE IS COMFORTED, AND THOU ART TORMENTED. AND BESIDE ALL THIS, BETWEEN US AND YOU THERE IS A GREAT GULF FIXED: SO THAT THEY WHICH WOULD PASS FROM HENCE TO YOU CANNOT; NEITHERCAN THEY PASS TO US, THAT *WOULD COME* FROM THENCE. THEN SAID HE, I PRAY THEE THEREFORE, FATHER, THAT THOU WOULDEST SEND HIM TO MY FATHER'S HOUSE: FOR I HAVE FIVE BRETHREN; THAT HE MAY TESTIFY UNTO THEM, LEST THEY ALSO COME INTO THIS PLACE OF

TORMENT. ABRAHAM SAITH UNTO HIM, THEY HAVE MOSES AND THE PROPHETS; LET THEM HEAR THEM. ANDHE SAID, NAY, FATHER ABRAHAM: BUT IF ONE WENT UNTO THEM FROM THE DEAD, THEY WILL REPRENT. AND HE SAID UNTO HIM, IF THEY HEAR NOT MOSES AND THE PROPHETS, NEITHER WILL THEY BE PERSUADED, THOUGH ONE ROSE FROM THE DEAD.

"I'm sorry, Bertha, I gave you every opportunity to repent,' said the Lord frowning. "Over and over again I chastised you, hoping that it would cause you to change your direction. But the correction you endured only phased you for the moment and you went back to your worldly ways."

Bertha stood silently listening to the Lord. "I allowed a lot of rain to come into your life," the Lord told her, "hoping that in your trials you would commit yourself unto Me and be saved. But," He continued, "as soon as you were delivered from your circumstances, you chose to ignore the eternal salvation I wanted to give you. And now, tragically," the Lord said, "after a life of pain and sorrow, I must send you to an eternity of suffering."

With remorse, Bertha looked up at the Lord and told Him tearfully in parting, "I must be a glutton for punishment."

PSALM 50:22: NOW CONSIDER THIS, YE THAT FORGET GOD, LEST I TEAR *YOU* IN PIECES, AND *THERE BE* NONE TO DELIVER.

JEREMIAH 2:32: . . . MY PEOPLE HAVE FORGOTTEN ME DAYS WITHOUT NUMBER.

"I'm not going to stand here and pretend I've never committed a sin," John told the Lord at the judgment. "Sure, I've had my days where I missed the mark. Yes," he continued, "there were times of carnality, times of animosity, times of vanity, times of profanity, times of obscenity, times of vulgarity and times of audacity."

"And there were times of bigamy and bigotry, interrupted the Lord. "And times of thievery . . . to name a few. "In fact, You made no attempt to live for Me at all after you confessed me as Lord and repented of your sins. Your prayer was only from the lips and not from the heart."

"But whose keeping track of a few earthly sins?" John asked, trying to make light of the situation.

"Just me," answered the Lord.

ROMANS 6:1-2: WHAT SHALL WE SAY THEN? SHALL WE CONTINUE IN SIN, THAT GRACE MAY ABOUND? GOD FORBID. HOW SHALL WE, THAT ARE DEAD TO SIN, LIVE ANY LONGER THEREIN?

HEBREWS 3:12 & 14: TAKE HEED, BRETHREN, LEST THERE BE IN ANY OF YOU AN EVIL HEART OF UNBELIEF, IN DEPARTING FROM THE LIVING GOD . . . FOR WE ARE MADE PARTAKERS OF CHRIST, IF WE HOLD THE BEGINNING OF OUR CONFIDENCE STEDFAST UNTO THE END; [SEE HEBREWS 3:6]

HEBREWS 10:26-29: FOR IF WE SIN WILFULLY AFTER THAT WE HAVE RECEIVED THE KNOWLEDGE OF THE TRUTH, THERE REMAINETH NO MORE SACRIFICE FOR SINS, BUT A CERTAIN FEARFUL LOOKING FOR OF JUDGMENT AND FIERY INDIGNATION, WHICH SHALL DEVOUR THE ADVERSARIES. HE THAT DESPISED MOSES' LAW DIED WITHOUT MERCY UNDER TWO OR THREE WITNESSES: OF HOW MUCH SORER PUNISHMENT, SUPPOSE YE, SHALL HE BE THOUGHT WORTHY, WHO HATH TRODDEN UNDER FOOT THE SON OF GOD, AND HATH COUNTED THE BLOOD OF THE COVENANT, WHEREWITH HE WAS SANCTIFIED, AN UNHOLY THING, AND HATH DONE DESPITE UNTO THE SPIRIT OF GRACE?

I JOHN 2:3-4: AND HEREBY WE DO KNOW THAT WE KNOW HIM, IF WE KEEP HIS COMMANDMENTS. HE THAT SAITH, I KNOW HIM, AND KEEPETH NOT HIS COMMANDMENTS, IS A LIAR, AND THE TRUTH IS NOT IN HIM. [SEE EZEKIEL 18:26-28 & REVELATION 20:12]

PSALM 5:4: FOR THOU ART NOT A GOD THAT HATH PLEASURE IN WICKEDNESS: NEITHER SHALL EVIL DWELL WITH THEE;

REVELATION 21:27: AND THERE SHALL IN NO WISE ENTER INTO IT [HEAVEN] ANY THING THAT DEFILETH, NEITHER *WHATSOEVER* WORKETH ABOMINATION, OR *MAKETH* A LIE: BUT THEY WHICH ARE WRITTEN IN THE LAMB'S BOOK OF LIFE.

As Greta stood in line with her daughter Bridgette, waiting to be judged, her head was pounding from all of the stress and anxiety. "I sure wish I had something for this headache," she told her daughter. "And just look at these hives. I'm all broken out," she said, "and the nearest doctor is a million light years away."

"Oh mom," her daughter replied, "you're always grumbling about something."

"Bridgette, don't you know what's going on up here?" she asked her. "This is the day of reckoning, honey—the moment we've been dreading all of our lives and there you are," she scolded, "carrying on as if we were at some picnic."

"Maybe you've been dreading it, mother," replied Bridgette casually, "but I've never even given it a second thought."

MATTHEW 24:37-39: BUT AS THE DAYS OF NOE [NOAH] *WERE*, SO SHALL ALSO THE COMING OF THE SON OF MAN BE. FOR AS IN THE DAYS THAT WERE BEFORE THE FLOOD THEY WERE EATING AND DRINKING, MARRYING AND GIVING IN MARRIAGE, UNTIL THE DAY THAT NOE [NOAH] ENTERED INTO THE ARK, AND KNEW NOT UNTIL THE FLOOD CAME, AND TOOK THEM ALL AWAY; SO SHALL ALSO THE COMING OF THE SON OF MAN BE.

"This is it—the grand finale!" exclaimed Maria, a former stage actress. Her friend, Ginger, was standing beside her at the judgment.

"Do I look okay?" Maria asked. "I want to put my best foot forward when the Lord calls my name. I've been rehearsing all my lines" she said, "so I'll know exactly what to say."

"And just what kind of an award winning act are you going to put on?" Ginger asked her. "And do you really think you can pull the wool over God's eyes?"

"It'll be comparable to a box office hit!" Maria exclaimed.

"But what if the Lord isn't impressed with your performance," she remarked. "You realize it could be 'curtains' for you."

"Well," said Maria, "Let's hope that doesn't happen, but if it does," she told Ginger, "then, unfortunately, I may have the lead role throughout all eternity in a horror movie.

PSALM 73:19: HOW ARE THEY BROUGHT INTO DESOLATION, AS IN A MOMENT! THEY ARE UTTERLY CONSUMED WITH TERRORS.

"I never knew there were this many people in the world," Frank said to Steve, his brother, in amazement. Just look at the line-up of souls waiting to be judged by God.'

"Do you think we'll make it, Frank?" his brother asked.

"I don't know, Steve," he answered. "We pulled some real capers in our day. Do you recall," he asked, "that time we parked mom's brand new car down the street and then told her it was stolen?"

"I sure do," answered Steve. "It was pretty funny," he said, "'til our insurance agent pulled up and said he had spotted a tow truck hauling it away with three or four tickets on it."

"Do you also remember the time we greased the pastor's steering wheel after washing and waxing his car?" asked Frank. "He was chasing us around like a tiger hunting prey."

"Yah," laughed Steve, reminiscing. "That was so hilarious," he exclaimed, "until, of course, the ambulance arrived and took him to the intensive care unit with that sudden heart attack!"

"The more I think about these things," Frank said nervously, "I believe our only hope is that the Lord develops amnesia by the time we get up there."

GALATIONS 6: 7-8: BE NOT DECEIVED; GOD IS NOT MOCKED: FOR WHATSOEVER A MAN SOWETH, THAT SHALL HE ALSO REAP. FOR HE THAT SOWETH TO HIS FLESH SHALL OF THE FLESH REAP CORRUPTION; BUT HE THAT SOWETH TO THE SPIRIT SHALL OF THE SPIRIT REAP LIFE EVERLASTING.

ROMANS 6:11-13: LIKEWISE RECKON YE ALSO YOURSELVES TO BE DEAD INDEED UNTO SIN, BUT ALIVE UNTO GOD THROUGH JESUS CHRIST OUR LORD. LET NOT SIN THEREFORE REIGN IN YOUR MORTAL BODY, THAT YE SHOULD OBEY IT IN THE LUSTS THEREOF. NEITHER YIELD YE YOUR MEMBERS *AS* INSTRUMENTS OF UNRIGHTEOUSNESS UNTO SIN: BUT YIELD YOURSELVES UNTO GOD, AS THOSE THAT ARE ALIVE FROM THE DEAD, AND YOUR MEMBERS *AS* INSTRUMENTS OF RIGHTEOUSNESS UNTO GOD.

JUDE 1:21: KEEP YOURSELVES IN THE LOVE OF GOD, LOOKING FOR THE MERCY OF OUR LORD JESUS CHRIST UNTO ETERNAL LIFE.

"Please raise your right hand," the angel told Patrick. "Do you swear to tell the truth, the whole truth, and nothing but the truth, so help you God?"

Patrick stood mute for a moment. He didn't know whether to run or take his chances. He hoped the Lord would overlook the sins of his former earthly life. After he had contemplated the situation for a few more seconds, he responded, "I'll be happy to tell the truth, Lord, but," he said fearfully, "in the best interests of my soul, could I give it to you with a grain of salt?"

I JOHN 2:28: AND NOW, LITTLE CHILDREN, ABIDE IN HIM; THAT, WHEN HE SHALL APPEAR, WE MAY HAVE CONFIDENCE, AND NOT BE ASHAMED BEFORE HIM AT HIS COMING.

PSALM 15:1-3: LORD, WHO SHALL ABIDE IN THY TABERNACLE? WHO SHALL DWELL IN THY HOLY HILL? HE THAT WALKETH UPRIGHTLY,

AND WORKETH RIGHTEOUSNESS, AND SPEAKETH THE TRUTH IN HIS HEART. *HE THAT* BACKBITETH NOT WITH HIS TONGUE, NOR DOETH EVIL TGO HIS NEIGHBOUR [NEIGHBOR], NOR TAKETH UP A REPROACH AGAINST HIS NEIGHBOUR [NEIGHBOR].

"It's going to be a stifling hot day in you-know-where," said Lenny to his friend, Jay, while they were waiting to be transported to the lake of fire. "Do you think the Lord will leave us there long?"

"Only throughout eternity," his friend replied looking panicky.

"I've got this canteen around my neck," Lenny said. "It's full of water." He lifted the strap over his head and handed it to Jay. "Would you like a drink," he asked. "As they say—'one for the road.'"

PSALM 9:17: THE WICKED SHALL BE TURNED INTO HELL . . . [SEE LUKE 16:19-30]

"But Lord, you can't do this to me!" shrieked Vicky. "I was a good person and my father was a clergyman who spent a lot of time in the pulpit.

"And my uncle, well, just ask anyone—he was a pillar of the church.

"And my sister, Lord, you know, yourself, she spent her whole life as a missionary in Africa.

"And my brother, Lord, he had the voice of an angel—a vocalist in the choir."

"And you, Vicky," replied the Lord. 'What were you—but a pagan in a pew!"

GALATIONS 2:16: . . . FOR BY THE WORKS OF THE LAW SHALL NO FLESH BE JUSTIFIED.

TITUS 3:5: NOT BY WORKS OF RIGHTEOUSNESS WHICH WE HAVE DONE, BUT ACCORDING TO HIS MERCY HE SAVED US, BY THE

WASHING OF REGENERATION, AND RENEWING OF THE HOLY GHOST;

EPHESIANS 2:8-9: FOR BY GRACE ARE YE SAVED THROUGH FAITH; AND THAT NOT OF YOURSELVES: *IT IS* THE GIFT OF GOD: NOT OF WORKS, LEST ANY MAN SHOULD BOAST.

"Time to bail out!" shouted the angel of the Lord to those who had been doomed to hell. "When you've put your parachutes on, line up single file and prepare to jump.

"Why do we need parachutes?" asked one of those who had been condemned.

"Due to the enormous flames, there's no airport runway or landing facilities in hell," replied the angel.

"Then am I to understand we'll be parachuting into hell without even so much as a single flying lesson?" Pete, one of the poor, unfortunate souls asked.

"It wouldn't make a difference," replied the angel. "Your eternal destiny is sealed."

"Then am I also to understand that this is not a round trip ticket?" Pete again questioned the angel.

"Hell is just a one-way excursion," came the reply. "But there must be some great attraction because there's a very huge crowd already there."

MATTHEW 7:13-14: ENTER YE IN AT THE STRAIT GATE: FOR WIDE *IS* THE GATE, AND BROAD *IS* THE WAY, THAT LEADETH TO DESTRUCTION AND MANY THERE BE WHICH GO IN THEREAT: BECAUSE STRAIT *IS* THE GATE, AND NARROW *IS* THE WAY, WHICH LEADETH UNTO LIFE, AND FEW THERE BE THAT FIND IT.

While they were waiting their turn to stand before the Lord in judgment, James and his wife, Dawn, watched as soul after soul was sentenced to an eternity in hell.

"Depart from me, you workers of iniquity," God said one by one to the sinners who had not been cleansed by His blood. "Depart into everlasting darkness and shame, you who have loved iniquity more than Me."

"This looks pretty serious," said James, working up a sweat. "I thought the Lord came down on me awfully hard during my lifetime," he shuddered, "but that's nothing compared to this!"

"I know what you mean," his wife replied. After watching all these souls get zapped into eternity," she said, trembling, "don't tell me that lightning never strikes twice in the same place!"

PSALM 18:13-14: THE LORD ALSO THUNDERED IN THE HEAVENS, AND THE HIGHEST GAVE HIS VOICE; HAIL *STONES* AND COALS OF FIRE. YEA, HE SENT OUT HIS ARROWS, AND SCATTERED THEM; AND HE SHOT OUT LIGHTNINGS, AND DISCOMFITED THEM . . .

HEBREWS 12:29: FOR OUR GOD *IS* A CONSUMING FIRE.

"What am I doing here?" asked Ted, a famous baseball player, stunned and confused by his new surroundings. "How did I get here?" He scratched his forehead and looked around trying to comprehend what had happened. "Where am I am?" he asked. "Just seconds ago I was making a home run and everyone was applauding me. I'm in the big leagues, you know."

"I'm the Lord," came the reply. "And you might say that this is the big leagues also. And like yourself," He said, "we play for keeps. You spent your life seeking fame and fortune," the Lord told him. You placed your career above everything—even your own soul.

"Up here," the Lord told him, "we don't give applause for fame or fortune, but rather for humility and a contrite spirit. But to put it in a language that you'll understand, Ted," the Lord declared, "Three strikes 'n you're out."

I CORINTHIANS 9:24-27: KNOW YE NOT THAT THEY WHICH RUN IN A RACE RUN ALL, BUT ONE RECEIVETH THE PRIZE? SO RUN, THAT YE MAY OBTAIN. AND EVERY MAN THAT STRIVETH FOR THE MASTERY IS TEMPERATE IN ALL THINGS. NOW THEY *DO IT* TO OBTAIN A CORRUPTIBLE CROWN; BUT WE AN INCORRUPTIBLE. I THEREFORE SO RUN, NOT AS UNCERTAINLY; SO FIGHT I, NOT AS ONE THAT BEATETH THE AIR: BUT I KEEP UNDER MY BODY, AND BRING *IT* IN SUBJECTION: LEST THAT BY ANY MEANS, WHEN I HAVE PREACHED TO OTHERS, I MYSELF SHOULD BE A CASTAWAY.

II CORINTHIANS 10:5: CASTING DOWN IMAGINATIONS, AND EVERY HIGH THING THAT EXALTETH ITSELF AGAINST THE KNOWLEDGE OF GOD, AND BRINGING INTO CAPTIVITY EVERY THOUGHT TO THE OBEDIENCE OF CHRIST.

PHILIPPIANS 3:14: I PRESS TOWARD THE MARK FOR THE PRIZE OF THE HIGH CALLING OF GOD IN CHRIST JESUS.

"Um . . . pardon me, Lord," Jack asked, "but did I understand you right? Did you say 'doomed to hell?'"

"That's right," answered the Lord. "It's undeniable that your record with the fire department is excellent and highly commendable. Nevertheless," the Lord told him, "we have no need for firefighters up here, unless, of course, they have been redeemed by the blood of the Lamb—Jesus Christ.

By this time, Jack was smoldering. "I'm not worried. I've been fighting flames for over twenty years and with great expertise I might add," he retorted.

"That's good, Jack," the Lord told him. "You're sure to get a lot of overtime where you're going," He said.

MARK 9:43: AND IF THY HAND OFFEND THEE, CUT IT OFF: IT IS BETTER FOR THEE TO ENTER INTO LIFE MAIMED, THAN HAVING TWO HANDS TO GO INTO HELL, INTO THE FIRE THAT NEVER SHALL BE QUENCHED:

"I tried to tell you," the Lord said to Martin when He had finished judging his works. "But you wouldn't listen.

Martin hung his head, not saying a word.

"Day after day of your earthly life," continued the Lord, 'I kept trying to impress on your mind the eternal consequences of your actions, but you ignored all the warnings I gave you. You would not heed the advice of those I sent to you. They warned you," he said, "over and over again that this day was coming."

Tears began to stream down Martin's face as he looked over at the angels who were waiting to take him away.

"For over fifty years you were given chance after chance to receive My grace and mercy but you chose instead to eat, drink, and be merry. And now," the Lord told him, "with a sad heart I must tell you that the 'party is over.'"

"I know things aren't looking good for me," Martin told the Lord sadly, "but if you change your mind, I guess you'll know where to find me. Right now I don't think it's going to be heaven!"

ACTS 28:24: AND SOME BELIEVED THE THINGS WHICH WERE SPOKEN, AND SOME BELIEVED NOT.

ROMANS 1:28 & 32: AND EVEN AS THEY DID NOT LIKE TO RETAIN GOD IN *THEIR* KNOWLEDGE, GOD GAVE THEM OVER TO A REPROBATE MIND, TO DO THOSE THINGS WHICH ARE NOT CONVENIENT . . .

WHO KNOWING THE JUDGMENT OF GOD, THAT THEY WHICH COMMIT SUCH THINGS ARE WORTHY OF DEATH, NOT ONLY DO THE SAME, BUT HAVE PLEASURE IN THEM THAT DO THEM.

"Are you saved and ready to meet Jesus?" Mary asked the young man standing behind her on judgment day.

"Yes, I think so," he replied looking somewhat apprehensive. "I've given my life to the Lord, asked forgiveness for my sins, and," he added, "Jesus is living in my heart."

"Then why all the frowning and doubting?" Mary asked.

The young man looked up at her fearfully and remarked, "There's just one problem," he said, "I'm a compulsive liar."

TITUS 2:6-9: YOUNG MEN LIKEWISE EXHORT TO BE SOBER MINDED. IN ALL THINGS SHEWING THYSELF A PATTERN OF GOOD WORKS: IN DOCTRINE *SHEWING* UNCORRUPTNESS, GRAVITY, SINCERITY, SOUND SPEECH, THAT CANNOT BE CONDEMNED; THAT HE THAT IS OF THE CONTRARY PART MAY BE ASHAMED, HAVING NO EVIL THING TO SAY OF YOU.

JAMES 2:19-20: THOU BELIEVEST THAT THERE IS ONE GOD; THOU DOEST WELL: THE DEVILS ALSO BELIEVE, AND TREMBLE. BUT WILT THOU KNOW, O VAIN MAN, THAT FAITH WITHOUT WORKS IS DEAD?

Craig stood nervously biting his fingernails as the Lord enumerated each diabolical deed.

"I declare," exclaimed Craig, "I had no idea I was such a rascal!" he told the Lord. "Did you get to the part yet where I became a boy scout?"

"Yes," replied the Lord. "But I don't find a single instance of you helping a little old lady across the street. Instead, if I remember correctly," He said, "you even tripped a few widows while swiping their handbags. Even worse," the Lord continued, "you snatched one elderly lady's dentures after they flew out of her mouth during her fall. And you laughed as you ran down the street with them."

"I forgot about all that stuff," said Craig. "I guess I was more of a hellion than I remember!" "But did you get to the part, Lord," he asked, "where I joined the church youth group? I got a gold star for attendance, you know."

"Only because you threatened to spray paint the teacher's new car if she didn't give it to you," replied the Lord.

Oh . . . er . . . I forgot about that," Craig said, realizing his deeds had caught up with him. "Lord," he pleaded, "doesn't a condemned man get a last request?"

"What is it?" the Lord asked him.

Craig looked up at the Lord. "How about a second chance?" he begged.

PROVERBS 29:1: HE, THAT BEING OFTEN REPROVED HARDENETH *HIS* NECK, SHALL SUDDENLY BE DESTROYED, AND THAT WITHOUT REMEDY.

"Mom," asked her daughter Brenda, "What happens if you don't pay your gas bill?

"Well, you get a shut off notice?" she replied.

"What happens is you don't pay your electric bill? She asked.

"Well, it's like the gas company, honey," she told her daughter. "You get a shut off notice."

"Mom," Brenda asked, "what happens if you don't pay your phone bill?

"Well, dear," she answered, "it's like the gas and electric company. You get a shut off notice."

Satisfied with her mother's answers, Brenda walked away, but only minutes later she returned. "Mom," she said, 'I've just got one more question."

"What is it?" her mother asked. "What happens if you don't pay your tithe?"

"Well," said her mother, thinking a moment, "Its kind of like the gas and electric company, except that instead of a shut off notice, God let's you slide until eternity and then He gives you a shove off notice."

MALACHI 3:8-11: WILL A MAN ROB GOD? YET YE HAVE ROBBED ME. BUT YE SAY, WHEREIN HAVE WE ROBBED THEE? IN TITHES AND OFFERINGS. YE *ARE* CURSED WITH A CURSE: FOR YE HAVE ROBBED ME, *EVEN* THIS WHOLE NATION. BRING YE ALL THE TITHES INTO THE STOREHOUSE, THAT THERE MAY BE MEAT IN MINE HOUSE, AND PROVE ME NOW HEREWITH, SAITH THE LORD OF HOSTS, IF I WILL NOT OPEN YOU THE WINDOWS OF HEAVEN, AND POUR YOU OUT A BLESSING, THAT *THERE SHALL NOT BE ROOM* ENOUGH *TO RECEIVE IT.* AND I WILL REBUKE THE DEVOURER FOR YOUR SAKES, AND HE SHALL NOT DESTROY THE FRUITS OF YOUR GROUND; NEITHER SHALL YOUR VINE CAST HER FRUIT BEFORE THE TIME IN THE FIELD, SAITH THE LORD OF HOSTS. [SEE GENESIS 28:22]

PROVERBS 3:9-10: HONOUR [HONOR] THE LORD WITH THY SUBSTANCE, AND WITH THE FIRSTFRUITS OF ALL THINE INCREASE:

"It is with a heavy heart, Christine, that I must sentence you to hell for all eternity," said the Lord to the teenage girl.

"Is this some kind of April fool's joke?" she asked, laughing nervously.

"No, I'm afraid not," replied the Lord ever so solemnly. "The time for jesting is over," he continued. "Each time the Holy Spirit called you to repentance, you dismissed him from your mind with ridicule and haughty laughter. The gift of salvation was not worthy of your time or consideration. Now you must pay the consequences."

"Maybe, so," replied Christine. "But my parents are not going to like it one bit if I'm not back by dark."

PROVERBS 10:28 & 30: THE HOPE OF THE RIGHTEOUS *SHALL BE* GLADNESS: BUT THE EXPECTATION OF THE WICKED SHALL PERISH . . . THE RIGHTEOUS SHALL NEVER BE REMOVED: BUT THE WICKED SHALL NOT INHABIT THE EARTH.

"Your new residence will be hell," the Lord told Milton.

"You will be sent there momentarily, but first I want to share some parting thoughts with you." With eyes of sorrow, the Lord told him of all the dreams that he had wanted so much to materialize for him. "I wanted so much to give you a glorious mansion, prepared just for you. I dreamed of us walking down streets of gold together, side by side, in fellowship. I longed to show you rivers of crystal clear water. But, Milton," the Lord said sadly, "you shunned all that I would have given you for a few fleeting years of sinful pleasure."

"Listen, Lord," just skip the mansion," said Milton. "I'm not used to living 'high on the hog' anyway. As for hell, I appreciate the free room and board," he told Him, "but if it's all the same to you, I prefer a cooler climate.

I CORINTHIANS 6:9-11: KNOW YE NOT THAT UNRIGHTEOUS SHALL NOT INHERIT THE KINGDOM OF GOD? BE NOT DECEIVED: NEITHER FORNICATORS, NOR IDOLATORS, NOR ADULTERERS, NOR EFFEMINATE, NOR ABUSERS OF THEMSELVES WITH MANKIND, NOR THIEVES. NOR COVETOUS, NOR DRUNKARDS, NOR REVILERS, NOR EXTORTIONERS, SHALL INHERIT THE KINGDOM OF GOD.

"Hey, what kind of raw deal is this?" objected Norman, a bearded gentleman, after the Lord sentenced him to eternal punishment,. "I may not be affluent enough to suit you, but I'm proud of the forty years I put in at the factory," he said. "I did an honest day's work for an honest day's pay."

"You're right Norman," answered the Lord. "You put forty years in at that factory, but how many years did you invest in a relationship with Me? You see, Norman," continued the Lord, "you spent a lot of time on the job—but none on Me. You never took the time to invite me into your life."

Not comprehending anything that was said to him, he snarled, "What is it, Lord? Have you got something against blue collar workers?"

"No," said the Lord. "But I do have something against wayward weasels."

JOHN 1:12: BUT AS MANY AS RECEIVED HIM, TO THEM GAVE HE POWER TO BECOME THE SONS OF GOD, *EVEN* TO THEM THAT BELIEVE ON HIS NAME:

JOHN 6:37: . . . HIM THAT COMETH TO ME I WILL IN NO WISE CAST OUT.

I TIMOTHY 2:3-6: FOR THIS IS GOOD AND ACCEPTABLE IN THE SIGHT OF GOD OUR SAVIOUR [SAVIOR]; WHO WILL HAVE ALL MEN TO BE SAVED, AND TO COME UNTO THE KNOWLEDGE OF THE TRUTH. FOR THERE IS ONE GOD, AND ONE MEDIATOR BETWEEN GOD AND MEN, THE MAN CHRIST JESUS; WHO GAVE HIMSELF A RANSOM FOR ALL . . . [SEE REVELATION 3:20 & ROMANS 1:16 & ROMANS 5:18

HOLIDAY HILARITY

A weekly church singles group gathered one evening to prepare for their annual Thanksgiving celebration. An invitation for turkey dinner, fellowship, and a drama presentation were generously extended to all the singles, home less, and abandoned individuals.

"We need a new title for this year's program," announced Helen, a middle aged spinster and leader of the group. Has anyone prayerfully considered the theme for this Thanksgiving celebration?

A visiting teenage granddaughter of one of the members was present that evening. Eager to participate, and without hesitation, she made her suggestion. "You are what you eat," she said.

COLOSSIANS 4:6: LET YOUR SPEECH BE ALWAY WITH GRACE, SEASONED WITH SALT, THAT YE MAY KNOW HOW YE OUGHT TO ANSWER EVERY MAN.

Trudy was a woman who only attended church on major holidays. "Sunday is my only day off," she said, trying to justify herself to her friend, Marge. "There's so much to catch up on when Sunday rolls around," she said, "and after all, cleanliness is next to godliness. Lord knows," she added, "I just don't have time to squeeze God in. And, besides," she said, "He's not there anyway. He wouldn't even notice my absence!"

Marge sat dumbfounded by all of Trudy's remarks. "But Trudy," just because you don't see Him is no reason to say He's not there," she argued. "His presence can be felt within."

"Well, that may be the case," said Trudy, "but I'm not going. That's one way I can avoid the Christmas rush of sinners."

I CHRONICLES 28:9: . . . IF THOU SEEK HIM, HE WILL BE FOUND OF THEE; BUT IF THOU FORSAKE HIM, HE WILL CAST THEE OFF FOR EVER.

ACTS 26:28: THEN [KING] AGRIPPA SAID UNTO PAUL, ALMOST THOU PERSUADEST ME TO BE A CHRISTIAN.

HEBREWS 2:3: HOW SHALL WE ESCAPE, IF WE NEGLECT SO GREAT SALVATION . . .

JOHN 8:24: . . . YE SHALL DIE IN YOUR SINS: FOR IF YE BELIEVE NOT THAT I AM *HE*, YE SHALL DIE IN YOUR SINS.

JOHN 5:40: AND YE WILL NOT COME TO ME, THAT YE MIGHT HAVE LIFE. [SEE JOHN 6:63 & 68-69; & JOHN 14:6]

Every Christmas, as is fitting for the occasion, Yvonne would get out her holy nativity scene to display on her fireplace mantle.

"I think this set has seen its better days," she remarked to her friend, Molly, showing her the assortment of damaged figurines, including a three-legged camel with a cracked hump, a wise man whose gift had been extracted several Christmases ago by her mischievous son. There were also some other badly maimed characters among which was Joseph whose left arm was amputated, the mother Mary whose blessed face had been victimized by a black marker, and two "Siamese" wise men who had been permanently joined together by a piece of gooey bubblegum that had since hardened like a fossil.

Nevertheless, in spite of their 'minor' handicaps, Yvonne reverently placed each figurine into its proper place within the stable.

"Where's the baby Jesus?" asked Molly, observing that the most important character—the babe wrapped in swaddling clothes—the Savior of the world was missing and most conspicuous by his absence!

"Well," replied Yvonne, "Last Christmas my little Tommy swiped him from the stable. The baby Jesus spent more time in the back of his toy truck,"

she said, "than he ever did in the manger and," she added, "wherever they drove off to, we haven't been able to find him since!"

MATTHEW 1:23: BEHOLD, A VIRGIN SHALL BE WITH CHILD, AND SHALL BRING FORTH A SON, AND THEY SHALL CALL HIS NAME EMMANUEL, WHICH BEING INTERPRETED IS, GOD WITH US.

Due to an unexpected layoff, Jack, a family man with a wife and five children to feed, had to immediately find work elsewhere. It was only after weeks of searching that he finally landed a steady job which, unfortunately, was nearly a thousand miles from home.

Living out of state, with finances tight and a busy work schedule to keep, it was impossible for Jack to fly home and see his family.

His wife, Anne, had already put their home up for sale, but with five very active and mischievous children things seemed to need continuous repair. The holes the children had dug in the yard and the black marker etchings on the walls were not among its best selling features.

After nearly a year of separation from their dad, the children were longing to see their father and missing him very much. "Could we surprise daddy and get him something special for Christmas?" they asked their mother as the Christmas holiday drew near.

"Of course," replied their mother with delight. "What did you have in mind?" Smiling from ear to ear, they all chirped in unison, "How about a new baby brother or sister to add to his collection?"

JAMES 2:17: EVEN SO FAITH, IF IT HATH NOT WORKS, IS DEAD, BEING ALONE.

With Mother's Day soon approaching, Shirley was reminding her son how much she liked flowers.

On the way to church one morning, he was scouting for a florist so that, when the time came, he wouldn't have to look for one at the last minute.

As they were driving along, he spotted a flower shop. In the window a sign read, MUMS-$3.99 A DOZEN.

Known for his quick wit, her son commented, "Wow, mom, you gals are getting cheaper every year. I can get a whole bunch of you for under five bucks!"

I TIMOTHY 5:10: WELL REPORTED OF FOR GOOD WORKS; IF SHE HAVE BROUGHT UP CHILDREN, IF SHE HAVE LODGED STRANGERS, IF SHE HAVE [HAS] WASHED THE SAINTS' FEET, IF SHE HAVE RELIEVED THE AFFLICTED, IF SHE HAVE [HAS] DILIGENTLY FOLLOWED EVERY GOOD WORK. [SEE PROVERBS 31:10-31; LUKE 1:38; & ACTS 9:36; LUKE 2:37

Kim was excited by all the Christmas gifts under the tree. She shouted for joy when her mother and father told her that all of the big boxes were hers.

"All of these are mine?" she asked, squealing with delight. "They sure are, sweetie," her father told her happily. "You can open two of them on Christmas eve and the rest of them on Christmas day."

"Now don't forget to thank God for his goodness toward us," her mother said lovingly.

"I won't! I won't! I promise!" she said excitedly. "I can't wait to open these boxes and see what's inside! I've been praying for a new bike," she said, "and that talking baby doll I showed you."

That night she kneeled beside her bed to pray. Trying to be earnest, she remembered what she thought were the words of her pastor and began repeating them:' Heavenly Father, we thank thee for thy 'presents' among us and for thy 'mountain full' of gifts that we are about to receive. Amen."

PSALMS 16:11: . . . IN THY PRESENCE IS FULNESS OF JOY; AT THY RIGHT HAND THERE ARE PLEASURES FOR EVERMORE.

Pastor Baines, one of the new assistant pastors was asked to lead the mother's day service with a short prayer. Caught off guard, he slowly walked to the podium, smiling nervously at the capacity crowd. "Dear Lord," he began to pray with a slightly detectable speech impediment and nervousness in his voice, "We ask you to bless all of the women present with us today, etc. etc. And finally, for those of us who have had mothers, . . . um, . . . er . . . I mean Christian mothers, we thank thee for this additional blessing in our lives."

By this time, Reverend Daniels, the Senior Pastor had joined him. "And for the rest of us, Lord," he joked, "who were hatched from an egg, we thank thee Lord that you didn't scramble us for breakfast."

JEREMIAH 1:5: BEFORE I FORMED THEE IN THE BELLY I KNEW THEE . . .

Job 33:4: THE SPIRIT OF GOD HATH MADE ME, AND THE BREATH OF THE ALMIGHTY HATH GIVEN ME LIFE. [SEE RUTH 4:13; ACTS 17:28]

SILLY SAINTS

A Christian woman had been praying and asking God for a husband—and not just any husband—but a certain man she hoped would propose marriage.

She decided to put out a fleece. "Lord," she prayed, "If he calls this Friday at 7:00 p.m. on the dot, I'll know you've answered my prayer."

When the phone mysteriously rang at exactly 7:00, she grabbed it excitedly and answered with an ecstatic "Yes! Yes! Yes!"

The party on the other end, momentarily stunned, replied, "Great! You must have been expecting our call. Then, unless we hear otherwise, we'll expect to see you in our church nursery this Sunday at 9:30 sharp. Oh," she remarked, cheerfully, "and I must say, I've never seen such willing enthusiasm for God's little lambs."

HEBREWS 6:10: FOR GOD IS NOT UNRIGHTEOUS TO FORGET YOUR WORK AND LABOUR OF LOVE WHICH YE HAVE SHEWED TOWARD HIS NAME, IN THAT YE HAVE MINISTERED TO THE SAINTS, AND DO MINISTER.

"I'm so excited," Robbie exclaimed. "My whole life has changed since I accepted Christ as my Lord and Savior."

"I'm so happy to hear that," her sister replied. "I've been praying for you a long time.

"Well," Robbie told her, "you'll be glad to hear I started a Bible study and I already have six new members attending.

"Wow, that's great!" her sister replied.

"Yah, I usually start out by reading something out of the Bible. So far I have quite a congregation at my feet."

"Really?" her sister said enthusiastically. "That's just awesome!"

"Yah," Robbie said. "My congregation includes four cats, one squirrel, and a stray dog.

PSALM 148:7 & 10: PRAISE THE LORD FROM THE EARTH, YE DRAGONS . . . BEASTS, AND ALL CATTLE; CREEPING THINGS, AND FLYING FOWL . . .

PSALM 150:6: LET EVERY THING THAT HATH BREATH PRAISE THE LORD. PRAISE YE THE LORD.

John had spent most of his life behind bars. As a habitual criminal, he was always dodging the police and in and out of jail continuously.

The only photographs his mother owned of him were the few treasured baby portraits she had taken. After that, the only time she saw John was in mug shots or on wanted posters. It seemed he was always in front of a camera but for the wrong reason.

Nevertheless, on John's death bed, in those last fleeting moments before he died, he cried out for mercy like the proverbial thief on the cross.

As he stood before the Lord in judgment, and his earthly deeds were made manifest, one of the angels overhead the former convict say, "Whew! I'm glad that's over! I felt like I was back in the police line up!"

I JOHN 1:9: IF WE CONFESS OUR SINS, HE IS FAITHFUL AND JUST TO FORGIVE US *OUR* SINS, AND TO CLEANSE US FROM ALL UNRIGHTEOUSNESS.

JOHN 6:37: . . . HIM THAT COMETH TO ME I WILL IN NO WISE CAST OUT.

PSALMS 103:12: AS FAR AS THE EAST IS FROM THE WEST, SO FAR HATH HE REMOVED OUR TRANSGRESSIONS FROM US.

ISAIAH 43:25: I, *EVEN* I, *AM* HE THAT BLOTTETH OUT THY TRANSGRESSIONS FOR MINE OWN SAKE, AND WILL NOT REMEMBER THY SINS.

ROMANS 5:20: . . . BUT WHERE SIN ABOUNDED, GRACE DID MUCH MORE ABOUND.

ROMANS 5:9: MUCH MORE THEN, BEING NOW JUSTIFIED BY HIS BLOOD, WE SHALL BE SAVED FROM WRATH THROUGH HIM.

ROMANS 8:1: THERE *IS* THEREFORE NOW NO CONDEMNATION TO THEM WHICH ARE IN CHRIST JESUS, WHO WALK NOT AFTER THE FLESH, BUT AFTER THE SPIRIT.

A newly married couple were out looking at homes for sale. Their real estate agent took them to a number of houses that were within the price range that they could afford. Most of the homes they looked at within their budget, however, needed a lot of repair.

One evening, though, while they were out looking at more homes they came across a very affordable place that impressed both of them. It was neat, clean, and appeared to have been well maintained.

Their agent handed them a flyer giving a complete description of the home.

"Honey, this place sounds like a real bargain," the man said to his wife chuckling. "It says the appliances are stainless 'steal' [steel]."

RUTH 1:16: AND RUTH SAID [TO HER MOTHER-IN-LAW, NAOMI, AFTER THEY HAD BOTH BECAME WIDOWS], INTREAT ME NOT TO LEAVE THEE, *OR* TO RETURN FROM FOLLOWING AFTER THEE: FOR WHITHER THOU GOEST, I WILL GO; AND WHERE THOU LODGEST, I WILL LODGE: THY PEOPLE *SHALL BE* MY PEOPLE, AND THY GOD MY GOD:

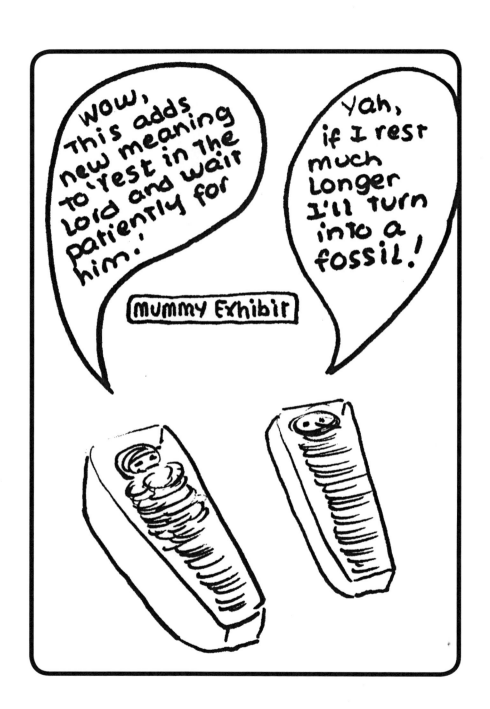

"For some reason this hot chocolate is not dissolving in the hot water," Alice said glancing into her cup.

"Well, we've had it quite awhile," her sister said. "Maybe we should tell mom that it needs to be thrown out."

All of a sudden Alice let out a shriek. "Ick!" she shouted. "That's not hot chocolate. It's live ants," she exclaimed, "and they're moving!"

"How awful!" her sister remarked. "When an *insect* gets in my food or drink it really *bugs* me."

NUMBERS 13:27 & 30-33: AND THEY [THE TWELVE SPIES MOSES SENT TO SEARCH THE LAND OF CANAAN GIVEN TO THE CHILDREN OF ISRAEL] TOLD HIM, AND SAID, WE CAME UNTO THE LAND WHITHER THOU SENTEST US, AND SURELY IT FLOWETH WITH MILK AND HONEY . . . AND CALEB STILLED THE PEOPLE BEFORE MOSES, AND SAID, LET US GO UP AT ONCE, AND POSSESS IT; FOR WE ARE WELL ABLE TO OVERCOME IT. BUT THE MEN THAT WENT UP WITH HIM SAID, WE BE NOT ABLE TO GO UP AGAINST THE PEOPLE; FOR THEY *ARE* STRONGER THAN WE . . . AND ALL THE PEOPLE THAT WE SAW IN IT *ARE* MEN OF A GREAT STATURE. AND THERE WE SAW THE GIANTS, THE SONS OF ANAK, *WHICH COME* OF THE GIANTS: AND WE WERE IN OUR OWN SIGHT AS GRASSHOPPERS, AND SO WE WERE IN THEIR SIGHT.

ROMANS 8:31: WHAT SHALL WE THEN SAY TO THESE THINGS? IF GOD *BE* FOR US, WHO *CAN BE* AGAINST US. [SEE I JOHN 4:4; I CORINTHIANS 15:57; ROMANS 8:37; PSALM 60:12; II CORINTHIANS 2:14; HEBREWS 11:33-34; I SAMUEL 17:37, I SAMUEL 14:6]

ACTS 5:38-39: AND NOW I SAY UNTO YOU, REFRAIN FROM THESE MEN, AND LET THEM ALONE: FOR IF THIS COUNSEL OR THIS WORK BE OF MEN, IT WILL COME TO NOUGHT: BUT IF IT BE OF GOD, YE CANNOT OVERTHROW IT; LEST HAPLY YE BE FOUND EVEN TO FIGHT AGAINST GOD.

Two women, Jean and Tonya, were grumbling about their dilapidated cars and how one or the other of them was always getting stranded when their car broke down.

"Why is it?" asked Jean, "that whenever your car breaks down, God sends someone right away to give you a hand whereas," she complained, "I'm usually left waiting for hours before help comes."

"Well, Jean," Tonya answered, "that's because, in a neighborhood like mine where violent crime abounds, if God didn't send an angel right away," she said, "He would have to send an undertaker later."

DEUTERONOMY 4:4: BUT YE THAT DID CLEAVE UNTO THE LORD YOUR GOD *ARE* ALIVE EVERY ONE OF YOU THIS DAY. [SEE PSALM 118:17; PSALM 112:7]

PSALM 34:17: *THE RIGHTEOUS* CRY, AND THE LORD HEARETH, AND DELIVERETH THEM OUT OF ALL THEIR TROUBLES. [SEE PSALM 34:19; PSALM 46:1 & ISAIAH 43:2]

PROVERBS 3:25-26: BE NOT AFRAID OF SUDDEN FEAR, NEITHER OF THE DESOLATION OF THE WICKED, WHEN IT COMETH. FOR THE LORD SHALL BE THY CONFIDENCE, AND SHALL KEEP THY FOOT FROM BEING TAKEN.

PROVERBS 14:26: IN THE FEAR OF THE LORD *IS* STRONG CONFIDENCE: AND HIS CHILDREN SHALL HAVE A PLACE OF REFUGE.

PROVERBS 27:1-3: THE LORD *IS* MY LIGHT AND MY SALVATION; WHOM SHALL I FEAR? THE LORD *IS* THE STRENGTH OF MY LIFE; OF WHOM SHALL I BE AFRAID? WHEN THE WICKED, *EVEN* MINE ENEMIES AND MY FOES, CAME UPON ME TO EAT UP MY FLESH, THEY STUMBLED AND FELL. THOUGH AN HOST SHOULD ENCAMP AGAINST ME, MY HEART SHALL NOT FEAR: THOUGH WAR SHOULD RISE AGAINST ME, IN THIS *WILL* I *BE* CONFIDENT.

PSALM 91:5-7: THOU SHALT NOT BE AFRAID FOR THE TERROR BY NIGHT; *NOR* FOR THE ARROW *THAT* FLIETH BY DAY; *NOR* FOR

THE PESTILENCE *THAT* WALKETH IN DARKNESS; *NOR* FOR THE DESTRUCTION *THAT* WASTETH AT NOONDAY. A THOUSAND SHALL FALL AT THY SIDE, AND TEN THOUSAND AT THY RIGHT HAND; *BUT* IT SHALL NOT COME NIGH THEE.

PSALM 91:10-12: THERE SHALL NO EVIL BEFALL THEE, NEITHER SHALL ANY PLAGUE COME NIGH THY DWELLING. FOR HE SHALL GIVE HIS ANGELS CHARGE OVER THEE, TO KEEP THEE IN ALL THY WAYS. THEY SHALL BEAR THEE UP IN *THEIR* HANDS, LEST THOU DASH THY FOOT AGAINST A STONE.

Kevin and Lorraine were out taking a drive and enjoying the early evening. The sky was ablaze with vivid colors of pink and orange just after the setting sun.

"Hasn't it been a gorgeous day?" Lorraine remarked to her husband, rolling down the window to enjoy the fresh smell of the fall air. "I love to see the falling leaves."

As they were driving along they stopped at a park near a vacant foot ball field. Slowly, they walked along with the leaves rustling under their feet enjoying the scenic view all around them. But while they were strolling through the park they happened to notice a stray cat all alone under some bleachers. It looked lonely, abandoned, and emaciated. Its desperate cries pierced their hearts.

"Honey!" Lorraine asked with a pleading voice, "Can we help that cat?"

"I was just about to suggest that very thing," he said walking over to the helpless animal. It seemed to be begging for food and attention.

Lorraine picked it up and cradled it in her arms. "Don't worry, 'Paws,' she lovingly called it. "We're here for you!"

Kevin and Lorraine got in the car with their newly found treasure stroking its matted fur. "We're going to fatten you up," she said tenderly, noticing its skeleton like appearance.

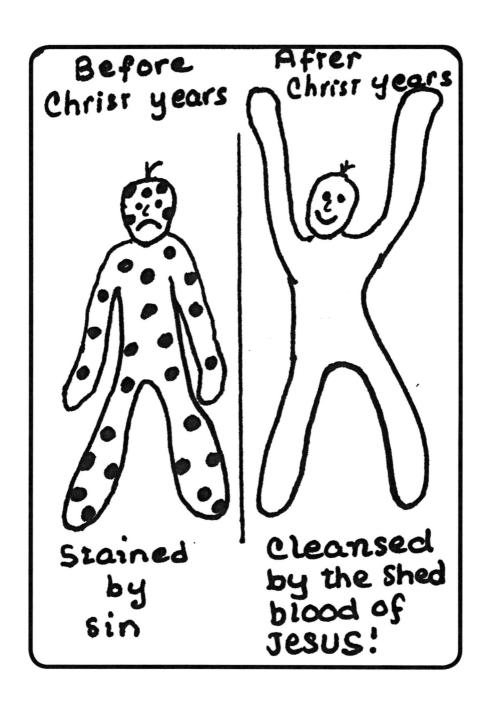

Paws curled up in Lorraine's lap as they drove to the pet store to get it some food, bedding, and a litter box. Its cries seemed to subside. They knew that it must have sensed that all would be well.

After its belly was full and it had been bathed and fluffed dry, Paws sat between Lorraine and Kevin on their loveseat and "the three of them" watched a Christian video.

Paws purred for the first time! She looked up at them as if to say, *Thanks to the Lord and the two of you I think everything's going to be simply purr-fect' for me from now on.*

Lorraine leaned over toward her husband and kissed him on the cheek. Then she laid her head on his shoulder glancing down at their new kitty. "I think God arranged this whole thing," she told her husband. "And what 'p-u-r-r-fect' timing," she said, stroking their furry little friend. "This is one story that has turned out happily ever after."

(Author's note: This is the feline version of Isaiah 26:3: Thou wilt keep him in purr-fect peace whose mind is stayed on thee.

ISAIAH 26:3: THOU WILT KEEP *HIM* IN PERFECT PEACE, *WHOSE* MIND IS STAYED *ON THEE*: BECAUSE HE TRUSTETH IN THEE.

Janice, the wife of a preacher, was confiding her troubles to another minister's wife.

"I just don't how to handle this situation," she said in frustration. "My husband's job seems to be going to his head."

"What's wrong?" asked Marie, her concerned friend.

"Lately he's been exhibiting strange behavior," Janice replied. Sunday we invited company over," she said, "and when our guests sat down to join us for dinner, my husband passed around an offering plate.

"My, you certainly have your problems," Marie sympathized.

"I wouldn't have said anything," said Janice, "but tonight things really got out of hand when he tried to baptize our bird and St. Bernard in the bath tub!"

PSALM 90:17: AND LET THE BEAUTY OF THE LORD OUR GOD BE UPON US: AND ESTABLISH THOU THE WORK OF OUR HANDS UPON US; YEA, THE WORK OF OUR HANDS ESTABLISH THOU IT.

A church service was about to begin. Two ladies, Francis and Anita, arriving a little later than usual, were trying to find an ideal place to sit. Since the bottom floor where they usually sat was full, they decided to try the balcony.

'Let's sit here," said Francis to Anita, seating herself. "We'll have a good view from up here and besides," she said, lowering her voice to a whisper, "the seats are still warm from when the last sinners sat here."

I JOHN 1:8-9: IF WE SAY THAT WE HAVE NO SIN, WE DECEIVE OURSELVES, AND THE TRUTH IS NOT IN US. IF WE CONFESS OUR SINS, HE IS FAITHFUL AND JUST TO FORGIVE US OUR SINS, AND TO CLEANSE US FROM ALL UNRIGHTEOUSNESS.

"And where have you been, Joey?" the Sunday School teacher lovingly asked a little three-year-old boy who had been absent for several weeks. "We've all missed you!"

Then the teacher looked up at his mother, courteously acknowledging her. "It's so nice to see you again, Mrs. Payne," she said. "And I can't tell you how thrilled we are to have little Joey back with us again."

"Thank you," his mother replied, "He would have returned sooner, but we've had him in storage."

"In storage?" his teacher asked, incredulous.

"Yes," his mother replied smiling. "He's been staying with his grandmother while we were traveling abroad."

MATTHEW 19:14: . . . JESUS SAID, SUFFER LITTLE CHILDREN, AND FORBID THEM NOT, TO COME UNTO ME: FOR OF SUCH IS THE KINGDOM OF HEAVEN.

When a fender bender occurred in the parking lot just after church had let out, the two parties involved, Marilyn and Dawn, both Christians, tried to maintain a Christ like attitude.

Though they were both a bit miffed over the incident, they didn't want to allow a piece of metal to come between their friendship or their Christian testimony. Maintaining a spirit of self control, they smiled and hugged one another. They weren't about to give Satan the satisfaction of losing their composure.

Later, one of the other church members was overheard remarking that "the church parking lot was the only place in the world where collisions occur with a smile."

PROVERBS 27:6: FAITHFUL ARE THE WOUNDS OF A FRIEND; BUT THE KISSES OF AN ENEMY *ARE* DECEITFUL.

Each month Reverend Roth invited new members to he publicly recognized. In order to honor them, he would invite them to come up on the platform.

The wife of one of the couples was suddenly struck with stage fright and did not accompany her husband to the front of the church.

When he reached the platform, the minister began speaking unaware that his wife was still glued to her seat.

"We would like to welcome the Coopers into membership this morning," he said. Reverend Roth then noticed, however, that his wife was not with him. "His wife," he added, "is not able to be with us in today's service due to illness, but we would certainly like to recognize her as well."

The husband then returned to his seat, joining his healthy, but blushing wife.

I JOHN 4:18: THERE IS NO FEAR IN LOVE; BUT PERFECT LOVE CASTETH OUT FEAR: BECAUSE FEAR HATH TORMENT. HE THAT FEARETH IS NOT MADE PERFECT IN LOVE.

"It sounds strange," Heidi told her friend, "but our dogs love the frozen style string beans. They've become a regular part of their diet," she said. "In fact, the way they devour them," she exclaimed, "you would think I had just handed them a juicy steak!

One day Heidi noticed that she was all out of their favorite treat. *I really should go get them some string beans*, she said to herself, *but there are so many things to take care of today that I doubt I'll have time before church.*

Heidi's busy schedule didn't allow her to make that stop at the grocery store. *Oh well, I'll get them tomorrow*, she said to herself a little disappointed.

That evening, as soon as she walked into church, one of the members approached her. "Hey, I was just wondering," she said, "could you use a huge kettle of green beans?" They were left over from that wedding reception we had here last night. We're trying to get the refrigerator cleared out so we can make room for some other things.

Heidi smiled and looked up toward heaven. *Lord*, she said, *You never cease to amaze me! I love You every bit as much for all the little things You do, but I never would have guessed You'd have a 'string bean' miracle on the list!*

PSALM 78:19: . . . CAN GOD FURNISH A TABLE IN THE WILDERNESS?

(Author's note: Heidi says, "Yes!" And I say, "Yes!")

Linda and her husband, Bill, hadn't been married very long. One day as they were coming out of church, their pastor asked them how things were going.

"They're going just fine," Bill said, "except that Linda is driving me to the edge . . ."

The pastor interrupted before Bill could finish his sentence. "I'm sorry, Bill and Linda, that you're having problems," their pastor said, looking concerned. "Would you like to come in for counseling?"

"Oh, it's not that kind of edge," Bill laughed. "I just meant she's driving me to the edge of the bed!"

"Yah," Linda joked, "he tries to get away from me but it doesn't work."

SONG OF SOLOMAN 7:10: I *AM* MY BELOVED'S, AND HIS DESIRE *IS* TOWARD ME.

After being laid off, Alex, a middle aged man, was having a hard time making ends meet. He tried to encourage himself by reading II Kings 4. It was the story of a woman about to lose her two sons because her life was in financial jeopardy. Her story gave him hope whenever he read it because it had a happy ending.

The problem was that every place Alex applied for a job, he was usually overwhelmed by someone younger, someone more qualified, or someone with a higher education.

Too proud to ask for help, he struggled along doing the best he could to keep his bills paid, but soon he found himself delinquent on several of his accounts.

Some people at the church who had heard about his dilemma collected an offering and, so as not to make him feel obligated, they simply signed the envelope, "A gift from the Lord."

One of the church members, Louis, who lived in the same neighborhood offered to drop it off. Twenty minutes later he was knocking at his door.

When Alex answered the door, Louis handed him the envelope. "The Lord wants you to have this," he said lovingly. He would have brought it himself but he's not making house calls these days."

PSALM 75:6-7: 6-7: FOR PROMOTION *COMETH* NEITHER FROM THE EAST, NOR FROM THE WEST, NOR FROM THE SOUTH. BUT GOD IS THE JUDGE: HE PUTTETH DOWN ONE, AND SETTETH UP ANOTHER.

PROVERBS 21:1: THE KING'S HEART [ANYONE IN A PLACE OF AUTHORITY] IS IN THE HAND OF THE LORD, AS THE RIVERS OF WATER: HE TURNETH IT WHITHERSOEVER HE WILL.

DANIEL 11:32: . . . THE PEOPLE THAT DO KNOW THEIR GOD SHALL BE STRONG, AND DO *EXPLOITS*.

PROVERBS 18:16: A MAN'S GIFT MAKETH ROOM FOR HIM, AND BRINGETH HIM BEFORE GREAT MEN.

PROVERBS 22:29: SEEST THOU A MAN DILIGENT IN HIS BUSINESS? HE SHALL STAND BEFORE KINGS . . .

I KINGS 11:28: AND THE MAN JEROBOAM *WAS* A MIGHTY MAN OF VALOUR [VALOR]: AND SOLOMON SEEING THE YOUNG MAN THAT HE WAS INDUSTRIOUS, HE MADE HIM RULER OVER ALL THE CHARGE OF THE HOUSE OF JOSEPH.

II CHRONICLES 27:6: SO JOTHAM BECAME MIGHTY, BECAUSE HE PREPARED HIS WAYS BEFORE THE LORD HIS GOD.

NEHEMIAH 4:6: SO BUILT WE THE WALL; AND ALL THE WALL WAS JOINED TOGETHER UNTO THE HALF THEREOF: FOR THE PEOPLE HAD A MIND TO WORK.

NEHEMIAH 4:21: SO WE LABOURED [LABORED] IN THE WORK: AND HALF OF THEM HELD THE SPEARS FROM THE RISING OF THE MORNING TILL THE STARS APPEARED.

I CHRONICLES 4:10: AND JABEZ CALLED ON THE GOD OF ISRAEL, SAYING, OH THAT THOU WOULDEST BLESS ME INDEED, AND ENLARGE MY COAST, AND THAT THINE HAND MIGHT BE WITH ME, ANDTHAT THOU WOULDEST KEEP *ME* FROM EVIL, THAT IT

my boss says he's going to fire me if I don't shave my beard.
Are you going to picket or pick it?

MAY NOT GRIEVE ME! AND GOD GRANTED HIM THAT WHICH HE REQUESTED.

GENESIS 28:10-17: AND JACOB WENT OUT FROM BEERSHEBA, AND WENT TOWARD HARAN. AND HE LIGHTED UPON A CERTAIN PLACE, AND TARRIED THERE ALL NIGHT, BECAUSE THE SUN WAS SET; AND HE TOOK OF THE STONES OF THAT PLACE, AND PUT *THEM* FOR HIS PILLOWS, AND LAY DOWN IN THAT PLACE TO SLEEP. AND HE DREAMED, AND BEHOLD A LADDER SET UP ON THE EARTH, AND THE TOP OF IT REACHED TO HEAVEN: AND BEHOLD THE ANGELS OF GOD ASCENDING AND DESCENDING ON IT. AND, BEHOLD, THE LORD STOOD ABOVE IT, AND SAID, I *AM* THE LORD GOD OF ABRAHAM THY FATHER, AND THE GOD OF ISAAC: THE LAND WHEREON THOU LIEST, TO THEE WILL I GIVE IT, AND TO THY SEED; AND THY SEED SHALL BE AS THE DUST OF THE EARTH . . . IN THY SEED SHALL ALL THE FAMILIES OF THE EARTH BE BLESSED . . . I WILL NOT LEAVE THEE, UNTIL I HAVE DONE *THAT* WHICH I HAVE SPOKEN TO THE OF. AND JACOB AWAKED OUT OF HIS SLEEP, AND HE SAID, SURELY THE LORD IS IN THIS PLACE; AND I KNEW *IT* NOT. AND HE WAS AFRAID, AND SAID, HOW DREADFUL *IS* THIS PLACE! THIS *IS* NONE OTHER BUT THE HOUSE OF GOD, AND THIS *IS* THE GATE OF HEAVEN.

GENESIS 32:30: [JACOB WRESTLED WITH A MAN UNTIL THE BREAK OF DAY] AND JACOB CALLED THE NAME OF THE PLACE PENIEL: FOR I HAVE SEEN GOD FACE TO FACE, AND MY LIFE IS PRESERVED.

Two factory workers, Alex and Ron, were complaining because everyone in the company was required to take a cut in pay. "I may not be much of a Christian," said Alex, "but one thing I can say for the Lord is that, in a world where you can't get your boss to pay you what you're worth, God always gives you what you've got coming.

ROMANS 6:23: FOR THE WAGES OF SIN IS DEATH: BUT THE GIFT OF GOD IS ETERNAL LIFE THROUGH JESUS CHRIST OUR LORD.

A woman was relating to her friend some things she had been fervently praying about. She was sure they were finally going to come to pass.

"What makes you so certain God is answering your prayers?" asked her friend, Rhonda.

"Because," she replied with exuberance, "A friend of mine called to say so! She said God had wakened her early this morning with a message for me. And, believe me, Rhonda, if he managed to get Christine out of bed, it had to be something pretty important!"

"So why didn't he just tell you and leave her sleeping?" Rhonda asked, doubting the validity of the message.

"Oh," she answered, "I always have my ear plugs in when I go to bed."

JOHN 10:27: MY SHEEP HEAR MY VOICE, AND I KNOW THEM, AND THEY FOLLOW ME. [JOB 33:14-17; II CORINTHIANS 13:1; GENESIS 46:2]

JOHN 8:47: HE THAT IS OF GOD HEARETH GOD'S WORDS . . . [SEE PROVERBS 3:5-6; II SAMUEL 5:19 & 23; ACTS 16:6-7; ACTS 21:4; JOHN 15:15; JOHN 16:13; AMOS 3:7; ISAIAH 46:10; DANIEL 2:22 & 47; LUKE 8:10]

JOB 33:14-17: FOR GOD SPEAKETH ONCE, YEA TWICE, *YET MAN* PERCEIVETH IT NOT. IN A DREAM, IN A VISION OF THE NIGHT, WHEN DEEP SLEEP FALLETH UPON MEN, IN SLUMBERINGS UPON THE BED; THEN HE OPENETH THE EARS OF MEN, AND SEALETH THEIR INSTRUCTION, THAT HE MAY WITHDRAW MAN *FROM HIS* PURPOSE, AND HIDE PRIDE FROM MAN. [SEE MATTHEW 2:12-13]

II CORINTHIANS 13:1: . . . IN THE MOUTH OF TWO OR THREE WITNESSES SHALL EVERY WORD BE ESTABLISHED.

I SAMUEL 3:10: AND THE LORD CAME, AND STOOD, AND CALLED AS AT OTHER TIMES, SAMUEL, SAMUEL. THEN SAMUEL ANSWERED, SPEAK; FOR THY SERVANT HEARETH.

PROVERBS 8:34: BLESSED *IS* THE MAN THAT HEARETH ME, WATCHING DAILY AT MY GATES, WAITING AT THE POSTS OF MY DOORS.

ROMANS 8:16: THE SPIRIT ITSELF BEARETH WITNESS WITH OUR SPIRIT, THAT WE ARE THE CHILDREN OF GOD.

JAMES 4:8: DRAW NIGH TO GOD, AND HE WILL DRAW NIGH TO YOU . . .

Because Ada was approaching thirty five and not yet married, she was worried that life might be passing her by.

"There just don't seem to be any eligible, Christian men my age," she told her friend, Heather, sighing.

Heather, who was never seen without a man at her side, replied, "If it's a husband you want, you're only a step away from meeting Mr. Right." She then gave Ada explicit instructions on what to do.

"Next Saturday morning, put on your nicest silk dress and heels," she told her. "Make sure every hair is in place and your nails are polished. Then, after you have prayed in faith, drive over to the men's breakfast gathering. Trespass until noon and I can guarantee that you'll come away with more than a ham on rye." Then she smiled reassuringly at Ada. "How do you think," she said, "that I found the smorgasbord I have!"

PROVERBS 3:5-6: TRUST IN THE LORD WITH ALL THINE HEART; AND LEAN NOT UNTO THINE OWN UNDERSTANDING, IN ALL THY WAYS ACKNOWLEDGE HIM, AND HE SHALL DIRECT THY PATHS.

PSALMS 37:4-5: DELIGHT THYSELF ALSO IN THE LORD; AND HE SHALL GIVE THEE THE DESIRES OF THINE HEART. COMMIT THY WAY UNTO THE LORD; TRUST ALSO IN HIM; AND HE SHALL BRING *IT* TO PASS.

GENESIS 24:27 & 48: AND HE SAID [ABRAHAM'S MASTER IN SEARCH OF A WIFE FOR ISAAC, ABRAHAM'S SON], BLESSED *BE* THE LORD GOD OF MY MASTER ABRAHAM, WHO HATH NOT LEFT DESTITUTE MY MASTER OF HIS MERCY AND HIS TRUTH: I *BEING* IN THE WAY, THE LORD LED ME TO THE HOUSE OF MY MASTER'S BRETHREN . . . AND I BOWED DOWN MY HEAD, AND WORSHIPPED THE LORD, AND BLESSED THE LORD GOD OF MY MASTER ABRAHAM, WHICH

HAD LED ME IN THE RIGHTWAY TO TAKE MY MASTER'S BROTHER'S DAUGHTER UNTO HIS SON.

GENESIS 24:16: AND THE DAMSEL *WAS* VERY FAIR TO LOOK UPON, A VIRGIN, NEITHER HAD ANY MAN KNOWN HER . . .

MATTHEW 6:33: BUT SEEK YE FIRST THE KINGDOM OF GOD, AND HIS RIGHTEOUSNESS; AND ALL THESE THINGS SHALL BE ADDED UNTO YOU. [SEE PSALM 84:11]

"Can I call you back, Roberta?" asked Dee. "Things are a disaster over here right now."

"Before I hang up," Roberta said quickly, "why don't you let me pray for you."

Without giving Dee a chance to get a word in edgewise, Roberta began praying from the depths of her soul. "Father," she cried. "I ask you to intervene in this crisis. Grant, I pray, the 'peace that passes all understanding.' Minister to the needs of this family. Comfort them with your endless love and mighty power, etc. etc. etc."

When she had finished, some five minutes later, Dee thanked her but then sheepishly admitted that, when she was referring to things being a disaster, all she was talking about was her kitchen!

'The Lord's helping me make some things for our Saturday bake sale," she said. It's the first time that I've ever attempted some of these pastries, bread and cinnamon rolls. With the Lord's assistance," she said confidently, "I believe they will turn out okay."

"Oh," said Roberta, feeling embarrassed, "You mean all my travailing in prayer was over bread and rolls?"

PSALMS 46:8: COME, BEHOLD THE WORKS OF THE LORD, WHAT DESOLATIONS HE HATH MADE . . .

"I'd like an order of manna to go," said Harry as he drove through a fast food restaurant.

"An order of w-h-a-t?" the waitress asked, confused by his strange request.

"An order of manna," he said.

"I'm sorry, sir," she said politely, "but we don't carry that here. In fact," she told him, "I don't think anyone carries that anywhere. Frankly, I've never even heard of it."

Slightly irritated by her reaction to his request, Harry replied, "What are you—some kind of heathen? That's what the children of Israel were fed for over forty years."

"Yes, sir," she said, trying to hide her anger over his comment, "I now recall hearing about it in the Bible. But," she asked sarcastically, "does this place look like some forsaken wilderness?"

EXODUS 16:15 & 35: AND WHEN THE CHILDREN OF ISRAEL SAW *IT*, THEY SAID ONE TO ANOTHER, IT IS MANNA: FOR THEY WIST NOT WHAT IT *WAS*. AND MOSES SAID UNTO THEM, THIS *IS* THE BREAD WHICH THE LORD HATH GIVEN YOU TO EAT . . . AND THE CHILDREN OF ISRAEL DID EAT MANNA FORTY YEARS, UNTIL THEY CAME TO A LAND INHABITED; THEY DID EAT MANNA, UNTIL THEY CAME UNTO THE BORDERS OF THE LAND OF CANAAN.

JOHN 6:47-51 & 58: VERILY, VERILY, I [JESUS] SAY UNTO YOU, HE THAT BELIEVETH ON ME HATH EVERLASTING LIFE. I AM THAT BREAD OF LIFE. YOUR FATHERS DID EAT MANNA IN THE WILDERNESS, AND ARE DEAD. THIS IS THE BREAD WHICH COMETH DOWN FROM HEAVEN, THAT A MAN MAY EAT THEREOF, AND NOT DIE. I AM THE LIVING BREAD WHICH CAME DOWN FROM HEAVEN: IF ANY MAN EAT OF THIS BREAD, HE SHALL LIVE FOR EVER: AND THE BREAD THAT I WILL GIVE IS MY FLESH, WHICH I WILL GIVE FOR THE LIFE OF THE WORLD . . . THIS IS THAT BREAD WHICH CAME DOWN FROM HEAVEN: NOT AS YOUR FATHERS DID EAT MANNA, AND ARE DEAD: HE THAT EATETH OF THIS BREAD SHALL LIVE FOR EVER.

"Honey," Ron said to his wife, "would you like me to do those dishes for you?" He could see that she had her hands full with laundry, unmade beds, and dirty dishes on the kitchen table.

On top of that, their dogs were looking at her with that expression that seemed to say, *It's chow time; don't you realize it?*

And meanwhile, their two year old twins were fighting over a toy that they both wanted control of.

"No honey," Ron's wife said, "you don't have to do the dishes.

"Well," he replied, "I'm going to do them anyway," he said, "because if I don't, I'll be setting a trap for myself that I'll be falling right into. And later tonight," he continued, "when I'm feeling amorous, you're liable to remember those dirty dishes I didn't do!

PSALM 127:3: THY WIFE *SHALL BE* AS A FRUITFUL VINE BY THE SIDES OF THINE HOUSE: THY CHILDREN LIKE OLIVE PLANTS ROUND ABOUT THY TABLE.

PSALM 23:5-6: . . . THOU ANOINTEST MY HEAD WITH OIL; MY CUP RUNNETH OVER. SURELY GOODNESS AND MERCY SHALL FOLLOW ME ALL THE DAYS OF MY LIFE: AND I WILL DWELL IN THE HOUSE OF THE LORD FOR EVER.

Continuing his series on the evils of drinking and gambling, Reverend Norton began delivering his sobering message on the consequences of such sins.

Only a quarter of the way through his sermon, a lady, who was paranoid of bugs, pulled out her insect repellent and began spraying it toward a fly that had landed nearby. The overpowering smell of the bug spray caused a dozen or so people to suddenly get up and leave.

Unaware of what the woman had done, the minister watched as several of his members walked out. "Just because you're living lower than a snake's belly," he bellowed, "is no reason to stomp out of here."

I CORINTHIANS 12:26: AND WHETHER ONE MEMBER SUFFER, ALL THE MEMBERS SUFFER WITH IT.

"Could I borrow a tissue?" whispered an elderly woman to the lady seated beside her.

"Certainly," she replied in a low voice as she began rummaging through her purse. Unfortunately, however, she didn't have a tissue or a hankie to offer the poor, wheezing woman.

Then it occurred to her, however, that she sometimes kept a napkin or paper towel in her coat pocket in case of an emergency. "Here you are," she whispered, handing the woman the napkin and glad that she was able to be of assistance.

"Thanks so much," whispered the woman next to her. But as she lifted it to her nose, she discovered that a twenty dollar bill was stuck to it."

"I'm not sure which of these you want me to blow my nose on," she teased, handing her back the twenty dollars "but I think Andrew Jackson would prefer that I used the tissue."

GALATIONS 6:2: BEAR YE ONE ANOTHER'S BURDENS, AND SO FULFIL THE LAW OF CHRIST.

MATTHEW 25:35-36, & 40: FOR I WAS AN HUNGRED, AND YE GAVE ME MEAT: I WAS THIRSTY, AND YE GAVE ME DRINK: I WAS A STRANGER, AND YE TOOK ME IN: NAKED, AND YE CLOTHED ME: I WAS SICK, AND YE VISITED ME: I WAS IN PRISON, AND YE CAME UNTO ME . . . INASMUCH AS YE HAVE DONE *IT* UNTO ONE OF THE LEAST OF THESE MY BRETHREN, YE HAVE DONE *IT* UNTO ME.

A sleepy-eyed, very hungry gentleman stumbled into church making his way up to the front row.

The pastor looked over at the man, noticing his pale countenance. "Are you alright?" Reverend Brady asked the weary looking gent.

"I'm fine, thank you, he said. "I had a rather sleepless night, though, followed by a hectic morning. In fact," he went on, "I had to skip breakfast in order to make it here on time. And I want you to know, Reverend Brady," he continued, that although my wife prepared a delicious, mouth-watering breakfast for me, I chose you over two eggs—sunny side up, bacon, and a banana nut muffin.

MATTHEW 11:30: FOR MY YOKE *IS* EASY AND MY BURDEN IS LIGHT.

As Sean's stomach growled loudly in church, he began squirming and nervously chewing his fingernails. Toward the end of the service, he was even gnawing the corners of his church bulletin. It was difficult for him to concentrate because all he could think about was a nice, thick, juicy steak.

The growling of Sean's stomach grew increasingly louder by the minute sounding like an off-key orchestra, and his thoughts of food only made the hunger pangs more apparent.

The church service, which seemed to last an eternity, finally ended with some profound words of wisdom from the Pastor. "That's my message for today," he concluded. "I think you'll all agree that this sermon has given you something to chew on."

"I'm glad to hear there is something to chew on," Sean whispered to his wife. "Let's just hope it tides me over until we get to the nearest restaurant!"

LUKE 5:4-6: NOW WHEN HE [JESUS] HAD LEFT SPEAKING, HE SAID UNTO SIMON, LAUNCH OUT INTO THE DEEP, AND LET DOWN YOUR NETS FOR A DRAUGHT. AND SIMON ANSWERING SAID UNTO HIM, MASTER, WE HAVE TOILED ALL THE NIGHT, AND HAVE TAKEN NOTHING: NEVERTHELESS AT THY WORD I WILL LET DOWN THE NET. AND WHEN THEY HAD THIS DONE, THEY INCLOSED A GREAT MULTITUDE OF FISHES: AND THEIR NET BRAKE.

MATTHEW 4:19: AND HE [JESUS] SAITH UNTO THEM, FOLLOW ME, AND I WILL MAKE YOU FISHERS OF MEN. [SEE ISAIAH 6:8 & ROMANS 10:15]

MATTHEW 5:14 & 16: YE ARE THE LIGHT OF THE WORLD . . . LET YOUR LIGHT SO SHINE BEFORE MEN, THAT THEY MAY SEE YOUR GOOD WORKS, AND GLORIFY YOUR FATHER WHICH IS IN HEAVEN.

PROVERBS 4:18: BUT THE PATH OF THE JUST *IS* AS THE SHINING LIGHT, THAT SHINETH MORE AND MORE UNTO THE PERFECT DAY.

MARK 16:15: AND HE SAID UNTO THEM, GO YE INTO ALL THE WORLD, AND PREACH THE GOSPEL TO EVERY CREATURE. [SEE ACTS 1:8]

EPHESIANS 6:19: AND FOR ME, THAT UTTERANCE MAY BE GIVEN UNTO ME, THAT I MAY OPEN MY MOUTH BOLDLY, TO MAKE KNOWN THE MYSTERY OF THE GOSPEL, [SEE REVELATION 12:11; JOHN 4:29]

ACTS 20:26-27: WHEREFORE I TAKE YOU TO RECORD THIS DAY, THAT I *AM* PURE FROM THE BLOOD OF ALL *MEN*. FOR I HAVE NOT SHUNNED TO DECLARE UNTO YOU ALL THE COUNSEL OF GOD.

PSALM 40:9-10: I HAVE PREACHED RIGHTEOUSNESS IN THE GREAT CONGREGATION: LO, I HAVE NOT REFRAINED MY LIPS, O LORD, THOU KNOWEST. I HAVE NOT HID THY RIGHTEOUSNESS WITHIN MY HEART; I HAVE DECLARED THY FAITHFULNESS AND THY SALVATION: I HAVE NOT CONCEALED THY LOVINGKINDNESS AND THY TRUTH FROM THE GREAT CONGREGATION.

PSALM 107:2: LET THE REDEEMED OF THE LORD SAY *SO*, WHOM HE HATH REDEEMED FROM THE HAND OF THE ENEMY;

PSALM 66:16: COME *AND* HEAR, ALL YE THAT FEAR GOD, AND I WILL DECLARE WHAT HE HATH DONE FOR MY SOUL.

ROMANS 1:16: FOR I AM NOT ASHAMED OF THE GOSPEL OF CHRIST: FOR IT IS THE POWER OF GOD UNTO SALVATION TO EVERY ONE THAT BELIEVETH . . .

MARK 8:38: WHOSOEVER THEREFORE SHALL BE ASHAMED OF ME AND MY WORDS IN THIS ADULTEROUS AND SINFUL GENERATION; OF HIM ALSO SHALL THE SON OF MAN BE ASHAMED, WHEN HE

COMETH IN THE GLORY OF HIS FATHER WITH THE HOLY ANGELS. [SEE I JOHN 2:28]

II TIMOTHY 2:12: . . . IF WE DENY *HIM*, HE ALSO WILL DENY US:

During every church service, little Ryan would sit quietly buried in the Word of God. It seemed that, whenever anyone looked over at him, he was always in earnest with his head stuck between the pages of his Bible.

"My, what an attentive son you have," remarked one of the members to his mother.

"Yes," she replied. "It's amazing that those comic books he tucks inside his Bible manage to hold his interest throughout the entire service."

PROVERBS 4:20-23: MY SON, ATTEND TO MY WORDS; INCLINE THINE EAR UNTO MY SAYINGS. LET THEM NOT DEPART FROM THINE EYES; KEEP THEM IN THE MIDST OF THINE HEART. FOR THEY *ARE* LIFE UNTO THOSE THAT FIND THEM, AND HEALTH TO ALL THEIR FLESH. KEEP THY HEART WITH ALL DILIGENCE; FOR OUT OF IT *ARE* THE ISSUES OF LIFE.

II TIMOTHY 2:15: STUDY TO SHEW THYSELF APPROVED UNTO GOD, A WORKMAN THAT NEEDETH NOT TO BE ASHAMED, RIGHTLY DIVIDING THE WORD OF TRUTH.

A string of robberies had taken place in one middleclass neighborhood. On one block in particular, every home with the exception of one had been burglarized. The irony was that, this house belonged to a single Christian woman who lived alone.

Several of her neighbors who had already been victimized wondered why she had escaped harm or burglary.

"I don't know," she said, "I pray over this house every day and I keep my radio on 24 hours a day. It's tuned into a Christian radio station. Maybe," she said, "they didn't want to hear a sermon."

Mrs Davis, my wife is still on the phone so I'm leaving her a note saying I'm taking you home.
Sure do wish that note was from our Lord saying He was taking me home!

"They couldn't steal anything from me anyway," she went on, "because I don't own a single thing! It all belongs to the Lord.

"And," she continued, "even if they rob Him blind they won't be able to keep it. I Timothy 6:7 says that 'we brought nothing into *this* world, *and it is* certain we can carry nothing out.'"

"But what if they steal your furniture?" one of the neighbors asked her?

"Then I reckon if the Lord allows them to take it," she said, "then it means He's fixing to give me something better to sit on."

"But what if they take your life?" her neighbor asked.

"My last breath on earth," she replied, "is my first one in heaven."

II CORINTHIANS 5:1: FOR WE KNOW THAT IF OUR EARTHLY HOUSE OF THIS TABERNACLE WERE DISSOLVED, WE HAVE A BUILDING OF GOD, AN HOUSE NOT MADE WITH HANDS, ETERNAL IN THE HEAVENS.

PHILIPPIANS 1:21 & 23-24: FOR TO ME TO LIVE *IS* CHRIST, AND TO DIE *IS* GAIN . . . FOR I AM IN A STRAIT BETWIXT TWO, HAVING A DESIRE TO DEPART, AND TO BE WITH CHRIST; WHICH IS FAR BETTER: NEVERTHELESS TO ABIDE IN THE FLESH *IS* MORE NEEDFUL FOR YOU.

ISAIAH 57:1: THE RIGHTEOUS PERISHETH, AND NO MAN LAYETH *IT* TO HEART: AND MERCIFUL MEN *ARE* TAKEN AWAY, NONE CONSIDERING THAT THE RIGHTEOUS IS TAKEN AWAY FROM THE EVIL *TO COME.*

As the communion plate was being passed to Jan and John one Sunday morning at church, John accidentally dropped it on the floor, leaving tiny pieces of bread scattered everywhere about their feet. Church members seated nearby stared in utter disbelief at what had happened.

A few minutes later, the pastor, unaware of what had just occurred, asked, "Has everyone been served?"

"I should say so!" whispered John with embarrassment to his wife as he glanced at the bread all around them. "And this time we sure got more than our share!"

I CORINTHIANS 11:23-31: FOR I HAVE RECEIVED OF THE LORD THAT WHICH ALSO I DELIVERED UNTO YOU, THAT THE LORD JESUS THE *SAME* NIGHT IN WHICH HE WAS BETRAYED TOOK BREAD: AND WHEN HE HAD GIVEN THANKS, HE BRAKE *IT,* AND SAID, TAKE, EAT: THIS IS MY BODY, WHICH IS BROKEN FOR YOU: THIS DO IN REMEMBRANCE OF ME. AFTER THE SAME MANNER ALSO *HE TOOK* THE CUP, WHEN HE HAD SUPPED, SAYING, THIS CUP IS THE NEW TESTAMENT IN MY BLOOD: THIS DO YE, AS OFT AS YE DRINK *IT,* IN REMEMBRANCE OF ME. FOR AS OFTEN AS YE EAT THIS BREAD, AND DRINK THIS CUP, YE DO SHEW THE LORD'S DEATH TILL HE COME. WHEREFORE WHOSOEVER SHALL EAT THIS BREAD, AND DRINK *THIS* CUP OF THE LORD, UNWORTHILY, SHALL BE GUILTY OF THE BODY AND BLOOD OF THE LORD. BUT LET A MAN EXAMINE HIMSELF, AND SO LET HIM EAT OF *THAT* BREAD, AND DRINK OF *THAT* CUP. FOR HE THAT EATETH AND DRINKETH UNWORTHILY, EATETH AND DRINKETH DAMNATION TO HIMSELF, NOT DISCERNING THE LORD'S BODY. FOR THIS CAUSE MANY *ARE* WEAK AND SICKLY AMONG YOU, AND MANY SLEEP. FOR IF WE WOULD JUDGE OURSELVES, WE SHOULD NOT BE JUDGED.

Three women were having coffee together. Ann, one of the ladies, began scratching herself incessantly.

"Did you ever wonder why the Lord made mosquitoes," she asked them. "Every time we go camping I get eaten alive."

"I hadn't given much thought to mosquitoes," replied Abby, seated at her left. "But speaking of pests," she complained, "I'm still trying to figure out what the Lord was thinking when he made my husband.!"

"That's easily explained," the third woman, Libby, quipped. "He wanted us to know the difference between good and evil."

GENESIS 6:5-6: AND GOD SAW THAT THE WICKEDNESS OF MAN *WAS* GREAT IN THE EARTH, AND *THAT* EVERY IMAGINATION OF THE

THOUGHTS OF HIS HEART *WAS* ONLY EVIL CONTINUALLY AND IT REPENTED THE LORD THAT HE HAD MADE MAN ON THE EARTH, AND IT GRIEVED HIM AT HIS HEART.

JEREMIAH 17:9: THE HEART *IS* DECEITFUL ABOVE ALL *THINGS*, AND DESPERATELY WICKED: WHO CAN KNOW IT?

PSALM 14:2-3: THE LORD LOOKED DOWN FROM HEAVEN UPON THE CHILDREN OF MEN, TO SEE IF THERE WERE ANY THAT DID UNDERSTAND, *AND* SEEK GOD. THEY ARE ALL GONE ASIDE, THEY ARE *ALL* TOGETHER BECOME FILTHY: *THERE IS* NONE THAT DOETH GOOD, NO, NOT ONE. [SEE PSALM 53:2-3]

ECCLESIASTES 7:20: FOR *THERE IS* NOT A JUST MAN UPON EARTH, THAT DOETH GOOD, AND SINNETH NOT.

ROMANS 3:19 & 23: . . . THAT EVERY MOUTH MAY BE STOPPED, AND ALLTHE WORLD MAY BECOME GUILTY BEFORE GOD . . . FOR ALL HAVE SINNED, AND COME SHORT OF THE GLORY OF GOD. [SEE ROMANS 5:12]

ISAIAH 64:6: BUT WE ARE ALL AS AN UNCLEAN *THING*, AND ALL OUR RIGHTEOUSNESSES *ARE* AS FILTHY RAGS . . .

Theresa was complaining to her husband, Al, about all of their troubles. "Our baby's due in two weeks and we can't even afford a crib," she cried.

"Can I help it if my attorney is bleeding me for every last cent so he can win that paternity case against me?" her husband said in frustration. "You know I only dated that girl once before we were married and now she accuses me of being the kid's father."

"Yah," muttered Theresa, "And now we can't even go to church without everyone staring at us. I'm starting to feel guilty about putting the Lord on hold," she said.

"Me too," replied her husband, "But until this whole mess is resolved, I feel too ashamed to face anyone."

"Well, all I know," said Theresa, "is that, no matter which way we turn, its either maternity, paternity, or eternity, and they all end with a big 'why?'"

I CORINTHIANS 13:12: FOR NOW WE SEEK THROUGH A GLASS, DARKLY; BUT THEN FACE TO FACE: NOW I KNOW IN PART; BUT THEN SHALL I KNOW EVEN AS I ALSO AM KNOWN.

PSALMS 34:19: MANY ARE THE AFFLICTIONS OF THE RIGHTEOUS: BUT THE LORD DELIVERETH HIM OUT OF THEM ALL.

As Pastor Olsen paced back and forth preaching with all his might, a gentleman in the balcony continually shouted "Praise God" and "Amen" to every sentence he delivered. It became quite distracting and annoying to those seated around him.

One lady in particular found his thunderous "amens" to be highly irritating.

Nearing the end of the service, the pastor said, "And now let us quiet our hearts before the Lord," at which point the lady glared at the noisy gentleman and howled out a "Double Amen!"

PSALMS 107:8: OH THAT MEN WOULD PRAISE THE LORD FOR HIS GOODNESS, AND FOR HIS WONDERFUL WORKS TO THE CHILDREN OF MEN!

PSALM 63:4: THUS WILL I BLESS THEE WHILE I LIVE: I WILL LIFT UP MY HANDS IN THY NAME.

PSALM 104:33: I WILL SING UNTO THE LORD AS LONG AS I LIVE: I WILL SING PRAISE TO MY GOD WHILE I HAVE MY BEING.

PSALM 113:3: FROM THE RISING OF THE SUN UNTO THE GOING DOWN OF THE SAME THE LORD'S NAME *IS* TO BE PRAISED.

PSALM 145:2: EVERYDAY WILL I BLESS THEE; AND I WILL PRAISE THY NAME FOR EVER AND EVER.

PSALM 146:2: WHILE I LIVE WILL I PRAISE THE LORD: I WILL SING PRAISES UNTO MY GOD WHILE I HAVE ANY BEING.

HEBREWS 13:15: . . . LET US OFFER THE SACRIFICE OF PRAISE TO GOD CONTINUALLY, THAT IS, THE FRUIT OF *OUR* LIPS GIVING THANKS TO HIS NAME.

PSALM 150:6: LET EVERY THING THAT HATH BREATH PRAISE THE LORD. PRAISE YE THE LORD.

REVELATION 5:12: SAYING WITH A LOUD VOICE, WORTHY IS THE LAMB THAT WAS SLAIN TO RECEIVE POWER, AND RICHES, AND WISDOM, AND STRENGTH, AND HONOUR [HONOR] AND GLORY, AND BLESSING. [SEE I TIMOTHY 1:17; PHILIPPIANS 2:10-11]

PSALM 95:6-7: O COME, LET US WORSHIP AND BOW DOWN: LET US KNEEL BEFORE THE LORD OUR MAKER. FOR HE *IS* OUR GOD . . .

Marianne, a young, love-struck woman, was trying to get a certain man from her church to notice her. She would go out of her way to walk past him and catch his attention with her prettiest dress.

Although he would smile and converse with her, he never came to the point of actually asking her out.

Finally, she decided to take matters into her own hands. One Sunday evening she approached him in the hallway of the church and handed him a note. *Dear Abe*, she wrote, *God told me in a prophetic vision that you would come to dinner at my place next Friday at 6:00 p.m. He also told me that you would appear at my door with a single, red rose in your hand.*

When church was dismissed and everyone was leaving, Abe walked over to Marianne. "I got your note," he said grinning. "I'd love to have dinner with you, Marianne, but," he said, "could we make it Saturday night instead. God must've forgotten that I have a 7:00 p.m. bowling tournament that night."

I TIMOTHY 5:14: I WILL THEREFORE THAT THE YOUNGER WOMEN MARRY, BEAR CHILDREN, GUIDE THE HOUSE, GIVE NONE [NO] OCCASION TO THE ADVERSARY TO SPEAK REPROACHFULLY.

PSALM 113:9: HE MAKETH THE BARREN WOMAN TO KEEP HOUSE, *AND TO BE* A JOYFUL MOTHER OF CHILDREN. PRAISE YE THE LORD.

I SAMUEL 1:10: AND SHE [HANNAH] *WAS* IN BITTERNESS OF SOUL, AND PRAYED UNTO THE LORD, AND WEPT SORE.

I SAMUEL 1:27: FOR THIS CHILD I [HANNAH] PRAYED; AND THE LORD HATH GIVEN ME MY PETITION WHICH I ASKED OF HIM:

GENESIS 29:31: AND WHEN THE LORD SAW THAT LEAH *WAS* HATED, HE OPENED HER WOMB: BUT RACHEL *WAS* BARREN.

GENESIS 30:17: AND GOD HEARKENED UNTO LEAH, AND SHE CONCEIVED, AND BARE JACOB THE FIFTH SON.

GENESIS 30:1: AND WHEN RACHEL SAW THAT SHE BARE JACOB NO CHILDREN, RACHEL ENVIED HER SISTER; AND SAID UNTO JACOB, GIVE ME CHILDREN, OR ELSE I DIE.

GENESIS 30:22-23: AND GOD REMEMBERED RACHEL, AND GOD HEARKENED TO HER, AND OPENED HER WOMB. AND SHE CONCEIVED, AND BARE A SON; AND SAID, GOD HATH TAKEN AWAY MY REPROACH:

RUTH 4:13: SO BOAZ TOOK RUTH, AND SHE WAS HIS WIFE: AND WHEN HE WENT IN UNTO HER, THE LORD GAVE HER CONCEPTION, AND SHE BARE A SON.

II KINGS 4:8-17: . . . ELISHA PASSED TO SHUNEM, WHERE *WAS* A GREAT WOMAN; AND SHE CONSTRAINED HIM TO EAT BREAD. AND *SO* IT WAS, *THAT* AS OFT AS HE PASSED BY, HE TURNED IN THITHER TO EAT BREAD. AND SHE SAID UNTO HER HUSBAND, BEHOLD NOW, I PERCEIVE THAT THIS *IS* AN HOLY MAN OF GOD, WHICH PASSETH BY US CONTINUALLY. LET US MAKE A LITTLE CHAMBER, I

PRAY THEE, ON THE WALL; AND LET US SET FOR HIM THERE A BED, AND A TABLE, AND A STOOL, AND A CANDLESTICK: AND IT SHALL BE, WHEN HE COMETH TO US, THAT HE SHALL TURN IN THITHER. AND IT FELL ON A DAY, THAT HE CAME THITHER, AND HE TURNED INTO THE CHAMBER, AND LAY THERE. AND HE SAID TO GEHAZI HIS SERVANT, CALL THIS SHUNAMMITE. AND WHEN HE HAD CALLED HER, SHE STOOD BEFORE HIM. AND HE SAID UNTO HIM, SAY NOW UNTO HER, BEHOLD, THOU HAST BEEN CAREFUL FOR US WITH ALL THIS CARE; WHAT *IS* TO BE DONE FOR THEE? WOULDEST THOU BE SPOKEN FOR TO THE KING, OR TO THE CAPTAIN OF THE HOST? AND SHE ANSWERED, I DWELL AMONG MINE OWN PEOPLE. AND HE SAID, WHAT THEN *IS* TO BE DONE FOR HER? AND BEHAZI ANSWERED, VERILY SHE HATH NO CHILD, AND HER HUSBAND IS OLD. AND HE SAID, CALL HER. AND WHEN HE HAD CALLED HER, SHE STOOD IN THE DOOR. AND HE SAID, ABOUT THIS SEASON, ACCORDING TO THE TIME OF LIFE, THOU SHALT EMBRACE A SON. AND SHE SAID, NAY, MY LORD, *THOU* MAN OF GOD, DO NOT LIE UNTO THINE HANDMAID. AND THE WOMAN CONCEIVED, AND BARE A SON AT THAT SEASON THAT ELISHA HAD SAID UNTO HER, ACCORDING TO THE TIME OF LIFE.

LUKE 1:7 & 13-14: AND THEY [ZACHARIAS & HIS WIFE ELISABETH] HAD NO CHILD, BECAUSE THAT ELISABETH WAS BARREN, AND THEY BOTH WERE *NOW* WELL STRICKEN IN YEARS . . . BUT THE ANGEL [WHO APPEARED TO ZACHARIAS] SAID UNTO HIM, FEAR NOT, ZACHARIAS: FOR THY PRAYER IS HEARD; AND THY WIFE ELISABETH SHALL BEAR THEE A SON, AND THOU SHALT CALL HIS NAME JOHN . . . AND HE SHALL BE FILLED WITH THE HOLY GHOST, EVEN FROM HIS MOTHER'S WOMB.

HEBREWS 11:11: THROUGH FAITH ALSO SARA HERSELF RECEIVED STRENGTH TO CONCEIVE SEED, AND WAS DELIVERED OF A CHILD WHEN SHE WAS PAST AGE, BECAUSE SHE JUDGED HIM FAITHFUL WHO HAD PROMISED.

Janice, a young woman, was making plans for her upcoming church wedding. As she began adding up the guest list, she confided in her friend the apprehension she was feeling about possibly insulting uninvited guests.

"I just don't know what to do," she shrugged, "If I invite this one, I have to invite that one, and before you know it," she sighed, "the list gets out of hand." She glanced up at her friend. "How can I afford to invite everyone I know?"

"I've got a solution to fit your budget," her friend, Melissa said chuckling. Invite all your friends and family to a Sunday morning church service. Then have your pastor include your wedding with his sermon. Make sure it's on a Sunday when potluck is scheduled. When the service is dismissed and you've been pronounced husband and wife, send them all to the church basement for food and fellowship!"

PHILIPPIANS 4:19: BUT MY GOD SHALL SUPPLY ALL YOUR NEED ACCORDING TO HIS RICHES IN GLORY BY CHRIST JESUS.

During a series of lectures on how to have a healthy and more successful marriage, Tina learned not to say negative things to her husband."

"Try to make uplifting, positive, constructive remarks," advised the Pastor during one of his sessions.

Tina was doing her best to follow through with his advice. For example, when her husband forgot and left her potluck casserole on the top of the car that he had placed there momentarily, she didn't call him insulting names. She simply said, "Honey, when that casserole flew off the top of our car at 70 miles per hour, I thought it was a U.F.O. but then I realized it was just your own sweet way of saving me from scrubbing another dirty dish."

And when he tripped on the kitchen rug and broke her favorite coffee mug containing a full cup of Cappuccino, she simply said, "You're not a clumsy oath, dear. You were just trying to wash the floor with something a little stronger than water."

And finally, when Tina saw her husband awakening from a loud snoring session in church, instead of yelling at him for embarrassing her, she gently thumped him on the forehead with the end of her umbrella and lovingly

said, "Honey, wake up. It's time for you to go home and climb into the dog house."

PROVERBS 16:24: PLEASANT WORDS ARE AS A HONEYCOMB, SWEET TO THE SOUL AND HEALTH TO THE BONES.

In a church that had a balcony and a few mischievous children on the loose, sitting on the main floor could be hazardous to one's health.

One gentleman found himself continually ducking airplanes, wads of paper, and other flying objects that came over the ledge like aimed missiles.

"You think it's bad tonight," exclaimed Vic, one of the surviving members, "you should have been here last week. I got thumped on the head by a couple of big marbles that felt like boulders. For a few seconds." he said, "in my dazed state of mind I thought the tribulation period was starting to rain hail stones!" Vic pointed at the lump still healing on the top of his head. "I was just getting ready to fire some ammunition back," he said vengefully, "when God spoke to me."

"What did he say?" asked the gentleman curiously.

"He told me to hang on to my marbles until He got there. "I don't know what He's got up His sleeve" Vic said, "but after seeing how he multiplied the two fish and five loaves I can't wait to see what He's going to do with these marbles! And," he told him, "I'm not sure whether He's coming with the canon or the c-a-n-n-on!"

REVELATION 16:17-21: [DURING THE LAST THREE AND A HALF YEARS OF THE GREAT TRIBULATION PERIOD JUST PRIOR TO CHRIST'S RETURN]: AND THE SEVENTH ANGEL POURED OUT HIS VIAL INTO THE AIR; AND THERE CAME A GREAT VOICE OUT OF THE TEMPLE OF HEAVEN, FROM THE THRONE, SAYING, IT IS DONE. AND THERE WERE VOICES, AND THUNDERS, AND LIGHTNINGS; AND THERE WAS A GREAT EARTHQUAKE, SUCH AS WAS NOT SINCE MEN WERE UPON THE EARTH, SO MIGHTY AN EARTHQUAKE, *AND* SO GREAT. AND THE GREAT CITY WAS DIVIDED INTO THREE PARTS, AND

THE CITIES OF THE NATIONS FELL: AND GREAT BABYLON CAME IN REMEMBRANCE BEFORE GOD, TO GIVE UNTO HER THE CUP OF THE WINE OF THE FIERCENESS OF HIS WRATH. AND EVERY ISLAND FLED AWAY, AND THE MOUNTAINS WERE NOT FOUND. AND THERE FELL UPON MEN A GREAT HAIL OUT OF HEAVEN, *EVERY STONE* ABOUT THE WEIGHT OF A TALENT: AND MEN BLASPHEMED GOD BECAUSE OF THE PLAGUE OF THE HAIL; FOR THE PLAGUE THEREOF WAS EXCEEDING GREAT.

Pastor Lane asked each of his new converts to stand up and give their testimony. Each person stood up and related the events that had led up to their decision for Christ.

When Ron, the last gentleman rose to share his story about accepting Jesus into his heart, he said, "I've always wanted to know God and to experience His presence. I think I have been searching for God all my life," he said, "but this is the first time I have ever been in a church where there was an altar call. And I thank God that I now have eternal life through Jesus Christ. I couldn't say 'no' to the Lord even if my life depended on it!"

II CORINTHIANS 5:17: THEREFORE IF ANY MAN *BE* IN CHRIST, *HE IS* A NEW CREATURE: OLD THINGS ARE PASSED AWAY; BEHOLD, ALLTHINGS ARE BECOME NEW. [SEE EZEKIEL 36:26-27; PSALM 51:7; PSALM 103:12; I JOHN 1:7 & 9; ISAIAH 1:18; ISAIAH 43:25; PSALM 86:5; ISAIAH 55:7; JOHN 6:37; JOHN 1:12]

Upon hearing some bad news, Laura was momentarily paralyzed with shock and too numb to cry. "I just can't believe it," she told her friend. Perhaps that's why I can't cry."

"I understand," said her Christian friend, but I just want you to know that whenever you want to cry on my shoulder, you've got a 'rain' check."

PROVERBS 17:17: A FRIEND LOVETH AT ALL TIMES . . .

PROVERBS 18:24: . . . THERE IS A FRIEND *THAT* STICKETH CLOSER THAN A BROTHER.

II SAMUEL 1:26-27: HOW ARE THE MIGHTY FALLEN IN THE MIDST OF THE BATTLE! O JONATHAN, *THOU WAST* SLAIN IN THE HIGH PLACES. I AM DISTRESSED FOR THEE, MY BROTHER JONATHAN: VERY PLEASANT HAST THOU BEEN UNTO ME: THY LOVE TO ME WAS WONDERFUL, PASSING THE LOVE OF WOMEN.

(Author's note: In the scripture above, David pays tribute to his dear friend, Jonathan, the son of King Saul. He describes his friendship as being so special that he esteemed it higher than the romantic love he had for women. In no way are we to assume that this was any kind of deviate lifestyle. It is, instead, a picture of the purest loyalty between friends . . . hence, "a friend that sticks closer than a brother.")

Describing a Christian friend of hers to a relative, Anne told her aunt, "Katie is the kind of person who would give you the shirt off her back." She then added, "Of course, the fact that she buys all her clothes at garage sales does make it a little easier to be so charitable."

MARK 12:41-44: AND JESUS SAT OVER AGAINST THE TREASURY, AND BEHELD HOW THE PEOPLE CAST MONEY INTO THE TREASURY: AND MANY THAT WERE RICH CAST IN MUCH. AND THERE CAME A CERTAIN POOR WIDOW, AND SHE THREW IN TWO MITES, WHICH MAKE A FARTHING AND HE CALLED *UNTO HIM* HIS DISCIPLES, AND SAITH UNTO THEE, VERILY I SAY UNTO YOU, THAT THIS POOR WIDOW HATH CAST MORE IN, THAN ALL THEY WHICH HAVE CAST INTO THE TREASURY: FOR ALL *THEY* DID CAST IN OF THEIR ABUNDANCE; BUT SHE OF HER WANT DID CAST IN ALL THAT SHE HAD, EVEN ALL HER LIVING.

While driving home from church one evening, a young man, Gerard, who seemed to have a bright future ahead, was involved in a serious car accident.

The party of the other car was seriously injured.

Gerard, the young man at fault was out on bond but was facing a court hearing and probable sentence. In the weeks following he was experiencing heavy anxiety and most fearful of the outcome.

Some of the other brothers and sisters in the Lord tried comforting him with their prayers and reassurance that God would be there in the midst working in his behalf.

"I'm sure that He'll be there," said Gerard, wringing his hands in despair. "It's just that, when he takes the stand to speak in my defense I'm not sure how the judge will react to a character witness who is invisible and will be pleading the fifth."

HEBREWS 9:28: SO CHRIST WAS ONCE OFFERED TO BEAR THE SINS OF MANY; AND UNTO THEM THAT LOOK FOR HIM SHALL HE APPEAR THE SECOND TIME WITHOUT SIN UNTO SALVATION.

HEBREWS 10:37: FOR YET A LITTLE WHILE, AND HE THAT SHALL COME WILL COME, AND WILL NOT TARRY.

TITUS 2:13: LOOKING FOR THAT BLESSED HOPE, AND THE GLORIOUS APPEARING OF THE GREAT GOD AND OUR SAVIOUR [SAVIOR] JESUS CHRIST;

REVELATION 1:7: BEHOLD, HE COMETH WITH CLOUDS; AND EVERY EYE SHALL SEE HIM, AND THEY *ALSO* WHICH PIERCED HIM: AND ALL KINDREDS OF THE EARTH SHALL WAIL BECAUSE OF HIM. EVEN SO, AMEN.

Reverend Edwards gave a stern and sobering appeal to those in his flock who were unsaved. He urged them to come forward and give their hearts to God. "There is a fire and brimstone judgment coming," he warned them emphatically. "Get right with God while you still have the chance!"

One of his listeners went home feeling quite apprehensive about the message. "Do we have fire insurance?" he asked his wife, puzzled by his sudden interest in the house. "Oh, and do we have the number of the fire department posted where it's clearly visible?" he questioned her.

"What is all this about?" she asked in a bewildered tone. "Are you expecting an asteroid to drop out of Jupiter's belt and hit this house?"

REVELATION 8:5-13: AND THE ANGEL TOOK THE CENSER, AND FILLED IT WITH FIRE OF THE ALTAR, AND CAST IT UNTO THE EARTH: AND THERE WERE VOICES, AND THUNDERINGS, AND LIGHTNINGS, AND AN EARTHQUAKE. AND THE SEVEN ANGELS WHICH HAD THE SEVEN TRUMPETS PREPARED THEMSELVES TO SOUND. THE FIRST ANGEL SOUNDED, AND THERE FOLLOWED HAIL AND FIRE MINGLED WITH BLOOD, AND THEY WERE CAST UPON THE EARTH: AND THE THIRD PART OF TREES WAS BURNT UP, AND ALL GREEN GRASS WAS BURNT UP. AND THE SECOND ANGEL SOUNDED, AND AS IT WERE A GREAT MOUNTAIN BURNING WITH FIRE WAS CAST INTO THE SEA: AND THE THIRD PART OF THE SEA BECAME BLOOD; AND THE THIRD PART OF THE CREATURES WHICH WERE IN THE SEA, AND HAD LIFE, DIED; AND THE THIRD PART OF THE SHIPS WERE DESTROYED. AND THE THIRD ANGEL SOUNDED, AND THERE FELL A GREAT STAR FROM HEAVEN, BURNING AS IT WERE A LAMP, AND IT FELL UPON THE THIRD PART OF THE RIVERS, AND UPON THE FOUNTAINS OF WATERS; AND THE NAME OF THE STAR IS CALLED WORMWOOD: AND THE THIRD PART OF THE WATERS BECAME WORMWOOD; AND MANY MEN DIED OF THE WATERS, BECAUSE THEY WERE MADE BITTER. AND THE FOURTH ANGEL SOUNDED, AND THE THIRD PART OF THE SUN WAS SMITTEN, AND THE THIRD PART OF THE MOON, AND THE THIRD PART OF THE STARS; SO AS THE THIRD PART OF THEM WAS DARKENED, AND THE DAY SHONE NOT FOR A THIRD PART OF IT, AND THE NIGHT LIKEWISE. AND I BEHELD, AND HEARD AN ANGEL FLYING THROUGH THE MIDST OF HEAVEN, SAYING WITH A LOUD VOICE, WOE, WOE, WOE, TO THE INHABITERS OF THE EARTH BY REASON OF THE OTHER VOICES OF THE TRUMPET OF THE THREE ANGELS, WHICH ARE YET TO SOUND!

MALACHI 4:1: FOR, BEHOLD, THE DAY COMETH, THAT SHALL BURN AS AN OVEN; AND ALL THE PROUD, YEA, AND ALL THAT DO WICKEDLY, SHALL BE STUBBLE: AND THE DAY THAT COMETH SHALL BURN THEM UP, SAITH THE LORD OF HOSTS, THAT IT SHALL LEAVE THEM NEITHER ROOT NOR BRANCH.

"Where did you get that straggly looking plant, Harry?" his wife, Gertrude asked.

"The Pastor's aunt gave it to me when I stopped by this afternoon to drop off her prescription," he replied.

"You don't honestly expect me to keep that green monstrosity in my living room, do you?" she asked, watching her husband place it near their television.

"I'm growing rather fond of it," he replied, tearing off some of the dead leaves. "But," he said, "I believe it needs a little more dirt."

"Good," she replied. "Let's bury it!"

PSALM 1:1-3: BLESSED IS THE MAN THAT WALKETH NOT IN THE COUNSEL OF THE UNGODLY, NOR STANDETH IN THE WAY OF SINNERS, NOR SITTETH IN THE SEAT OF THE SCORNFUL. BUT HIS DELIGHT IS IN THE LAW OF THE LORD; AND IN HIS LAW DOTH HE MEDITATE DAY AND NIGHT. AND HE SHALL BE LIKE A TREE PLANTED BY THE RIVERS OF WATER, THAT BRINGETH FORTH HIS FRUIT IN HIS SEASON; HIS LEAF ALSO SHALL NOT WITHER; AND WHATSOEVER HE DOETH SHALL PROSPER.

Feeling convicted about wearing too much makeup, Sally asked Reverend Taylor, "Do you think it's a sin to wear makeup?"

"Excuse me for a minute," said the minister rushing to the men's room. When he got there, he gazed into the mirror, looking intensely at himself, studying every pore, every blemish, and every wrinkle. He took out his comb and styled his hair three or four different ways. Then he straightened his tie and brushed the lint off his clothing.

When he returned, he apologized to Sally for the delay in responding to her question. "I've just looked in the mirror," he told her. "I don't think I look that bad," he said, "but if you feel a little makeup would improve my looks, I'm open to suggestions."

EPHESIANS 5:27: THAT HE MIGHT PRESENT IT TO HIMSELF A GLORIOUS CHURCH, NOT HAVING SPOT, OR WRINKLE, OR ANY SUCH THING; BUT THAT IT SHOULD BE HOLY AND WITHOUT BLEMISH.

After going up for prayer faithfully each week, it seemed that God's ear was deaf to Janet's prayers.

"Everything I've prayed about remains unchanged," she told a friend woefully. "I guess God isn't interested in my petty problems. I've been standing in the prayer line every Sunday for months now. Still nothing in my life has been resolved."

Her friend pondered the situation for a few minutes and then responded thoughtfully, "Are you sure you're standing in the right line, Janet?" she asked.

HABAKKUK 3:17-18: ALTHOUGH THE FIG TREE SHALL NOT BLOSSOM, NEITHER *SHALL* FRUIT *BE* IN THE VINES; THE LABOUR [LABOR] OF THE OLIVE SHALL FAIL, AND THE FIELDS SHALL YIELD NO MEAT; THE FLOCK SHALL BE CUT OFF FROM THE FOLD, AND THERE SHALL BE NO HERD IN THE STALLS: YET I WILL REJOICE IN THE LORD, I WILL JOY IN THE GOD OF MY SALVATION. [SEE HEBREWS 11:32-40; PSALM 39:7; PSALM 130:5; HEBREWS 6:10 & 15; HEBREWS 10:23 & 35-36]

I PETER 1:7: THAT THE TRIAL OF YOUR FAITH, BEING MUCH MORE PRECIOUS THAN OF GOLD THAT PERISHETH, THOUGH IT BE TRIED WITH FIRE, MIGHT BE FOUND UNTO PRAISE AND HONOUR [HONOR] AND GLORY AT THE APPEARING OF JESUS CHRIST: [SEE I PETER 4:12-13]

Cheryl was telling her friend, Sue, about the difficult labor her sister had experienced giving birth to her baby.

"My sister was in a lot of pain," she explained. "After being in labor all day, the baby still hadn't come."

"It sounds like it was a trying ordeal," Sue replied.

"It sure was," she answered. 'The doctor finally decided not to let her have the baby by natural childbirth so they performed a 'tonsillectomy' to remove the baby."

want to always do the things that please our Lord.

GALATIONS 6:15: FOR IN CHRIST JESUS NEITHER CIRCUMCISION AVAILETH ANY THING, NOR UNCIRCUMCISION, BUT A NEW CREATURE.

One night, after church services had concluded, a little lady approached the minister. "That was a great message, Pastor Dan," she exclaimed. There were a few places where I wanted to shout out an 'Amen.'"

"Then you should have," insisted the pastor. "No, I'm afraid not," she replied.

"There's no telling what my husband might do if he's awakened during a deep sleep."

I THESSALONIANS 4:14: FOR IF WE BELIEVE THAT JESUS DIED AND ROSE AGAIN, EVEN SO THEM ALSO WHICH SLEEP [THE DEAD] IN JESUS WILL GOD BRING WITH HIM.

Each year Reverend Ames church had a progress banquet and a State of the Church message immediately following the dinner.

Because the banquet was scheduled on a night when the singles class met, a notice was posted on the front door canceling the meeting. It read: "DUE TO PROGRESS BANQUET, SINGLES GROUP IS CANCELED.

That same weekend a wedding had taken place. When the newlyweds received the pictures back that had been taken, they were amused by one picture in particular. In the background of a photo, in which they were embracing, was the message of the singles group which had been partially blocked out because of the couple's presence in front of the door when the picture was taken. Part of the sign, still visible read as follows: DUE TO PROGRESS, SINGLES IS CANCELED.

THE SONG OF SOLOMAN 2:16: MY BELOVED *IS* MINE, AND I *AM* HIS . . . [SEE GENESIS 24:27, 40, & 48; PROVERBS 18:22; PROVERBS 30:18-19]

REVELATION 21:9-10: . . . COME HITHER, I WILL SHEW THEE THE BRIDE, THE LAMB'S WIFE. AND HE CARRIED ME AWAY IN THE SPIRIT TO A

GREAT AND HIGH MOUNTAIN, AND SHEWED ME THAT GREAT CITY, THE HOLY JERUSALEM, DESCENDING OUT OF HEAVEN FROM GOD.

The day to day drudgery of dishes, laundry, and cooking became monotonous to Rhonda, a housewife. "There is nothing in the world I'd rather be than a housewife and homemaker," she told her friend, Amy, "but there are days when I'd enjoy a diversion."

"Why don't you join the church choir?" Amy asked. "You could ride along with me," she told her. "It's only twice a week," "so you'd still have plenty of time to get your housework done. "Besides," she said, "you've got a good voice, so why not use it for the Lord."

"It sounds like a great idea, Amy," Rhonda replied. "It would be an avenue to minister to people. And it would also give me a break a couple times a week from slaving around in the kitchen."

"Sure," Amy said. "You'd be going from the frying pan into the choir."

PSALMS 40:3: AND HE HATH PUT A NEW SONG IN MY MOUTH, EVEN PRAISE UNTO OUR GOD.

II CHRONICLES 20:22: AND WHEN THEY [THE CHILDREN OF ISRAEL BEGAN TO SING AND PRAISE, THE LORD SET AMBUSHMENTS AGAINST THE CHILDREN OF AMMON, MOAB, AND MOUNT SEIR, WHICH WERE COME AGAINST JUDAH; AND THEY WERE SMITTEN. [SEE ACTS 16:25-32; HEBREWS 13:15]

PSALM 149:6: LET THE HIGH PRAISES OF GOD BE IN THEIR MOUTH, AND A TWOEDGED SWORD IN THEIR HAND;

PSALM 18:3 I WILL CALL UPON THE LORD, *WHO IS WORTHY* TO BE PRAISED: SO SHALL I BE SAVED FROM MINE ENEMIES.

After receiving an unsolicited dating application in the mail, a Christian woman sent back a polite refusal informing them that she did not need to enlist their services.

Please do not send me any further mailings, she wrote. *I already belong to a dating service that is out of this world.* She went on to explain, *God sends me all the Christian male friendship I need. His service is absolutely free of charge, and the men in my life are Bible totin', sin smotin', born-again, blood bought believers who love the Lord and know how to treat a woman in a dignified, respectable manner.*

A few days later, she received a note in the mail from a woman who was an employee of the dating service. "Could you tell me," she asked, "where to find one of those men you wrote about?

NUMBERS 12:7: MY SERVANT MOSES . . . WHO *IS* FAITHFUL IN ALL MINE HOUSE . . .

JAMES 2:23: . . . ABRAHAM BELIEVED GOD, AND IT WAS IMPUTED UNTO HIM FOR RIGHTEOUSNESS: AND HE WAS CALLED THE FRIEND OF GOD.

NUMBERS 32:12: . . . CALEB THE SON OF JEPHUNNEH THE KENEZITE, AND JOSHUA THE SON OF NUN: . . . THEY HAVE WHOLLY FOLLOWED THE LORD.

ACTS 13:22: AND WHEN HE [GOD] HAD REMOVED HIM [SAUL], HE RAISED UP UNTO THEM DAVID TO BE THEIR KING; TO WHOM ALSO HE GAVE TESTIMONY, AND SAID, I HAVE FOUND DAVID THE *SON* OF JESSE, A MAN AFTER MINE OWN HEART, WHICH SHALL FULFILL ALL MY WILL. [SEE I SAMUEL 13:14]

I SAMUEL 18:14: AND DAVID BEHAVED HIMSELF WISELY IN ALL HIS WAYS; AND THE LORD *WAS* WITH HIM.

I SAMUEL 18:28: AND SAUL SAW AND KNEW THAT THE LORD *WAS* WITH DAVID . . .

ACTS 9:15: . . . HE [PAUL] IS A CHOSEN VESSEL UNTO ME, TO BEAR MY NAME BEFORE THE GENTILES, AND KINGS, AND THE CHILDREN OF ISRAEL:

ACTS 20:26-27: WHEREFORE I [PAUL] TAKE YOU TO RECORD THIS DAY, THAT I *AM* PURE FROM THE BLOOD OF ALL *MEN*. FOR I HAVE NOT SHUNNED TO DECLARE UNTO YOU ALL THE COUNSEL OF GOD.

JOB 1:1: THERE WAS A MAN IN THE LAND OF UZ, WHOSE NAME *WAS* JOB: AND THAT MAN WAS PERFECT AND UPRIGHT, AND ONE THAT FEARED GOD, AND ESCHEWED EVIL.

ROMANS 16:19 [FAITHFUL MEN OF GOD] FOR YOUR OBEDIENCE IS COME A BROAD UNTO ALL *MEN*...

ACTS 6:5: ... STEPHEN, A MAN FULL OF FAITH AND OF THE HOLY GHOST ...

DANIEL 5:12: FORASMUCH AS AN EXCELLENT SPIRIT, AND KNOWLEDGE, AND UNDERSTANDING, INTERPRETING OF DREAMS, AND SHEWING OF HARD SENTENCES, AND DISSOLVING OF DOUBTS, WERE FOUND IN THE SAME DANIEL, WHOM THE KING NAMED BELTESHAZZAR ...

ACTS 10:1-2: THERE WAS A CERTAIN MAN IN CAESAREA CALLED CORNELIUS, A CENTURION OF THE BAND CALLED THE ITALIAN *BAND*, A DEVOUT MAN, AND ONE THAT FEARED GOD WITH ALL HIS HOUSE, WHICH GAVE MUCH ALMS TO THE PEOPLE, AND PRAYED TO GOD ALWAYS.

"It's hard to imagine that when I was conceived, I started out as just a blob of nothingness," said Gilbert.

"That's not true, Gilbert," replied his Sunday School teacher. "Even in your earliest beginnings, when you were little more than a tiny speck of a person, God had already started to make you intricately unique from any other person before you. At the moment of conception, God had already planned all the wonderful details of your features—how tall or short you would be, how thin or how wide you would be, whether you would have a fair or dark complexion, even down to the most complex details of your being—the color of your eyes and hair, the size of your nose, every little crevice, nook and cranny that makes you look like you and me look like me.

"Are you telling me that God is the one responsible for my existence?

"That's right," replied his teacher.

"And to think," said Gilbert, "that all this time I've been blaming this face on my parents!"

PSALMS 119:73: THY HANDS HAVE MADE ME AND FASHIONED ME. [SEE GENESIS 2:7 & 21-23; PSALM 139:14-16; JOB 33:4; JEREMIAH 1:5]

JOB 31:15: . . . DID NOT ONE FASHION US IN THE WOMB?

After a couple of extensive evangelism endeavors, Brian the missions director, was welcomed back by his pastor.

He picked up the microphone and thanked everyone for their cards and letters. He told them how much he had missed each and everyone.

"Hopefully," he said, "It'll be awhile before I have to leave you again."

He then turned to the staff members. "But if the Lord sends me back to the mission field," he told them, smiling, "I would like to put each one of you in a suitcase and take you with me. As for my wife," he teased, "I need to give that a little more thought."

HEBREWS 11:8-10: BY FAITH ABRAHAM, WHEN HE WAS CALLED TO GO OUT INTO A PLACE WHICH HE SHOULD AFTER RECEIVE FOR AN INHERITANCE, OBEYED; AND HE WENT OUT, NOT KNOWING WHITHER HE WENT. BY FAITH HE SOJOURNED IN THE LAND OF PROMISE, AS *IN* A STRANGE COUNTRY, DWELLING IN TABERNACLES WITH ISAAC AND JACOB, THE HEIRS WITH HIM OF THE SAME PROMISE: FOR HE LOOKED FOR A CITY WHICH HATH FOUNDATIONS, WHOSE BUILDER AND MAKER *IS* GOD.

ISAIAH 30:21: AND THINE EARS SHALL HEAR A WORD BEHIND THEE, SAYING, THIS *IS* THE WAY, WALK YE IN IT . . . [SEE ISAIAH 6:8; PSALM 31:15; PSALM 37:23; PROVERBS 16:9; PROVERBS 20:24]

MATTHEW 10:7-8: AND AS YE GO, PREACH, SAYING, THE KINGDOM OF HEAVEN IS AT HAND. HEAL THE SICK, CLEANSE THE LEPERS, RAISE THE DEAD, CAST OUT DEVILS: FREELY YE HAVE RECEIVED, FREELY GIVE.

"The baby is coming!" Faith told her husband.

He quickly took her bags and loaded them in their van. "Here, take my arm," he told his wife, helping her into the car.

When they arrived at the hospital, his wife was quickly ushered up to the labor and delivery room.

"We have a few rules and regulations you should be aware of here in the 'matrinity' ward," the nurse told Faith's husband. "As you know," she said, "this hospital is a Christian facility and we only allow three visitors at a time—God the Father, God the Son, and a holy guest, which, in this case is you!"

I JOHN 5:7: FOR THERE ARE THREE THAT BEAR RECORD IN HEAVEN, THE FATHER, THE WORD, AND THE HOLY GHOST: AND THESE THREE ARE ONE.

"Would you like some tea and crumpets?" Anne asked her friend, Martha.

"Thanks, that would be delightful," Martha replied. "I think I'm suffering from jet lag," she said. "It's a long trip from the U.S. to England. It's so nice just to be able to stretch my legs." "You'll have plenty of opportunity to do that," Anne said. "We want to show you all of the sights here."

Then, handing Mary a cup of tea, she said, smiling, "Here in England we have our own version of the beatitudes: Blessed are the tea makers!"

MATTHEW 5:9: BLESSED ARE THE PEACEMAKERS: FOR THEY SHALL BE CALLED THE CHILDREN OF GOD.

Velma had missed several Sunday night and Wednesday night services. "I sure hope the Pastor hasn't noticed I've been gone," she told her friend, Emma.

"Don't worry about it Velma," Emma said. "The pastor's had to do several funerals lately," she said, "and all of those people have been missing, too."

PSALM 17:15: AS FOR ME, I WILL BEHOLD THY FACE IN RIGHTEOUSNESS: I SHALL BE SATISFIED, WHEN I AWAKE, WITH THY LIKENESS.

As Marianne was sorting through boxes of used clothing and knick knacks at a church auction, she commented on the incredible bargains they had. "A lot of these things are like new!" she exclaimed.

"You think this stuff is a bargain," remarked one of the workers, "just wait until you get to the gymnasium. They've got all kinds of furniture in there that was donated for the auction. And," she said, "if you'll pardon the expression, I think you'll find the prices are a 'real steal.'"

"Great!" replied, Marianne. "Our place could sure use a face lift. My furniture is really sagging and badly worn," she said. "I'll go check it out."

Just as the worker had told her, they were practically giving it away just to get it off the premises.

Later that evening, showing off her new sofa, loveseat, and end tables, Marianne bragged to her friend, "Where else but church could you get a complete living room outfit for 75 cents!"

EZRA 8:22: . . . THE HAND OF OUR GOD *IS* UPON ALL THEM FOR GOOD THAT SEEK HIM; BUT HIS POWER AND HIS WRATH *IS* AGAINST ALL THEM THAT FORSAKE HIM.

Jeff was filling out checks to cover his monthly bills. *Let's see*, he said to himself, sorting through the bills, *which of you guys would mind waiting awhile?*

He picked up the gas statement. *My good friend, the gas company*, he said sarcastically. *You always keep in touch.* Jeff looked at the bill a little more closely. *Whoa*, he shrieked, *it says here that you want to be paid within thirty days or I freeze!* Jeff quickly wrote out a check. *Okay boys, relax*, he said, *don't get your feathers ruffled; it's in the mail.*

Then he picked up his electric bill. *Too many kilowatts, and not enough cash, hey?*" he said, shaking his head. "*Okay fellas, hold your horses*," he declared, "*the check's on the way.*" Then he looked upward throwing his arms up in the air. *Wow, Lord,* he said, *when you created light I bet you had no idea what the electric company would do when they got involved!*

Next Jeff fished through the pile of delinquent accounts for his phone bill. When he saw the staggering amount he owed, he gasped. *I'm sorry I found that one!* he exclaimed.

He shuffled through some other bills. *And now here's the happy little house payment*, he said with a sinister snicker. *With the way things have been going for me*, he said to himself, *the termites will have this place eaten before I ever get it paid off.* Nevertheless, he filled out the check and put it in the envelope.

And now, last, but not least, Jeff said, *it's your turn, God. Ten percent, right? Okay, Lord, you're getting it with no back talk from me.* Without thinking, Jeff made the check payable to 'Jehovah.'

A week later, the check was returned to him from his church.

This came for you," his elderly mother said, handing him the envelope.

When he opened it and saw the returned check he showed it to his mother. "What's the matter, mom?" he remarked with a chuckle, "doesn't God accept personal checks anymore?"

HEBREWS 13:8: JESUS CHRIST THE SAME YESTERDAY, AND TO DAY, AND FOR EVER.

Dad, if there were no freezers in hell and I was a giant ice cube, how long would it take me to melt after I got there?
well son, that would depend on how well the air conditioning system works down there.

As the deacons were preparing to pass the offering plates, Rose pulled her wallet out of her purse so that her tithe and offering would be ready when the plate was passed.

Russell, her son-in-law and a new Christian, was eager to please his new mother-in-law by attending church with her one Sunday morning when his wife was working.

Misinterpreting her actions, he assumed that the large wad of bills must be for something other than the offering plate. He knew that her income was limited and assumed that she would never give that much to the church.

Then it suddenly dawned on him as he glanced at the wad of money that she had once told him about tithing. She had explained that it was not only a command, but a privilege to give God at least ten cents out of every dollar. "After all," she said, "It's a pretty good arrangement if you ask me. You give the Lord ten cents out of every dollar," she said, "and you keep ninety cents. He could have asked for ninety cents and made you keep the ten cents. But the way I see it," she continued, "even if He had asked for the larger amount, it's a small thing to give when you consider that He gave all."

JOHN 3:16: FOR GOD SO LOVED THE WORLD, THAT HE GAVE HIS ONLY BEGOTTEN SON, THAT WHOSOEVER BELIEVETH IN HIM SHOULD NOT PERISH, BUT HAVE EVERLASTING LIFE.

A crippled and elderly widow who had been suffering for months hobbled up to the altar for prayer. "Besides healing, I'm up here to receive all that the Lord might have for me," she told the minister and his assistants.

The pastors and deacons surrounded themselves around her and laid their hands on her head. A few seconds later because of so many hands on her, she began to sense her hair piece sliding off. As a result she decided to hurry things along.

"Praise God," she exclaimed, pushing her toupee in place. "The Lord just touched me from 'taup' to bottom."

(Author's note: In Revelation 9:8, we read about some very strange creatures with hair like women's, but with a diabolical nature coming straight from the pit of hell.)

REVELATION 9:1-11: AND THE FIFTH ANGEL SOUNDED AND I SAW A STAR FALL FROM HEAVEN UNTO THE EARTH: AND TO HIM WAS GIVEN THE KEY OF THE BOTTOMLESS PIT. AND HE OPENED THE BOTTOMLESS PIT; AND THERE AROSE A SMOKE OF A GREAT FURNACE; AND THE SUN AND THE AIR WERE DARKENED BY REASON OF THE SMOKE OF THE PIT. AND THERE CAME OUT OF THAT SMOKE LOCUSTS UPON THE EARTH: AND UNTO THEM WAS GIVEN POWER, AS THE SCORPIONS OF THE EARTH HAVE POWER. AND IT WAS COMMANDED THEM THAT THEY SHOULD NOT HURT THE GRASS OF THE EARTH, NEITHER ANY GREEN THING, NEITHER ANY TREE; BUT ONLY THOSE MEN WHICH HAVE NOT THE SEAL OF GOD IN THEIR FOREHEADS. AND TO THEM IT WAS GIVEN THAT THEY SHOULD NOT KILL THEM, BUT THAT THEY SHOULD BE TORMENTED FIVE MONTHS: AND THEIR TORMENT *WAS* AS THE TORMENT OF A SCORPION, WHEN HE STRIKETH A MAN. AND IN THOSE DAYS SHALL MEN SEEK DEATH, AND SHALL NOT FIND IT; AND SHALL DESIRE TO DIE, AND DEATH SHALL FLEE FROM THEM. AND THE SHAPES OF THE LOCUSTS *WERE* LIKE UNTO HORSES PREPARED UNTO BATTLE; AND ON THEIR HEADS *WERE* AS IT WERE CROWNS LIKE GOLD, AND THEIR FACES *WERE* AS THE FACES OF MEN. AND THEY HAD HAIR AS THE HAIR OF WOMEN, AND THEIR TEETH WERE AS *THE TEETH* OF LIONS. AND THEY HAD BREASTPLATES, AS IT WERE BREASTPLATES OF IRON; AND THE SOUND OF THEIR WINGS *WAS* AS THE SOUND OF CHARIOTS OF MANY HORSES RUNNING TO BATTLE. AND THEY HAD TAILS LIKE UNTO SCORPIONS, AND THERE WERE STINGS IN THEIR TAILS: AND THEIR POWER *WAS* TO HURT MEN FIVE MONTHS. AND THEY HAD A KING OVER THEM, *WHICH IS* THE ANGEL OF THE BOTTOMLESS PIT, WHOSE NAME IN THE HEBREW TONGUE *IS* ABADDON, BUT IN THE GREEK TONGUE HATH *HIS* NAME APPOLLYON.

SATAN SHAKERS

"It's the F.B.I. and the C.I.A.! Please open your door!" came the chorus of voices behind Vern's apartment door as they knocked loudly.

"But I haven't done anything wrong!" cried Vern speaking through the crack of his door. "I've never even had a traffic ticket."

"Please open up!" they persisted. Vern slowly opened his door, wondering what fate would befall him by doing so. He looked fearfully at the three gentlemen standing before him dressed in black suits.

"We didn't mean to frighten you," one of them told him. We're from the F.B.I. and the C.I.A."

"There must be some mistake," said Vern. I probably just resemble somebody you're looking for."

"We're not picky," answered another gentleman.

"What do you mean, you're not picky?" Vern said indignantly. "Is this some kind of a joke? If it is," he told them angrily, "I fail to see the humor in it." He glared at the three men and then asked to see their identification."

"Here's my identification," said one of the gentlemen holding up his Bible as he smiled from ear to ear.

"Who are you and what's going on?" Vern demanded to know.

"We're from the church down the street," one of the men answered politely. "We're going door to door witnessing," he told Vern. "We're not picky," he said, "because neither is Jesus. God is no respecter of persons.

"And as for the F.B.I.," he continued, "that stands for 'Faithful Believers, Inc.'"

"And the C.I.A. stands for Christian Inspiration Association," replied another gentleman.

"Do you have any idea how much you scared me?" Vern asked. "You should be ashamed of yourselves."

"We apologize," said one of the men, "but we figured it would be better for you to be scared for five minutes than for all eternity."

II CORINTHIANS 5:11: KNOWING THEREFORE THE TERROR OF THE LORD, WE PERSUADE MEN;

HEBREWS 10:31: *IT IS* A FEARFUL THING TO FALL INTO THE HANDS OF THE LIVING GOD.

MATTHEW 10:28: AND FEAR NOT THEM WHICH KILL THE BODY, BUT ARE NOT ABLE TO KILL THE SOUL: BUT RATHER FEAR HIM WHICH IS ABLE TO DESTROY BOTH SOUL AND BODY IN HELL.

(Author's note: I do not recommend the approach to witnessing that they used in the story above! Our Lord Jesus told us to be 'wise as serpents but harmless as doves.)

MATTHEW 10:16: BEHOLD, I SEND YOU FORTH AS SHEEP IN THE MIDST OF WOLVES: BE YE THEREFORE WISE AS SERPENTS, AND HARMLESS AS DOVES

Just shortly after buying a new motorcycle, Ray was the victim of a hit and run driver. Not having latched the strap on his helmet, it flew off during the accident.

A pedestrian who witnessed the ordeal saw the helmet roll down the road. In the midnight darkness, he mistook it for Ray's head.

"Whew, that was a ghastly sight," he told Ray. "I thought your head was rolling down the pavement!"

"When the doctors delivered me," Ray joked, "they told my mother that no assembly was required, but ever since I got this bike," he said, "I've been put back together more times than a jigsaw puzzle! I think the devil's been trying to kill me," he chuckled, "but with God's help, I'm not making it easy for him!"

EPHESIANS 6:10-17: FINALLY, MY BRETHREN, BE STRONG IN THE LORD, AND IN THE POWER OF HIS MIGHT. PUT ON THE WHOLE ARMOUR [ARMOR] OF GOD, THAT YE MAY BE ABLE TO STAND AGAINST THE WILES OF THE DEVIL. FOR WE WRESTLE NOT AGAINST FLESH AND BLOOD, BUT AGAINST PRINCIPALITIES, AGAINST POWERS, AGAINST THE RULERS OF THE DARKNESS OF THIS WORLD, AGAINST SPIRITUAL WICKEDNESS IN HIGH *PLACES*. WHEREFORE TAKE UNTO YOU THE WHOLE ARMOUR [ARMOR] OF GOD, THAT YE MAY BE ABLE TO WITHSTAND IN THE EVIL DAY, AND HAVING DONE ALL, TO STAND. STAND THEREFORE, HAVING YOUR LOINS GIRT ABOUT WITH TRUTH, AND HAVING ON THE BREASTPLATE OF RIGHTEOUSNESS; AND YOUR FEET SHOD WITH THE PREPARATION OF THE GOSPEL OF PEACE; ABOVE ALL, TAKING THE SHIELD OF FAITH, WHEREWITH YE SHALL BE ABLE TO QUENCH ALL THE FIERY DARTS OF THE WICKED. AND TAKE THE HELMET OF SALVATION, AND THE SWORD OF THE SPIRIT, WHICH IS THE WORD OF GOD:

Amanda was a young Christian woman whose determination to witness was unparalleled.

Her automobile was literally buried under a barrage of religious bumper stickers.

The front and back door of her house was also plastered with Christian stickers. In each window was a scripture promise. Her walls were covered with plagues and pictures, so much so that folks who visited her thought they'd just entered a shrine.

Amanda, herself, was a walking sermon. Her clothing was covered with a mass of pins, all containing scriptures and religious sayings. Her handbag, weighing just under a ton, was filled with tracts and Christian literature. Everything, including the dog's dish, was laced with scriptures of various sorts—from salvation messages to the promise of the Lord's return.

When asked why she had gotten so carried away with proclaiming the gospel, she replied with Acts 4:20: For we cannot but speak the things which we have seen and heard."

PSALMS 111:97: OH HOW LOVE I THY LAW; IT *IS* MY MEDITATION ALL THE DAY.

PSALM 1:2: BUT HIS DELIGHT *IS* IN THE LAW OF THE LORD; AND IN HIS LAW DOTH HE MEDITATE DAY AND NIGHT.

JOB 23:12: NEITHER HAVE I GONE BACK FROM THE COMMANDMENT OF HIS LIPS; I HAVE ESTEEMED THE WORDS OF HIS MOUTH MORE THAN MY NECESSARY *FOOD.* [SEE JOHN 6:63; JOHN 7:46]

JEREMIAH 15:16: THY WORDS WERE FOUND, AND I DID EAT THEM; AND THY WORD WAS UNTO ME THE JOY AND REJOICING OF MINE HEART: FOR I AM CALLED BY THY NAME, O LORD GOD OF HOSTS.

DEUTERONOMY 6:5-9: AND THOU SHALT LOVE THE LORD THY GOD WITH ALL THINE HEART, AND WITH ALL THY SOUL, AND WITH ALL THY MIGHT. AND THESE WORDS, WHICH I COMMAND THEE THIS DAY, SHALL BE IN THINE HEART: AND THOU SHALT TEACH THEM DILIGENTLY UNTO THY CHILDREN, AND SHALT TALK OF THEM WHEN THOU SITTEST IN THINE HOUSE, AND WHEN THOU WALKEST BY THE WAY, AND WHEN THOU LIEST DOWN, AND WHEN THOU RISEST UP. AND THOU SHALT BIND THEM FOR A SIGN UPON THINE HAND, AND THEY SHALL BE AS FRONTLETS BETWEEN THINE EYES. AND THOU SHALT WRITE THEM UPON THE POSTS OF THY HOUSE, AND ON THY GATES. [SEE PROVERBS 4:20-23]

PSALM 92:2: TO SHEW [SHOW] FORTH THY LOVINGKINDNESS IN THE MORNING, AND THY FAITHFULNESS EVERY NIGHT,

Geraldine, a seamstress, invited a dozen or more ladies to her home one evening for a sewing bee. "I thought it would be nice," she told them, "if we could all work together and make a quilt for the pastor's wife's birthday. It's next month," she continued, "so we don't have much time."

Only nine of the invited guests were present. Geraldine had some refreshments prepared for her guests which she served when they were finished working on the quilt. "And now," she said, "I think we should take time out for devotions." She ended their time with the Lord with an invitation to receive Christ for those from the church who might not yet know Him personally. All nine of the ladies bowed their heads, asking to receive Jesus into their lives.

Astonished at the miracle of salvation that had taken place in her home, Geraldine related to a friend, "This adds new meaning to 'a stitch in time saves nine!'"

PSALMS 96:2: SING UNTO THE LORD. BLESS HIS NAME; SHEW FORTH HIS SALVATION FROM DAY TO DAY.

I CHRONICLES 16:23: SING UNTO THE LORD, ALL THE EARTH; SHEW FORTH FROM DAY TO DAY HIS SALVATION.

"For whatsoever is not of faith is sin," quoted Reverend Chapman from Romans 14:23. "Do you know what that means, flock?" the Reverend asked his audience. "It means that worrying could be classified as sin and," he said, "that's exactly what the devil wants you to do."

He went on to admonish them not to be idle. He explained that the devil often gets the upper hand when a believer is not occupied with Christian duties. "Keep your mind on Christ and stay busy helping others," he said, "and you'll find that you won't have much time to think about yourself. And I can guarantee you," he continued, "speaking from my own experience, you'll be too tired to worry!"

One distraught woman passed the minister on the way out. Noticing her sad countenance he asked if something was wrong.

"Yes, Reverend Chapman," she said. "To be honest with you," she sighed, "Living by myself there's not much to do around my place. I'm worried that all my idle time will be spent the way it always is—worrying."

"Oh, that's no problem," the Reverend told her. "Just go home and drink eight glasses of water every hour and you'll have lots of things to do."

EPHESIANS 4:27: NEITHER GIVE PLACE TO THE DEVIL.

PHILIPPIANS 4:8: FINALLY, BRETHREN, WHATSOEVER THINGS ARE TRUE, WHATSOEVER THINGS ARE HONEST, WHATSOEVER THINGS APE JUST, WHATSOEVER THINGS ARE PURE, WHATSOEVER THINGS ARE LOVELY, WHATSOEVER THINGS ARE OF GOOD REPORT; IS THERE BE ANY VIRTUE, THINK ON THESE THINGS.

ROMANS 8:35, & 37-39: WHO SHALL SEPARATE US FROM THE LOVE OF CHRIST? SHALL TRIBULATION, OR DISTRESS, OR PERSECUTION, OR FAMINE, OR NAKEDNESS OR PERIL, OR SWORD? NAY, IN ALL THESE THINGS WE ARE MORE THAN CONQUERORS THROUGH HIM THAT LOVED US. FOR I AM PERSUADED, THAT NEITHER DEATH, NOR LIFE, NOR ANGELS, NOR PRINCIPALITIES, NOR POWERS, NOR THINGS PRESENT, NOR THINGS TO COME, NOR HEIGHT, NOR DEPTH, NOR ANY OTHER CREATURE, SHALL BE ABLE TO SEPARATE US FROM THE LOVE OF GOD, WHICH IS IN CHRIST JESUS OUR LORD.

"I was delighted to finally see your husband up at the altar today," commented Pastor Perkins to Helen, the wife of the new convert. "The devil had him for such a long time, but now, thank God," he said smiling, "he's under new management and I bet the devil is shivering in his shoes about that!"

"Yes, I'm thrilled too," she told the Pastor. "All it took was some heavy prompting by the Holy Spirit and a banana peel under his foot."

"A banana peel?" the pastor asked, grinning.

"Sure, Pastor Perkins," she said, "he would've slid up sooner but he needed that extra momentum."

ACTS 3:19: REPENT YE THEREFORE, AND BE CONVERTED, THAT YOUR SINS MAY BE BLOTTED OUT, WHEN THE TIMES OF REFRESHING SHALL COME FROM THE PRESENCE OF THE LORD . . .

"I'm sorry, sir," said the librarian, "but this book is long overdue. I'm afraid you're going to owe a rather large fine." As she began looking up the amount of the fee, the gentlemen began whistling a happy tune. He smiled as if he wasn't the least bit bothered over the penalty.

Meanwhile, the librarian calculated the fine and told the gentleman the amount he owed. Still, he appeared not be disturbed by it.

"For someone who owes us $25.00," she remarked, "you certainly seem to be good natured about it."

"Miss," he said joyfully, "any fine incurred is well worth what I received from this Book."

"And just what is that?" The librarian asked, setting aside the overdue Bible.

"Eternal Life!" he told her.

"In that case," she said, picking up the Bible, "maybe I should read it myself."

I JOHN 2:25: AND THIS IS THE PROMISE THAT HE HATH PROMISED US, *EVEN* ETERNAL LIFE.

HEBREWS 7:25: WHEREFORE HE [JESUS] IS ABLE ALSO TO SAVE THEM TO THE UTTERMOST THAT COME UNTO GOD BY HIM, SEEING HE EVER LIVETH TO MAKE INTERCESSION FOR THEM.

HEBREWS 6:19: WHICH *HOPE* WE HAVE AS AN ANCHOR OF THE SOUL, BOTH SURE AND STEDFAST . . .

I PETER 1:4: . . . AN INHERITANCE INCORRUPTIBLE, AND UNDEFILED, AND THAT FADETH NOT AWAY, RESERVED IN HEAVEN FOR YOU,

I PETER 1:8-9: WHOM HAVING NOT SEEN, YE LOVE; IN WHOM, THOUGH NOW YE SEE HIM NOT, YET BELIEVING, YE REJOICE WITH JOY UNSPEAKABLE AND FULL OF GLORY: RECEIVING THE END OF YOUR FAITH, EVEN THE SALVATION OF YOUR SOULS.

GALATIONS 1:11-12: BUT I CERTIFY YOU, BRETHREN, THAT THE GOSPEL WHICH WAS PREACHED OF ME IS NOT AFTER MAN. FOR I NEITHER RECEIVED IT OF MAN, NEITHER WAS I TAUGHT *IT*, BUT BY THE REVELATION OF JESUS CHRIST. [SEE II PETER 1:20-21]

PSALM 19:7: THE LAW OF THE LORD *IS* PERFECT, CONVERTING THE SOUL: THE TESTIMONY OF THE LORD *IS* SURE, MAKING WISE THE SIMPLE.

ACTS 17:11: THESE [THE BEREANS] WERE MORE NOBLE THAN THOSE IN THESSALONICA, IN THAT THEY RECEIVED THE WORD WITH ALL READINESS OF MIND, AND SEARCHED THE SCRIPTURES DAILY, WHETHER THOSE THINGS WERE SO.

JOHN 14:6: JESUS SAITH UNTO HIM, I AM THE WAY, THE TRUTH, AND THE LIFE: NO MAN COMETH UNTO THE FATHER, BUT BY ME.

Reverend Brown had an unsurpassed reputation for preaching on the judgment and wrath of God.

One night, in the middle of one of his fiery messages on the eternal flames of hell, a young man came rushing down to the altar and dropped to his knees in prayer.

The pastor was overwhelmed with emotion at seeing such a moving response to his message. He walked over and knelt beside the broken man, hoping the reason for his presence was a desire for salvation. "What brings you to the altar?" he asked him tenderly.

"I can't exactly explain it," said the man. "I felt compelled to come down here. I listened to your message on hellfire and brimstone. I guess it reminded me of a nasty sunburn I experienced years ago. Ever since then, I've always had enough sense to come in out of the heat."

II PETER 3:10: BUT THE DAY OF THE LORD WILL COME AS A THIEF IN THE NIGHT; IN THE WHICH THE HEAVENS SHALL PASS AWAY WITH A GREAT NOISE, AND THE ELEMENTS SHALL MELT WITH FERVENT HEAT, THE EARTH ALSO AND THE WORKS THAT ARE THEREIN SHALL BE BURNED UP.

"Class, I'd like you to turn in your book reports today," Miss Chelsea told her students.

"Melinda," she said, "Would you pick up everyone's report, please."

Melissa nodded and began collecting the book reports.

After all of them were handed to Miss Chelsea, she gave her tenth grade students some study time to complete another assignment she had given them.

Meanwhile, she began looking through the papers, noticing page after page had the same student's name on it.

"Bobby," she whispered, "would you come here a moment."

The young man walked up to her desk.

"Bobby," she said rather sternly, "nearly two thirds of these papers have your name on them! Did you do book reports for some of the other students?"

"No," replied Bobby. "They're all mine."

"But, Bobby," Miss Chelsea told him, "you only had to read one book."

"Yes, I know, Miss Chelsea," he said. But I chose the Bible and everybody knows there's sixty-six books in it!"

PSALMS 119:105: THY WORD IS A LAMP UNTO MY FEET, AND A LIGHT UNTO MY PATH.

PSALM 138:2: . . . FOR THOU HAST MAGNIFIED THY WORD ABOVE ALL THY NAME. [SEE I JOHN 5:7; MATTHEW 4:4: PROVERBS 4:20-23; PROVERBS 30:5]

JOHN 5:39 & 46: SEARCH THE SCRIPTURES; FOR IN THEM YE THINK YE HAVE ETERNAL LIFE: AND THEY ARE THEY WHICH TESTIFY OF ME . . . FOR HAD YE BELIEVED MOSES, YE WOULD HAVE BELIEVED ME: FOR HE WROTE OF ME. [SEE LUKE 24:44; ACTS 13:33-35]

JOHN 6:63: . . . THE WORDS THAT I [JESUS] SPEAK UNTO YOU, *THEY* ARE SPIRIT, AND *THEY* ARE LIFE. [SEE JOHN 1:1 & 14]

A salesman went door to door trying to sell life insurance policies. When he entered one woman's house, he was told that she wouldn't need any.

"I already have insurance," she told him. "Rapture insurance," she said excitedly, "and you can cash in on it whether you're dead or alive!"

"Hmmm," he said, rather skeptical. "I don't believe I've ever heard of it."

"Then sit down," she exclaimed, "And I'll tell you all about the provisions you're entitled to under the full-coverage plan!"

ROMANS 8:11, 14, 17: BUT IF THE SPIRIT OF HIM THAT RAISED UP JESUS FROM THE DEAD DWELL IN YOU, HE THAT RAISED UP CHRIST FROM THE DEAD SHALL ALSO QUICKEN YOUR MORTAL BODIES BY HIS SPIRIT THAT DWELLETH IN YOU . . . FOR AS MANY AS ARE LED BY THE SPIRIT OF GOD, THEY ARE THE SONS OF GOD. AND IF CHILDREN, THEN HEIRS; HEIRS OF GOD, AND JOINT-HEIRS WITH CHRIST: IF SO BE THAT WE SUFFER WITH HIM, THAT WE MAY BE ALSO GLORIFIED TOGETHER.

II CORINTHIANS 4:14: KNOWING THAT HE WHICH RAISED UP THE LORD JESUS SHALL RAISE UP US ALSO BY JESUS, AND SHALL PRESENT *US* WITH YOU.

JOHN 11:25: JESUS SAID UNTO HER, I AM THE RESURRECTION, AND THE LIFE: HE THAT BELIEVETH IN ME, THOUGH HE WERE DEAD, YET SHALL HE LIVE:

JOHN 14:19: . . . BECAUSE I LIVE, YE SHALL LIVE ALSO.

I THESSALONIANS 4:15-18: FOR THIS WE SAY UNTO YOU BY THE WORD OF THE LORD, THAT WE WHICH ARE ALIVE *AND* REMAIN UNTO THE COMING OF THE LORD SHALL NOT PREVENT THEM WHICH ARE ASLEEP. FOR THE LORD HIMSELF SHALL DESCEND FROM HEAVEN WITH A SHOUT, WITH THE VOICE OF THE ARCHANGEL, AND WITH THE TRUMP OF GOD: AND THE DEAD IN CHRIST SHALL RISE FIRST: THEN WE WHICH ARE ALIVE *AND* REMAIN SHALL BE CAUGHT UP TOGETHER WITH THEM IN THE CLOUDS, TO MEET THE LORD IN THE AIR: AND SO SHALL WE EVER BE WITH THE LORD. WHEREFORE COMFORT ONE ANOTHER WITH THESE WORDS.

"Someone's thinking of you," the mailman told Annette, handing her a big package.

"It's my birthday," she said, excited by the unexpected gift. "And it's from a close friend of mine whom I haven't seen in months."

"Well, I didn't think it felt like a bomb," the mailman teased, also handing her a couple of letters.

Annette tore open the package as soon as she got inside. *How beautiful*, she said to herself, admiring the intricately embroidered plague given her.

Then she picked up the enclosed note which read: *Dear Annette, I couldn't afford to buy you a present but I think you'll like the embroidered scripture just as well. Love from your friend, Neva.*

Annette picked up the plague, studying each carefully stitched word of Numbers 6:24-26: "The Lord bless thee, and keep thee: The Lord make his face shine upon thee, and be gracious unto thee: The Lord lift up his countenance upon thee, and give thee peace.

Annette wasn't sure where she wanted to hang it. But then it occurred to her that a number of family members who frequently visited were atheistic in their views. *I know the perfect place to put it,* she said to herself, hanging it on the wall in front of the toilet. *Sooner or later they'll be in here and it'll be waiting to speak to them!*

I SAMUEL 25:6: . . . PEACE *BE* BOTH TO THEE, AND PEACE *BE* TO THINE HOUSE, AND PEACE *BE* UNTO ALL THAT THOU HAST.

DEUTERONOMY 28:2-6: AND ALL THESE BLESSINGS SHJALL COME ON THEE, AND OVERTAKE THEE, IF THOU SHALT HEARKEN UNTO THE VOICE OF THE LORD THY GOD. BLESSED *SHALT* THOU *BE* IN THE CITY, AND BLESSED *SHALT* THOU *BE* IN THE FIELD. BLESSED *SHALL BE* THE FRUIT OF THY BODY, AND THE FRUIT OF THY GROUND, AND THE FRUIT OF THY CATTLE, THE INCREASE OF THY KINE, AND THE FLOCKS OF THY SHEEP. BLESSED *SHALL BE* THY BASKET AND THY STORE. BLESSED *SHALT* THOU *BE* WHEN THOU COMEST IN, AND BLESSED *SHALT* THOU *BE* WHEN THOU GOEST OUT.

PSALM 103:1-5: BLESS THE LORD, O MY SOUL: AND ALL THAT IS WITHIN ME, *BLESS* HIS HOLY NAME. BLESS THE LORD, O MY SOUL, AND FORGET NOT ALL HIS BENEFITS: WHO FORGIVETH ALL THINE INIQUITIES; WHO HEALETH ALL THY DISEASES; WHO REDEEMETH THY LIFE FROM DESTRUCTION; WHO CROWNETH THEE WITH LOVINGKINDNESS AND TENDER MERCIES; WHO SATISFIETH THY MOUTH WITH GOOD *THINGS; SO THAT* THY YOUTH IS RENEWED LIKE THE EAGLE'S.

PSALM 68:19: BLESSED *BE* THE LORD, *WHO* DAILY LOADETH US *WITH BENEFITS, EVEN* THE GOD OF OUR SALVATION. SELAH.

PSALM 84:11: FOR THE LORD GOD *IS* A SUN AND SHIELD: THE LORD WILL GIVE GRACE AND GLORY: NO GOOD *THING* WILL HE WITHHOLD FROM THEM THAT WALK UPRIGHTLY. [SEE ROMANS 8:32]

III JOHN 4:2: BELOVED, I WISH ABOVE ALL THINGS THAT THOU MAYEST PROSPER AND BE IN HEALTH, EVEN AS THY SOUL PROSPERETH.

Janet and Emily were out taking a walk with Janet's black lab when they happened to pass by a beautiful ornate church with stained glass windows. They happened to notice that the front doors were wide open. "That's odd," said Janet, "maybe there is a wedding or funeral planned for today."

Emily suggested they take a peek inside. "We won't go in, of course," she said, "but we can get close enough to the front of the building to see what it looks like inside.

Suddenly, however, Janet's black lab got loose and headed straight toward the doors. It ran like lightning down the front aisle and straight up to the altar wagging its tail.

Out of nowhere one of the maintenance workers appeared.

Janet and Emily profoundly apologized and grabbed the dog's leash.

"Don't be too hard on him," the worker said, patting the dog on the head. "He has more sense than most of the members here. Some of them have never come down to the altar even once!"

GENESIS 8:20: AND NOAH BUILDED AN ALTAR UNTO THE LORD . . . AND OFFERED BURNT OFFERINGS ON THE ALTAR . . .

GENESIS 22:8-9: AND ABRAHAM SAID, MY SON, GOD WILL PROVIDE HIMSELF A LAMB FOR A BURNT OFFERING: SO THEY WENT BOTH OF THEM TOGETHER. AND THEY CAME TO THE PLACE WHICH GOD HAD TOLD HIM OF; AND ABRAHAM BUILT AN ALTAR THERE . . .

EXODUS 17:15: AND MOSES BUILT AN ALTAR, AND CALLED THE NAME OF IT JEHOVAH-NISSI . . .

JOSHUA 8:30: THEN JOSHUA BUILT AN ALTAR UNTO THE LORD GOD OF ISRAEL IN MOUNT EBAL . . .

I SAMUEL 14:35: AND SAUL BUILT AN ALTAR UNTO THE LORD: THE SAME WAS THE FIRST ALTAR THAT HE BUILT UNTO THE LORD.

II SAMUEL 24:18-19 & 24-25: AND GAD CAME THAT DAY TO DAVID, AND SAID UNTO HIM, GO UP, REAR AN ALTAR UNTO THE LORD IN THE THRESHING FLOOR OF ARAUNAH THE JEBUSITE. AND DAVID, ACCORDING TO THE SAYING OF GAD, WENT UP AS THE LORD COMMANDED . . . AND THE KING SAID UNTO ARAUNAH, [WHO GRACIOUSLY OFFERED HIM EVERYTHING FOR FREE FOR THE ALTAR AND SACRIFICES] NAY; BUT I WILL SURELY BUY *IT* OF THEE AT A PRICE; NEITHER WILL I OFFER BURNT OFFERINGS UNTO THE LORD MY GOD OF THAT WHICH DOTH COST ME NOTHING. SO DAVID BOUGHT THE THRESHING FLOOR AND THE OXEN FOR FIFTY SHEKELS OF SILVER. AND DAVID BUILT THRE AN ALTAR UNTO THE LORD, AND OFFERED BURNT OFFERINGS AND PEACE OFFERINGS. SO THE LORD WAS INTREATED FOR THE LAND, AND THE PLAGUE WAS STAYED FROM ISRAEL.

II CHRONICLES 5:13-14: IT CAME EVEN TO PASS, AS THE TRUMPETERS AND SINGERS *WERE* AS ONE, TO MAKE ONE SOUND TO BE HEARD IN PRAISING AND THANKING THE LORD [AND THE LEVITES & PRIESTS STANDING AT THE EAST END OF THE ALTAR IN THE DEDICATION OF SOLOMAN'S TEMPLE]; AND WHEN THEY LIFTED UP *THEIR* VOICE WITH THE TRUMPETS AND CYMBALS AND INSTRUMENTS OF MUSICK [MUSIC], AND PRAISED THE LORD, *SAYING*, FOR *HE IS* GOOD; FOR HIS MERCY *ENDURETH* FOR EVER: THAT *THEN* THE HOUSE WAS FILLED WITH A CLOUD, *EVEN* THE HOUSE OF THE LORD: SO THAT THE PRIESTS COULD NOT STAND TO MINISTER BY REASON OF THE CLOUD: FOR THE GLORY OF THE LORD HAD FILLED THE HOUSE OF GOD.

"You don't really believe in the devil do you?" Max asked his friend. "You're too sensible to fall for that," he said. "The Bible is nothing but a bunch of fairy tales."

"Have you ever read the Bible before?" his friend asked him.

"No, not exactly," Max said. "I don't want to waste my time on fiction. I quit believing in Santa when I grew up and I also quit believing in Satan."

"Well then," his friend told him, "it appears to me you were much smarter when you were a little kid! It's dangerous to doubt the Bible. And besides," he said, "it's no sweat if a big guy dressed up in a red suit drops down your chimney, but when the devil drops in, he doesn't leave!"

"I'm starting to think you've fallen for the lie about the little red man with the pitch fork!" Max told him.

"Well," his friend replied, "Not only do I believe it, someone much more powerful, brilliant, and influential than myself believes it."

"And who would that be?" Max asked him.

"God!" he replied.

(Author's note: We can only hope that the scales will be taken off of Max's eyes and that he will know the truth. Actually, though, he was right about one thing. Satan isn't some little red man with a pitch fork. The Bible says that he was created as a beautiful angel. He was corrupted by his own self centeredness and greed for power. He wanted to jump up on the throne and knock God off. The problem is, he overlooked one thing. God's omnipotence!)

ISAIAH 14:12-17: HOW ART THOU FALLEN FROM HEAVEN, O LUCIFER, SON OF THE MORNING! *HOW* ART THOU CUT DOWN TO THE GROUND, WHICH DIDST WEAKEN THE NATIONS! FOR THOU HAST SAID IN THINE HEART, I WILL ASCEND INTO HEAVEN, I WILL EXALT MY THRONE ABOVE THE STARS OF GOD: I WILL SIT ALSO UPON THE MOUNT OF THE CONGREGATION, IN THE SIDES OF THE NORTH. I WILL ASCEND ABOVE THE HEIGHTS OF THE CLOUDS; I WILL BE LIKE THE MOST HIGH. YET THOU SHALT BE BROUGHT DOWN TO HELL, TO THE SIDES OF THE PIT. THEY THAT SEE THEE SHALL NARROWLY LOOK UPON THEE, *AND* CONSIDER THEE, *SAYING, IS* THIS THE MAN THAT MADE THE EARTH TO TREMBLE, THAT DID SHAKE KINGDOMS; *THAT* MADE THE WORLD AS A WILDERNESS, AND DESTROYED THE CITIES THEREOF . . .

EZEKIEL 28:13-18: THOU HAST BEEN IN EDEN THE GARDEN OF GOD; EVERY PRECIOUS STONE *WAS* THY COVERING, THE SARDIUS, TOPAZ, AND THE DIAMOND, THE BERYL, THE ONYX, AND THE

JASPER, THE SAPPHIRE, THE EMERALD, AND THE CARBUNCLE, AND GOLD: THE WORKMANSHIP OF THY TABRETS AND OF THY PIPES WAS PREPARED IN THEE IN THE DAY THAT THOU WAST CREATED. THOU *ART* THE ANOINTED CHERUB THAT COVERETH; AND I HAVE SET THEE *SO:* THOU WAST UPON THE HOLY MOUNTAIN OF GOD; THOU HAST WALKED UP AND DOWN IN THE MIDST OF THE STONES OF FIRE. THOU *WAST* PERFECT IN THY WAYS FROM THE DAY THAT THOU WAST CREATED, TILL INIQUITY WAS FOUND IN THEE. BY THE MULTITUDE OF THY MERCHANDISE THEY HAVE FILLED THE MIDST OFTHEE WITH VIOLENCE, AND THOU HAST SINNED: THEREFORE I WILL CAST THEE AS PROFANE OUT OF THE MOUNTAIN OF GOD: AND I WILL DESTROY THEE, O COVERING CHERUB, FROM THE MIDST OF THE STONES OF FIRE. THINE HEART WAS LIFTED UP BECAUSE OF THY BEAUTY, THOU HAST CORRUPTED THY WISDOM BY REASON OF THY BRIGHTNESS: I WILL CAST THEE TO THE GROUND, I WILL LAY THEE BEFORE KINGS, THAT THEY MAY BEHOLD THEE. THOU HAST DEFILED THY SANCTUARIES BY THE MULTITUDE OFTHINE INIQUITIES, BY THE INIQUITY OF THY TRAFFICK; THEREFORE WILL I BRING FORTH A FIRE FROM THE MIDST OF THEE, IT SHALL DEVOUR THEE, AND I WILL BRING THEE TO ASHES UPON THE EARTH IN THE SIGHT OF ALL THEM THAT BEHOLD THEE.

REVELATION 12:9: AND THERE WAS A WAR IN HEAVEN: MICHAEL AND HIS ANGELS FOUGHT AGAINST THE DRAGON; AND THE DRAGON FOUGHT AND HIS ANGELS, AND PREVAILED NOT; NEITHER WAS THEIR PLACE FOUND ANY MORE IN HEAVEN. AND THE GREAT DRAGON WAS CAST OUT, THAT OLD SERPENT, CALLED THE DEVIL, AND SATAN, WHICH DECEIVETH THE WHOLE WORLD: HE WAS CAST OUT INTO THE EARTH, AND HIS ANGELS WERE CAST OUT WITH HIM.

REVELATION 12:12: . . . FOR THE DEVIL IS COME DOWN UNTO YOU, HAVING GREAT WRATH, BECAUSE HE KNOWETH THAT HE HATH BUT A SHORT TIME. [SEE JUDE 6 & REVELATION 20:10]

I PETER 5:8: BE SOBER, BE VIGILANT; BECAUSE YOUR ADVERSARY THE DEVIL, AS A ROARING LION, WALKETH ABOUT, SEEKING WHOM HE MAY DEVOUR. [SEE LUKE 22:31; JOB 1:6-12; GENESIS 3:1-5; ZECHARIAH 3:12-2]

JOHN 8:44: . . . HE WAS A MURDERER FROM THE BEGINNING, AND ABODE NOT IN THE TRUTH, BECAUSE THERE IS NO TRUTH IN HIM. WHEN HE SPEAKETH A LIE, HE SPEAKETH OF HIS OWN: FOR HE IS A LIAR, AND THE FATHER OF IT.

II CORINTHIANS 11:3: BUT I FEAR, LEST BY ANY MEANS, AS THE SERPENT BEGUILED EVE THROUGH HIS SUBTILTY, SO YOUR MINDS SHOULD BE CORRUPTED FROM THE SIMPLICITY THAT IS IN CHRIST.

II CORINTHIANS 2:11: LEST SATAN SHOULD GET AN ADVANTAGE OF US: FOR WE ARE NOT IGNORANT OF HIS DEVICES.

II CORINTHIANS 11:14: AND NO MARVEL; FOR SATAN HIMSELF IS TRANSFORMED INTO AN ANGEL OF LIGHT.

COLOSSIANS 2:8-10: BEWARE LEST ANY MAN SPOIL YOU THROUGH PHILOSOPHY AND VAIN DECEIT, AFTER THE TRADITION OF MEN, AFTER THE RUDIMENTS OF THE WORLD, AND NOT AFTER CHRIST. FOR IN HIM DWELLETH ALL THE FULNESS OF THE GODHEAD BODILY. AND YE ARE COMPLETE IN HIM, WHICH IS THE HEAD OF ALL PRINCIPALITY AND POWER. [SEE GALATIONS 6:1 & 7; I TIMOTHY 4:1-4; II TIMOTHY 4:3-4; I JOHN 4:1; & II CORINTHIANS 11:13-14; LUKE 4:1-13; EPHESIANS 4:27]

I CORINTHIANS 2:2: FOR I DETERMINED NOT TO KNOW ANY THING AMONG YOU, SAVE JESUS CHRIST, AND HIM CRUCIFIED.

MICAH 5:7: HE HATH SHEWED THEE, O MAN, WHAT IS GOOD; AND WHAT DOTH THE LORD REQUIRE OF THEE, BUT TO DO JUSTLY, AND TO LOVE MERCY, AND TO WALK HUMBLY WITH THY GOD.

ECCLESIASTES 12:13: LET US HEAR THE CONCLUSION OF THE WHOLE MATTER: FEAR GOD, AND KEEP HIS COMMANDMENTS: FOR THIS IS THE WHOLE *DUTY* OF MAN. FOR GOD SHALL BRING EVERY WORK INTO JUDGMENT, WITH EVERY SECRET THING, WHETHER *IT BE GOOD*, OR WHETHER *IT BE* EVIL.

ABOUT THE AUTHOR

I am an ambassador of Christ as is each one of us who embrace Him and represent His cause.

When I think of an ambassador, I think of someone far more noble than myself. But because of Christ's shed blood, I am made worthy to proclaim His glorious gospel.

He is my reputation, my identity, my righteousness. Without him I am lost without a Shepherd, but with Him I am an over comer, an heir, and a child of Almighty God. I am defined by my Master and not my mistakes! And as long as I shall live on this earth, with every breath that is within me, I want to proclaim the good news of his salvation to all who will listen. I want to hear the heart's cry of others. I want your needs to become my prayers.

I became a Christian over 40 years ago and Jesus has been my passion ever since.

In 1999, after receiving my ministerial license, I was given the privilege of sharing Him over the air waves in mid Michigan on a half an hour program that airs in Owosso and Corunna. It is called the Tidal Waves Ministries and produced through the King of Kings video productions.

My beloved husband, Roger, and I now host this program together sharing the Lord Jesus Christ and His saving grace.

In addition to that, some of my poetry has been featured in newspapers and in anthologies both in the United States and in England.

I also enjoy oil painting. The chairman and owner of Kelly Services has displayed some of my paintings in his Harbor Springs, MI home.

As I mentioned in the dedication of my book, I am the proud mom of three wonderful children, Lisa, the oldest, Clifford, next oldest, and Joey, the youngest. One of the greatest joys of my life has been the experience of parenting and training them up in the Lord. Nothing has been more satisfying than to see them honor Jesus in whatever they say and do.

I am also the proud grandmother of three adorable, beautiful grandchildren: Wyatt, Liam, and Isabella. It is my heart's desire that they serve Christ all the days of their lives.

I would love to hear from you! Please email me as follows:

GIVEPRAISE2JESUS@COMCAST.NET or please write, including your prayer requests and comments. You can contact me as follows:

CAROL DOLD
P.O. BOX 33272
BLOOMFIELD HILLS, MI 48303

Thank you, dear reader, for taking time out of your schedule to read my book. May the Lord Jesus bless you in all that you endeavor to do in spreading the gospel as you pick up your cross and follow Him. May He keep you healthy and well in body, soul, and spirit. May He bless you physically, spiritually, emotionally, and financially. May he fulfil all the godly desires of your heart. I pray that in your journey of faith you will be able to say, like myself, "Look what the Lord has done!"

I would be remiss in not mentioning my dear friends & family who have been there (and were there) for me over the many years since we have been part of one another's lives. Their love and encouragement has been a fountain of refreshment. Their faith has most certainly boosted my own. We have laughed together and cried together, some by way of phone calls, some by way of cards & letters, and some by way of litres . . . litres of soda pop, cups of coffee, tea, juice and an endless number of prayers and pizzas. They are listed below in alphabetical order:

Kenneth & Lenore Ashenden

Pamela Ashenden & family

Phil & Sue Ashenden & family

Jackie Binder

Thomas Brown

Wilma Duley

Ethel Frazier

Lisa Freeman

Chris & Lori Gilbert & family

Barb Goddard

Rosie Hahn

Frederica Hanmore

Reverends Chris & Yvonne Hardwick

Jim & Betty Hardwick

Peggy Hicks

Robin Jones & family

Rose Jones

Carrie Kim

Mike Lefebere

Steve & Reverend Deborah LeFrancois

Marc & Sharon Lollio & family

Margie Martin & family

Beverly Jean Maynard

Tricia Maynard

Carol Nicols

John O'Donnell (Deceased)

Tom Robillard

Malloy and Reverend Patsy Shumate

Reverends Harvey & Roberta Whittle

Debbie Whittle

I also wish to acknowledge Rey August from Author House Publishing for her very helpful and professional assistance.

I also wish to acknowledge Dr. William D. Campbell, DDS, 5555, Suite 100, Metro Parkway, Sterling Heights, MI for his kindness and generosity toward my family. (#586-977-8888) If you need a dentist, he is highly recommended!

I also wish to acknowledge Derek Ball, 15160 Goutz Rd., Monroe, MI 48161 (#734-241-1226 & www.derekscomputers.com) for his expertise and help when my computer crashed in the process of compiling my manuscripts. He, likewise, is highly recommended.

I also wish to recognize my faithful pastor and his wife, Reverend Robert and Judy Cholette as well as their staff (listed below). They are the shepherds of Troy Assembly of God, 3200 Livernois, Troy, MI 48083. You may reach them at 248-689-1270 or email them at TROYAG@SBCGLOBAL.NET. (For spiritual enlightenment and the uncompromising truth of the gospel of our Lord Jesus Christ, I highly recommend this church if you live in this area.

Also listed below are precious believers in Christ who attend our church, many of whom are so near and dear to my heart.

Mike & Winifred Azzopardi	Chuck Foster
Rebecca Barrett	Sue Foster
James & Cheryl Bailey	Bernie & Wilma Garnett
Kim & Cheryl Branson	Orville & Marilyn Garnett
Jim, Judy, & Matt Bridges	Will & Joan Garrett
Pastor Fred & Emily Betcher	Robin Glover
Suzi Brown	Al & Robin Griffin
Glenn, Barbara, & Rod Carter	Brendan & Cathy Hahn
Elsie Chanay	Jerry & Jeannie Harrison
Daniel & Cerita Cholette	Donna Haskins
Jonathan & Theresa Cholette	Linda Hartlage
Michael Cholette	Paul Jablonski
Robert & Nikki Cholette	Debbie Jablonski
Pastor Scott & Kellie DeClaire	Chris & Sandy Jacobson
Billie Clendenin	Alan Johnson
Claude & Edna Cline	Johnie Johnson
Ron & Grace Clute	Dan & Karen Kasprzak
Sarah D'Silva	Adolph & Rosemary Kipper
MJ Dawood	Robert Kirkpatrick
Linda DeWitte	Dave & Deniese Krall
Pastor Jed & Tracy Durrant	Blake & Dawn Kittle
Dorothy Dye	Aatto & Heimi
Clyde, Sarah, & Kim Fletcher	Judy Kwiatkowski

Rick and Sherry Lisiecki
Bobbie Lovins
Evelyn Mean
John, Maria Middleton
Terri Mazurek
Rose McWilliams
Reba Merglewski
Nina Morgan
Laurie Najm
Al Neusius
Carmen Parker
Laura Podczervinski
Sherry Patterson
Kathy Rainey
Bradley & Julie Richardson
Brad & Lana Sawicki
Pat Savage
Bob & Lynda Schodowski
Rick Schroeder
Herb & Sandy Scott
Wayne & Sandy Sharp
Dennis & Ruby Sviontek

Jeff & Sherry Patterson
Bruce Rittenhouse
Rose McWilliams
Reba Merglewski
Nina Morgan
Laurie Najm
Dick & Linda Rofkar
Chris & Rosa Russell
Rob & Charlie Porter
George & Denise Saputo
Jeff & Mary Saputo
Steve & Diane Saunders
Wayne & Sandy Sharp
Ruth Smith
Lois Stover
Mostafa & Andrea Tale Ghani
Darrell & Phyllis Taylor
Jim & Rachel Taylor
Bill, Lucille, Tammy, & James Turner
Jeff & Sheree Weddell
John Yaworsky

(If anyone's name has been omitted, it is purely unintentional)

CPSIA information can be obtained at www.ICGtesting.com
Printed in the USA
BVOW030858081111

275503BV00003B/2/P